Praise for
THE FUNDAMENTALS

"Gordon relates this story...on engagingly human levels. By the time Alexa finds herself lined up against the powerful Bell, readers will directly feel the stakes involved in the conflict."

— Kirkus Reviews

"An absorbing probe into lives transformed not just by stances on community issues, but by forces from the outside which affect choices in education, belief systems, and interactions. Gordon is as astute at showing how these processes connect people as she is at charting how they divide...a community whose school board lies in the eye of a storm shaking the nation. A compelling story of unexpected encounters and transformation."

— Midwest Book Reviews

"Brava! *The Fundamentals* is a truly wonderful achievement! The tension starts high and ratchets higher in each woman's voice. The poignancy of their journeys will really stay with me."

— Emma Gates, award-winning author of Walking to Israel

THE
FUNDAMENTALS

a novel

LYDIA
GORDON

THE
FUNDAMENTALS

2019

1

Alexa: Thursday, August 15

They were almost to Ecstasy when the tire blew. One minute they were cruising at 80, the early morning sun behind them, and the next—bang!—the car dropped on the driver's side and Alexa fought the steering wheel as her olive-green Hyundai pulled hard to the left and traveled over the center line into oncoming traffic.

"Hold on!" she yelled to her daughter Lucy, her urge to throw out a protective arm overridden by the need to control the car.

Think, think! Don't brake. Steer into the skid. Or was that for ice? It wasn't working; the car was flying at breakneck speed diagonally toward the ditch on the other side of the road. They would hit hard, maybe flip and roll. Alexa tapped the brake to test it and, when there was no response, trod harder. At the same time she steered away from the ditch, hoping to miss the big SUV coming dead at them in the farthest lane. She heard the squeal of the SUV's brakes as her own car spun and reversed direction, suspending itself on two wheels for what seemed a tiny eternity, the hazy horizon standing still while insects speckled the windshield and the scent of earth drifted in from the open fields. Then they bounced as their other two wheels hit the road, their wild trajectory sending them back across three lanes of traffic. Tires screeched as more drivers swerved to avoid them. They reached the shoulder just ahead of an enormous semi, which blew its horn as it missed them by inches and thundered past. The brakes caught when they hit the gravel, spraying stones, and Alexa and Lucy were thrown forward against their seatbelts as the car came to a stop.

Alexa's heart slammed in her chest. She forced herself to breathe, then turned to Lucy.

"Are you alright?"

Lucy, white and shaking, nodded. Her hazel eyes were huge.

"Don't take off your seat belt yet," said Alexa. "We have to get Olive's tail end off the road."

The back of the Hyundai was still in the path of traffic. Alexa eased her foot off the brake and the car crept forward. She gave it some gas, then turned the wheel to bring the back end to the shoulder, but the blown tire on the left front caused the rear of the car to swing to the right and over the edge of the ditch beside the road. The Hyundai teetered, then tipped and rolled backwards down the incline until it hit bottom, throwing them forward, then back. The suitcases on the top of the car slid out of the luggage rack restraints and into the wet ditch.

Alexa groaned.

"Okay, Mom," said Lucy, "what do we do now?"

"We get out," said Alexa. "Very carefully."

Lucy exited easily, but Alexa's seatbelt was jammed. She worked the button for several minutes before it gave. The driver's side of the car was low, and Alexa's door wouldn't fully open. She climbed across Lucy's side of the car, dragging her purse behind her, and pulled herself free. Standing at last, she took Lucy by the shoulders and looked her over.

"You're not hurt?"

"I told you Mom, I'm fine," said Lucy, squirming from her embrace. "I'm fine." Her arms crossed over her chest as if to ward off danger, but her usual peevish tone had returned.

Alexa checked to make sure the car wouldn't move any farther, then started toward the back end to retrieve the fallen bags. The grass was damp and slippery, and she decided not to chance it; falling into a wet ravine would not improve her day. She turned and started back up the incline to find that Lucy was fighting a similar lack of traction. They slipped and fell on their knuckles more than once on their way to the top.

As Alexa called for help on her cell phone, Lucy took pictures of the ditched Hyundai on hers, posting them on Instagram before Alexa had even connected to the garage in Ecstasy. The tow-truck dispatcher told her it would be at least half an hour; there was nothing to do but wait. Alexa called the moving van, which turned out to be an hour behind them, then dialed the lawyer, John Jeffers, who agreed to meet the van at the house and stay there until they arrived. Alexa hung up and paced the shoulder. Lucy busied herself with her phone, then slumped cross-legged to the gravel, scowling, as her battery went dead.

"You *had* to make us do this," she whined. "And look what's happened. It's a sign."

"It's not," Alexa countered, but she understood her daughter's mood; she'd been just as unhappy when her own mother plucked her from school and friends and moved her to a new town. And for Lucy, halfway through high school, it was worse.

Alexa shielded her eyes and looked at the miles of planted rows in every direction. Soybeans, she thought, from their size and shape, though she didn't know enough about crops to be sure. One lone farmhouse with a barn and silo stood in the distance, and above that only sky, unmarred but for a vapor trail catching the morning sun. As she watched, it lengthened slowly, as if of its own accord. A couple of hours out from the glitter and grit of Chicago—lake, skyscrapers, airports—and the planes were too high, too far away to be seen or heard.

The traffic passed them in waves, some drivers slowing when they saw them, as if to stop. Alexa held up her cell phone and waved them on, but the gravel crunched as a battered blue pickup pulled onto the shoulder some distance in front of their car. A slim young man got out and walked back to where they waited by the road.

"Looks like you need some help," he said.

"Thanks, but there's not much you can do," said Alexa. "We've called a tow, and they'll be here in just a bit." He seemed like a nice kid; he was dressed in a torn t-shirt and jeans, but his clothes and hands were clean. Sandy hair, farmer's tan, twenty-four, maybe twenty-five years old.

"Those your suitcases in the ditch?" He grinned. "Would you like 'em out?"

He didn't wait for an answer, but slid down the bank in his thick work boots and hauled the first one up. Soon all their luggage was piled by the road.

Alexa was impressed. "I can't thank you enough."

"Yes, thank you," said Lucy, emerging for the moment from her pique and boredom. She seemed to like him. Alexa noticed the lowered gaze, the softened voice. If the young man was aware, he didn't let on. He dried his hands on a bandana from his pocket. "I'm Ben Miller."

"Pleased to meet you, Ben. I'm Alexa Moss, and this is my daughter Lucy."

Ben glanced up and down the highway. "I'll wait with you, see you're safe 'til the tow truck comes." He pushed the hair out of his eyes and looked at them more closely. "You ladies headin' up to ECM?"

"ECM? What's that?" asked Lucy.

"Ecstasy Christian Ministries. Big church just north of town. The one on TV. Folks come from all over the county."

"Actually, we're moving here—to Ecstasy," Alexa said.

"Oh, I see. Whereabouts?"

"Collins Road."

He nodded. "I've done some work over there."

On closer inspection, Alexa noticed his youth was balanced by a hint of shrewd intelligence around the eyes, and a lean efficiency in the lines of his body. Maybe not such a kid at that.

"What type of work do you do?"

"I'm a carpenter, when I can find jobs. The rest of the time I work the factory."

"What kind of factory?" Lucy asked.

"Amos Windows, same as most folks 'round here."

A big white tow truck finally appeared, and they watched the driver maneuver to find the right angle to haul the Hyundai out of the ditch. Satisfied finally with his position, the driver hopped down from his perch and headed toward them. Ben turned to take his leave.

Alexa pulled a bill from her purse.

"Wait, Ben. I'd like you to have this for your trouble."

"No," he said. "I couldn't. I was happy to help."

Alexa thought about pressing him, then remembered something and took out her phone. "You said you're a carpenter. Experienced?"

The tow truck driver swayed from foot to foot impatiently.

"Yes, ma'am. A cabinetmaker too."

"Can you give me your number?"

"Sure. You hire carpenters?" He looked slightly amused.

"Sometimes." She didn't elaborate.

"How 'bout that." He fired off some digits Alexa entered into her phone. "I hope you'll give me a call." He held out a callused hand. "Ladies, it was a pleasure."

The noise from his tailpipe faded as he drove away. The tow-truck driver shook his head. When their car was out of the ditch at last, Alexa and Lucy climbed into the cab of the truck with the driver, the Hyundai in tow behind.

As they rolled along, the stale-smelling driver peppered them with questions. Where had they come from? Why were they here? Alexa did her best to dodge them without being rude, but he seemed to feel entitled to answers. He quizzed her about the accident, judging Alexa's response.

"You gals could have been killed," he insisted, "traveling alone like that."

Gals. Alone. When Alexa didn't reply, he shrugged and turned up the volume on his country radio station. Lucy was unusually quiet, hunched against the door of the cab, chewing her cuticles. Alexa wondered how much the blowout had rattled her—not to mention the blustery driver, or the thought of a new town and school.

As they exited the ramp from the highway, the flat and featureless farmland they had passed for hours gave way to subdivisions, and they slowly started to climb. Ecstasy was built near the bluffs overlooking the Hawthorne River. Pioneers had named the town, but citizens a century ago had changed the name to Pine Bluff. Now, for some reason she couldn't fathom, it was Ecstasy again. Alexa remembered the landscape from her childhood. Her father had grown up here, and they'd traveled back each summer to stay with his sister Margaret and visit his family and friends. That is, before her father's death and her mother's breach with Margaret.

Her mother, Sheila, was vehemently opposed to this move, and Alexa's choices in general. Their last phone conversation had covered it all.

"It was bad enough you lost your job," Sheila had reproached her. "Why can't you act like normal people? What is it with you and authority?"

"It wasn't like that. I simply disagreed." Alexa wrapped the coiled cord of their condo's old kitchen landline around her fingers. She could hardly *be* less confrontational, professionally or personally.

"You don't 'disagree' with the boss, dear, if you have a daughter to feed."

"I listened to what the clients wanted—"

"Pfft! It doesn't matter. You insisted on this 'career' instead of motherhood, and look at your life: no job, no marriage, no religion. You and Margaret always were two peas in a pod. Willful. Reckless."

"I *am* a mother. And be careful how you speak of the dead." Alexa wouldn't allow her memories of Margaret to be defiled. Especially now.

"Why should I—now that Margaret is reaching beyond the grave to steal my only grandchild? And you abetting her, running off to that God-forsaken place."

She knew she should laugh at her mother's theatricality, but her teeth clenched, and the tips of her cord-bound fingers flushed blue.

"It'll only add a few hours to our trips to Grand Rapids. We can afford to see you more often now." That is, if Sheila could learn to behave herself. "This inheritance coming along when it did has really saved us."

Sheila snorted. "Sometimes the devil's temptations are disguised as the Lord's provisions." She paused for effect, then went on. "You know you're breaking Lucy's heart."

Alexa had cut their call short and extracted herself from the tangled cord, leaving it to twist against the wall. But she couldn't deny the evidence that she'd failed as a wife and maybe as an architect, or shake the fear that she might now fail as a mother.

In the past few months, their lives had been quickly and stunningly upended. One morning in April she'd lost her job, then endured months of sleepless nights and unproductive interviews while scrounging for freelance drafting work to keep them fed. Just when it looked like they might go under, she'd gotten the call from Mr. Jeffers, followed by a messenger with a thick brown envelope containing the will.

She hadn't known that Margaret was ill; it had been almost 30 years since she'd seen her. In the last ten years, they'd exchanged a few holiday cards and letters, a fact she'd hidden from her mother. But Alexa had never made the trip back to Ecstasy, never taken Lucy to Margaret's house, a fact she now regretted. Margaret was buried, Mr. Jeffers told her, and her life already celebrated by a few close friends. She had no children of her own and no other family.

Lucy at first had been thrilled by the inheritance: a big old farmhouse, 20 acres of land, and money for her college and graduate school. She pored over the blueprints and photographs enclosed with the will, and asked what seemed a hundred questions about the property and Margaret. Alexa had answered them as well as memory allowed.

But it didn't take long for Lucy to realize the move would be permanent. Her eyebrows drew together as the knowledge dawned on her.

"Seriously? We're not just going to stay there on the weekends?"

"No, hon. It's a condition of the will. We would have to move." Alexa sighed. "Under the circumstances—"

"You promised me when you lost your job that we'd be alright. You said we'd just have to be careful with our money for a while. You didn't say anything about moving!"

"We *will* be alright. I promise you," Alexa said, though her own knotted neck and shoulders had yet to get the message.

"Everything I have is here—my school, my friends," Lucy wailed. "What about my science?" Her delicate, silver-ringed fingers raked her hair.

"The science department at the high school has an excellent reputation. The department head has great credentials—"

Lucy took another tack. "This is totally unacceptable," she argued in her most adult voice. Then, adversely, she planted her feet and dug her toes into the rug, the way she had as a toddler. "I'm not moving, and you can't make me."

Alexa looked at her sadly. A moment of silence passed between them. Despair washed over Lucy's face. "You can't do this to me! It's not fair!"

"Lucy," Alexa began again, but her daughter was past listening. Alexa watched Lucy's face close like a curtain before she turned and ran from the room. In the six weeks since the decision was made, Lucy's tears, her wrath, her sarcasm had nearly spent her mother. And since that day, that curtain between them had not lifted.

She glanced now at Lucy, who watched the passing scenery with hooded eyes, and a tender rush went through her. She ached to pull her daughter close, to fold her arms around her like in the old days. But Lucy was having none of that now. Yes, Alexa was making Lucy unhappy, at least in the short term. Yet she couldn't allow her daughter's academic potential to be wasted. Lucy deserved the best education, without the late start Alexa had had or the hobbling student debt she still carried. If Alexa could just do this one thing right, the rest of it—her marriage, her career, her personal life—didn't matter.

On the radio, Martina McBride sang about "God-fearin' women," and the tow truck slowed. As they entered the city limits, the strip malls yielded to older storefronts, interspersed with a few chain stores and mid-century office buildings. They pulled into a gas station on Main Street with canopied pumps, a handful of auto service bays, and a squat convenience store. Alexa spoke with a tall woman in gray coveralls who assured them that a mechanic named Rodrigo would assess the damage within the hour. Fortunately, it was Thursday morning. The place didn't look very busy.

They bought a couple of sodas and sat in the glassed-in waiting room. Alexa filled out the paperwork while Lucy slumped, chin on her chest, in a vinyl and chrome chair. It was almost half an hour later when Rodrigo emerged. He was a short, square man with close-set eyes, features redeemed by a beautiful smile that made him almost handsome.

"The damage isn't extensive," he told them. "It could have been worse. The blowout was caused by a sidewall bubble—a manufacturing defect, usually. The tire was new?"

"Yes, I replaced it a month ago, when we were planning this trip."

"That air bubble, under pressure, causes the inner layers to separate and gets between them, looking for somewhere to go. You can sometimes see the bulge in the tire."

"Wow. I didn't notice a bulge. Is this something I could have prevented?"

"I doubt it. Tire pressure can play a part, but it's trouble waiting to happen. Was anybody hurt?"

"No," Alexa and Lucy replied at once.

"Then it's your lucky day. Somebody up there likes you." Rodrigo pointed toward the ceiling and gave them a luminous smile.

Alexa didn't believe in either luck or divine providence. But she and Lucy were safe, and today she was not inclined to argue.

Rodrigo gave them the price to change the flat, balance the tires, and do a four-wheel alignment. The rims weren't damaged, but the right front tire had lost some tread in the skid and should be replaced. Alexa agreed and signed. The car would be ready in two or three hours. Alexa and Lucy decided to walk around for a while, then have lunch at the diner across the street.

The garage was near the edge of town, close to the subdivisions. Despite some empty storefronts, this area of Ecstasy had a well-kept, touristy feel, with small boutiques selling clothes and knickknacks, a bookstore, and an ice cream and coffee shop. After browsing through a few of the stores with a sulking Lucy, Alexa suggested her daughter go on while she rested on one of the benches that lined the street. It was a comfortable mid-August morning, with a strong breeze blowing clouds across the sun. She made a second call to John Jeffers to update him on the timing.

Resigned to the fact that she'd done all she could, Alexa began to relax. It was then her hands began to shake. That was always the way—her body's delayed processing of stress and adrenaline. She remembered the nights in emergency rooms with her daughter's fevers, ear infections, once a green-stick fracture of her arm. In those moments of crisis, Alexa was comforting with Lucy, calm and clear-headed with the staff. But once they were over, she'd always felt the full effect on her nerves. She tried not to think about what might have happened this morning, had there been more cars on that road.

She distracted herself from her pounding heart by watching the passing pedestrians. The people here looked much as they did in the suburbs of Chicago—young mothers with small children, businessmen and women, uniformed tradesmen—though the crowd was smaller and less racially diverse. Maybe small-town life wouldn't be so different. Sure, they were more conservative here, but cable TV and the internet were everywhere, and she assumed that rural culture would be much more like the city's now than it had been when she was a kid. In those days her Aunt Margaret's house had seemed a quieter, slower world away.

Through one of the large shop windows, she could see Lucy trying on hats. Turning one way and then another before a mirror, she brushed her gold-brown hair to one side for a cloche, then tucked it under a fedora. A salesclerk offered a piece of jewelry. Alexa could make out the gleam of the necklace against Lucy's smooth young skin. Poised, engaging, and lovely in a slender, slightly bookish way, her daughter had a confidence that she herself had not had at that age. Alexa would hate to see that change. She wondered for the umpteenth time if she were doing the right thing.

Lucy frowned as she left the store and crossed the street to rejoin her mother. She carried a bag of undisclosed items, probably bought with the last of her babysitting money. Alexa hoped that the purchase would bring her comfort. The sky began to cloud and they were getting hungry, so they walked down the street to the diner.

"Sandy's" was one of those narrow restaurants built into a railroad car: lunch counter on one side, booths on the other, a harried waitress working the aisle between. They were guided to a booth with a window directly overlooking the garage across the street. They could see their Santa Fe on the rack in the middle service bay.

"At least we'll know when she's ready," said Alexa, then scanned the menu. It looked and smelled as if everything at Sandy's was grilled. A waitress came and took their order: Alexa chose a Caesar salad, Lucy a cheeseburger and lemonade. They ate in silence. A tinny speaker in the corner played vocalists from the 1950s; Perry Como caught a falling star. When they finished, Lucy fidgeted and stared out the window, bored without her phone.

"You seemed to enjoy the shops," said Alexa.

"The shops are lame. Just like the rest of this place." Lucy fingered an earring and refused to meet her mother's eyes.

"Okay, it's different, but I'm asking you, Lucy, to keep an open mind."

"What am I supposed to do in this town?"

Alexa lowered her voice, hoping Lucy would do the same. "Go to school, make friends, grow up."

Lucy sat up straight and glared at Alexa.

"Are you kidding me? I had *great* friends. And if you remember, a life. Good grades, too. And all for nothing. Grow up? Now I'm supposed to start again like I was in kindergarten!"

"I don't think it will be quite that bad."

"Oh, don't you?"

Alexa changed her tone. "That's enough now, Lucy. I'm moving too. I'm starting over as well."

They were interrupted by the thump—thump—thump of a vehicle's audio, the diner's windows buzzing with the beat. A late-model bright red pickup had pulled into the service station across the street. The truck had barely come to a stop when a young woman flew out of the passenger side as if she'd been pushed. A purse was thrown after her. The large male driver leaned over the seat and slammed the door, then executed a 3-point turn, missing the girl by a foot. She gave him the finger, thrusting with her whole arm. He hit the gas, pulled onto the street, and roared away.

The young woman stood in place for a moment, teetering in tall heels, then picked up her bag and searched for something in its depths. She looked to be in her early twenties. Even from across the street, Alexa could see her dark hair was wild, her makeup smeared, and those, she'd bet, were last night's clothes the girl was wearing: a spangled top too dressy for this time of day, a short black skirt. Seeming at last to find what she sought, she rounded a corner of the building and stopped before a bank of old pay phones. She pumped in a few coins and punched some numbers, then cradled the receiver between chin and shoulder as she pulled a cigarette from her purse, lit it, and exhaled.

Alexa's phone rang. She and Lucy jumped. Their car was ready.

As they left the diner and crossed the street to the gas station lot, Alexa and Lucy could hear the dark-haired girl on the pay phone plead with someone, then slam the receiver down and punch in more numbers. While they waited for their vehicle, the same young woman walked through the convenience store to the bathroom in the rear. A trio of pretty teenage girls loitering in the candy aisle turned to stare. Alexa heard them whispering, and they pointed and laughed when the young woman reappeared. She had cleaned the makeup from her face and tamed her hair, but her skin was pale and mottled with emotion. She wore the air of someone humbled, yet defiant. As she paid for a Red Bull and bag of chips, she returned the gaze of the smirking cashier until he dropped his eyes. Then she turned to the teenage girls, who silenced themselves at once. The first drops of rain began to fall as she left the store and headed up the street. The trio of girls burst into laughter again.

Ten minutes later, Rodrigo of the brilliant smile delivered Olive to them "as good as new." He routed them to Collins Road and Aunt Margaret's house on a map. "Alternate route. More accurate than your GPS. Fifteen minutes, tops," he told them, and waved to them as they pulled onto the street. It was almost two o'clock, and as their luck today would have it, raining hard. Alexa hoped the movers had finished before the weather.

They'd traveled half a mile when they saw her, soaked and shivering, trying to thumb a ride. Her feet were bare; she carried her high heels in her hand. Her spangled top was bedraggled and clung to her breasts.

"Look!" cried Lucy. "We have to help her."

Alexa had no time to consider. A silver sedan a few car lengths in front of them pulled to the curb, and the young woman climbed inside.

2

Rachel: Thursday, August 15

She heard Caleb's wedding ring click against the steering wheel as he pounded his hands against it for emphasis. "Rachel, what were you thinking?"

The sky was dark, and the rain poured down the silver Subaru's windshield so fast the wipers could barely keep up. Soaked through, she shivered in the air conditioning, and he shot her a look as she leaned forward to close the vents instead of answering him. His mouth twisted, and Rachel waited for the words she knew would come. When they stopped for a red light at Chestnut, he turned to her.

"How could you call the house?"

"I tried Sarah first, but she wouldn't come. Then your cell, but you didn't pick up. I didn't have any choice. You know the buses don't run that way this time of day, and I didn't have money for a cab."

"We're both damned lucky Rebecca just hung up on you. She didn't call your brother. This time. If Daryl Green hadn't texted me, you'd still be wandering the streets in that outfit, shaming the family."

Daryl, the smirking convenience store clerk. What business was it of his? But Rachel noted that Caleb swore, something he rarely did.

"I'm sorry about Rebecca, Caleb. Do you think she knows you're with me?"

"No. Not this time. But if this keeps up, she'll figure it out soon enough. I can't be lying to her, Rachel. I can't be running to bail you out of your troubles. You made your bed."

The light turned green, but soon they slowed to a crawl as Main Street ran with water and every vehicle sent up a spray. The windows steamed, and Caleb told her to open the vents again.

"If you're cold, you can use my jacket. It's on the seat behind you."

Rachel wrapped herself in the denim and the scent of Caleb she remembered from their youth. She could always count on her older cousin to look out for her, to be her friend. Her ally. Until the day she had disobeyed— they would say *betrayed*—the family. Now he and his wife Rebecca were lost to her, and their children too. Rachel's best friend Sarah as well. She felt it keenly. She watched Caleb in profile as he drove—the same lanky frame, the same light hair and eyes—and she wanted to put her hand on his, to make him look at her and see the Rachel he knew as a child. But his face was set, and his kind eyes were not for her. He was only here to save the family from talk.

They turned left on River Road and headed south, toward the factory and the older, dirtier neighborhoods in its shadow.

Caleb spoke. "I'm not even going to ask you what happened. Frankly, I'm too disgusted."

She wouldn't have told him anyway. But she couldn't stop the tears that slid silently down her face and onto the spangled top, the denim jacket.

"You've got to stop this," he told her. "The drinking, the whoring. It's dangerous. You're ruining your life. Not to mention imperiling your soul. Worst of all, you're getting a reputation, and you know that Cyrus won't stand for that once he gets wind."

Rachel shuddered at the mention of her uncle's name.

Caleb made a few more turns, then pulled up to the old brick building where Rachel rented a furnished room and bath. Rachel gathered her courage. It was the worst time to ask, but she wasn't sure when she'd have another chance.

"Caleb ... how is Phoebe?"

"Rachel, you know I can't talk about that, especially with you."

"*Please*, Caleb. She's my sister. I need to know."

Caleb looked out through the windshield at the lessening rain. He pounded the steering wheel once more, then sighed and dropped his shoulders. He kept his eyes averted when he finally spoke.

"She's not any better. If anything, she has more seizures now."

Rachel began to cry harder.

"Stop," said Caleb. "Your lack of faith is hurting her. Pray for her, Rachel, and mend your ways. Stop offending God. Then maybe things will start to change for Phoebe." He still refused to look at her.

"*Caleb* ... "

He held up his hand. Rachel threw off his jacket and fled the car.

It took three tries to unlock the deadbolt to her apartment. She dropped her purse and threw herself on the sagging bed in the middle of her room.

It must be true. It was her fault. She remembered those nights, awakening to the shaking of the bed they'd shared, Phoebe rigid, her teeth clenched, the headboard banging against the wall, the smell of urine as Phoebe's bladder emptied; Rachel's own prayers and entreaties, the helplessness as she held her sister's bucking body close to hers to keep her from falling, injuring herself; the clammy skin, the blue lips, the long, slow recovery of sense and clarity. It was as if Phoebe's soul had left and had to find its way back home.

Phoebe had been *her* responsibility. A relief, really, when their mother Ruth Ann had given up, after years of unsuccessful attempts to pry Phoebe's jaws open during her "fits" and hold a spoon over her tongue. She had eight other children to care for, she said, and as the oldest daughter, it was time Rachel earned her keep.

Rachel would step out of the room to make her siblings' lunches or do a load of wash, leaving Phoebe at the dining room table with her blond head bent over her homeschool work—then, suddenly, the banging would start. Phoebe would be sprawled where she'd fallen, her head pounding the floor until Rachel got to her. There were more and more days like that, and they haunted Rachel.

Thank God Phoebe had no memory of her attacks, and had at first seemed to suffer no ill effects beyond headaches afterwards. She was embarrassed, as most young people would be, but Phoebe rarely left the house, and the family had gotten used to her affliction. Aunt Eunice would come and lay hands on her, and everyone would pray. The seizures would stop for a few days or a few weeks, but they always returned. "A difficult case," Aunt Eunice would say. All illness was illusion, lack of faith. The explanation was obvious: someone in the house was not right with God.

If that was the case, Rachel had no doubt who it was. She had done bad things, made wrong choices, and Phoebe had suffered for it. Rachel had paid the price. Cast out of her family, never to see her sister again, she could only hope Phoebe was well taken care of. Caleb was right: as much as it hurt, it was better to keep her distance from Phoebe, steeped in sin as she was.

Exhausted, Rachel closed her eyes and fell into a troubled sleep.

She awoke several hours later to the sound of traffic rumbling under her window. The sky was still light, but barely. Her damp clothes had dried and stiffened into wrinkles while she slept; the spangled top was ruined. She peeled them off and inspected herself in the full-length bathroom mirror. Despite the sleep, there were new shadows under her blue eyes. Her nipples were chafed, and bruises blossomed along one inner thigh and above her elbow. She turned her head and shifted her dark hair. Yes, she could see the marks his fingers had left on her neck when he'd forced himself on her this morning. Harley was a big man. She had resisted. She didn't remember leaving the bar with him last night, but she'd never forget waking up with him this morning.

Her mouth was parched and cottony. She took a few aspirin and drank a full tumbler of water from the tap before showering, then pulled on jeans and an oversized t-shirt to make her run for milk and vodka and cigarettes. She could hear the TV laugh tracks and smell other people's dinners as she descended the worn stairway from her apartment to the street.

The night was warm and muggy, but the rain had stopped. This part of town looked better after dark. The trees, the brick and stucco buildings seemed far less sooty and neglected under the moon. Further on, the neon shop signs were reflected by the puddles in the street. She bought only the few items she could carry from the small grocer's down the block. When she entered the liquor store, she noticed two men who worked on the window-factory floor. One elbowed the other when she came in, and they followed her to the cashier.

"Hey honey, aren't you that girl from the office?" the stocky one asked.

She could see they'd had plenty to drink already and avoided eye contact with them.

"I work at Amos, if that's what you mean."

The taller, darker one inched closer. "And what do you do up there in the air-conditioning?"

"I take orders for you guys to fill." She wanted to take it back as soon as she said it.

"I'll give you an order–and fill it, too." They both laughed. She didn't turn to see the gesture she was sure would accompany that. "Why don't you come and party with us?"

"Sorry, I'm busy."

"Fellas, what can I do for you?" asked Mel, the owner, as he scanned her liquor, her bottle of cranberry juice, and her cigarettes.

As they pointed to something behind the counter, Rachel edged away. An old-fashioned bell clanged against the door as she passed from the cool stale air back into the humid night. She walked quickly but carefully home along the broken sidewalk, with her purchases in her arms. The men must have had somewhere else to go; they didn't follow her. As she entered her building's tiny foyer, she stopped in surprise. In the row of long-tarnished mailboxes, hers was most often empty. But tonight through the grid she detected the edge of an envelope. She put down her groceries and fumbled for the key in her purse, her heart jumping when she opened the box and saw the familiar blue logo. Her GED test results, after weeks of waiting. She pressed the envelope between her lips to free her hands for the groceries and climbed the steps.

Inside her apartment, she placed the envelope unopened on her bedside table, put away her groceries, and fixed a drink. She found the ritual calming: first, the fluted texture of the kitchen tumbler, then the crack of the plastic ice tray and clink of cubes in the glass. Next, the serrated cap of the vodka bottle against her fingertips as she twisted it; the lift, the pour; the action repeated with cranberry juice, its portion a fraction smaller every day. Then lastly, the ruby-colored liquid held to the light in a silent salute (to who or what, she couldn't imagine), the scent as she brought the glass to her lips, the swallow, the sweetness, the warmth. And sometime later, if only for an hour, peace.

But not tonight. Tonight there was an envelope.

Would it be worth it? The time, the money, the trips on the bus to take the GED preparation class? So many evenings she'd dragged herself to that stark community college classroom and listened to the pale instructor drone tips, tricks, and admonishments to a roomful of anxious students, giving them little real help or tutoring. She still didn't get the math.

Her family hadn't thought math was important for girls. They were going to be mothers; basic arithmetic would do. Though she'd aced the test for the homeschool kids and begged to go to the public high school, her mother held firm that an eighth-grade education was enough. They'd complied with the law, and she'd continued to test until age 16, but most of that time was spent teaching the younger ones.

She'd read what she could. The books in the house were Bibles or other religious texts, but her father read the newspaper every day, then dropped it into a box to go out with the trash. Rachel often crept back to the kitchen late in the evenings and borrowed only a section or two, so its absence wouldn't be noticed. She'd hid the pages under a pile of towels or clothes from the dryer and slipped into the downstairs bathroom to read. All her knowledge of the world outside her family, her church, had come to her this way.

One drink finished, Rachel poured another and lit a cigarette as she put macaroni on to boil on the single burner hot plate. The blue box had always looked cheerful when she was making lunch for her family. But now Rachel mixed the bright orange powder with milk and noodles and butter and sat down to dinner as she did each night: alone. The cheerfulness was gone. She missed the noise and chaos of her large family, despite the structure of prayer and strict routine. As she washed her dishes in the chipped sink, she thought of her parents, her brothers and sisters, well in bed by now. She knew they'd never speak of her—or to her—again, but did they think of her, as she so often thought of them? Would she be able to make a life without them? She walked to the bedside table and picked up the white-and-blue envelope.

It had been the math that worried her. The battery of tests was long and hard, the tension of the test-takers palpable, and the proctor roving the aisles with a stopwatch had done nothing to ease her distress. Rachel had found the reading and writing parts challenging, but manageable. The social science part was tough, but she'd already passed the required Constitution tests, and she'd thought she had a chance.

The surprise had been the science. Chemistry, anatomy, biology, physics. The natural world. She'd foolishly thought she knew the basics. She had cared for children, cooked meals, worked a garden. She knew the names of the parts of the body, the types of clouds, the traits of mammals. Gravity, inertia, centrifugal force. But it seemed there was so much more to it than that. The topics and questions had startled her. *Why* do certain chemicals react with one another? *How* do plants grow? What determines the sex of a child? How do species change? How did the universe begin? In her faith and family, the answer to each of those questions had been God.

Courage. She slit the envelope open with a knife. Inside were two sheets of paper: one titled *Official Transcript*, the other *Interpreting GED Results*. On the transcript, the scores and percentiles of each individual test were listed. She needed a 410 in each subject and an average of 450 for the entire battery. She scanned the columns and rows. Reading and writing: good scores, high percentiles. Social science: better than she'd thought. In math she just scraped by with 430. Okay, a relief. She held her breath. Science: 360. *Oh.*

She'd made her 450 battery average easily, but it wasn't enough. There, on the bottom, two little boxes: pass, non-pass. The X was in the latter.

Maybe she'd made a mistake. She studied the second sheet, to make sure she'd read her transcript correctly. For nearly ten minutes, Rachel scoured the page for hope, but in the end, it was painfully clear she hadn't passed.

She fixed herself a third cocktail and took several drinks, then set it on her nightstand next to the envelope and lay down on her bed, fully dressed. She couldn't even cry any more. She could take the whole test over, or just the science part. But she was tired. She couldn't afford another class. How would she do better? And if she didn't, she knew she couldn't keep her job. Her boss would only cover for her for so long.

She found the remote in the night table drawer and turned on the small TV that had come with the furnished room. Watching it had been strange at first. Their TV at home had only been used with an old VCR: Disney films or Bible stories for the little kids, programs or movies selected by their parents for the rest. She'd been too busy to watch herself, but had found relief occasionally by sitting her younger siblings in front of the set. Now TV had become a lifeline which allowed her to sleep at night. She turned the sound low at bedtime and slept to the hum of flickering, muted conversations. It was almost like being at home in a house full of people.

Tonight, as she listlessly clicked through the channels, she stopped and sat upright. She'd heard a name on the late-night local news.

"Is the teaching of evolution hurting your kids? Coming up, we'll be hearing from Cyrus Bell, the pastor of Ecstasy Christian Ministries. Stay with us."

Uncle Cyrus. Rachel lit a cigarette and changed the channel. A familiar commercial: a bankruptcy lawyer, blind to the evidence that he couldn't act. She could barely hear his words over the rush of blood in her ears.

Cyrus. Her physical reaction came first: rapid heartbeat, churning stomach, sweat. Then the memory.

"Uncle Cyrus, please, I can explain."

Cyrus fixed his gaze on her from behind his huge glass desk. She'd been called into his church office, more than a year ago now, after the Sunday midday service. Her parents were there, as well as her brother Aaron, who stood at Cyrus' side. Cyrus was still in his purple and silver vestments, colors Rachel was sure had been chosen to set off his full head of white hair and violet eyes for the cameras. His charisma had the crowd of worshippers alternately on its feet, then on its knees that morning: a thousand people singing, clapping, lifting their hands to the Lord with tears in their eyes. She was only one person, a woman at that, and she felt very small standing before him.

"There's no excuse for your behavior, for your insolence to God and your family." Rachel prepared to answer, but Cyrus went on. "The question is not if you've sinned, but what should be done with you." She felt as if his eyes bored into her body. Aaron leaned in and whispered something in Cyrus' ear. Cyrus turned to Rachel's parents. "Why isn't she married?"

"Cyrus, with all due respect—" her mother began.

"Ruth Ann," said Cyrus to his sister, "let your husband speak."

Rachel's mother closed her mouth and picked invisible lint from the skirt of her dress. George's voice was low when he spoke, and his eyes were downcast in respect.

"Well, you know, Cyrus, Ruth Ann and I needed her at home. For the little ones, and to care for Phoebe—"

"And you see how that turned out." His voice was not harsh or menacing, but his tone held a terrible judgment.

George nodded. Cyrus's gaze bore into Rachel. "The devil has tracked you a long time, girl. Looks like he's caught up to you."

Rachel fought the panic rising in her breast. When Cyrus mentioned the devil, it wasn't good.

There was a knock on the office door. Aaron exchanged a glance with Cyrus, then cast a smug look at Rachel. Rachel had seen that look on Aaron's face when she was sixteen, and he caught her being kissed on the mouth by Daniel Carleton. Rachel had been whipped soundly. That punishment, as far as she knew, was not administered to Daniel.

"Come in," said Cyrus.

Rachel was surprised to see Harold Waters.

"Cyrus," he said, and bowed a bit in the pastor's direction before he took a seat.

Harold was an unpleasant, pretentious man in his fifties whose wife had been a good friend of Ruth Ann's. Her battle with cancer hadn't stopped him from eyeing young women at church suppers, and when she had died three months ago, he hadn't seemed especially grieved.

"Rachel, Harold has offered to solve your problems. Although you've disgraced yourself, he's agreed to have you."

"Have me?"

"Marry you. Your parents can't seem to control you. You need a husband."

Rachel couldn't speak. She looked to her mother and father. Her parents were silent at first, her father contemplating the backs of his rough workman's hands. Then he raised his head, looked from Cyrus to Ruth Ann and cleared his throat.

"Rachel, you're twenty-two. Maybe it's time."

She knew if it wasn't for Phoebe they would have married her off years ago. There were young men who'd asked to court her, but her parents had run them off so she could care for the kids and the house. She had known they'd choose a husband for her eventually. But Harold Waters? They'd guarded her virginity so carefully for *him*?

"No," said Rachel.

Uncle Cyrus rose to his feet. His jaw tightened, and his white eyebrows drew together until they touched. His voice was commanding, chilling.

"Rachel, you'll do as your father says."

She looked to her mother.

Ruth Ann returned her eyes to her skirt. "It's for the best, Rachel."

"No."

Rachel squared her shoulders and looked at each of them in turn. She knew they would not back down, but this time, neither would she. In her whole life, she'd rarely taken a stand. Aaron could barely hide his amusement. She knew that something awful would happen now.

"No?" roared Cyrus.

"No." She held his eyes.

"Then you leave me no choice." He sat down at his desk and folded his hands. "Rachel Whitman, you're disfellowshipped."

Disfellowshipped. Shunned. Cast out. Rachel's knees started to give. She caught herself on Cyrus' desk and pulled herself upright to face him.

"No—" her mother pleaded with Cyrus, who cut her off.

"That's enough, Ruth Ann. You can see that she's been led astray. Better to cut ties now than to harbor a snake in your midst. Once this faithless child is gone, Phoebe will get better."

He turned his attention back to Rachel.

"You turn yourself around, young woman, and leave this place. Do not go home. You are banned from any contact with your family or this church. May God forgive you before you face his wrath."

Aaron strode to the door and opened it. Rachel cast one last, pleading look at her parents, which they didn't dare return.

She hardly knew how to move her feet across the threshold, but somehow she did. The door closing at her back was the final blow.

She couldn't watch Cyrus on the television now, didn't want to, but she found herself changing the channel back, returning to the local news. She'd missed the interview, but now there was footage of Cyrus on the steps of Ecstasy City Hall with the mayor. The real snake, her brother Aaron, was at his side.

3

Lucy: Monday, August 19

The stupid screen door was banging again. Lucy hated this old Victorian house, and it seemed to return the feeling. Tired wallpaper, peeling paint, dark wood everywhere. Not that their old place was so great, but at least there she knew how to live, to be. This was a freaking foreign country.

She could smell fresh paint from the third floor, and her muscles ached. They'd worked long into the night to finish, and she would be able to move her things upstairs in a few days. But Alexa was deluded if she thought a big bedroom with a turret would make Lucy happy here. She was almost sixteen—seriously past the princess stage—and this was no fairy tale. She missed her friends. She wanted to go home.

Her mother was moving boxes again. For the last few days, their lives had been one big scavenger hunt, without any of the fun. Alexa had labeled cartons with the names of the rooms they should go to, but the movers had stacked one on top of another wherever they found space. Kitchen utensils turned up in the bedrooms, boxes of books in the bath. At the moment, Alexa was dragging cartons marked "garage" out to the porch, the screen door squeaking open on its rusty spring, then slamming shut behind her every time. Lucy made her way to the ugly kitchen at the back of the house and popped a couple of frozen waffles into the toaster.

Her phone pinged with a text from Haley, who was fighting with Josh again. At least Lucy had this one link to her real life back home in Elm Ridge. She sent a quick, sympathetic reply, then texted Nicole and Olivia, the other half of the quartet of friends who'd been hanging out together since 6th grade. They were comparing their new fall schedules, learning which teachers they had in common, consulting on each other's outfits for the upcoming first day of school. And she wasn't there. It hit her again that she would miss *everything*. Hanging out. Homecoming. Driver's Ed. They had talked since freshman year about all the things they'd do, the places they'd go, as soon as they learned to drive.

As she ate her waffles, she tried to imagine what high school was like in this town. How would she compete for state and national science awards, get junior-level internships with biotechs, scholarships for college? She was one of the few kids her age who knew exactly what she wanted in life, but she didn't have any faith at all that she could get there from here.

Her mother called her from the living room. She ignored her at first, poured herself a glass of orange juice, and watched a few TikTok videos on her cell phone. There was no way she was going to make this easy on Alexa. Lucy felt a twinge of longing for the way things used to be between them: shopping for music and clothes together, dancing around the kitchen to the radio, trying new recipes, sharing a passion for science documentaries, *HGTV*, and board games. Lucy's friends had loved Alexa and hung out at their apartment so often her mother was occasionally forced to point them toward the door. Though she'd had her rules, her mother had been reasonable and easy to talk to. But that was before. Before Alexa dropped the bomb. Before the news they'd be moving to Ecstasy.

The third time Alexa called Lucy's name, she recognized a certain tone in her mother's voice and ambled toward the front of the house. In the foyer, Alexa looked up from her cartons, obviously annoyed.

"There you are. Why didn't you answer?" She looked Lucy over and sighed.

"What?" Big deal. So she was still in the loose boxer shorts and tank top she'd worn to bed.

"It's after noon. Did you forget Mr. Jeffers is coming at 1:00?"

"Oh Mom, come on. Do I have to be there?"

"I think it's a good idea."

"Fine." She turned her back and headed upstairs, making as much noise as possible on the way. She didn't get why she had to see this lawyer, this "executor," whatever that meant. It wasn't like *she* got to make any decisions.

As she showered and washed her sweaty hair, she yawned. Tired as she had been last night, it was still too hot to sleep much. The first night they stayed here, they'd put air conditioners in the bedroom windows, but of course the ancient fuses had blown the moment they'd turned them on.

She pulled on a pair of jean shorts and a boxy green t-shirt that brought out her hazel eyes. She added a little makeup, but left her long hair damp, afraid that plugging in the dryer would fry the wiring. As she finished, she heard the screen door again and a man's voice at the bottom of the steps.

Lucy found them in the dining room. Mr. Jeffers stood as she entered and motioned for her to join them. She took a seat on one long side of the antique table, her back to the old-fashioned sideboard. Her mother continued her conversation with the lawyer, who seated himself again and answered Alexa's questions about the trust and estate. Bored already, Lucy focused on the glittering dust motes that danced in the sunbeams coming in through the bay windows. In this light, John Jeffers's silver hair and mustache shone, and Lucy was surprised to see a few strands of that same silver in the highlights of her mother's auburn hair. She also noticed subtle new lines around Alexa's large gray eyes.

The adults finally turned toward her.

"Lucy, Mr. Jeffers and I would like to make sure you understand all this. He's come today to fill us in on the details and get my signature on some forms. When we first talked about this, you were upset, and probably didn't get all the facts. Do you have any questions now?"

Lucy crossed her arms in front of her on the table.

"I remember what you told me," she said, glaring at her mother. "You get the house and land, and I get an education. I don't get any say in this. I just do what I'm told."

"Lucy," Alexa began, but John Jeffers held up his hand and stopped her.

"Please, allow me." He turned to Lucy, his manner friendly, but firm. "Young lady, I know you think this doesn't suit you right now. And you're right; it's difficult. But your mother has made a good decision on your behalf. She's given up quite a lot to come here, just as you have. And when the terms of the will are met, you'll be happy she did."

Who did this old guy think he was? And why should she listen to him?

"I don't care about the money. I'm good in science; I'll get scholarships. Or grants."

"I have no doubt that you will."

Yeah, sure. A thought came to Lucy. "Wait—you said, 'when the terms of the will are met.' What did you mean by that?"

"The will says that you must live on the property for five years and use part of the insurance money to renovate. The property can't be sold in that time, and the college portion of the insurance can only be tapped once the work is done. If those terms aren't met, the whole twenty acres, and the money, too, will go to charity."

"Who gets to say if we get the money or not?"

"As executor," Mr. Jeffers said, "that would be me."

"And why are you the executor?"

"Lucy!" Alexa exclaimed.

"It's okay, Alexa," John Jeffers said. "I imagine Margaret named me, Lucy, because we were friends for many years."

"If you knew her so well, can you explain why Aunt Margaret would do this to us? Why wouldn't she just give us the money? Or *you*, if you were her friend."

Mr. Jeffers tilted his head and lifted his eyes, remembering. "Margaret's great-grandfather built this house, and she wanted it to stay in the family. She started the renovations, but most of her money went to her medical bills. In later years, her Parkinson's kept her from working on the place herself. She refused to sell off the acreage, though, and kept paying on the life insurance, hoping to save it all. Your mother is her closest living relative; Margaret knew that she's an architect."

"So we moved here, away from my school and friends and life, and if we don't fix this place to your satisfaction, I might not get the college fund anyway?"

"I know you will," he said, looking at Alexa.

Lucy opened her mouth to speak again, but the doorbell rang, and Alexa went to answer it. Lucy could hear a young woman's voice.

"I'm Kelly. The notary?"

"Oh, hi. Come in. There are just a few things to sign."

Lucy watched her mother sign the documents. When Mr. Jeffers, smiling, shook her mother's hand, Lucy jumped up from the table and ran outside.

She skirted the cars in the driveway and crossed the property diagonally toward a few outbuildings she hadn't yet explored. Approaching them, she found herself drawn to the old stone shed her mother called the spring house. It was built into the side of a hill, with a heavy door and an iron bolt that slid back reluctantly. Lucy stepped inside and shut the door. The air was moist and refreshing, maybe fifteen or twenty degrees cooler than outside. She was surprised to see a large stone pool, which took up most of the space. The water looked about three feet deep, and the surface was still, though she could hear a trickling from somewhere. One small window set high on the wall sent a narrow shaft of light through the gloom. As her eyes adjusted, she noticed glints of green and gold in the water. There were ledges along the sides of the pool, under the water line, and on them sat a watermelon and a couple of bottles of beer.

She heard voices, then the cars in the driveway started and drove away. The screen door slammed. Lucy sat on the edge of the pool and reached down toward the bottles. The water was icy; by the time she pulled one bottle up, her arm had started to ache. She looked at the label—some brand she'd never heard of. She hid the beer in a corner of the spring house, behind a crate. Something for later.

"Lucy ... "

Her mother was calling her, but it was cool here and Lucy wasn't in the mood to talk. Alexa called her name again, then Lucy heard the land line in the kitchen ring, and all was quiet. She considered staying where she was for the afternoon; she felt distant here from both her mother and her own emotions. Calm. She took deep breaths and closed her eyes, imagined herself on the beach in that Mexican beer commercial, lounging to the sound of surf next to a mysterious stranger. As he leaned in to kiss her, she could feel his fingertips on her skin. She opened her eyes and looked down at her thigh, where a huge brown spider was crawling. Muffling a scream, she brushed it off and flew from the spring house back in the direction of the house.

The front porch looked much friendlier now, and Lucy sank into one of the painted rockers Margaret had left behind. Her mother finished her conversation and came out just as the postman pulled up to the box. Alexa went out to the road to introduce herself. The balding postman leaned out of his jeep and gave her mother a smile. The usual. Lucy wouldn't call her mom a beauty, but men paid attention to her.

A blue convertible filled with teens sped past the house. A red-haired boy was driving, and Lucy thought she recognized the girl in the front seat. She wondered where they were going and what there was to do in this place on an August afternoon.

The postman spent almost fifteen minutes flirting with her mother. He'd brought mail, though, their first in Ecstasy. Alexa attempted to speak to her as she climbed the peeling porch steps with a stack of it in her arms, but Lucy turned away, feigning interest in the yellow roses that grew on that side of the yard. Her mother dropped Lucy's copy of *Discover Magazine* on the table near the rocking chairs and slipped into the house without further comment.

She knew she should go in and help Alexa with the unpacking, but she'd had days of that already. Besides, it was nice out here. Despite the heat, her skin was still cool from the spring house, and the porch was shaded in the afternoon. A ceiling fan—one of the few things that worked around here—kept the porch at least as cool as it was inside the house. She lounged in the rocker, reading her magazine. The familiar summer sound of cicadas built to a crescendo around her, then ebbed to almost nothing, only to start all over again.

In the late afternoon, she heard a car approach and the sound of laughter. The teens in the blue convertible were passing again, returning from wherever they'd been. She stood to see them better, and her movement caught their eyes. The car pulled over down the road and backed up until it was directly in front of the house. A blond girl got out and waved her hand in greeting. Lucy froze for a moment and thought about dodging inside for cover, then realized how that would look. What could she do but wave in return? The blond girl beckoned, and Lucy walked toward her. The rest of the teens were lined up on the sidewalk by the time she got to the gate. They had evidently come from swimming; the boys wore trunks and tee shirts, and the girls' bikini tops showed through their clothes.

"Hi. Are you the new owners?" the blond girl asked. "You bought the Moss property?"

"We didn't exactly buy it," said Lucy. "Margaret Moss was my great aunt."

"Your aunt? I used to do yard work for her," said a dark-haired boy with a narrow face. "That is, until she passed."

"Oh, I see."

"Nice lady."

There was an awkward pause. The blond girl looked toward the porch.

"Are those rockers antiques?"

"Uh, yeah. I guess so."

To Lucy's surprise, the girl started past her toward the house.

Lucy hesitated, then turned to the others. "I'm Lucy. Would you like to come up to the porch? I could get you some Cokes ..."

They required no persuading and were soon sprawled on the rockers and wicker, smelling of tanning oil. The blond girl introduced herself as Jordan. She was obviously calling the shots.

"This guy is David," said Jordan, pointing a thumb toward the red-haired boy on her left. "And that's Maddie and Logan."

Maddie had a round face with freckles and glossy brown hair that reminded Lucy of one of her dolls, packed away in a box of mementos upstairs. Logan was the dark-haired boy. His eyes were gray, like Alexa's. They were all good-looking and confident; Lucy guessed they were popular.

"I'd give you a tour," Lucy told them, "but we've only been here since Thursday. Right now, there's nothing but boxes all over the place."

"That's cool," said David. "No worries."

Lucy retreated into the house. She heard them continue to talk as she poured soft drinks in the kitchen. Alexa must have heard them too, but she didn't appear.

Well, what do you know? There was life in freaking Ecstasy. These people were clearly here to check her out. She'd never been the new kid before and didn't know how this went. Would they like her? Then again, why should she care? It wasn't like they were her friends. But she was trapped here, for now, and it wouldn't be wise to pointlessly piss off the natives. She threw a bag of taco chips into a bowl, filled a smaller one with salsa, and headed back out to the porch. It took several trips to pass out the drinks and snacks.

"So where are you from?" David asked, when she took a seat.

"Elm Ridge," Lucy told them. "It's right outside Chicago. I go to ER."

"What—the hospital?" asked Maddie.

"No, Elm Ridge High School."

"So you're not going to go to Pine Bluff?"

Oh yeah … Pine Bluff. That was the name of the high school in Ecstasy.

"Well, actually, I am," said Lucy. "I guess we're living here now." It was the first time she'd admitted as much, even to herself.

"So you're from Chicago?" asked Maddie. "We went on a field trip there last year. Saw some museums, went to Willis Tower, Navy Pier …"

"Willis Tower?"

"Yeah, you know, the tallest building. With the observation deck?"

"Are you sure you're from Chicago?" Jordan asked, and the others snickered.

"Oh, I know what you mean. Most of us call it the Sears Tower. Because that's what it was named when it was built."

"Whatever," said Jordan, and smiled. "I hear it's not the tallest anymore."

Something about the tilt of her head made Lucy remember: Jordan was one of the trio of girls she'd seen in that convenience store on her first day in Ecstasy.

Her visitors went on to other subjects, talking and laughing about the kids they'd seen at the pool. Their conversation and ease with each other made Lucy feel like the total outsider she was. She wondered if it was meant to.

Logan seemed to pick up on her thoughts.

"Hey, Lucy," he said. "We're going to the pool again Friday. Think you'd like to come?" The group laughed again, and Logan reddened. "What I meant was—"

"I know what you meant," said Lucy.

Then she smiled. What the hell. She'd have to blend in with the flora and fauna, at least for a while. Might as well start now. She'd go to the pool.

"Sure," said Jordan. "You're on our way. It's half a mile south of here. We'll pick you up."

They exchanged phone numbers. Jordan entered Lucy's number into her cell, then flipped her hair away from her face with manicured fingertips. She had large green eyes and a killer shape. Which, it appeared, she knew very well how to use. Both boys watched as she shifted on the wicker loveseat, crossing and recrossing her legs.

She studied Lucy. "By the way, what church do you go to?"

Her tone was casual, but she leaned toward Lucy as she asked, and it was difficult to miss the gold cross swinging close to Jordan's breasts.

"We don't really go to church."

Jordan exchanged a look with Maddie that Lucy couldn't read.

"Well, you're welcome at ours. Everybody is. We're part of the youth group there, at ECM."

That was the second time Lucy had heard of this place in the four days she'd been here.

"Sure, I'll think about it."

They stood and left almost as suddenly as they'd arrived, trooping down the porch steps and across the yard, waving from the blue convertible as they pulled away.

Lucy sat on the porch for nearly an hour, thinking. Shadows lengthened on the front lawn, where robins alighted to look for worms. The scent of the yellow roses wafted over the porch. It was pleasant here, but it wasn't home. Her mother might have a plan for their lives, but Lucy had one too. And it sure wasn't Ecstasy.

She thought about Aunt Margaret's will. The thing was not a done deal; there were conditions. Maybe a way out. What if the renovations didn't get done on time? Would they lose the property? What if she failed a semester in school? Would Alexa admit that this was a mistake and take her home?

She felt like Dorothy, except that she was stuck in Kansas instead of Oz. And she wouldn't just stand here clicking her heels in the stupid ruby slippers. She would help herself. Lucy could see there was more than one way to get back home to Elm Ridge.

Her stomach was growling. She hadn't heard a sound from Alexa, and she wondered if there would be dinner. Lucy rose from the rocker and entered the house, letting the screen door slam.

4

Alexa: Friday, August 23

The butler's pantry would have to go. She could see it was the only place for the kitchen expansion and first-floor powder room. She wouldn't have the heart to raze it if it had the original fixtures, but someone in the 60s had switched out the cabinets, substituting shellacked wood and Formica. It matched the 50-year-old kitchen, which John Jeffers told her had been there when Aunt Margaret inherited the house.

Her first view of the house on Collins Road had been a shock. Its peeling Victorian frame had worn shabby since she'd seen it twenty-odd years ago, and the sheeting rain she ran through from her car to the sagging wraparound porch didn't help the impression. She had hardly noticed the inside of the house at first, concerned as she was with the state of her damp furniture and the cardboard boxes piled in every room.

John Jeffers, as promised, had been there when they arrived—a tall, thin man in his mid-to-late sixties, with silver hair and mustache. Beside Alexa and Lucy, he was evidently the closest thing Aunt Margaret had to family. He listened sympathetically as they told the tale of the blown-out tire, then offered them refreshments from the refrigerator he'd stocked. Alexa was grateful to learn he'd had the movers set up their beds. He'd also made sure they had water and electricity, but after the air conditioners blew several fuses, she feared to put them to the test again. Despite the intense humidity, they'd have to make do with the ceiling fans. John had handed her the keys and promised to return on Monday to discuss Aunt Margaret's will. Alexa had watched him drive off in the rain, then sighed, looking around her. So much work already, and this was just the beginning.

The success of their first few months, Alexa reasoned, depended on Lucy, so she dedicated the first weekend to her daughter's room. To some extent, that strategy failed; Lucy never let up about wanting to be back in Elm Ridge with her friends. But Alexa could see that she was charmed by the third-floor bedroom, with its circular turret overlooking both the broadleaf maple in front of the house and the beautiful side-yard garden. On Saturday morning, they'd gone to Ecstasy for paint—the deep shade of rose that Lucy loved—and also bought her a pale gray comforter. They had cleaned and masked and painted together, with Lucy rolling the wall color on, Alexa working the white trim with a brush. They listened to the radio, occasionally singing along, and lapsed into near camaraderie, until Lucy remembered again that she was angry.

Alexa had spent the next few days pacing the 1890s farmhouse, estimating the damage. She took in the state of the walls and woodwork, pulled up carpet to look at the floors, peeled back the old wallpaper. The double parlor and dining room had a fireplace each, and she could see that the mantels and the sweeping staircase in the foyer would be impressive once they were stripped and refinished. But the plaster walls in the dining room were beyond repair and needed to come down. Ditto the walls in the den. The kitchen was a total gut job, along with the butler's pantry. A large second pantry off the kitchen could be divided for food storage and a mudroom.

Surprisingly, the second floor was in better shape. The full bath needed a patch and paint, but the fixtures and original tile were in fairly good condition. The three bedrooms on the second floor had been drywalled sometime in the last decade, and the maple floors refinished. The same was true of the one large bedroom on the third floor—Lucy's—which had new walls, a new oak floor, and a closet and bath carved out of the attic space.

The electric and plumbing repairs were anyone's guess, and she didn't yet know the state of the foundation or the roof. Her biggest immediate concern was to get back on the grid.

On their trip into town, Alexa had noticed a small computer store on Main Street with refurbished laptops and monitors in the window. On Tuesday, she'd gone back to talk with the IT people there. Behind the canvas awning and hand-lettered sign—*Prometheus Computer Sales and Diagnostics*—she'd found two men in their mid-thirties: Jeremy, tall, with a red-blond topknot and black-framed glasses, and Chad, shorter, thicker, with dark hair that was shaved on one side, and black plug earrings. They turned out to be the owners and sole employees of the place.

"Chad and Jeremy?" Alexa suppressed a smile.

"Yeah, we're aware," said Chad good-naturedly. "We'll sing you a few bars of 'Summer Song' when we get to know you better. What can we do for you?"

Alexa explained her need to set up internet access for her CAD equipment, scanner, and drafter. Jeremy queried her on her configuration and began to search online. Chad showed her a router more powerful than the one she owned and a few pieces of auxiliary equipment. He was by far the more talkative of the two, commenting on everything from her operating system to the traffic in Ecstasy.

The pair had agreed to come out to Margaret's place today to coordinate with the electrician. Alexa took a break in the midafternoon to clean up for her meeting with them. The water pressure in the shower over the clawfoot tub was low, and she had some trouble rinsing the lather from her hair. But the water cooled and relaxed her, and the view of the 20 acres from the bathroom window was beautiful, just as she remembered: the orchard, the raspberry bushes, the spring house, the now-crumbling carriage barn. She had played here as a child with some distant cousins, chasing fireflies, playing hide and seek at dusk, then taking baths with the girls in this huge old tub before bed. The smell of Aunt Margaret's Ivory soap was all that was missing from her reverie.

Those kids had moved to other states years ago, and as she tended to her face in the mirror of the old medicine cabinet above the sink, she wondered where they were now.

The new cover-up was working well, even in this humidity. She first blended several colors to get the right shade and applied it to her cheek, then brushed on the setting powder, closed her eyes, and applied the setting spray. Then blush, and done. Not bad. These days no one but Lucy ever had to look at the port-wine mark that had stained her left cheek from birth. Thank goodness for modern advances in cosmetics.

"What's that on your face?" The refrain still echoed through her mind. She had heard it in this very bathroom from the cousins, and nearly every day at school or play in the rest of the world. The adults stared at the spot, too polite to speak of it, but the children were direct and cruel. "Why do you have that?" "What's wrong with you?" They gathered around on every first day of school, in every new place she went, pointing their fingers. In class, she sat, elbow on her desk, her left hand raised to hide the spot on her cheek.

Her mother, Sheila, refused to let her cover it. Alexa wanted a bandage or some makeup, as soon as she was old enough to realize there was such a thing. Sheila called this vanity, and she wouldn't have it. The birthmark, her mother told her, was shaped like a descending dove, a special gift from heaven that set her apart. It set Alexa apart alright, and she truly hated it.

The flat reddish-purple stain hadn't changed much over the years; it was still the same irregular ellipse with ragged extensions. Not a dove. Perhaps a comet, or the tulip a face painter had drawn around it the summer she was eight. She'd slept on her back for a week to keep that artwork intact, and had felt almost like a normal girl until it faded and her mother made her wash the remnants away.

But in truth, the birthmark looked like a flame, red and hot. The other kids called her "fire face" for most of her youth.

She still loathed being singled out, hated crowds and any occasion where she was the center of attention. This move had stirred up a lot of those anxieties, being new to and so different from this rural community. But she'd just have to deal with it, big-girl style. The makeup, thankfully, helped.

Hearing a car turn into the driveway, Alexa pulled on a pair of khakis and one of her nicer t-shirts and headed downstairs. Someone was leaning hard on the doorbell, sending the sound of chimes throughout the house. Well, at least one thing in this place didn't need to be fixed.

Alexa opened the screen door to the electrician, a tall man in clean white coveralls who shook her hand formally. His name was Ivan, he said, his accent eastern European, his smile guarded but polite. Alexa led him down to the basement fuse box, then up through the house, explaining the scope of the planned renovations, and her need to be up and running on the second and third floor while they were taking place.

Chad and Jeremy arrived, and Alexa showed the three men to the middle-sized bedroom on the second floor, which she intended to use as her drafting office until she could move to the renovated den or restore the carriage barn. She gave them a sketch of her preferred layout, and together the four of them figured out the particulars: how much power was needed, where the electric outlets should be, where the cable should come in, and how the router should be positioned.

Ivan the electrician opened the walls in several spots with a special cutting tool he'd brought and determined that—in that room at least—there was no old knob-and-tube wiring. That would simplify things. He squatted, testing outlets with a handheld meter. Finally he stood, scribbled some figures, and handed them to Alexa.

While the IT guys took a look at her hardware and software, Alexa walked Ivan back to the front door. Standing under the antique chandelier in the foyer, they finished their discussion about the job. Ivan suggested 300-amp service and new circuit-breaker panels for the house. He couldn't know all he was dealing with until the first-floor gut, but he would install the first panel and make sure the wiring in her office and the bedrooms were able to carry the load they'd need.

That meant the internet. Work. That meant air conditioning.

"When can you start?"

"Tomorrow, in the afternoon."

Alexa was surprised, and at the same time saddened. The easy availability of skilled tradespeople spoke directly to the economy in this town.

"That'll be fine."

"You hired a contractor? I know a man."

"I have a call in to one who was referred to me. Have you heard of him? George Whitman?"

"Yes, I know him a little bit. Good work if you pay attention."

Alexa laughed. "I know what you mean. As architect and designer, I'll be overseeing the work."

"Then I think, okay. Big job. But you will succeed." Ivan paused, then touched a finger to his temple. "Ah! There are some few things I forgot to check," he told her. "I must do it before I leave."

He drifted into the dining room as a blue convertible pulled up on the road in front of the house and the driver blew its horn. Lucy came down the stairs in a short print dress, the thin straps of her emerald-green swimsuit visible at the shoulders.

"Are you going to the pool now?" Alexa asked her. "Where is it? And when will you be home?"

"Mom," Lucy said with mock patience as she pulled on a pair of canvas flats by door, "chill out. The pool is just a couple miles down the road. I'm going with those kids from the school. I'm fine. I have my phone."

"Okay, let me know if you'll be home for dinner—" but Lucy was out the door, then climbing into the vehicle's back seat, the other teens moving over to make room. Alexa raised her hand to wave, but none of them looked back as they pulled away. Her daughter was doing as she'd asked, making friends. But Alexa didn't know these kids. She'd assumed they'd come in; such a rookie mistake for a seasoned single parent. She was losing her touch.

Alexa rejoined the computer guys in the would-be office. Jeremy inspected her equipment and cables as Chad suggested hardware and software upgrades.

"The router signal needs to reach the first floor and front porch, if possible, and Lucy's room upstairs. Any problem with that?" Alexa asked.

"Probably not. We can set up a signal here and check it out. Can you show us your daughter's room?"

The three of them climbed the stairs to the third floor. Lucy had left her small TV on and tuned to the local news, probably the only channel she could get here without cable. As Jeremy took measurements, Alexa's attention was drawn to the program on the screen. Theme music played as the camera panned across the image of a giant, glittering church. Its tall, sloped roof and steeple made of mirrored glass reflected the sky, and seemed, at least from some camera angles, to disappear completely. The large cross at the top of the steeple, by virtue of this illusion, looked like it was floating in the air. The caption on the screen read "Sky Cathedral, Ecstasy Christian Ministries."

The shot dissolved to a middle-aged man in a black suit and clerical collar seated across from one of the station's reporters. On the wall behind them, the church's logo—a white cross and circle containing the letters ECM in scrolling script—was backlit in violet light. He had a mane of wavy silver hair, high cheekbones, and a long, rather flat nose that gave him a leonine look. But it was his intense eyes that captured the camera. There was something strangely iconic about the man.

"Oh, *this* asshole," said a voice over her shoulder. It was Chad.

In Alexa's experience, those who called others assholes often fit the criteria themselves. She didn't know Chad well, so she suspended judgment and merely turned to him, one eyebrow raised.

"One of those idiot creationists," said Chad, gesturing at the set. "He's getting this poor girl to sue the high school for not teaching Genesis in science class."

"The public high school?"

"Yeah. Pine Bluff. And the local stations are giving him time, as if this stuff is legit. He's been all over the news here for a week."

The stiffly coiffed blond announcer spoke directly into the camera.

"Welcome back. We're speaking with Cyrus Bell, pastor of Ecstasy Christian Ministries." She turned to Bell and addressed him deferentially. "Tell us why you, as the plaintiff's pastor, became involved in this suit against the high school."

"Thanks, Ashley. An important question. The girl comes from a humble Christian family here in town. She was quite distressed to be forced to study a version of the earth's origins that contradicts the Bible. She came to me, concerned, for my advice. As her pastor, my choice was simple. It's my duty to set an example for our children.

"The Pine Bluff science department claims to be doing what's 'rational.' But let's be clear: by teaching evolution, they're teaching the atheist faith. They're teaching scorn for the word of God, the Holy Scriptures. That's not only *ir*rational, but foolish. Naturally, I will fight it. It's commanded by God that we have no other god before him, even if they call it science."

"Oh, he's good," said Chad. "He's very good. The bastard."

The news anchor faced the camera again.

"Tomorrow we'll have more in our continuing series, 'Evolution vs. the Bible in Ecstasy.'" The program broke for commercials.

Alexa made a mental note to speak to someone at the high school. Before she'd considered moving, she had contacted the science department and verified that they offered the courses Lucy needed, with well-credentialed instructors. Surely that curriculum wouldn't be jeopardized by this nonsense!

Jeremy had calculated the optimum router placement to reach Lucy's desk, so they started downstairs to check out the kitchen and porch. Halfway to the second-floor landing, they heard a shriek from below. They raced down the steps to find Ivan standing stock-still in the middle of the parlor, wailing and covering his head with his arms as a sparrow flew through the room. The bird was as crazed as Ivan, tracing figure eights near the ceiling at top speed. The approach of Alexa and the IT men threw it into an even wilder frenzy, and it flung itself against the windows, looking for escape. Ivan lunged through the foyer and fumbled with the screen door hook before spilling himself onto the front porch, where he stopped, his hand to his chest. The whole thing would have been comical but for the look on Ivan's face. Alexa followed him out.

"Are you alright, Ivan?"

He gasped, then shook his head. "A bird in the house."

"Are you afraid of them?" Alexa asked.

"Not outside, no. But inside?" He crossed himself.

Alexa wasn't sure how to respond. Chad stuck his head out the door and asked for a broom.

"There are a couple of brooms in the kitchen," she told him, and turned again to Ivan, who was fleeing toward his car. "Wait!" she called. "You'll be here tomorrow, right?"

"No. No," he said. Then, "Maybe. We'll see. I'll call you." And with that, he started his engine and sped toward the road.

Alexa stood there a moment, speechless. What the hell? Then she reentered the house to find Chad and Jeremy herding the bird into the foyer with the brooms. She opened the screen door, and thankfully, the bird chose the offered portal and launched itself into the still, hot afternoon. It passed close enough to Alexa that she could see the subtle patterns in its dun-colored feathers. She watched it fly away.

"Poor little thing. I hope it's okay. I hope they're *both* okay."

"The bird wasn't as scared as Ivan," Chad observed with a chuckle.

"I wonder what it is with him," said Alexa. "Some phobia?"

"Superstition," offered Jeremy. "My grandmother was the same. Bad luck. They believe a bird in the house means someone will die."

"Really? An omen?" Alexa shook her head. "Wow. People in this day and age really believe that's a harbinger of death?"

"Trust me," Jeremy replied. "They do."

"It must have flown down the chimney. I'll have to remember to check the flue."

The men finished their measurements and left, promising on their way out to return when the cable and electricity were in.

Alexa was relieved to have the house to herself for the first time since they'd moved. Yes, she liked people—a few at a time—and enjoyed being around them. But social interactions sapped her, and she recharged by spending time alone. She reveled in uninterrupted thoughts as she washed and chopped vegetables for salad and brewed iced tea in the kitchen where for so many years, Aunt Margaret had done the same. Alexa could envision the tall, thin woman in jeans and sneakers, her hair pulled away from her face in a style that showed off her prominent cheekbones.

Her cell phone rang. Alexa looked at the caller—her mother, Sheila—then ignored it. She wasn't in the mood. She was happy her mother had never learned to text.

The last time Sheila and Margaret spoke had been in this kitchen when Alexa was eleven years old, and her father, Margaret's brother, had been dead just over a year.

Alexa had heard loud voices and came into the room to see her mother and Margaret turn their backs to one another and busy themselves with chores. The next morning, her mother had packed up the car and they'd driven home, several days earlier than planned. That's the last time either one of them had seen Margaret.

Alexa took her tea and a plate of salad into the front parlor, where she'd draped Margaret's sofa with sheets and placed it in front of the ancient, rabbit-eared TV. There was no remote, so she stood at the set and dialed through channels to find some that were clear. The cable man was coming tomorrow; tonight her choices were limited to an inane network reality show and a *Big Bang Theory* marathon. *Big Bang* won, hands down. She worked on her tablet as she watched, entering measurements and notes for her remodeling designs, thankful for 4G, however spotty.

Lucy texted that they were going for pizza in town. She asked to be out until eleven. "Everyone's nice. I'll get a ride home."

Alexa consented on condition that Lucy send her the names and numbers of some of her companions. Lucy complained but complied.

A breeze fluttered the curtains and the leaves on the trees outside the house. Thunder rumbled; a cool front was moving in. At ten thirty, the national news began. Alexa looked up to see Cyrus Bell talking to another reporter. His tone, though, was quite different for the national show.

"It's clearly a case of *academic freedom*," the pastor was saying. "The young lady's rights as a Christian are being denied. Intelligent Design is good science. Why is only one set of theories allowed to be taught in the classroom? Education requires *critical thinking,* a skill that every student needs to acquire."

Chad was right. The guy was good.

There was more thunder, closer now, and doors started slamming upstairs. Alexa went through the house and closed most of the windows. She left the ones in their bedrooms open just a bit, and also those in the still-stifling front parlor, to which she returned.

"The problem," Cyrus Bell was saying, "is carbon-dating. It's not—as the scientists claim—reliable."

Alexa winced, knowing some listeners would believe him. They continued to discuss the lawsuit, but the student plaintiff was still not identified. Alexa wondered about her—how she was raised, how at such a young age she was so sure of the story she'd been told that she was willing to fight in court.

"It's about faith," said Pastor Bell.

Yes, thought Alexa, it *is* about faith. Not faith in the first sense—a confidence that comes from one's experience with an idea or thing or other human being—but rather, faith in the second sense, the kind that lets you believe in something without any evidence. Many could manage this sort of faith, and she didn't begrudge them, as long as they didn't encroach on anyone's rights. Or education. But she herself couldn't manage that faith. Not since she was young.

The wind was whipping the trees. Something—maybe the metal downspout—was groaning as if it protested. Alexa grew uneasy. When the wind blew hard, she always felt that the world was wild, unpredictable, everything pushed to its limit. The air itself could become a weapon to tear apart the life you'd built from planks and bricks. Or love.

She remembered the storm at the county fair the year that she was ten. On a visit to Ecstasy, her mother had made a sudden decision to go to the fair, which was probably less about quilts and pies and livestock, Alexa realized now, than it was about escaping the good intentions of family and friends. Her father had been gone four months by then, dead of a brain aneurism no one had known he'd had. Gone—her father, her hero, her confidante, who had read to her, and listened to her, and taught her to play the piano.

Her mother was young and husbandless, but it was not her nature to weep. Practical and pious, she prayed and got on with it. She expected the same from her only child, and Alexa disappointed her daily, crying and mourning, shutting herself in her room to read, or playing the piano. By the time school let out in June, her mother had had enough. The piano disappeared, and Alexa was ordered outside to play. Her mother kept her busy that summer with swimming lessons, ballet classes, and vacation Bible school. Until their visit to Ecstasy in August. There, her father's sister Margaret, his cousins and friends, were awash with memories and emotions unwelcome to Sheila.

So Alexa and her mother went to the fair. The day was hot and humid, with oppressive clouds that seemed to hang a few feet above their heads. By midafternoon a breeze moved in, followed fast by great sheets of rain that sent them scurrying for shelter. Her mother pulled her into one of the bigger tents where the large antiques were sold. Thirty or forty other people had taken refuge there. The wind grew stronger, then really fierce as the downpour continued, trapping them all in the tent and forcing them toward the center, away from the buffeted sides. A few brave souls volunteered to wrestle the whipping tent flaps. The top of the structure beat like great wings, as if it would scoop them up any moment and fly them away with the storm.

Soon the rain was coming faster than the fairgrounds could absorb. Water rushed under the sides of the tent, soaking them all to the ankles as they huddled together, listening to the wind and thunder, watching the silhouettes of trees flash against the canvas as the storm lit up the sky.

"What if lightning strikes?" Alexa asked her mother, clutching her skirt. "We'll be electrocuted!"

"It's alright. It's just rain. The Lord will protect us." Then her mother bent her head and clasped her hands.

Alexa tried her best to do as her mother did, screwing her eyes shut, plaiting her fingers until they hurt, asking God to still the wind and the rain. Instead, she heard something roaring like an animal and opened her eyes to witness the tent flaps breaking their ties to fly loose. Antique china and glassware pieces rattled and shattered against one another as one shelf after another toppled, the furniture near the tent sides first, and then some pieces amid the crowd. An elderly woman cried out as a massive breakfront fell and pinned her to the sodden ground. Others rushed to pull it from her, but Alexa could see that the woman was unmoving and gravely injured.

Alexa began to scream. "She's dead! She's dead!"

Her mother moved to shield Alexa's view. She took her daughter's shoulders, stood in front of her, and looked her in the eyes. Her voice was firm and strangely without emotion.

"That's enough, Alexa. She's probably not dead. Everything is alright."

That moment was the first time Alexa rebelled against her mother. Her father would have listened to her, been honest with her, saved her—or if that was impossible, comforted her in his arms.

This time it was Alexa who'd had enough.

"It's *not* alright!" she screamed. "It's *not* alright!" She balled her hands into fists and beat them on her thighs. "It's *not* alright! I want my dad! I want my dad!"

She screamed so hard and so long, that others forgot their fear of the storm and gathered around to watch the child with the purple flame on her face melting down in their midst. She cried until she was hoarse, until the storm passed and the ambulance came and the people had dispersed. She cried as they waded through mud and water, picked their way over fallen debris to their car. As they drove back to Aunt Margaret's through the surrounding towns, they saw ruined houses and dozens of downed trees. The radio told them three separate twisters had touched down near them that day.

"See?" Alexa told her mother, her breath still wracked with spasms.

"Yes, I see," said her mother. "God in his grace has spared us."

Alexa was unconvinced. "What did that old lady do, that God wouldn't spare her?" she asked. And then her real question: "What did *Daddy* do?"

Her mother had no answer, and they drove the rest of the way back to Margaret's in silence. That day's events put an end to Alexa's faith in the second sense.

She shook her head. This house brought back too many memories, both painful and sweet. The TV flickered. The final close-up of Cyrus Bell showed the man had violet eyes. At the sound of a car in the driveway, Alexa went to unhook the screen door for Lucy, and the two of them closed the rest of the windows just as the rain set in.

5

Lucy: Friday, August 23

It was the fourth Friday in August—the end of the longest, hottest week of Lucy's life— when Jordan texted her. Since they'd moved to the farmhouse in Ecstasy, there had been no air conditioning, no friends, no life—nothing to do but sweat and unpack. The house was filled with workmen. She fantasized about stealing the keys to her mother's car and heading back home—if only she had her license. She had to settle for giving Alexa the silent treatment. She was pissed and bored, and agreed to go to the pool with these people just to have something to do.

Sandwiched between Maddie and Logan in the back seat of the small sleek car, hot country wind blowing through her hair, the radio playing some twangy song she'd never heard, she felt like a foreigner. Actually, more like a foreign object. *Which one doesn't belong?*

"So how are you liking Ecstasy?" Jordan asked her from the front passenger seat, shouting over the noise of the rushing air.

Lucy clutched her hair in one hand and raised her voice to match. "Well, I haven't really seen much of it yet. We've been busy painting, getting stuff organized ..."

"Did you register for school yet?"

"Yeah, on Wednesday."

"What're your classes? I hope you don't have Mr. Malloy for English."

"No, I think it's a woman. I also have history, math, and AP physics and bio."

"Another smart one," Jordan said, with a tinge of sarcasm. "Logan's in AP bio, too."

Lucy met Logan's eyes. "Great."

Logan smiled as Jordan continued, "Do you have a boyfriend?"

"Not at the moment. Hey, what kind of car is this?"

"It's a BMW 4 series," answered David, the red-headed guy who was driving. "My dad got it into the lot last week." Logan explained. "His father owns a car dealership, so he gets to borrow some pretty sweet rides."

"So David usually drives," said Jordan. "What do you guys have?"

Lucy wasn't about to admit to their 11-year-old Hyundai, no matter how fond she was of Olive.

"Nothing like this. How far is it to the pool?" Every question she asked was one they couldn't ask her. It sucked being the newbie.

"Another couple of blocks." Jordan checked her look in the mirror, but kept at it. "What does your dad do? Do you have any sisters or brothers?"

"No, he's not in the picture; it's just me and my mom. She's an architect. She's renovating the house."

"So that's why you moved here? Why didn't you just sell it?"

"Long story …"

At that, Jordan, thankfully, seemed to lose interest, faced forward again, and began to detail her latest conversation with someone named Brad, most of which was lost to the wind before it got to Lucy. David honked the horn as they pulled into the pool lot, and several teens waved back at them. He found a shaded spot to park, and they all piled out of the car.

It was the last weekday of summer vacation, and half the high school must have been at the pool. Everyone was dark from the sun, there being, Lucy figured, little else to do here in August. The volume was deafening—radios, laughter, splashing boys and shrieking girls, the lifeguard blowing his shrill whistle, trying to keep order. The group headed to a corner near the deep end, put down towels, and arranged some deck chairs. She had heard the buzz as they came in, evidently the norm for Jordan, but attention was focused on Lucy too, some probably wondering how she had crashed Jordan's group.

It was rough to make her debut to this crowd in her swimsuit; everyone eyed her up and down when she took off the sundress, taking in every part of her not covered by her emerald-green bikini.

As the group settled themselves by the pool, the scrutiny faded. Except for occasional curious glances, almost everyone ignored her. People came and went in that first hour, paying court to Jordan. Lucy took cover behind her sunglasses, sweat collecting between her breasts and trickling toward her navel as she lay on a deck chair watching them, listening to their conversations. When the group was left to themselves again, Jordan returned to her favorite subject: her boyfriend who'd just left for college.

"Brad calls every night and says he misses me. They just started classes, but they've had some parties and concerts and stuff, and he says it's great, that we have to get there and visit as soon as we can." Lucy had learned on the ride to the pool that "there" was Blackrock Christian College.

"How long does it take to get there?" Logan asked.

"A couple of hours, more or less. Close enough for Brad to come back home some weekends. I can't wait. It's a whole eight days until I see him again." Jordan hugged her knees to her chest and rocked back and forth on her deck chair.

Maddie sat down next to her and put an arm around her. "Jordan, don't start. You'll end up crying again."

And indeed Jordan's eyes had begun to fill.

"What am I going to do? It's a whole year! I could finish Pine Bluff in January, if I add one more class this semester. But my dad said no way—he's not sending a seventeen-year-old daughter off unsupervised, even to a Christian college." Jordan scanned the faces of those around her. "It's *forever*. What if Brad meets someone? There are plenty of girls who want him."

A beach ball landed at Lucy's feet, and she threw it back to the kids who had been playing with it in the pool. The diving board rang as a pudgy preteen cannonballed into the deep end.

Maddie's voice was sympathetic and soothing. "But you and Brad are perfect for each other."

David chimed in. "Why would he give up someone like you? I don't think you have to worry."

"I know. But ..." Jordan's voice trailed off as she noticed a gorgeous blond guy walking toward their group.

"What are you doing here?" Jordan asked him as he approached.

"Mom dropped me off. She's taking the Lexus into the shop—something about a recall. Dad has the Jeep, so I'd be stuck at the house all afternoon. I figured I might as well hang out here, and maybe David could run me to Tyler's later?"

"Sure," David answered.

"Thanks."

"Did you bring any money?" Jordan asked.

The gorgeous guy grinned. "I don't get my paycheck 'til tomorrow, but Mom spotted me a few bucks."

"Get us some Cokes?"

"Okay."

"And some nachos."

"Come and help me carry."

Jordan sighed and looked around for a stand in. "Oh, I almost forgot. This is Lucy. She's from Chicago. Lucy, this is my baby brother Jake."

"Yeah—no." Jake shook his head and smirked. "I'm younger by fourteen minutes. I'm her twin." Jake looked Lucy over appraisingly and smiled.

"Good to meet you," she said. He was tan and well built, with surfer-boy hair, a cleft chin, and unsettling azure eyes. The fact that he was Jordan's twin meant that he was a senior. She'd never seen a high-school boy look like *him*.

"Let's walk, Chicago Lucy, and get us some nachos."

She was delighted he asked. They followed a line of wet footprints around the pool to the whitewashed concession stand.

"So you just moved here?"

"Yeah. A week ago."

"And Jordan found you already." He laughed. "My sister misses nothing."

"Is she okay? I mean … "

"Brad?" he asked. Lucy nodded.

"Yeah, she will be." He turned to the girl behind the counter. "Six Cokes, three nachos." He smiled at Lucy. "I know how these people can eat." Then his expression grew more serious. "Brad, it happens, is the chink in Jordan's otherwise impervious armor. They've been going out for two years. It's going to take a while for her to adjust. But trust me, she will."

"*Impervious.* Impressive vocabulary."

He laughed. "Impervious. *Imperious.* That about sums it up."

Being Jordan's brother, he probably had plenty of reason to know the word *imperious*. Still, it was nice of Jordan to bring the new kid along today, and she said as much to Jake. He looked pleasantly surprised. "Yeah, she *is* nice, actually; a lot of people don't get that about her."

Lucy carried the cardboard tray of drinks while Jake managed the nachos. An old man in a tiny Speedo crossed their path, and they looked at each other and laughed. Wow. She felt the warmth of Jake's attention as a new thing, a new color. Nothing up to the present moment had ever been anything like it. As they moved together through the crowd, time slowed and stretched to encompass the sun, the pool sounds, the smell of chlorine and coconut, the feel of the rough pavement under her feet. She thrilled to it all, especially the humor and frank appreciation in Jake's eyes.

The moment was not to last. As they approached the group, Lucy could see her seat had been taken by a dark-haired girl in a well-filled yellow bikini, who smiled when she caught sight of Jake, revealing perfect teeth.

"Sophiiia." Jake teased out the second syllable of her name, then bent to give her a quick kiss on the lips.

Introductions were made as they passed out the drinks and nachos, then Sophia stood and ceded her lounge chair to Lucy. The boys dragged more chairs into two rows in their corner of the pool deck. They were seven now. Jake and Sophia went back to concessions to get another Coke.

Lucy tried hard to stay quiet, but finally couldn't resist. "Is that his girlfriend?"

Jordan sent her a knowing look. "Yeah, they've been together for a while. They have their ups and downs."

"She's beautiful."

Jordan shrugged. "The guys like her."

Damn. It made sense that he'd have a girlfriend who looked like a movie star. As the dark and sexy Sophia walked away with Jake, the other boys watched her with hooded eyes. Lucy knew then she didn't stand a chance with Jake, but suspected that knowledge might be completely useless against her emotions.

The truth of that was made apparent later in the evening. Hungry from their day at the pool, the group invited Lucy to go with them to a place in town, a strip mall's attempt at an old-world pizzeria. The venue didn't matter to Lucy; the food wasn't really the thing. She spent most of the evening watching and listening. Logan attempted to talk with her, but her eyes were drawn to Jake and Sophia nuzzling one another. David and Maddie seemed to be an item, too. They sat close together holding hands, although most of David's attention was directed to Jordan, who gossiped about other students. As in Elm Ridge, there was a lot of talk about the upcoming new school year.

After the pizza, they went to a bookstore café at Ecstasy Christian Ministries. Lucy was stunned at the size of the complex. One of the buildings was obviously intended for worship, with a mirrored glass roof and a huge cross on the top. But the rest looked more like a shopping mall, with stores, restaurants, and recreation areas. It covered what would be blocks in the city, with parking for acres around it.

Jake worked as a barista at the coffee shop—this being one of his nights off—and the Christian kids met there often in the evening. Tonight, Jake had brought an acoustic guitar, into which, Lucy noticed, amazed, he'd carved Bible verses in a stunning swirl pattern, making the instrument a work of art. They had stopped to pick up Tyler, who'd brought a bass. The place was filled with high-school kids moving among the small round tables, talking and sipping their lattes. At their urging, Jake and Tyler moved to the mic and tuned their instruments.

A few minutes later, they introduced themselves and announced their opening song: "Who Am I," by Casting Crowns. Lucy expected the typical rock star wannabe sound from the two boys on the stage. Instead, she heard the expertly played opening chords of a contemporary Christian song. The light caught the golden hair on Jake's forearms as his fingers flew across the strings, his voice as beautiful as his face: strong, clear, resonant, and very adult. This was no amateur. The lilting, lovely melody, Jake's nuanced and compelling delivery, the message of humility and love had everyone leaning forward, listening, or closing their eyes as if praying. Lucy and her friends had been moved by music, but this was different: nakedly emotional, a group experience that seemed to dissolve the borders between the performers and audience.

In five minutes, Jake had somehow moved to the center of Lucy's world. Her face burned with an embarrassment she tried to hide from the others. Sophia had her back to her; there was nothing to stop Lucy from gazing intently at Jake, trying to absorb his very essence. They played for nearly half an hour, ending with "Learning to Be the Light," the students raising their hands and swaying side to side, singing the chorus and the refrain, "Whoa, whoa-oh-oh." As Jake and Tyler gave up the mic and walked to their table, Lucy knew for certain that things would never be the same.

Jake sat in the empty seat next to hers and asked what she thought of their performance.

"Amazing!" she answered.

Jake looked pleased.

"We play most Sundays at the church," he told her, and smiled his megawatt smile. "You should come."

"Yeah," she said. "Maybe I will."

6

Rachel: Friday, September 6

"You're late," said Yolanda, as if Rachel didn't know. Rachel turned from her workstation in the four-woman cubicle to face her. The three other women eyed their computers, but she could tell by their body language they wouldn't miss a word.

Yolanda wore a short, fitted red jacket over a black pencil skirt, with lips and nails to match her red-framed glasses. Her bleached hair, fashionably dark at the roots, had been cropped into a slightly different style this week, and she looked—if it was possible—even more tan than usual. The effect, as Yolanda was surely aware, was fairly intimidating.

"I'm sorry, the buses weren't running. Or at least mine wasn't this morning. I had to walk."

Yolanda shifted her weight to one hip and crossed her arms. The face of her expensive watch reflected the dull fluorescent lights that studded the soundproof ceiling.

"Where do you live again?"

"Center Street."

"South?"

Rachel knew the question was meant to humiliate. No one wanted to live on South Center Street. Or to admit it. "Yes."

Yolanda managed a tight smile. "And it takes that long to walk from there? Why didn't you start earlier?"

"I waited for the bus first. When it didn't come, I decided I'd better walk."

"You know I'll have to write you up," she said with feigned regret. "This tardiness, after you missed some days last month without calling in."

"*One* day, and you know I did call in, Yolanda, just not until afternoon." Yolanda, in fact, was the one who had taken the call.

"Yes. Sick, you said. Well, you can explain it to *him*. He wants to see you."

"Now?"

"Not now. At ten thirty, when his meeting is over." Yolanda leaned close and lowered her voice, but just barely. "Even *he* can't save you if you keep screwing up like this."

With that, she turned on her spike heels and went back to her own much larger cubicle. Most of the women hated Yolanda. As supervisor she'd divided and conquered, making favorites of some of the workers, scorning others. Rachel was definitely not one of her pets. She turned back to her computer and opened a page to retrieve the latest orders.

"He" was Tom Marshall, head of Human Resources at Amos Windows. Rachel had met him at a local job fair a year and a half before, about a month after she'd been disfellowshipped. She'd been looking for work everywhere, dressed in a thrift-store suit, trying to hide the fact that she was living in a shelter. Not to mention that she'd never actually graduated from high school. The prior weeks had been a deluge of rejection. The job fair, held at a local hotel, began on a Friday morning. She'd arrived early only to find that the line to get in already wrapped around the block. The sun was out, but the spring wind was strong; by the time she got to the entrance, she was cold and tired, hungry, and close to tears.

Inside, the line was longest for Amos Windows and their table was the largest at the fair. The positions were mostly customer service, and she knew she could do the job. Her duties as liaison between her strict parents and her siblings had taught her tact, salesmanship, and empathy. She'd learned multiple ways to approach a problem, propose solutions, and placate almost any unhappy human being.

Three interviewers sat at the Amos table: a dark-haired man with acne-scarred skin, a blond woman with red glasses, and a very tall man with thick, brown hair, who, even sitting, towered over the others. The dark-haired man, who introduced himself as Orrin, waved Rachel to the chair in front of him. The job entailed filling phone and online orders from distributors. Could she handle that? He looked over her application and frowned. "No work experience?"

"I haven't had an actual paying job, but—"

"Geez. What are you doing here?" He scanned the page. "Where did you go to high school? Here in town?"

"I was homeschooled."

"Yeah. Do you have a diploma?"

"Well, I—no, not exactly."

The man rolled his eyes to the ceiling. "Honey, we don't even hire for the factory floor without one." He gestured around the room. "And neither do the rest of these guys."

She was obviously dismissed. Rachel grabbed her application and crumpled it, then tried to control her face as she stood and walked away. She heard a voice from the Amos table behind her.

"Miss?"

She kept going.

"Miss?"

She turned. The very tall man was standing.

"Miss? Could I speak with you?" He gestured to a seat at the table across from him. She sat. The man looked her over with curious brown eyes.

"I couldn't help but overhear. I apologize for Orrin. I'm Tom. Why don't you tell me about yourself? Maybe I can help."

Rachel was confused, but what the heck. It couldn't hurt. So she told the tall man the carefully edited version of her history she'd rehearsed.

"It's almost two," Tom observed when she was finished. "Have you had lunch?"

He took her to a coffee shop near the hotel. By the time they left, Rachel had a job, provided that she work for and get her GED; Tom had a date with her later in the evening.

The month that followed seemed like heaven to the homeschooled girl. They went to restaurants, bars, and movies in Ecstasy and surrounding towns. Rachel had never been to such places. Tom dressed well, complimented her, brought her flowers, bottles of wine. She smoked her first cigarette with him. She felt sophisticated, like she was waking, coming alive to a new world. She began the job at Amos and did well.

The fourth week they were dating, Tom asked to make dinner for Rachel at his apartment. She knew a girl could get into trouble alone with a man, and she was already doing so much that was immoral: dating unchaperoned, drinking, smoking, kissing with her mouth open. But according to her family, her church, she was already going to hell.

He took her virginity that night. She had loved the preliminaries: the kissing, the heat, the rubbing together like matches waiting to catch. But this was different. Too stark, too fast, too personal. Painful at first, and then just humiliating.

She never grew to like the sex, but he didn't much care; he preferred the oral kind. She was shocked and disgusted the first time she understood what he wanted, and it took him three weeks to convince her. She gagged through it time after time, but he wouldn't give up; she got the knack, eventually, and pleased him just enough. He didn't complain. She thought that was the worst of it, until he called her into his office at work one day, shut the door, and unzipped his fly.

She knew why he wanted to see her today at ten thirty. They'd broken up nearly a year ago. After that first blush of romance, Tom had slowly pulled away. First they were dating, then "hanging out," and then just hooking up. He started to criticize her hair, her clothing, her apartment. Even her one slightly crooked front tooth; she was prettier, he claimed, when she didn't smile.

He was seeing one of the window saleswomen now. But every week he called Rachel into his office, asked about her progress on the GED, locked the door, and unzipped. He swore that no one at Amos knew, but the looks the men gave her told her otherwise. She wanted to scream, to kick him, to quit ...

"Rachel." Yolanda stood at the mouth of their cubicle. "He's ready for you now."

Rachel thought of the envelope on her bedside table, then rose and walked the long aisle to his door.

* * *

She was so sick of men. She could see the spittle shine at the corners of Orrin's mouth as he brought his pitted face close to hers.

"Hey, little girl. How 'bout I buy you a drink?" He was with Brett Earl, one of the men she'd seen several weeks ago on her run to the liquor store.

She had thought she could avoid those guys at a place like this: a pub that served dark beer and roast beef sandwiches, with wood paneling and an older crowd who danced to jukebox oldies. The last strains of "Twist and Shout" were just fading, and the gyrating couples stopped and returned to their seats. Rachel had found she liked to dance; she had gone to clubs in those first blue months after Tom had dumped her, but she was stunned by the music volume, the crudeness of patrons in various states of stupor. Yet she'd found herself in the arms of a stranger more than once, just for some human connection, some company. The shame was nearly unbearable, but she had to admit if she had the chance, she wasn't sure she'd return to her former life.

Now, she swiveled her stool to face the bar. If they couldn't get you to look at them, they eventually went away. But Orrin knew her. He wasn't about to give up.

"Don't turn away from *me*, Miss Rachel. I know what you are, our sexed-up little no-diploma girl."

When Rachel didn't answer, he grabbed her arm and wrenched her around on the stool. Brett put his thigh to hers to stop her from spinning and left it there. She tried to pull away, but Orrin held tight.

"See how good we are together?" he said in her ear.

Faces flashed through Rachel's mind. Her mother, her father, Cyrus, Aaron. Harold Waters, Daniel Carleton, Tom. Elton John's voice rang from the jukebox: *this is your song.*

"That's enough." Rachel spoke at the top of her voice and stood, facing the men. "Take your hands off me and leave me alone."

Orrin was caught by surprise. Both men backed away a few inches and looked around at the crowd. A young man came to stand behind Orrin, then, two women. The bartender moved toward them down the bar. The motion around them stopped for a moment, as the crowd stared in their direction. Orrin lost some of his bravado, but didn't give up more ground.

Rachel lowered her voice. "I don't think Tom would like to hear about this."

She wasn't a fool. She knew Tom didn't respect her any more than Orrin did, but she'd bet that wouldn't stop him from defending his territory.

Orrin knew it too. He threw up his hands. "Okay, okay. No need to make threats. We were just kidding around." He and Brett turned tail and left the bar.

Rachel was floored. She had never spoken to anyone like that, let alone a man. She was pretty sure she would pay for it later, one way or another. But at the moment, she was relieved.

Rachel thanked the people gathered. The women returned to their seats. The young man sat in the stool next to hers and asked if he could buy her a drink. *Out of the frying pan, into the fire,* her mother used to say. But there was something she liked about this man, something friendly and calm. And more, some instant symmetry between them.

"I'm Ben," he told her. "And you are?"

"Rachel."

"Well, Rachel, I like your style. It looks like you know how to take care of yourself."

Did she? She knew how to take care of others, surely, but look at her life—the boring job, the awful apartment, the string of less-than-wonderful men ...

Ben seemed like a normal person, and an attractive one. Rangy, sandy hair, strong jaw. But, history considered, she wasn't such a great judge of character. Her drink came, and she downed half of it quickly. Several TVs above the bar flickered with the Cardinals game, and patrons at a corner table erupted in cheers when a crucial run was scored.

"Ben, you look familiar to me. Do you work at the factory?"

"Sometimes. When they need extra workers, I pick up some hours there."

A day laborer. Even she knew that was a step beneath any regular job at the plant. But his quietly confident manner impressed her. "Luckily, I don't have to do it this month. I'm working over on Collins Road, for a woman architect there."

"An architect?"

He took a long pull at his beer, rubbed his thumb over the label, smiled at her. "Yeah, I'm a carpenter when I can find the jobs. This lady called me after some other guy ruined her woodwork. She's renovating an old house. The trim is really beautiful, and this clown gouged up a whole section of it trying to remove the paint. I'm replicating it for her, so the new section matches the old."

"You mill your own woodwork?" Impressive.

"Yeah. It's pleasant work, and she likes the results, so I'm doing the rest for her: stairway spindles and stringers, a couple of mantels, pocket doors, that kind of thing. It's quite the grand old place. 'Course," he took another swig, "the contractor isn't happy; it was his guy. He doesn't care much for the fact I'm stepping in."

"Who's the contractor?" Rachel asked him. She could feel her pulse in her neck.

"George Whitman."

She knew her face betrayed her.

"Did I say something wrong?"

"No," she said. "He's my father. Or he *was*."

"Your father? Oh, I'm sorry, I didn't—what do you mean, he *was*?"

Rachel finished the rest of her drink and signaled the bartender for another. She noticed that Ben noticed, but he didn't remark on it.

"I used to have a family," she told him. "But not anymore."

"What happened? Did he leave you?"

"No, I left. I was asked to."

"Asked to leave?"

"Yes; disfellowshipped."

Ben's blue eyes narrowed. He knew what that meant. He was the only person she'd met on the outside who did.

"Why?" he asked her, his voice intense.

She shifted on her stool and leaned on the bar. "It's too long a story."

"I don't think it is, for someone who's interested."

She didn't know how to read him. She could hear both anger and something like compassion in his voice. "First, tell me *why* you're interested."

"Let's say I grew up in a similar situation."

Rachel doubted that, but who knew? She spun her cocktail on the coaster, listening to the cubes in the glass. Then held it up to the light, admired the color and took a drink. Then several more. Someone chose "Unchained Melody" on the jukebox. She really needed a cigarette, but she didn't want to get up and leave him to smoke. In a year and a half, she hadn't told anyone, even Tom, why she really left her family. Now she was about to confide in this stranger. She looked around; no one else was listening. She focused her gaze on her drink.

"My sister has fits. They started when she was seven and have gotten worse ever since. It was my job to take care of her. My family—" she stopped and twirled the tip of a finger in her glass. "My family doesn't believe in doctors. We pray and take care of our own."

She glanced sideways up at Ben, who was very still, waiting for her to continue.

"My Aunt Eunice is a healer. She can help, sometimes, if the patient and the family have enough faith. She laid hands on Phoebe, and her seizures did go away sometimes, for a week or two, but they always came back, stronger and more often than before." Rachel took a deep breath, and stole another look at Ben, who was staring ahead. He was watching her face in the back-bar mirror, she realized. Their eyes met over the bottles of flavored rum, then looked away.

She went on. "We believe there's no such thing as illness; it's all lack of faith. It's usually the person himself, Aunt Eunice says, unless the patient is a child, and then it can be someone else in the family."

Ben's eyebrows drew together. "They thought it was you?"

She took another sip and swallowed hard.

"It had to be. My faith wasn't pure. I wasn't sure—I'm still not sure—that Phoebe's illness isn't real."

Ben recoiled. "You were disfellowshipped for *that*?"

"Not that, no, though they were watching me. No, it was for disobeying the family." She turned and looked into his eyes. Fueled now by the alcohol, she continued.

"We were buying shoes. That's the reason we were out. They never let us go anywhere, especially Phoebe, but Aaron, my older brother, was going to town. Phoebe had outgrown her shoes and worn through every old pair of mine. She had to have new ones. So Aaron dropped us off at the shoe store, and Phoebe had a fit.

"It was a bad one. I was alone with her, except for a few shoppers and two clerks. When they saw Phoebe on the floor convulsing, one of them called 911."

Ben let out a long breath, nodded and closed his eyes.

Rachel's voice trembled with the memory. "I let her go in the ambulance. I knew how they'd feel about that, but for the first time I was more scared for Phoebe than I was of my parents or even Uncle Cyrus. In emergency they took her for a CT scan and MRI. Our family has no insurance, but that wasn't the worst. The worst part was their questions: they wanted to know how long she'd had seizures, who her doctor was, what medication she was on. I kept saying 'I don't know. I don't know.' I didn't tell them. But they weren't satisfied, and there was an investigation."

Rachel drained the rest of the ruby liquid from her glass.

"I was kicked out before the investigation began. Fortunately for my family, it came to nothing. It turns out faith healing—even on kids—is legal in Illinois, if the parents have a religious objection to doctors and hospitals.

"I miss her—Phoebe. And I worry." Rachel started tearing up. Why was she imposing on this stranger? She straightened, wiped her eyes.

"You mentioned your Uncle Cyrus. Is that Cyrus Bell? The guy from ECM?"

"It is."

"Oh, Rachel." He put her hand over hers, and she let him. "Is he for real?"

Flustered in more ways than one, she answered, "I ... what do you mean?"

"Does he believe what he preaches? Or is he in the church business for other reasons—money, power, that sort of thing?"

Rachel thought about that for a moment. "Well, it's true he seems to enjoy the power," she told him. "But why wouldn't he believe?"

"There are pastors who don't." Ben raised his eyebrows.

"But Cyrus has the calling, the gift; it was given to him by God." Ben looked skeptical, so she continued. "My mother tells the story about it. When she and Uncle Cyrus were little kids in West Virginia, their mother ran off with a traveling musician. Their father couldn't get over it, and after a couple months of grieving, he threw himself in front of a train."

"Did he die?"

"Yes, instantly, and they were orphaned, more or less. Their grandfather, who—according to my mother—was not a patient man, took them in. My mother was seven, but Cyrus was only four years old, and he started refusing to eat, or dress, or use the toilet. He acted up: biting and kicking, hitting his head against the walls, things like that.

"The old man was a regular fire-and-brimstone type, afraid that Cyrus would grow up like his mother. So he took both kids to church every day and made them memorize Bible verses, hitting their hands with a birch switch if they forgot the words. My mother's hands, she told me, were always stung and sore, but Cyrus excelled at the task. It was like a miracle: his behavior improved, and he learned the Bible verses so well that he and his grandfather tried every day to see who could remember more."

Ben was listening, rapt.

"One day, Cyrus recited his verses perfectly, but their grandfather forgot his. It might have been senility, my mother says, or the start of it, considering what came later. Whatever the reason, the old man held out the birch switch to Cyrus and put out his own hands. Cyrus looked tempted, but bowed his head, went down on his knees, and handed the switch back to their grandfather, thanking him—and God—for his religious instruction. Cyrus got his first and only embrace from the man that day."

There was a moment of silence, then they looked up to find the bartender standing in front of them. "Last call," he told them. "Can I get you anything?"

Rachel shook her head, as did Ben, who took the opportunity to finish the last few ounces of his beer. He chewed his lip on one side, lost in thought.

"So Cyrus kept this up throughout childhood?"

"He did. Pretty soon he was quoting Bible verses in church, then preaching sermons, and even speaking in tongues. People came from miles around to see him. At eighteen, he went off to the Baptist Seminary, but came back when the pastor died and took over the church. He was twenty-one."

"Wow."

"He renamed it Church of the Living Waters and took it on the road in summer, preaching and baptizing across three states. My mom went with him as his assistant; that's how she met my father in Wheeling. When Pine Bluff put out the call for a pastor ten years ago, Cyrus came and charmed them."

She crunched on an ice cube left in her glass while they settled up with the barman. "Everyone seems to love Cyrus," she said, as she pocketed her receipt.

"Well, not everyone," Ben said with a twitch of one cheek.

Rachel could see the face of his watch. It was almost eleven, and the pub's crowd was thinning out. She'd been talking for more than an hour, to a man she knew nothing about.

"Tell me about you," said Rachel.

"There's not much to tell," he said. "I'm ex-Amish. Born in Arcola. Raised on a farm. Worked in a furniture business and learned my trade."

Ex-Amish. That's why he knew about being shunned, disfellowshipped. "Were you kicked out, too?"

"No, I left on my own."

"You did?" Rachel couldn't imagine that. "Why did you go?"

Now it was Ben's turn to stare into his empty beer bottle, as if he were weighing his words.

"I realized pretty early that I don't believe in a god."

"You don't believe in God?" She was incredulous. "Aren't you afraid of hell?"

"I don't believe in hell, or heaven, or anyone to judge me and send me there."

Wow. She'd read about these atheists, been warned about them in church. They lay in wait for good Christians, to turn them away from the Lord. He didn't *feel* evil. But maybe she herself was now so evil she couldn't tell.

Still, he'd been very nice to her; she didn't want to be rude ... "Well," said Rachel, "I suppose I really shouldn't judge, since I seem to be headed in that direction myself."

He shook his head.

"Really," she said. "You have no idea."

"I think I *do* have some idea," he told her. "I've known plenty of people raised in religion who ended up outside their faith, voluntarily or not. They all have one thing in common: when they leave the group, they find freedom but lose their families, their community, a lot of times any sense of who they are."

That had been Rachel's experience exactly.

"Unfortunately, they often end up swinging to the other extreme: lots of drinking, drugs, gambling, sex—all the things they couldn't do before—treating themselves and sometimes others badly. They figure they're already damned to hell."

Rachel shifted uncomfortably in her seat.

"A lot of them return to their religions, just to feel there are morals in the world. They never even recognize there's any middle ground."

"Middle ground? How is that possible? Either you're sinning or you're not."

Ben clasped his hands together before him. "The idea of sin is the problem. The truth is, if you separate your sense of good and evil from belief in a god, you can keep your freedom and still choose to be good." His hands slowly opened. "Good for its own sake, not for future reward or punishment."

Rachel's head was spinning, as much from Ben's words as from drink. His assertions were foreign and frightening to her, though they carried some intriguing new ideas. She didn't know what to say. They stared at each other. Several moments passed.

"I suppose it's futile now to ask for your number."

This made Rachel laugh, until she was once again wiping tears from her eyes.

"You have a lovely smile," he told her.

She entered his number in her prepaid phone, giving herself the option to call or not. They said good night outside the pub, and he put her in a cab.

Later, lying alone in bed, she thought about his hair, his eyes, the touch of his hand. He was wrong about religion. No doubt about it. And yet, where she herself was concerned, he'd landed uncomfortably close to the truth.

He didn't believe in God, he said. Before she'd lost her home and family, she'd never even known that was an option.

7

Lucy: Friday, September 27

D r. Reynolds rapped on his desk. "Okay, I need your attention," he said. The students broke off their conversations and the room quieted. "The procedure today is an interesting one. I think you'll have fun with it, but there are a few things you need to know before you begin. I need a volunteer. Sam? ... No, Logan. Come up here with me. The rest of you take your stations."

Logan moved to the front of the room, while Lucy and the rest of the students shuffled to their places at the lab stations. Each group of lab partners had several planters of delicate yellow flowers before them. Next to those were placed the bee sticks they'd constructed the day before: actual dead bee thoraxes impaled and glued on seven-inch wooden sticks.

"Logan will demonstrate. We discussed in previous classes the difference between self- and cross-pollination. Wisconsin Fast Plants—*Brassica rapa*—do not self-pollinate. *We* will be the pollinating agent today, cross-pollinating the plants with the help of our bee sticks." Logan picked up a bee stick, waved it like a magic wand, and grinned. "We will transfer pollen from the anthers of one plant to the stigma of another, repeating the process until all are pollinated. Mark your plants to keep track of the ones you've done. I've put out some colored toothpicks for this purpose."

Several students picked up the toothpicks and rattled them in their plastic containers. "We'll use the blue ones to mark this group of pollinated specimens."

"Now for the technique," Dr. Reynolds continued. "The most effective way is to *gently roll* the bee thorax over the anthers of the flower." Logan bent to his task, his wavy dark hair falling forward over one eye. He rolled the bee thorax back and forth, then held it aloft, covered with yellow pollen.

"Good. Now roll that pollen onto the stigma of a flower from another plant." Logan did. "Since we have selected out these F1, first-generation plants for the same trait—trichomes—we can use the same bee stick for multiple flowers as long as the thorax holds up."

A girl named Kaitlyn raised her hand. "Is there a reason we're not using cotton swabs or paint brushes to pollinate, like the lab manual says we can?"

"Good question. Other experimenters have found that using bee sticks yields a higher seed count. And since we'll be planting those seeds to produce our F2 generation, we should probably give ourselves every advantage we can." The students, including Kaitlyn, looked satisfied. "Anyone else?" He paused, but there were no more questions. "I've also set up microscopes at station 1, with slides of *Brassica* reproductive organs. Sometime during this class period, take a look and identify them."

He turned to Logan. "You can return to your place."

Logan bowed deeply, drawing hoots and applause from the class.

"Okay, people, you may begin. Take your time and pay close attention to what you're doing. When you're finished, be sure to record this procedure and all observations in your notebooks. I want *sketches*, too." Several students groaned. "And don't forget to water your plants enough to get them through the weekend."

As Logan made his way toward her, Lucy was glad again for her lucky choice of lab partners. If she was to brave the "science geek" label at this school (a curse that even hot-for-an-older-guy Dr. Reynolds couldn't seem to lift), she needed people to work with who weren't screwing around. Logan, she'd found out with relief, took AP Biology seriously, as did Sam, who wanted to be a doctor.

Sam had transferred into their class several weeks into the semester. Everyone was partnered in twos or threes already, and Dr. Reynolds added her to their group. Her real name was Samantha, but she liked her more androgynous nickname, a preference that extended to her haircut, which was short and spiked up at the top. Petite and fit, she dressed in a retro 80s style, wearing slim jeans and sneakers, dark t-shirts and boxy suit jackets with the sleeves rolled up. She had big brown eyes that turned down at the corners, and a wicked sense of humor.

Today she sported a swollen bruise along her cheek and similar marks on the knuckles of one hand—maybe the reason Dr. Reynolds had passed her over for the demonstration. A fight of some kind, probably. Lucy thought it better not to remark on it. Logan, though, was not so restrained.

"What happened to *you?*" he asked as he reached them and took a look at Sam's face.

"Slight altercation. Nothing to worry about." Sam's voice and expression let Logan know any further inquiry was unwelcome.

So of course, he opened his mouth to speak again.

Lucy jumped in. "We can split the plants into three groups," she said, putting several planters in front of each of them. "I'll take pollen from mine and move it to Logan's. Logan can pollinate yours, Sam, and you can do mine. It'll be easier to keep track of them that way."

There was no more talk about Sam's face as they set to work with their bee sticks.

Lucy already felt at home in this lab in a way she knew she never would in the farmhouse. One lab was similar to another, yet each had its own character, housing different equipment, holding new discoveries. Rows of plants and cages of animals, scales, test tubes, acrid chemicals, periodic tables. Bleached and pinioned skeletons, fossils and rocks and minerals—all were burned into her memory since elementary school, when they'd raised white mice and coated pennies with zinc sulfate to turn them gold. She remembered the thrill of those early experiments, cause and effect, which taught her that *she* could use the laws of nature to make things happen. Laws that held the key to every wild and unknown thing in the universe.

Science was an emotional subject for her. Not that everyone needed to know that.

Their unit of study this semester covered natural selection as an agent of evolution. Natural selection was difficult to observe in a lab, especially in the time they had, so Dr. Reynolds had chosen this project on artificial selection. It was similar to one that Lucy had done in middle school, but at this level the students were required to make their own observations and decisions. They would plant the *Brassica*, then observe the resulting F1 generation, identifying heritable traits like flower color, stem color, or number of plant hairs (trichomes) on the leaves. After choosing one, they'd select out 10% of the F1 plants for that trait. Those plants would be cross-pollinated, and the results observed and recorded. Further generations and the other 90% of the F1s could be crossed and studied for different or combined characteristics, an opportunity that leant itself nicely to Lucy's interest in genetics and need for competition-level projects.

The class had first researched the best way to plant and light the *Brassica*. They settled on light banks constructed of PVC piping and fluorescent bulbs, and planters fashioned from recycled plastic bottles and nylon wicking. They'd need to add fertilizer, water, soil, and vermiculite before planting the seeds. Class time was short, and Dr. Reynolds offered extra credit to those who could come after school and put the materials together. Lucy, Logan, and Sam had volunteered.

"I think that's it," Logan said, putting his bee stick down.

"Looks like it." Lucy pushed her last blue toothpick into the soil, marking the final plant as pollinated. She looked at the clock. "Let's get the microscope slides identified."

They waited a few minutes behind another group at Station 1, then a space at the microscopes opened and they stepped up to take a look.

Logan sighed. "I'll never be able to draw that."

"I'll draw; you label," Sam told him, as she pulled a fancy mechanical pencil from a pocket of her jacket. They'd worked like this together before: Sam, the artist among them, sketching what she saw in their notebooks, Lucy and Logan identifying and labeling.

They finished just before the bell.

"Make sure to put your *Brassica* back under the lights," said Dr. Reynolds. "And any bee sticks *you haven't used* should go here." He pointed to a container by the door. "Not so fast, Sean," he said to a boy who was leaving station 4. "You forgot to water your plants."

The rest made for the door and squeezed themselves through it several at a time.

"Later," called Logan, as he dashed down the hallway to try to make his last class on the far side of the building.

Sam and Lucy walked together, Sam's eyes scanning the crowd, as if she were looking for someone. Suddenly she stopped.

"I just remembered I left something in the lab," she said, and was gone before Lucy could tell her to have a good weekend.

Lucy continued down the hall, past a clot of football players known as "the Bison." That was the name of all the school's sports teams, but everyone knew "the Bison" referred to these five guys—six, sometimes, with Jake. Just past the jocks was her friends' rendezvous point at Maddie's locker. Every day before seventh period, Jordan and company met here and firmed up plans for the evening or the weekend.

Jordan hadn't arrived yet. She'd been pressuring Lucy to come to their ECM youth group on Sunday night. Also, the anti-Halloween harvest party next month. Lucy asked Maddie what the group was like.

"It's pretty big. Like 80 kids, but only 30 or so show up every week. We play video games, watch movies—stuff like that. Sometimes we do volunteer projects, like witness to seniors, or work at the food pantry. But the party is special; everybody comes. We dress up as Bible characters, do skits and stuff, have a scavenger hunt. The parents bring food and punch. Then Jake and his friends play music, and we sing. It's good."

"Any dancing?"

"No, not really. Some of the kids have families that don't like it." Maddie pushed a wing of shiny brown hair from her freckled face. "Hey, isn't that your mom?" She pointed toward a woman walking down the hall, slowing before each classroom to look at the number.

Lucy fought down her embarrassment and answered as casually as she could. "Yeah, that's her."

"What's she doing here?"

"She just wanted to check on some scholarship stuff for college."

"Oh." Maddie pulled a book from her locker and tossed another one in. She closed the door and spun the lock, then turned, pressed her back to the locker, and stared into space.

Lucy hadn't known Maddie very long, but even she could tell that something was different. The bright-faced, upbeat girl she'd met on her aunt's front porch seemed to melt away these past few weeks, leaving someone older and more serious in her place. Today she seemed especially distracted. Lucy was about to speak when Maddie straightened and waved; she'd caught sight of David as he made his way toward them through the crowd. Usually, Maddie and David looked around for teachers and then locked lips immediately, making the most of the five-minute passing period. This time David drew Maddie aside with a hand at her elbow, and pressing the side of his face to hers, whispered something into her ear.

It was clear they wanted to be alone. Jordan had not shown up at all, and Lucy was left to look on awkwardly.

"I'll see you in class," Lucy mumbled and made her escape down the hall.

Thank goodness Maddie was too distracted to notice Alexa was headed toward the labs. Her science career was beginning to be a sore subject with Lucy. She was different enough because of her interests; she wished her mother would just stay out of it.

Lucy's first days at Pine Bluff had been a surprise. Most of the teens here wore the same styles, followed the same music, used the same social media as her friends did in Elm Ridge. There were kids with tattoos in places their parents wouldn't see them, even a few with studs in their lips and eyebrows. But here, the religious kids were the popular ones, dominating clubs, and sports, and student government. There were prayer groups and Bible study clubs, and girls who flaunted purity rings their *fathers* had given them. Many of them dressed modestly in school.

Jordan and her friends, however, morphed into hot girls in leggings or short skirts the moment the last bell rang. David chose a car from his father's lot every week and they'd drive around town. Since the dealership was on Collins Road, David picked Lucy up for school every day and drove her home as well. Maybe these kids weren't exactly her type, but she was grateful not to ride the bus like a child.

In one way, there was curiosity value in being the new kid. In other ways, she could see she would have to earn her place with them. It turned out that behind their friendly Christian exterior were people who cared for and were deeply loyal to their own. Most of them had known one another since childhood; why they'd taken her into the group was beyond her, though she suspected that as a heathen she was something of a project to Jordan. They had nicknamed her "Chicago." Sometimes that felt okay, sometimes not. Mostly it meant different.

She missed her friends in Elm Ridge and their own brand of smart and funny, the witty marathon conversations where they riffed off one another for hours just for the joy of it. Now those friends weren't calling or texting as much anymore, though they often Skyped on the weekend.

Lucy took her seat in AP English several minutes before the bell. Last period, thank goodness. And Friday, too. The class was restless and talkative, excited for the weekend. Toward the front of the room, she saw Jake's well-muscled shoulders, his blond head bent over his book; he was probably—like half the class—trying to read the assigned short story at the last possible moment. The girl in the next seat spoke to him, and he turned to her as she talked and gestured, twirling her highlighted hair around two fingers.

Lucy could think of no one else since the day she'd met Jake at the pool. She'd gone to the coffee shop often to hear him play, and each time it was more amazing. Despite her crush, he put her at ease and seemed to like her.

And Jake was available again. It was two weeks since Sophia had broken up with him, after meeting a first-year Air Force cadet at some kind of family party. To Lucy's surprise, Jake didn't seem too heartbroken, and in fact had been flirting with a number of girls, herself included. He often showed up when she hung out with Jordan's group after school, and always made a point of sitting near her, talking to her. He teased her about her interest in science, which she had begun to downplay as much as she could. But she knew he wouldn't stay free long; if Lucy wanted a chance with him, she'd have to take it this weekend. She would go to the ECM youth group.

The bell rang and Maddie snuck in a few seconds later, looking pale and distracted. Lucky for her, Mrs. Kirchner was running late as well, entering a minute after Maddie. Mrs. K's long hair was drawn up in a clip as usual; the full sleeves of her tunic flowed around as she readied her materials for class. Today they were discussing Hemingway's "Hills Like White Elephants."

"Tell me about the setting of the story. Why is it significant?" Mrs. Kirchner queried.

"Well," Jake's friend Tyler ventured, "one side of the landscape is dead. The other side, that the woman likes, has wheat, a river, and some trees."

"And what themes might that resonate with in the story?"

He looked stumped. Then, "Um ... maybe life and death?"

"Whose life and death?" Mrs. Kirchner prodded.

A girl in the back of the class volunteered, "The baby's. Either the baby will have a life, or it'll die."

"That's one possibility. Anything else?"

"Well, yeah," Jake answered. "It also goes to the woman's feelings. I mean, she knows her life will be pretty bleak if she goes through with the 'operation.' When she looks at the growing side with the wheat, she says 'we could have everything.'"

Jake *had* finished reading the story.

"Good. Both of these are reasonable interpretations, and both are probably true in this instance. Why set the story in a train station?"

The class went quiet.

"What is the significance of the train?"

Lucy spoke up. "Maybe time. The train is coming in forty minutes, and that's all they have to make this decision, before they can move on."

"True. And have they moved on?"

"Well, not really," Lucy continued.

"Why?"

No one in the class had any idea.

"So in the end," Mrs. Kirchner prompted, "he takes the bags over to the lush side of the tracks but can't see the train coming. And she's on the barren side, saying she's fine. What is going on there?"

"Well," a student named Molly answered, "they're both kinda trying to see the other's point of view. You don't know what the decision will be, but you know at least one person won't be happy."

"And why does the couple never get on the train? Why does Hemingway end the tale where he does?"

Tyler said, "Well, maybe he wants to leave us there, in that moment."

"Why?"

"I guess because it will really never be over. No matter where they go from here, they'll always remember that moment, and that choice."

"Very insightful," said Mrs. Kirchner. "Let's talk about the language here, and just how Hemingway accomplishes all of this."

They spent several minutes discussing understatement in the story.

"I'll say it was *understated*," blurted one girl toward the front of the room. It was Grace Hubbly, who pulled her lanky frame to its full height and stood next to her desk. A handful of students sighed. Everyone knew that Grace and her family were suing the school for failing to teach intelligent design.

"It's *abortion* they're talking about. How can they be so casual?" Grace's voice was low but filled with emotion, and her fists were clenched at her side. "It's a *sin*. That's bad enough. But then they talk about it as if it were nothing. As if they could be happy afterwards, just go on with their lives as if they hadn't *killed their child*."

Lucy was surprised to hear a smattering of applause. Her eyes were fixed on the long braid falling the length of Grace's back, past the waist of her old-fashioned denim skirt.

Suddenly Maddie, looking paler than ever, rose and bolted from the room. Lucy stood to follow her, but Mrs. Kirchner cleared her throat.

"Lucy, Grace, please take your seats."

Lucy returned to her desk. After a few additional minutes on Hemingway, Mrs. Kirchner wrote Monday's assignment on the board and dismissed the class a moment before the last bell. Jake was waiting as Lucy gathered her books and Maddie's and walked to the front of the room.

"That was some class."

Lucy nodded.

"I heard you're coming to the group on Sunday night."

"Yeah," she replied. "I promised Jordan I'd check it out."
Five weeks in a small town, and she had already been
talked into going to a Christian youth group. Geez. Her
friends in Elm Ridge would never believe it. Hell, she
wouldn't believe it herself, if she didn't know her reasons.
Reason.

"Cool." He smiled at her.

Okay, maybe it was worth it.

"I'll see you later. I have to go check on Maddie," she
said. Lucy hurried down the hallway to the nearest girls'
bathroom. Several stalls were occupied, and Lucy waited until
they were all empty but one, and the other girls had left.

Lucy called softly, "Maddie? Are you in there?" She
heard a rustling sound. "Maddie?"

A toilet flushed. Maddie emerged and went to the sink,
crying silently. Lucy's heart went out to her; she looked so
miserable.

"What's wrong?" she asked, as gently as she could.

Maddie hesitated. "You can't tell *anyone.*"

"I won't." Lucy wasn't sure what she was promising.

Maddie pulled a piece of plastic from her purse. It
looked like a thick, flat marker with a pink cap. On one
side in a little window there were two parallel pink lines
and some words on the plastic shaft next to them: one line,
not pregnant; two lines, pregnant. Two lines. Lucy gasped.

Maddie, white and shaking, slid her back down the
tiles until she sat on the floor. "I don't feel so good," she
moaned.

"I'm here with you." Lucy joined Maddie on the floor
and put her arms around her.

"Does David know?" Lucy asked.

Maddie shook her head. "Not for sure. I just got the
test at lunchtime. He's waiting in the parking lot now."
There was a long pause, then Maddie cried, "What am
I going to do?"

She covered her face with her hands and began to weep again. The lights above the bank of sinks illuminated the flowing script on the silver ring on her finger: "True love waits."

8

Alexa: Friday, September 27

A lexa braved a turbulent sea of high-school students between classes. She'd been virtually alone in the hallway when a bell rang and she was engulfed by teenagers pouring out of every door, laughing, talking, and jostling her on their way. Then as quickly as the human deluge had started, it was over.

The bell rang again just as she found the science lab. Dr. Reynolds, Lucy's science teacher and the chair of Pine Bluff's science department, had been absent on the high school's parent night. So Alexa had requested a one-on-one. He looked up when she entered, smiled and shook her hand, and gestured for her to take a seat at one of the lab stations near the front of the classroom. The lab was colorful and fascinating with its charts and posters, models, equipment, plants, and animals. It was empty now; evidently he had no last period class on Fridays.

Eric Reynolds was tall and trim, with wavy brown hair. Friendly and accommodating, he answered her questions as he watered plants, wiped down counters, and put away equipment. He showed her the *Brassica* experiment and complimented Lucy highly.

"She's an exceptional student and a natural scientist, as I'm sure you're aware, Mrs. Moss. Lucy has an intuitive curiosity which helps her see less obvious patterns and think in creative directions."

His green eyes, she noticed, were warmly expressive behind his horned-rimmed glasses. He had picked the right frames for his face shape, which was masculine, yet refined.

"Ms."

He looked at her quizzically.

"It's *Ms.* Moss, awkward as that sounds. Moss is my maiden, not my married name."

She glanced at his ring finger reflexively and saw a wide gold band. Catching herself and nearly blushing, she steered her attention back to the subject at hand.

"I'm concerned, Dr. Reynolds, when I hear talk about this lawsuit. Is it true that you could be forced to teach intelligent design?"

Reynolds was silent for a moment. "Any answer would be speculation at this point," he finally said. "Some elements in the community do oppose the teaching of evolution, or at least, uh, would like to supplement it with other theories." He appeared to be choosing his words very carefully.

"What would that mean for the standing of the school? How would college science programs view my daughter's application?"

"It wouldn't help. I've been frank about this, and other issues, with the board."

Alexa frowned. "Is this already affecting the science program here?"

"Not the classes themselves, no. And I've got state science standards to back me up, at least for the moment. But the budget has been cut for some extracurricular activities. Participation in certain competitions will no longer be underwritten by the school."

"You mean the ones my daughter needs."

"Exactly the ones your daughter needs. But," he said, brightening, "she can enter as an individual. Homeschooled students do it all the time. Of course there would be a fee. But I'd be happy to do all I can to support and mentor her. Frankly, I haven't had a student at this level for quite some time, and I'd be willing to work with her on extra projects."

"That's very generous, Dr. Reynolds," Alexa countered, "but what about the other kids?" Cyrus Bell's televised interviews crossed her mind. "Should they be subject to these restrictions for one conservative religious student's sake?"

Reynolds ran a hand through his hair and sighed. "Oh, if there were only one. Our community has changed significantly in the past few years."

"What can be done to combat this?" Alexa asked him. "What's the plan?"

Reynolds broke eye contact and busied himself filling rows of small food dishes for the lab animals.

"We're doing all we can within the proper channels," he said at length. "The school district has a lawyer."

He sounded resigned. Alexa watched him until she caught his eye again. There was a spark—she was sure of it—but one obscured, a star behind a cloud. She waited for him to continue.

"I understand your concerns," he told her. "But there's really minimal impact on our program now. Don't worry. We'll prepare Lucy well for college, and if you have questions, you can always call. I'll be happy to keep you updated."

A polite dismissal, just as the last bell rang. When he offered his hand, it was warm and dry and lingered in hers a second longer than she'd expected. An interesting, but ultimately frustrating encounter. Alexa thanked him and trundled off to Lucy's guidance counselor, with whom she had an after-school appointment. Maybe this Mrs. McLeary would be more helpful.

Alexa sat in the waiting area outside the counselors' offices. It appeared there were only three counselors for the hundreds of students at the school. Eventually, a striking blond woman appeared in one of the doorways and called out.

"Mrs. Moss?"

Alexa stood. There was something familiar about the woman; Alexa was dead certain she'd seen her before.

"It's Ms."

"I'm Heather McLeary," the woman said, holding out her hand.

"Good to meet you, Mrs. McLeary." Alexa passed into the woman's tiny office and took one of two seats facing the counselor's desk. Again, she felt a strange familiarity. The voice, the eyes. Though surely she would have remembered this woman's lush blond waves.

Heather McLeary sat, then studied her, her gaze appearing to fall on Alexa's cheek. Alexa brought her hand to her face and fought the urge to root through her purse for the mirror that would tell her if her foundation was still in place.

Mrs. McLeary knit her brows. "Do you mind if I ask your first name, Ms. Moss?"

"It's Alexa."

Heather McLeary smiled broadly then. "I thought so."

"Do we know each other?"

"It's been a while. Don't you recognize me? I'm Heather Robinson. Well, McLeary now."

Heather Robinson. Of course. Alexa was transported back in time to their first meeting in the Pine Bluff Library. Heather was seven, Alexa eight. Alexa was an avid reader and Heather's mother, the librarian. Heather had been a tiny child with straight, pale hair that clung to her head so tenaciously her ears always stuck out. She had offered Alexa a mini Tootsie Roll in the children's section. It was the beginning of a fast friendship.

"Heather! How many years has it been?"

"I'm not sure. Last time I saw you, we were 10 or 11 years old."

"I *thought* I knew you! Your hair—"

"I have a body wave now. And you—"

"I cover my birthmark."

"Wow, you look great. Still reading Nancy Drew?"

Alexa laughed. "Occasionally, I have to admit. My daughter loves her, too." Or at least she used to. It had been a while.

"This daughter?" Heather consulted her file. "Lucy?"

"That's the one."

Heather glanced at the clock on her desk, then through her window at the filled chairs in the waiting room.

"Unfortunately, I'm booked tight today, so we'll have to get down to business. But let's make a date to get together for lunch so we can catch up."

"That'd be great."

They settled on October 12th, at a Mexican restaurant in town. Heather's attention then returned to her file.

"Now let's talk about Lucy. What's on your mind?"

Alexa filled Heather in on the situation and her conversation with Reynolds.

"You can see why I'm concerned, Heather. What do you know about this?"

Heather leaned forward and lowered her voice. "There's not much I can tell you in an official capacity. We're not allowed to discuss the lawsuit. But Reynolds is right: there's no immediate change to the curriculum."

"But?" said Alexa, sensing the same withholding of information she had felt with Reynolds. "What do you really think will happen here?"

Heather hesitated, as Reynolds had. In the end, however, she opted to be more candid. "Alexa, I'd like to tell you it will work itself out. And that's what we're hoping. It's hard to say in the current political climate. I don't know which way you lean … " She paused.

"I've always been an independent, actually, but that's changing," Alexa answered. "I don't care at all for the turn things have taken since the 2016 election."

Heather raised her eyebrows and nodded. She looked relieved for a moment, then concern crossed her face again. "There are federal laws that protect the teaching of evolution and require that subjects taught in science classes be grounded in the discipline. But they're being challenged more and more. Quite a few states are passing laws allowing either criticism of evolution, climate change, etc., or allowing the public schools to teach 'alternatives' like intelligent design outright. Even more liberal states like ours aren't exempt from this pressure. These 'religious freedom' lawsuits are meant to challenge our state laws in federal courts. And this administration is appointing sympathetic federal judges as quickly as they can."

Alexa was aware of this but had tried not to think about it. What, after all, could one person do? But now she had Lucy and her future to consider.

"Will the high school fight it?" Alexa wanted to know.

Heather sat back in her chair and shook her head. "I really don't know. The truth is it will come down to timing, and whether this actually goes to court. The current board is conservative and likely to favor 'teaching the controversy' over defending the school in a lawsuit. Four of the seven board seats are up for election in April, and how this is handled will largely depend on who is sitting on the board when it does."

"That's not very comforting."

"True. But between the three of us—you, me, and Dr. Reynolds—we can make sure that your daughter, and students like her, get what they need to succeed. And that's the most important part, isn't it?"

Was it? What if what high-school students needed was the truth?

That question weighed on Alexa's mind as she took leave of Heather and drove home through the late September evening.

9

Rachel: Wednesday, October 2

R achel toyed with her food, a lump in her throat. The diner sounds and aromas she loved couldn't cheer her now, while her life was crumbling around her. Her only comfort: Ben was with her, holding her hand across the table.

At first she hadn't trusted him. It was difficult to get past the word "atheist." All her life she'd been warned about the unchurched, the godless, how the devil dwelt in their hearts and minds and worked through them to poison the world. After she'd taken Ben's number in the bar, she'd spent a week of restless evenings, mulling the whole thing over.

On one hand, his views defied everything she'd ever believed. On the other, the very people who had taught her to believe those things had used her up, then pushed her out, unprepared, unprotected. They'd lied about life—so much of that was clear to her now—and she was still sifting through the rubble, deciding what to keep or to toss. She suspected it might be a lifelong process.

In the end she decided new people, new ideas were a good thing. She picked up the phone and called Ben.

They spent the next week talking for hours every evening. Rachel asked Ben a lot of questions. She learned, relieved, that atheists aren't Satanists, indeed don't believe in Satan at all. No heaven or hell. No original sin—only good and bad decisions and behavior, for which we're individually responsible. That seemed like a benefit, or at least a fair trade. She hadn't been looking forward to heaven anyway, especially if it was anything like her former family life.

But mostly she and Ben talked of everyday things: his job, hers, their common interests and differences. They both loved live music, nature, simple food, and dogs— though neither one was allowed to have pets where they lived.

They got to know one another slowly. He spoke of his work, the joy he felt holding oak or maple or walnut in his hands, shaping it into something useful that would last a generation. Like Rachel, he came from a big family, and he told her stories of his Amish childhood: the kindness of his late mother, her cherry pies, his favorite horses, the brothers and sisters he would never see again.

"Your choice or theirs?" she asked him.

"Both."

Rachel couldn't imagine that. "How could you give up your family voluntarily?"

"Most of them shunned me when I left, though one of my younger brothers and my sister Louisa still spoke with me once in a while. But then my mother died. They didn't tell me when she fell sick, and my father didn't want me at the funeral."

"Oh, I'm so sorry, Ben."

"She'd been in the ground three days before I knew. That's when I washed my hands of them."

Though they came from different cultures, they understood one another. She looked forward to the evening hours in her rented room, talking to Ben on the phone, and found him better than vodka for calming her nerves at the end of the day.

On their first date they met at a coffee shop at Rachel's request, so she might feel more secure. But there was nothing scary about Ben; in fact, she found him magnetic— the pitch of his voice, the touch of his hand when he reached for hers across the table. Later, after he drove her home, and walked her to her door, he leaned in and kissed her on the cheek, and the scent and warmth of him left her wanting more.

For their second date, Ben had picked her up in the Amos Windows parking lot in his ancient truck (he'd fixed his muffler for the occasion), while Yolanda, Rachel's supervisor, stopped before her brand new Buick to look on in disdain through her red-framed glasses. Somehow that made Rachel feel better instead of worse, and it set the tone for the evening.

Ben headed northward out of town on the road that climbed the bluffs. Rachel snuck glances at him as he drove, admiring the sandy hair on his lean muscled forearms, the outline of his long thighs in worn jeans.

"Where are we going?" she asked him.

"It's a surprise," he said with the mischievous lift of an eyebrow, "but I'll tell you the first part. I packed a picnic dinner for us. I thought we'd eat it on the bluffs, overlooking the river."

"That sounds nice." A lovely evening for it. Rachel was intrigued about what would follow.

They left the main road and climbed higher on a gravel track half hidden by pine trees. At one point, Ben had to stop and unlock a gate that stood across the road. Soon after that, they passed a large log cabin-style house, and at last reached a clearing at the peak of the bluffs. Ben pulled up the pickup and went around to open the door for Rachel.

The spot overlooked a bend in the river, which flowed both to the north and west of them. The early evening sun played over the tops of the trees below, endowing some with bright green crowns as it filtered through translucent leaves and threaded among the deep blues and greens of the pines. There were touches too of gold and of red. The legendary colors of autumn were still a few weeks away, but it was hard to imagine a more beautiful view than this. The river winked and tumbled in the light.

"Where exactly are we?" asked Rachel. "Is this a park?"

"Actually, we're on private land. You saw the house? My friend Ray Ingersoll owns it. I worked for him, helped him build that place, and he lets me keep a key to the gate and come up here when I want."

"It's gorgeous."

Ben spread several blankets on the rocky soil, then retrieved an insulated bag and a small cooler from the truck. He tuned the radio to a soft country station before unpacking their dinner. First, he produced a couple of bottles of good beer, some thin crackers, and a wedge of cheese—not the grocery-store cheddar Rachel was used to, but something white and pungent, with a strong, sweet aftertaste. As they drank and ate, they talked about their day, their lives, their individual hopes for the future. Ben was hoping to buy a small farm, with a barn he would use to start his own carpentry business. Rachel simply wanted to pass the GED and get a better job so she could care for her sister Phoebe.

"And now for the main course," Ben said by and by, and pulled a foil-wrapped package from the bag. It carried a familiar logo; as Ben unwrapped it, Rachel laughed with delight. Inside the package were two slabs of barbequed ribs. Rachel had told Ben that on rare occasions, her father would bring home baby back ribs from Jessup's, a grill near town. The meal was her favorite. Ben unpacked some thick paper plates and cut her a large serving.

"And there's plenty more," he told her. They pulled the tender meat from the bones, their hands and faces sticky with the sauce. Rachel ate a half slab of ribs. When they were done, he produced a package of lemon-scented wipes, and as she cleaned her fingers, he leaned toward her and gently removed some sauce from the edge of her mouth. Their eyes locked for a moment, and Rachel felt the force between them, pulling them toward one another and yet holding them inches apart. Something brand new stirred inside her.

Ben packed up the leftovers and moved the blankets to the bed of the truck, where he placed a couple of cushions against the cab. They reclined and watched the sunset, pointing out shapes to each other in the brightly colored clouds. As darkness descended Ben checked his watch, then told her to sit tight. He hopped into the cab and turned the pickup, facing the truck bed toward the east.

"Watch," he told her when he returned, pointing to the horizon.

Soon she saw a golden glow behind the trees, then an arc of light against the sky, the leading edge of some vast orb. Rachel gasped when she realized it was the moon. Huge and orange, it dwarfed the stars around it.

"The harvest moon," Ben told her.

Rachel knew about harvest moons from her earliest childhood in West Virginia. Her parents used to take the family out at night to view the firmament, as they called it. It was usually an excuse for a sermon, but she'd learned then that the harvest moon was the full moon nearest the autumnal equinox.

"I can't afford a telescope, but I picked this up at a tag sale near the river, and it does the job." Ben handed an old-fashioned brass spyglass to Rachel. Now the whole moon was visible above the horizon, and Rachel could see the dark and light spots on its face as she put the glass to her eye.

"What are those dark places?" she asked him.

Ben explained the craters, the rays, the lava-filled "Seas" of Serenity, Tranquility, Rains, Storms, Fertility. "I like those words. They're cyclical, rhythmic," he said.

As the moon rose higher, more golden in the night sky, he pulled her closer and kissed her. His lips on hers were soft at first, then more insistent. Her body responded immediately, intensely, every heartbeat heightened, every nerve bathed in warmth and longing. She wanted to be devoured, swallowed whole. He seemed to sense this, and reluctantly pulled away from her, his breathing as heavy as hers.

"Darlin', you're wonderful," he whispered. Then sighed. "I think it's probably best if I took you home."

Rachel assented, though in truth she felt she was home already.

Over the next week, she could barely think of anything but Ben. He was an interesting mix of contradictions. He worked with his hands, oftentimes at menial jobs, but he was intelligent, confident. Strong, but kind. Practical, but passionate, receptive to the world. And he was more than willing to share his world with her. They continued to speak on the phone every evening, her favorite part of the day.

She suspected that her feelings for Ben would jeopardize her job at Amos. Shortly after their second date, Tom called her into his office overlooking the floor of the window factory, expecting to be flattered and serviced as usual. But this time, when he ushered her in and locked the door, she went back to the door and unlocked it, then asked him in a professional tone why he had wanted to see her. He went red, coughed, then made an excuse and released her back to the customer service department. She knew that would not be the end of it.

And she was right. From that day forward, her supervisor Yolanda was laser-focused on Rachel's performance. She and Tom were waiting, she knew, for an error. Because she so desperately needed the job, Rachel doubled her efforts and output. But eventually, predictably, they found their opportunity. Rachel had one customer she could never please, who owned a small hardware store several towns away. The man placed custom window orders, then tried to change or cancel them, often claiming he had ordered something different than he had.

This morning Rachel had been called into Tom's office. Yolanda was waiting there with him. "A customer" had complained that Rachel had botched his latest order and then denied it. He had let them know he was taking his business elsewhere. That was unlikely; shipping from another factory across the state would cost the man a fortune. But Rachel understood this was not the point.

Tom cleared his throat: "In looking over your records, it appears you never graduated from high school. Is that correct?"

"That's true, but I've been working toward my GED." *As you very well know.*

"That's all well and good, but the job requirements clearly state a high-school diploma is required. In light of these complaints, I'm afraid we're unable to make an exception in your case."

A smug Yolanda walked Rachel to her desk to collect her belongings, then security escorted her out of the building. It all happened in less than an hour.

She called Ben and he'd picked her up and brought her to Sandy's. He said all the right things to comfort her, but Rachel knew there was little he could do to help. Despite her best efforts at composure, she broke down in tears halfway through the meal. Sandy herself, a buxom matron with platinum hair piled high on her head, brought several extra napkins and handed them to Rachel.

"What's all this, then?" she asked her. Rachel couldn't find her voice to answer.

"She'll be okay, Sandy. She just lost her job," Ben said.

Rachel wiped her eyes, amazed that Ben seemed to know almost everyone in this town.

"Sorry. That's rough." Sandy's eyes narrowed and looked Rachel over, seeming to size her up. "Can you serve?" she asked her.

Rachel drew herself together. "I'm sorry. What?"

"Can you serve? Wait tables."

"Well, I never have, in a restaurant. But I cooked for and served my younger brothers and sisters most of my life."

Sandy nodded, then said. "Give me a minute."

She came back shortly with an application and placed it in front of Rachel.

"Fill this out."

"Wow. Really? Thank you."

"Don't thank me yet. We got a girl that's pregnant," said Sandy. "Eighth month, having a time of it. She went to the doctor yesterday. He told her preeclampsia—one of my daughters had that. You got to stay off your feet with that. So we're short one. I hire experienced, usually, but I'll give you a try if you can start tomorrow."

"Okay, I'll be here," Rachel said, relieved. Sandy moved on to wait on another table. Rachel looked at Ben, who gave her hand a squeeze.

"You'll be a perfect waitress, darlin'."

She wasn't sure of that, but in the short run, at least, she wouldn't starve, and she had Ben to thank for it.

10

Alexa: Saturday, October 12th

"**M**rs.?"

George Whitman stood in the doorway of the second-floor bedroom Alexa was using as an office. It was the third interruption in as many hours. And she'd asked the man repeatedly not to call her "Mrs." It gave her the creeps. Nevertheless, she forced a smile. "Yes, George?"

"We need the plans."

The plans? She searched the face of the stocky, crew-cut workman. "I'm not sure what you mean."

"The plans, the blueprints, Mrs. They're not on the wall."

The renovation specs had hung on the dining room wall for weeks.

"Really? Are you sure one of your men didn't move them?"

"Oh no, they didn't touch them, Mrs. Maybe you moved them and forgot?"

Alexa shook her head.

"Well then, it was probably your young carpenter fellow or that foreign electrician. My men are always tripping over their mess. The wires and wood are everywhere."

"This is Saturday, George, and your crew doesn't normally work the weekends, so Ivan and Ben have been doing their big jobs then. We didn't expect you today."

Ivan and Ben disliked Whitman so much they worked weekends to avoid him. Alexa preferred not to upset

Ivan, spooked as he was by the incident of the bird in the house. She'd managed to coax him back to the project with determination, charm, and a bit more money. He still looked over his shoulder and crossed himself every so often.

"Well, I thought that would be obvious, since we couldn't make it on Thursday," Whitman continued with a frown. "We like to stay on schedule. That's the problem with more than one contractor. I can't be held responsible if things get lost or the work starts to fall behind."

The fact that Alexa was architect and general contractor on her own project seemed to insult him personally, left him shaking his head and muttering, even when things were going well.

"You'll just have to get along, I'm afraid," Alexa told him. "At least for today. The plans will turn up. Or I'll print new ones. We'll rework the schedule on Monday to give you workers more space from each other. The kitchen wiring is nearly complete. You need that inspected before you drywall, so Ivan's work has priority. If you concentrate on mudding and sanding the walls you've done in the main rooms, Ben can trim them out next week while you work on the kitchen."

"Sounds like a plan." Ben had come up behind George Whitman. Whitman gave him a dirty look, shouldered past him, and huffed down the steps.

"Sorry to bother you, Alexa, but if you have time, I'm ready for you to look at the stains." Alexa resigned herself to packing in her project for the morning. She didn't mind working with Ben, however. He was polite, and more importantly, talented. He'd managed to completely restore the grand old staircase in the foyer in the space of a few weeks. Now it was time to pick out the finishes for the staircase, floors, and trim. Alexa followed Ben down the steps to the parlor, where he'd laid out samples with various stains and finishes applied. She made her choices, honoring but updating the original colors, and Ben promised to bring samples for the kitchen cabinets next week.

As they finished their discussion, their attention was drawn to the window. Lucy, in a neon pink tank top, was dragging gardening equipment to the side yard and marking out a space along the fence.

"What's she planting?" Ben asked Alexa.

Alexa laughed. "Who knows?" she said. "Whatever has the most interesting genetic properties."

"Come again?"

"Experiments. She's preparing the ground and planting a few bulbs and other things for spring. She'll keep track of all the plant traits and record her results. She's studying to become a geneticist. I think the chance to plant a garden is the only thing she's liked about moving here."

Ben let out a long low whistle. "Well, good for her! A scientist. How'd she get into that?"

"Well, I think, to be honest, it started in the bathtub. She used to spend hours in there as a child, pouring water, sinking and floating things. Elementary physics, I guess. And then it was animals. Any kind of animals. We nearly lived at the zoo."

"Then she liked science classes in school, I suppose?"

"She could hardly believe it the first time she saw a lab. The teachers couldn't get her out of there at the end of the day. They had to start a science club in middle school to oversee her experiments."

Ben ran a hand through his sandy hair and looked thoughtful. "How is she in math?"

"Also a whiz, though she prefers when it applies to science."

"She's fifteen, you said? Has she ever had a job?"

Alexa thought that an odd question coming from her carpenter. "Well, babysitting and the like. One summer she mowed a neighbor's lawn."

"Do you think she might like to tutor someone?"

"Another student, you mean?"

"Well, yes, strictly speaking. Though she's older, in her twenties. She needs some help to pass her GED. Particularly the science part."

"Hmm." It occurred to Alexa that any suggestion from herself to Lucy was likely to be rebuffed. "I'm not sure what she'd say. Why don't you ask her yourself?"

"Okay if I talk to her now?" he asked, carefully placing the samples back into his large canvas duffle bag.

"Sure; I don't think you'll need any more input from me today. I have a lunch meeting, but you can call me if anything comes up."

"I'll do that," said Ben. "Have a good one."

Then he exited through the gutted kitchen and walked around the back of the house to the side yard. Lucy rose from her garden as he approached. Alexa couldn't hear them, but she could read Lucy's body language from long familiarity. Her daughter was surprised, then hesitant, but finally her shoulders relaxed as Ben spoke to her and gestured. She nodded, and they laughed. The first days Ben had been on the job, Alexa could have sworn that Lucy was attracted to him. There seemed to be none of that now, however. Maybe she'd been mistaken. Or was there, perhaps, someone else in Lucy's life?

Alexa's phone rang. Her mother, Sheila. Alexa let it go to voicemail, mentally vowing to return the call later in the day. She wondered if twenty years from now, Lucy would be avoiding *her* calls. She fervently hoped their relationship would be better than hers and Sheila's.

In half an hour, she was scheduled to meet Heather McLeary in town. She ran upstairs to change her clothes, then waved to Lucy and Ben, still chatting in the side yard, as she headed for the garage.

As she drove into town, Alexa was amazed at the change in the foliage. Suddenly, fall colors had emerged and deepened, painting the landscape with oranges, golds, and caramel browns, patterned against the sleek black bark of the trees. A haze of mid-October wood smoke lingered against the blue sky.

Alexa reflected on her visits with Dr. Reynolds and Heather. She'd spent a few restless evenings wondering how far this lawsuit could go. Living in a liberal suburb she'd made certain assumptions—that separation of church and state in public schools, for example, was a given. But as she browsed the internet, she found that concept was now being challenged all over the country. Prayer in public schools, town meetings, and athletic events was common. *In God We Trust* plaques were hung in school hallways. Science and history textbooks were changed to include Christian claims and perspectives. Certain literature was banned. Religion was rapidly breaching secular institutions, and legislatures in conservative states were passing laws to allow it.

The fundamentalists were up in arms, claiming discrimination against them, while filing lawsuits allowing *them* to discriminate in hiring, health care, providing business and even social services like homeless shelters and adoptions. All in the name of religious freedom. Alexa had stayed up after midnight, reading.

But at least now, as she parked in front of the Mexican restaurant, she had a frame of reference for her meeting with Heather McLeary. Heather was waiting at a small table near the windows. On spotting Alexa, she grinned and stood to give her a hug. Her gold waves were set off by a black sweater, and her blue eyes shone. Her earnest friendliness soon put Alexa at ease.

The restaurant was casual, its white stucco walls tiled halfway up in turquoise and sunny yellow. After the waiter took their orders, they settled into conversation, catching up. Heather was married to Alan, a pediatrician, and they had two sons, the younger one in middle school, the older one a freshman at Pine Bluff. Heather had been a guidance counselor there for years. She liked the job, but it was harried; they were as understaffed as most schools were these days.

"How about you? You have one daughter; are there more kids, a husband? You have to tell me how you ended up back here."

"There was a husband, long ago, but Lucy's my only child." She told Heather a bit about her former life in Elm

Ridge, then explained Aunt Margaret's bequest and its exacting terms.

Heather was surprised. "You'd give up a career in architecture to live in Ecstasy?"

"I've never had that much of a career. I got married early and dropped out of college when I was pregnant with Lucy, then worked as an admin to put my husband Luke through medical school. Later, when we got divorced, I finished college, then got a job." She shook her head. "That was just before the housing market crashed. I was laid off less than nine months later: last one in, first one out. For years I did freelance drafting, mostly, and then finally, a few years ago, I was hired by a new firm in Chicago. I left there in June, because of—um—artistic differences."

She had supported the homeowners' wish to keep the walls in their iconic Chicago bungalow, rather than demolishing them for a totally open concept.

"I can do drafting work from here," she continued, "and maybe build my own business. At least I hope so; that's the plan."

"You said your ex is a doctor. Don't you get child support?"

Alexa took a sip of her iced tea and shook her head. She decided against telling Heather the rest of the story: brand new doctor meets stunning nurse from Belarus, leaves his family, performs lucrative but unethical procedures, loses his license, and leaves the country. Stops sending money. In five years, calls his daughter once from somewhere in Eastern Europe.

She realized that Heather was watching the changing expressions on her face.

"We were happy in Elm Ridge," said Alexa. "We had good lives, good friends. The people there, the schools were wonderful. But the value of our condo went down, the taxes went up, and the cost of living became prohibitive. And I still owed on my student loans. We were just barely making it. Then this summer we inherited the house and money for Lucy's education. It seemed like a no-brainer at the time."

"And now?"

"Well, I'm glad to meet up with *you* again. This is certainly a pleasure. And the chicken quesadillas here are terrific," she added as she spooned on some sour cream and took a bite. "I can see," she said, when she finished chewing, "that some of my fears were unfounded. Ecstasy has a lot to offer. The house itself will really be something once it's renovated. But it *has* been an adjustment. At first, I was really worried about Lucy; she was so upset. Lately, though, she seems to be fitting in and doing well. My big concern at this point is the threat to the school's science program. I don't want to see all she's accomplished go for naught."

"I see your point. But I don't think you need to worry."

Alexa wasn't so sure. "Where did this big church come from, Heather? And why are they interfering in the schools?"

Heather looked at the half-filled tables around them. She crumpled her napkin, then motioned the waiter over and asked for the check. She waited until he was out of earshot to speak again. "There's a little park down the block; let's walk and talk."

"Sure," she said. They paid for their food, then strolled past lampposts, seasonal flower beds, and shops decorated with pumpkins and Halloween garlands. They sat on the steps of a war memorial, basking in what was probably one of the season's last good days. Some children and a few adults passed in costume; there must have been a Halloween party nearby. A redhaired boy of six or seven trailed his mother, dragging his feet. He wore an old-fashioned plaid flannel shirt and a sullen expression.

"Why?" he whined, pointing to the costumed children. "Why can't I go trick-or-treating this year? I want to be Batman. Mom? Mom! Why can't I?"

His mother grabbed his hand and pulled him along, until his little plaid shirt disappeared around a bend. Odd. Alexa didn't even pretend to understand this town.

"Okay," said Alexa, "I have a few questions. I hope you're not in a rush to get somewhere."

"Not at all. Fire away."

"Well, first of all, the town name. How did it become Ecstasy again?"

"Funny you asked, since you mentioned the church." Heather rearranged herself on the step. "As you probably remember, this has always been a churchy town—'more steeples than people' my dad used to say—but fourteen or fifteen years ago, things got way more conservative.

"You know, I was raised a Methodist," Heather continued. "We're generally a reasonable, fairly mainstream denomination. United Methodists are, at least. But there's an evangelical branch as well, and a family moved to town from one of those churches in the south. They joined our congregation and started to challenge everything. They believed in the literal truth of the Bible. Unfortunately, they convinced quite a few of the others. Church leadership split and a few years of nasty infighting followed.

"The fundamentalists eventually lost—I'm not sure they would today—and fifteen or twenty of them formed their own new church, the 'Light' of something. At first they rented a storefront in town, then held services at the movie theatre on Sunday mornings. Every time you went to the movies, you'd see a commercial for the church before the film. It worked—their membership grew quickly, and they started saving for a building."

Two fat squirrels chased one another around the women, making them laugh. They watched the pair scamper off across the park. Then Heather grew serious again.

"In the meantime, religion seemed to be merging with politics," she continued. "Especially in the smaller towns like ours. All of a sudden, you weren't supposed to be pro-choice, pro-gay, or pro-sex ed anymore if you were a Christian. As town librarian, my mother went through— and *still* goes through—a tough time defending *Harry Potter* and *Twilight*, even adult books like *The Handmaid's Tale,* from being banned. Attendance at the mainstream churches tapered off. We lost more than half of our members. The Presbyterians went under—there's an antiques mall where they used to be—and Pine Bluff United Church of Christ sold their building and merged with another UCC thirty miles away. The fundamentalist 'Light' group attracted some folks with money. Amos, the window factory guy. People like that."

Heather stopped for a breath and picked a fallen leaf from where it had blown into Alexa's hair. Alexa noted how much she instinctively trusted Heather already; she could see why she'd be a wonderful school counselor. As they talked, the sun had moved to the west, sending golden rays horizontally across the park.

The stone step was making its contours felt, and Alexa leaned back on her elbows. "And this 'Light' church turned into Ecstasy Christian Ministries?"

"Yep, you guessed it. They started their search for a pastor nine, ten years ago. That's when Cyrus Bell and his family came to town."

Alexa narrowed her eyes at the pastor's name.

"Oh, I see that you're familiar with him. Cyrus charmed the hell out of them," said Heather. "He's the one who decided on Ecstasy for the church name. Religious ecstasy and all that, I guess. Plus, I think he knew the name was marketing gold. They hired him in a flash as pastor, and it only took him a couple of years to raise the rest of the money to build the new church. Most of us never realized it was going to be so big."

"Wow," said Alexa. "And what about the town?"

"Well, the longer Cyrus Bell's been here, the more influence he's had. As the church got bigger and richer, they started their own cable show on Sunday mornings, with entertainment and Cyrus's fiery sermons. And that building. When people saw that on their TV screens, they came out in droves to get a look for themselves. Now thousands go there every week. The sad part is, I don't think they really know what they're getting, behind all that glitter and hype." Alexa remembered the mirrored roof and steeple, and the cross that looked like it hung free in the sky. It was pretty impressive.

"So ECM is more conservative than most of them realize."

Heather scrunched her face and nodded.

"Yeah, in more ways than one. It wasn't long until Bell was buddies with most of the politicians in the county. Then he threw his weight into local affairs. He's careful not to publicly back candidates—doesn't want to lose that tax-exempt status—but even so, the town council, library board, and school board are loaded with his picks. Cyrus wanted the name of the town changed back to Ecstasy, so it was. He couldn't get the votes to change the high school's name. Sentimental alumni, I guess. So that's still Pine Bluff, at least for the time being."

"It sounds as if the town is in his pocket."

"That's partly true. People's jobs have disappeared when they differ with him."

Maybe Heather's and Reynolds' jobs as well. And others. That shed some light on the high school's reluctance to take on Bell.

"Are you still a Methodist?"

"Yep. Our church is pretty moderate, but we've had a small uptick in numbers lately, possibly an anti-ECM reaction. The Lutheran church is still holding on, as well as Temple Beth Israel and the Catholics at St. Sebastian. We're involved with all of them in the Interfaith League." Heather tilted her head to the side and looked at Alexa. "What about you?" she asked. And then a beat later, "You're welcome at our church anytime."

Alexa gazed out over the park. "Oh, I'm not a believer."

"Not at all?"

"Not since I was a kid."

"Atheist or agnostic?"

Alexa sighed. "I don't know. Either. Both. Those labels don't seem to fit me—or at least not completely. They say what I don't believe, rather than what I do. I believe in the Golden Rule, being decent to other people, living ethically. But I don't think you have to believe in a deity to do that."

"Good without a god?"

"Exactly."

Heather rummaged in her purse and pulled out a card. She handed it to Alexa; it said Mark Robinson, Vice President, Pine Bluff Humanists for Good. Underneath in smaller letters was an email and web address. Then: Member, National Humanist Organization.

"You might want to check these people out. The group is local," Heather said, "but part of a larger, national group. My brother—you remember Mark?—he's a member. I think they'd be a good fit for you."

Alexa was intrigued. She'd never known there was such an organization.

The sun slipped lower in the sky and disappeared behind a building, casting them into shade. It was suddenly cooler. They stood, brushing leaves from their pants and jackets.

"One more thing," said Alexa. "You mentioned sex education. Has that been an issue at the high school too?"

Heather's lips tightened into a straight line. "The curriculum is under review. An abstinence-only program has been proposed."

Alexa sighed. "I'd say 'God help us' if I thought it would do any good."

Heather gave her a rueful smile. "I'll say it for you. That okay?"

"What if you say it *instead* of me, and I look for another—um—more practical route?"

Heather laughed. "I can live with that."

Thank goodness. Alexa stood and gave her a hug.

11

Alexa: Thursday, October 31

Halloween day dawned crisp and cold. Alexa spent the morning running errands: gas station, dry cleaners, pharmacy, bank, and the town hall in Ecstasy, where she picked up and paid for a copy of her house renovation plans. Not only were the plans from the dining room missing, but the files on her computer had disappeared. She had long ago backed them up to a flash drive, which also held several client projects and a preliminary design for her studio in the carriage barn. The flash drive was gone, too.

Alexa knew that the plans disappearing from all three places at once was no accident. She remembered Lucy's vow to get back to Elm Ridge, whatever it took, and felt heartsick to think that her daughter might do something so irresponsible and mean. Lucy had looked at the floor and gone quiet when Alexa mentioned the loss. Not a good sign.

"Do you know anything about this?" Alexa had pushed.

"How would I know where your stupid plans are?" Lucy had answered, and stomped off.

Alexa didn't follow her. She was loath to make such an accusation unless she was completely sure.

Fortunately, she'd had to file the plans with the town for her permits. They were charging her to make duplicates, but at least she wouldn't have to start again from scratch.

Her client projects and carriage-barn plans were another story: several weeks of work lost, work not easy to make up.

As she drove past Kranston's Market, she spied boxes of bright pumpkins in one corner of their parking lot. Alexa made a U-turn and doubled back. She'd had so much on her mind she'd almost forgotten: it was Lucy and Alexa's tradition to carve jack-o'-lanterns on the Sunday evening before each Halloween. They'd never missed a year; they had homemade popcorn balls and hot cider and made a party of it. Lucy's friends often joined them, and sometimes a few of Alexa's as well. Everyone had a great time carving, and the jack-o'-lanterns were lit and set out on the balcony for all the neighborhood to see. Their record, set last year, had been seven pumpkins; Alexa still had the pictures on her phone. They'd rounded out those evenings watching old horror movies on TV, gasping together at the scary stuff, making fun of the nuttier parts. Alexa ached with the memory.

Well, they'd missed that Sunday this year, but there still was time—perhaps in more ways than one. Pumpkins as a peace offering; she liked the idea. Alexa rooted through the bins of picked-over pumpkins until she found two small but fairly well-shaped candidates. Heartened, she traveled the grocery aisles picking up molasses, butter, popcorn, cider, and miscellaneous groceries, along with some candy for the kids who would come to the door.

At home she unloaded the pumpkins and groceries, and carried them up to the makeshift kitchen they'd set up in a second-floor bedroom while the first floor was renovated. They had a small table, a microwave, and a two-burner hotplate. Until the kitchen was finished, they were doing dishes in the second-floor bathroom sink. Even up here, the demo dust was everywhere. First the black dust, soon the white. Alexa wiped the table clean, put several things away in the tiny temporary fridge, and called for Lucy, who came down the stairs and went straight to the grocery bags as usual, pulling out and examining the contents. She didn't comment on the pumpkins.

"So what do you think?"

"About what?" Lucy asked, not bothering to look at her.

"About the pumpkins. They look like good ones."

Lucy shrugged. "Mom, don't you think I'm getting too old for that?"

"I wasn't aware of an age requirement. You've always loved carving them."

"Not this year. I'm not in the mood. And anyway, where would we do it?" She gestured around the small room crammed with all their kitchen equipment.

"I don't know. The front porch, maybe?"

Lucy scrunched her face in dismissal. "I'm going out tonight." She pulled a banana from the bunch on the table and began to peel it down.

"Oh? Where to? And with whom?"

"With *whom*?" Lucy said around a mouthful of banana. "Geez, mom, do you *hear* yourself?"

Alexa brushed aside her rising frustration. This was just a phase—one she hoped wouldn't last too long. "Don't change the subject. Who are you going out with, Lucy? Tell me what's happening."

"There's a party tonight. You don't have to worry; it's at a church. No drinking or wild sex or anything. I'm going with a guy named Jake."

"Is that one of the kids who give you a ride to school?"

"He's the brother of one of the girls. You'll get your chance to meet him tonight. I told him he had to come to the house so you could pass judgment on him."

"Not the best way to phrase it, but I do want to meet him. Especially since it will be your first date. Ever, that I know of." She gave Lucy a sentimental look, despite her awareness of how it would be received.

Lucy rolled her eyes. "Not a big deal, Mom. I have to go get ready. He'll be here at six-thirty."

Lucy headed upstairs, and Alexa could hear the door to her third-floor bedroom close—not slam, exactly, but close enough.

She comforted herself with a cup of tea and a copy of the *Wednesday Gazette*, the local newspaper she'd picked up at

Kranston's Market. An article on page one caught her eye. "Halloween Alternatives: Local Organizations Offer Parties, Activities Without the Occult." Apparently, some Christian parents objected to their kids "being fed a seasonal diet of sinners, demons, and ghouls." As one young mother put it, "We want our kids to celebrate the harvest season without this unwholesome glorification of dark creatures and acts."

Traditional costume parties and trick-or-treating were called into question. The *Gazette* reported that schools, civic groups, and churches were offering substitute activities with "more appropriate" themes. One local grade school was holding a fall festival with carnival rides, games, prizes, and treats. That explained why the doorbell had only rung twice in the hours after school. Alexa remembered the young Batman wannabe in the plaid flannel shirt. According to the article, Ecstasy Christian Ministries had several options planned, including a party for teens.

Alexa remembered the Halloweens of her youth, before her father died—the excitement of weeks spent planning a costume, the mask or makeup that would cover her face and make her feel completely free for a day. And then the class party: crepe-paper streamers, black cats and ghosts the students had cut from construction paper, candy corn, colorful frosted cupcakes, and cookies the room mothers had made.

Later, and best of all, was the thrill of going door to door with her friends and her shopping bag. They ran and played in the dusk with little supervision, attempting to trick or spook one another, and stuffed themselves with treats until they were too cold and tired to walk another step. Then they'd dump all their candy on kitchen tables to tally and sort the booty they'd carry in their lunches until nearly Thanksgiving.

At six-thirty the doorbell rang, and Alexa went down the stairs to answer, leaving footprints in the dust as she did. When she opened the door, before her stood a tall blond teen, handsome as hell, his surfer-boy looks a contrast to the blue and white biblical robes he was wearing. He held a stuffed camel under one arm; he smiled and offered her the other hand.

"Hello. Mrs. Moss? Great to meet you. I'm Jake. I'm here to pick up Lucy."

Alexa shook Jake's hand and ushered him into the foyer, such as it was. The drywall was up but not finished, the chandelier was draped for dust, and the floors were covered with tarps. There was nowhere to sit and have a conversation, get to know this boy.

Alexa struggled to hide her surprise when Lucy appeared. She was dressed in a flowing magenta head scarf and robe edged in gold trim, over a pale pink tunic. She wore eyeliner and dangling filigree earrings, and held Alexa's blue-glazed pitcher. She looked both exotic and innocent.

Alexa's eyes met Lucy's. "I didn't realize it was a costume party."

Lucy opened her mouth to speak, but Jake answered. "We do it every year. It's all characters from the Bible. We're going tonight as Isaac and Rebecca."

"Oh," was all that Alexa was able to manage.

Lucy sent her mother a look. *Don't screw this up for me.*

Alexa gave a small sigh, resigned. "What time will you be home?"

"Don't worry," Jake said, "I'll take good care of Lucy and have her back by midnight."

"Okay, but leave your phone on, Lucy, and let me know if there's any change in plans."

"Sure, Mom. Bye."

"It was very nice to meet you, Mrs. Moss."

The screen door slammed as the two draped figures headed out into the cool autumn evening.

"Ms," Alexa said to the empty foyer.

She returned to their makeshift upstairs kitchen and microwaved a TV dinner, then ate it standing in front of the tall, uncurtained window, watching the lights come on in the houses further down the ridge. No shrieks of Halloween mirth from the lawns in Ecstasy. That was too bad.

Alexa headed back to her office to google ECM. Their home page was innocuous enough. Photos of the building and its congregation scrolled across the top of the page. People doing fun things in a gorgeous setting: raised-hand worship, live music, all magnified on giant screens next to the stage. The Ecstasy Christian Ministry campus was like its own city: a coffee shop and Christian bookstore, pizza and ice cream restaurants, a play area for children, a game arcade, even an athletic wing with basketball and tennis courts and a rock-climbing wall. Also ATMs where you could do your banking or donate to the church.

Attendees were encouraged to join the many small groups, which catered to varied interests, ranging from knitting to addiction recovery. Speakers were scheduled most nights of the week. A top-billed Christian rock group would appear there in early November. It was an entertainment complex unequalled in this region of small towns and farms.

Several menu lists in, hidden behind other subjects, she finally found a tab titled "What We Believe." It stated the obvious, bolstered with Bible verses. They believed in original sin, salvation through the son, that the Bible was the literal, inerrant word of their god. They believed in grace through faith, not works, and the eternal conscious punishment of nonbelievers after death. Unmerciful, but hardly different from many other churches out there.

And yet, she was sure this wasn't the whole picture. She searched further on the internet, found articles on these mega churches and their marketing as "destination centers." There were over 1,500 mega churches in the U.S., most of them larger than ECM. Many were open almost 24/7—barely requiring folks to leave the premises— while Christian music and messaging were piped in.

Alexa thought about Cyrus Bell—his mane of silver hair, leonine demeanor, and violet eyes. When he gave a Sunday sermon, she was sure people paid attention.

She remembered Chad, the IT guy, and his "asshole" comments. Alexa and Chad had worked together on several occasions to get her system set up. He said she could call about anything. He probably didn't mean quizzing him about ECM on Halloween night. Nevertheless, she shot him a text:

"Hi Chad. If you have the time this week, could you tell me what you know about ECM? And while you're at it, have you heard of a local group called Pine Bluff Humanists for Good?"

Twenty minutes later, she got a reply: "Sending you some docs by email." Not long after that, she found and opened Chad's message.

Alexa –

To answer your first question, I've attached some articles on the history of ECM, lawsuit, etc. Have been keeping a file on these bastards for some time. I think you'll find attachment 3 especially interesting—a page entitled "Core Beliefs" I captured from their website the first year, before they took it down. They are not as open about this stuff now.

To answer your second question, I'm a member. Will touch back tomorrow or next day and we'll talk.

Chad

Several of the articles covered the basic facts Heather had provided: new church, new pastor, etc. Alexa noticed there was little on Cyrus Bell's background, only that he'd been the pastor at a Church of the Living Waters in West Virginia, which was now defunct. Information on the high-school lawsuit rehashed what she'd heard on TV.

But Chad was right, the interesting piece was the "Core Beliefs" screenshot. Along with the tenets stated on their current website was a list of "Affirmations" that were far less benign.

- that the earth was created six to ten thousand years ago

- that through woman's first sin, all of mankind was born in sin thereafter
- that marriage is between one man and one woman, and all sexual behavior outside that framework, including fornication, adultery, homosexuality, and masturbation, is sinful
- that woman's God-given role is to bear and care for children and be a submissive helpmate to her husband
- that life begins at conception, and termination of pregnancy for any reason is against God's plan and sinful
- that men have spiritual and "corporeal" (meaning *bodily*, Alexa realized) authority over members of their households
- that no women may hold an oversight or teaching position over a man
- that due to the utter depravity of human nature, a constant vigil must be kept against the devil, who will tempt the weakest members of the community and work through them.

Alexa shuddered at the thought of women's and children's bodies under the "authority" of men. What exactly, Alexa wondered, was Lucy getting into?

Dismayed and weary of the subject, Alexa changed into sweats and sank into the loveseat in her office to drink hot cider and surf the TV channels for something spooky to watch. She settled on *Invasion of the Body Snatchers*. The story was simple enough: alien beings come to earth on a solar wind and take root as lovely pink flowers, which grow into pods that replicate any sleeping humans nearby. The humans then crumble into dust, leaving alien copies of themselves to take over the earth. The remaining humans eventually must stay awake to survive. When the aliens find a human, they point and emit an ear-splitting shriek to alert the others of their kind.

That shriek still ringing in her ears, Alexa heard a car pull into the drive. She surreptitiously went to the window. The vehicle was idling, but all she could see of the interior was a gleam of gold from the edge of Lucy's headscarf. She forced herself to back away from the window and sit at her desk. Nearly twenty minutes passed before she heard Lucy's footfalls on the stairs.

Alexa called to her as she passed the office. "Hi hon, how did it go?"

Lucy turned back and stepped into the room. Her color was high, her shiny pink lip gloss smeared. Her expression was excited but restrained, at least in front of her mother.

"It was fine. A lot of kids were there."

"All dressed in biblical costumes? What did you do?"

"There was a scavenger hunt, and music and food. It was fun." Lucy turned to leave.

"And Jake? Are you going to see him again?"

Lucy stopped and turned in the doorway. Alexa tried to read her face and failed; that curtain between them was still firmly in place.

"Yeah. He's great. A gentleman. You don't have to worry. I wouldn't have gone out with him otherwise."

"Well, I'm glad to hear that." Alexa paused. "Guess what I saw tonight?"

"What?" asked Lucy, her interest momentarily piqued.

"*Invasion of the Body Snatchers*. It's an old film from 1978, but it's great. I recorded it for you."

"Oh," Lucy said, unwrapping the head scarf and shaking out her hair. "Don't you think those movies are kind of *dark*? I mean, why spend your time on all those demons and ghouls?"

Almost the very words that Christian mother had used in the *Wednesday Gazette*.

"They were aliens, actually," said Alexa dryly.

"They were evil, right?"

"That's pretty much the point."

"Well, I just think ... why not concentrate on something more positive?" She kicked off her shoes and picked them up, dangled them from her fingers and wriggled her toes. Then she yawned. "We can talk more in the morning; I'm going to sleep."

Who was this pod child and what had she done with Lucy?

"Okay, good night."

Alexa reflected on all she'd learned as she prepared for bed. The church stuff was disturbing on so many levels and heightened her concern for Lucy. Her daughter was changing, and not in a direction Alexa liked. Par for the course for parents, she knew, and yet there was something more fundamental here. *Fundamental.* That was the word. Everything seemed to revolve around this invasive church, its effect on the town's population. Even her scientist daughter did not seem to be immune. Alexa remembered the small pink flowers from the movie—so lovely, but so deadly.

There were moderate believers like Heather. But even they equated good with religion and didn't ask too many questions. Most of the members of ECM had likely never investigated the true tenets of their church. Like the victims in the *Body Snatchers*, they slept as others stole their essence and substituted something very different in their names.

Alexa wiped the omnipresent demo dust from the bathroom mirror, then scrubbed the makeup from her face. Her port wine birthmark blazed in this private light.

She remembered the other shoppers at Kranston's: the crosses around so many necks, the Jesus fish on the cars in the parking lot. She had walked down those aisles, a stranger to this little town, and no one had stared at her. Alexa could pass for one of them, she realized. But she was a fraud. If they knew her heathen heart, they would point and shriek.

And her heart began to pound as she realized that she was the one who would have to stand and fight. It wouldn't be Heather; it wouldn't be Reynolds. This stained person in the mirror, this live-and-let-live woman who loathed the limelight was going to have to sound the alarm, wake the others. Run for the freaking school board.

She barely had time to pull back her hair before she was sick in the sink.

12

Lucy: Friday, November 8

Her phone was chiming with Jake's special ringtone, but Lucy ignored it as she buttoned her jacket and paced the porch, scanning Collins Road for David's car. She didn't want to lie to Jake if she could help it.

Being with him this past month had been amazing. The youth group meetings in early October had sealed the deal. Of all the girls he might have had, Jake had chosen her.

She'd always loved the fall in Elm Ridge, but that couldn't compare to this country autumn with Jake. They went on hayrides with other kids and took long hikes through the fallen leaves. He kissed her and kissed her under the colorful trees. They tried everything the town had to offer: restaurants, movies, the bowling alley. They drove to the county Fall Festival—part harvest fete, part renaissance fair—where they sampled root beers, ate kettle corn, and watched costumed jesters and jousters. Lucy bought Jake a replica of a medieval sword, and he chose a fake but beautiful jeweled coronet for her. "Milady," he said, with a courtly bow, "thou art the fairest in the land." Corny, but totally thrilling nonetheless. They posted their photos to Instagram, and hundreds of students liked and commented.

Her new friends were different from the old, but still fun to hang with. Yeah, they were more religious, but there was something weirdly attractive about that; their lives seemed deeper, more purposeful somehow. Lucy went to youth group often. She didn't know how her mother felt about that. She didn't ask.

Jake had turned her on to Christian rock, which often touched her on an emotional level that secular music had not. She still wasn't into the God thing—her science background made many of the church's claims absurd—but she could see the comfort there for those who believed. She didn't discuss her views with Jake, who insisted that global warming was fake and the earth was 6,000 years old. She hadn't changed her mind about the origins of the universe, but maybe Jake was right when he said her soul was more important than any career. He was older, wiser, showing her what life was about, willing to guide her. And she was willing to follow.

Their only disagreement so far had been about Sam. The Bison, Jake's friends on the football team, had been harassing Sam since the start of the school year. Lately it had gotten more physical. Sam fought back when she could, but she was outnumbered. Jake told Lucy it was just hazing, and to forget it. Sam herself had told her the same thing. "I'm fine. Please just stay out of it," she'd said when Lucy asked her to report it. "If the school gets involved, these guys will just take it off campus and it'll be worse."

Since there wasn't much that Lucy could do about it, she held her tongue, wanting to stay on Jake's good side.

But what she was up to now could wreck their relationship for good.

Her phone pinged with a text from Jake. "where r u?"

She wanted to ignore the message but knew from experience that Jake wouldn't quit until he got an answer.

"not feeling good" Lucy texted back. "staying home today"

"stomach or cold?"

"stomach" She added a green-faced rabbit GIF.

"weird davids sick too"

"we all ate popcorn yesterday from the same bowl maybe germs?"

"sorry feel better call you later ❤"

"k thanx ❤ ❤ ❤"

Lucy sighed. It didn't feel good to deceive him. She spent a few more jittery minutes on the porch before she saw David's car turning into the drive. If she was this nervous, she couldn't imagine how Maddie felt.

"How is she?" Lucy asked as she got in.

"She's a wreck."

"Understandable."

David looked tense and pale, and Lucy wondered whether it was the actual procedure that concerned him or something more. He picked up Logan and the three of them rode in edgy silence to Maddie's neighborhood.

It had been six weeks since Lucy had helped a sobbing Maddie off the high-school bathroom floor—still clutching her positive pregnancy test—and taken her out to the parking lot where David was waiting for the news. Maddie had begged Lucy not to tell anyone, and she hadn't. Not Alexa, not Maddie or David's parents, not even Jake or Jordan. David had confided in Logan, and the four of them had carried the heavy secret together through weeks of school. Maddie was terrified at the thought of telling her parents. But scared, too, about the procedure, she'd spent most of the month in tears. She'd always wanted children, but not *now*. Her plan was to be an art teacher, not a high-school dropout with a little kid at home.

David was not convinced. They were Christians. How could they end their own child's life? What kind of people would that make them? And yet, in the end, he admitted he couldn't wrap his thoughts around an actual baby. He was supposed to go to college, then to medical or dental school. How would he do that now with a child to support?

Logan researched abortion clinics, so no one would find the information on Maddie and David's phones. The one clinic near Ecstasy had closed its doors two years before, victim of picketing and harassment, including a daily pro-life vigil by members of ECM. Now the closest clinic was in Peoria, nearly two hours away. To make an appointment there, they realized, they'd have to go on a school day. They planned the trip for a day when Maddie's parents would be out of town. They'd call one another in sick for school, meet at Maddie's house that Friday morning, and get on the road by 9:00 a.m.

Lucy, Logan, and David parked across the street from Maddie's house and waited for her signal. A formation of honking migrant geese filled, then emptied the cold blue sky, heading southwest. The wind blew some withered leaves from the trees and scraped them across the cul-de-sac. David had chosen a used car in a muted color from his father's lot, hoping the neighbors wouldn't recognize him.

They saw Maddie's younger brother Jamie leave the house and walk to his bus stop, his backpack stuffed with all he'd need to stay overnight at a friend's. Several minutes later Maddie's attached garage door opened—their "all clear" signal—and David pulled inside. When the door closed again, they left the car and entered Maddie's kitchen through the side door.

Maddie didn't look good at all. She was sitting on the sofa in the family room, her brown hair disheveled, her head in her hands, weeping. Lucy sat down next to her and hugged her.

"Are you okay?" Maddie shook her head. "How can I help?" Lucy asked her.

Maddie raised her tear-streaked face, almost colorless now. Even her freckles seemed faded. The lids of her pale blue eyes were puffy. She probably hadn't slept at all.

"I'm not sure I can go through with it."

Lucy glanced at David. "You don't have to if you don't want to," he said." We'll think of something else."

"What else? What alternative do we have?" She sounded panicked, and David took Lucy's place on the sofa, holding Maddie to calm her.

"I don't know—" he began.

"Am I going to hell?" Maddie asked him.

"What?"

"Am I going to hell?"

David looked stricken. "If you are, then so am I."

They all fell silent.

"But my parents ..." Maddie began to cry again. The others stood around her, helpless. The minutes ticked past. Eventually she quieted, then straightened, sniffed, and wiped her tears. "I can't tell my parents. We have to go," she said at last. "We have to go now, right Logan?"

Logan checked his phone. "If you're sure this is what you want, Maddie, we really need to leave now."

"There's another reason we need to be quick," David told them. "When I was on the phone to you this morning, Maddie, my sister Chloe overheard me."

They all turned to look at David.

"She came in while I was talking about going to Peoria. I don't know what else she heard. I swore her to secrecy. I told her we were just skipping and promised to buy her apps for her phone and a pair of earrings if she didn't tell. I think that'll work; she didn't say a word to my parents, but we'd better not take any chances. Let's get on the road."

Maddie locked the kitchen door behind them, and they arranged themselves in the car, David driving, Maddie in front—she got carsick easily now. Maddie pressed the garage door remote, and David began to back out.

Then he stepped on the brake, rocking them all in their seats.

A car had pulled across the base of the driveway, blocking their exit. They knew that car; it was the one Jake and Jordan's parents had just given them for their birthday. The twins got out of the vehicle, leaving it parked where it was. Jordan locked the door and pocketed the clicker. Logan groaned. The group got out of the car to talk to them.

"There you are," Jordan said to Maddie. "Where are you going without us?"

David cut in. "Jordan—"

"I *knew* something was up," she said. "All the mood swings and stomach problems and private conversations. I didn't put it together until Chloe called me. You lied to us."

Maddie hung her head.

Jordan pressed on. "Maddie, are you pregnant?"

Maddie was silent.

"Look," David said. "I know you're shocked, and I'm sorry we didn't tell you. But we don't have time for this conversation. We have an appointment. We have to get on the road."

Jordan's eyes narrowed. "What kind of appointment?"

No one responded. Jordan searched their faces, their guilty expressions.

"Really?" she shrieked. "You're going to have an abortion?"

"Please, Jordan," David begged, looking around at the neighboring houses. "Keep your voice down."

Lucy looked at Jake, but he was texting, his head bent over his phone.

"I will *not*. This is wrong. You're Christians. What are you thinking?"

David turned to Jake. "Will you move the car?"

Jake held up one hand but didn't budge.

"How could you do this?" Jordan was raging now.

David gathered himself. "It's our decision, Jordan. Me and Maddie's. We've made up our minds. Now please move your car."

"No," Jordan said, and folded her arms. "I won't let you do this. It's a sin. You'll regret it. You won't be able to live with yourselves." She pointed to Lucy and Logan. "And you two, helping them! How could you?"

Lucy met Jake's eyes for the first time that day, and he looked away. Her stomach clenched.

"It was our decision," David countered. "Lucy and Logan were just being good friends."

"Some friends," Jordan spouted.

"*Jordan, move your car or give me the keys.*" She shoved her hands in her pockets and shook her head.

Then Jake spoke, finally, to David. "No."

Maddie moaned and leaned on Lucy.

"What right do you have?" David asked him, angrily. "Who are you to say?"

"We're your friends. Your *true* friends. This is for your own good. You'll see that later."

David flushed to the roots of his red hair. He balled his fists and stepped toward Jake. Logan moved to position himself between them. "C'mon guys, let's take this conversation inside."

Reluctantly, they turned and filed through the garage into the family room. Inside there were more recriminations, more raised voices and tears. Jake stayed in the kitchen on his phone. When he joined them, he nodded to Jordan and went back to arguing with David.

Maddie, oddly, was in the arms of Jordan now, still crying. Jake left off with David and took Lucy by the arm. "Are you responsible for this?" he growled in her ear.

"What? No. I just kept their secret."

He gave her a scathing look and turned away. She had blown it, lost him.

Someone knocked at the front door. Logan looked through the peephole and gasped. David's parents were standing on the front porch. Logan whispered the news to the room, as the doorbell began to ring insistently. David paled and sat on the sofa.

"Good. You're here," Jake said, when he opened the door. It was clear he had texted the Larkins.

Mr. and Mrs. Larkin seemed to bring the cold air in with them. It clung to their expensive coats, trendy haircuts, and angry expressions.

"It seems," said Mr. Larkin, "we have a situation here."

Mrs. Larkin took off her gloves and laid them on the coffee table. "Maddie, go wash your face, dear," she said. "Get control of yourself. Then we'll talk."

Mr. Larkin pulled David into a corner and spoke in low tones. David looked guilty and petrified; his father stern, then determined. Lucy studied her hands while Logan glanced around uncomfortably.

When Maddie returned, they were all told to put on their coats and get in the Larkin's big SUV.

"Where are we going?" Lucy asked. Her mother thought she was in school.

"Just come with us," Mrs. Larkin told her. "No sense in trying to go to class now, and we're certainly not letting you all run free for the day."

The couple herded the young people into their car. Lucy sat in the third row of seats, wondering how much trouble she'd be in. Jake sat next to her but ignored her. She'd lied to him and let him down, and she had no idea what he must think of her now. She wondered if they'd made a mistake in not telling Jake and Jordan from the start. She sensed they were more upset about being out of the loop than they were about the abortion. But the choice had not been hers.

Lucy realized eventually they were on their way to ECM. That didn't bode well for Maddie and David. Both of their fathers were elders there. The car was quiet. When they arrived, they were ushered into a Bible-study room with chairs arranged in a circle.

A woman in a tight suit beckoned to David and his parents, who followed her out. Twenty minutes later, Jake and Jordan were summoned, too. The others waited with growing apprehension. Morning light filtered through the window and fell on a wooden cross on the wall. A table clock ticked off endless seconds. Lucy sat next to Maddie, trying to comfort and calm her. They were waiting, they knew, for the pastor, Cyrus Bell.

Lucy had only seen the pastor once before, in the halls of the ECM complex, surrounded by attentive, busy people. He was impressive: a tall man, wearing a dark gray suit that set off his square shoulders and silver hair. His eyes exuded confidence and command. The overall effect was magnetic, and Lucy found it hard to look away. Now she wondered queasily what he'd say to them. Nearly an hour had passed.

Finally, they heard voices approaching and the others returned to the room. Cyrus Bell was among them. He was dressed in black, with a silver stole draped over his shoulders.

Jake still wouldn't look at her. David stuck close to his parents; Maddie noticed and hung her head. Lucy took Maddie's hand.

Mr. Larkin addressed them first.

"Listen up, everyone. The pastor has graciously agreed to forego other pressing business to advise us in this situation."

Mrs. Larkin nervously fingered the gemstone cross around her neck. Her eyelids were puffy and red.

The pastor stood in the circle. "First," he said, "Some introductions are in order. I'm Pastor Bell."

His tone was kindly, and he extended his hand toward Lucy. She did the same and the pastor covered her hand with both of his. It was comforting and at the same time vaguely alarming.

"I'm Lucy," she barely managed to answer.

"I'm very glad to meet you, Lucy. Though other circumstances would have been better."

Lucy was surprised by the pastor's deep, smooth voice. She blushed and cast her eyes down, too nervous to speak.

Bell turned his attention to Logan. "I've seen you here once or twice before."

"Yes, sir. Logan Hartman."

Logan attended the synagogue across town with his parents but hung out at the café with Jake and Jordan.

Pastor Bell took a seat in the circle, adjusting his robes as he did.

"Maddie's parents, the Gibsons, have been notified and are on their way. It'll be some time before they get here."

Maddie said nothing, but removed her hand from Lucy's to cover her face.

Pastor Bell said, "Let's begin with a prayer."

They all bowed their heads, so Lucy did the same.

"Almighty father, we thank you for all you have given us, for your abundance, your guidance, and your protection. We thank you for your wisdom, though we might not always fathom your reasons or your ways. We thank you for this new life among us, surprise though it is, and acknowledge that your will is ever perfect and right. Please help David and Maddie and their families accept this gift. Please help these young people look to you and follow your ways, turning sin into penance, patience, and responsible Christian parenthood, learning and growing in righteousness as they go. In Jesus' name we ask this. Amen."

"Amen," the others echoed, and raised their heads.

"Now," the pastor began, his tone darkening, "unfortunately, we need to address your choices and actions today."

He suddenly seemed to fill all the space in the room.

"David, Maddie, you indulged your lustful bodily passions, and then, when faced with the consequences, decided to take a human life. There is no bottom to the disappointment we feel in you today. You've been raised in the Lord. You, of all young people, should have known better."

David closed his eyes. Maddie looked as if someone had struck her.

"Your parents and I will work with you in the coming weeks to restore your godly outlook and prepare you for what's to come. There will be serious consequences, both at church and at home."

David's father nodded.

"Jake and Jordan, your actions were nothing short of heroic today," Bell continued. "You saved your friends not only from further grievous sin, but from everlasting torment. You are to be commended."

Jake looked humbled and a little conflicted, but Jordan raised her chin, clearly proud.

"Logan, we'll leave it up to the Larkins and Gibsons to decide if they want to contact your parents. The Jewish laws and values are sometimes different from ours, but I'm sure this kind of deception is not condoned."

Logan looked surprisingly calm. Maybe *his* parents would understand. Lucy wasn't sure about Alexa.

Cyrus's gaze then turned to her. "Lucy, you're new to this town, I understand." Lucy nodded, dreading whatever came next. "Jake tells me that your parents are atheists?"

"It's just me and my mom. She has no religion."

"She doesn't believe in God?"

"Not really," she answered.

"And how about you?" the pastor asked her, training those intense eyes on her face. She could feel her heart jump and flutter in her chest.

Lucy hesitated. "I don't know," she finally admitted. "I've never believed in God before. We never went to church. But I've begun to like Christian music, and the feeling that it gives me." She looked at Jake, who stared at the floor. "I don't know," she said again.

"Well then, Lucy." The pastor's voice softened a little, drawing her in. "I don't think it would do much good to contact your mother. We can hardly hold you responsible for something you've never been taught. Your upbringing seems woefully short of spiritual truth and values." He paused for a moment, maybe waiting for a reaction from her. Lucy didn't know what to say.

"I'll tell you what," Pastor Bell continued. "Why don't you give us a try? I invite you to come to church on Sunday and explore that feeling you mentioned. It's not an accident we've crossed paths. Perhaps the Lord has been looking for you." He smiled. "Will you do that for me?"

"Okay." If that was all, she was getting off pretty lightly. Lucy was too frightened not to agree.

The tight-suited matron came to the door and gestured to Pastor Bell, who rose, surveying those in the room. "You'll be hearing from me," he told them. "Maddie and the Larkins will remain with me until Maddie's parents can join us. Jake and Jordan will see Lucy and Logan home. I trust you will spend the rest of the day thinking about what you've done."

The minute the pastor left the room, it felt like the air went with him. Lucy hugged Maddie and David, and followed Jake and Jordan to their car. She found her knees weak as she climbed into the front seat. Except for a few logistical comments between the twins, they drove in silence. They dropped Logan off first, and Jordan, too.

Logan had lived next door to the twins from childhood, which must have made his secret-keeping seem more of a betrayal. That was bad. But the tension in the car was even worse when they were gone.

As they headed toward Lucy's house, Jake kept his eyes on his driving. Lucy was desperate to explain, to reach out and touch him. "Jake, please, you have to understand ..." she began.

"Lucy, don't try to defend yourself." Jake's handsome face grew distorted with disgust. "I can't believe you were part of this. Is this what kids do where you're from?"

Lucy tried her best to stay calm. "Jake, I think it happens everywhere."

"Yeah? Well, that's not how we solve our problems here."

She took a deep breath. If she allowed herself to argue, to feel anything, she knew she would break down. Maybe that's what he wanted—some sign of remorse.

"Look, I'm sorry we didn't tell you, but Maddie and David swore us to secrecy."

Jake's lip curled in disdain. "You didn't tell us because we'd try to stop them."

That much may be true, but she couldn't help feeling the "procedure," as they'd been calling it, would have been the best thing for them. What were they going to do now—sixteen and seventeen years old with a baby?

And the hardest part for Lucy to grasp was that Maddie's wishes didn't count at all. Pastor Bell had listened to everyone *but* Maddie. And now she had no choice. Her parents would follow the church, and she would become a mother, whether she wanted to or not.

Jake pulled up in front of Lucy's house. She turned to him. If he was going to dump her, she wanted to know.

"What will happen to us?"

Jake sat silent a moment. "Pastor Bell wants me to forgive you and to mentor you. To show you the right path." He paused. "I'm not sure I want to right now." He looked at her then. There was hard judgement in his blue eyes. "You should do what he says. Start going to church.

Start thinking about your actions. It's not me who has to forgive you."

"Okay. I'll think about it," she said. But she knew she didn't have much choice if she wanted to be with Jake.

"Don't text me or call me for a while," he told her. "I'll talk to you when I'm ready."

Lucy kept it together until she got inside and Jake had driven away. Then the tears came.

13

Rachel: Friday, November 29

Rachel stepped out of her uniform and pulled on her best skirt and sweater, such as they were. Checking herself in the mirror, she took down her dark hair and shook it out, then reapplied her lip gloss and smoothed her straight brows. An old radiator hissed in the corner of the tiny, overheated room the diner staff used for changing. It was five o'clock on the day after Thanksgiving, and her shift was finally done. Her feet ached from days of waiting tables, serving lonely patrons their solitary turkey dinners—and then, the moment that was over, the shoppers their Black Friday lunches.

That was okay; she was grateful for the job. Sandy turned out to be gruff, but fair, and seemed satisfied with her work. Rachel hoped she might be kept on even after Charlene returned from having her baby. But the shifts were long and busy, and the meager wage and tips were not quite enough to pay her rent. She didn't know yet what she'd do about that.

Ben was due to pick her up any minute. Alexa and Lucy had invited them to their place for a belated holiday dinner. Ben had warned her it might be Chinese, as the Mosses didn't have a kitchen yet. That was fine with Rachel; she was heartily sick of the smell of giblet gravy and pumpkin pie.

She lit a cigarette, wrestled open the sticky window over the parking lot, and waved out the smoke. As she watched for Ben's truck, she thought about him: his strong rough hands, his warm smile, his wry sense of humor. She'd only known him a few months, but in that time he'd become the best friend she'd ever had. He actually seemed to *like* her as a person. It was a new sensation for Rachel, and one that drew her closer to Ben by the day.

And yet they had not made love. He wanted to wait, he said, until they really knew one another. He was more patient than she was. They kissed and petted, and he claimed her erotically inch by inch. His plan, she saw, was to light a long fuse, so when they exploded, they'd fill the night sky like that brilliant harvest moon.

Several taps on the truck's horn brought her back to the present. Rachel ground out her cigarette and waved in some fresh air before she closed the window. A former heavy smoker himself, Ben was trying to get her to quit, so she fanned the odor from her clothes as she headed out of the diner to greet him. She leaned in to kiss him, then picked up the warm pie Ben had placed on the passenger seat and held it on her lap as they drove to Alexa's. The scent of it permeated the truck; fortunately for her, it was cherry.

Ben seemed happy just to see her, as always. She relaxed and stretched her legs before her, grateful to be sitting. Darkness had fallen early. The streetlights turned Ben's profile on and off as they drove, and his voice seemed to hang in the intimate air of the truck's cab when he spoke. He told her about his work at Alexa's, the antics of the men he shared a house with, some holiday doings in town he and she could attend. The truck's heater rattled, the shocks protesting every patch of uneven road, but Rachel was more content than she had ever been.

On the way through town, they passed the Pine Bluff Library, a 1930s brownstone on the grounds of one of Ecstasy's public parks. Rachel liked the tall façade, the window bays, the stacks of books you could actually smell from the street when the doors were open. The only thing Rachel could afford in this town was a library card, and she'd made good use of it. All the stories forbidden to her in her youth were there to be feasted on now as she pleased.

And feast she did, checking out fiction and nonfiction books by the armloads. They lit her squalid room like candles, transported her from her own life to the joy and excitement of other worlds.

She had studied at the library for her GED, checking out textbooks, drilling herself at the scarred wooden tables. But some things wouldn't stay in her brain. The algebraic formulas, the names for all those chemicals, the physiological terms. It was like they were written in a language she'd never heard. She needed a translator, and for more reasons than one. She had researched epilepsy in the first days of her disfellowship but didn't really grasp most of what she'd read. If she could understand science, perhaps she could learn how to help her sister Phoebe.

Rachel remembered her first meeting at the library with Lucy, how she had nervously paced the first-floor stacks, keeping her eye on the door. When Ben had told her he had hired a tutor, Rachel wouldn't agree to it. He couldn't afford that any more than she could. When she learned the girl was a high-school student, Rachel was even more humbled. But Ben had assured her that Lucy was qualified and eager to help. And Rachel knew she couldn't go on without an education.

When Lucy entered the library, Rachel had known her instantly from Ben's description: golden-brown hair, hazel eyes, heart-shaped face. She was smaller, finer-boned than Rachel and looked her 15 years. She stood near the information desk, hesitant, scanning the room, but when Rachel approached her, Lucy greeted her with a firm handshake and a flash of perfect white teeth.

It was a good match. Lucy seemed to have a natural affinity for teaching. She tried various methods, until she found several that fit Rachel's style of learning. After that, to her own surprise, Rachel progressed very quickly.

In her turn Rachel understood that, being slightly older, she was somehow glamorous to Lucy, who noticed every detail of her hair, her makeup, her clothes, and asked endless questions.

"Are you Ben's girlfriend?" Lucy asked at one of their early sessions.

Rachel thought for a moment. She'd never been called a girlfriend before. It seemed a trivial term for all she wanted to be to Ben. But she realized Lucy was only asking whether either of them was dating someone else.

"I suppose I am."

Lucy rested her chin on her hand and looked off into the distance before turning her eyes back to Rachel. "So is it ... romantic?"

"You mean candy and flowers romantic?" asked Rachel, suspecting what Lucy really wanted to know was if they were having sex.

"Well, yeah ... and other things."

Rachel answered carefully, trying to provide a good example, even if she really wasn't one. "Ben is wonderful to me."

"How did you know he was right for you?" Lucy pressed.

A library assistant passed their table and gave them the eye. They lowered their voices.

"I didn't, at first. Some of his ideas were very different than mine. But he was kind to me, and we had fun, and one day I realized that his opinion of me was the one I cared about." Lucy looked at her, clearly disappointed. "Plus," Rachel added by way of a concession, "he's *very* cute."

Lucy perked up. "Do you love him?"

"I think it's too early for that," Rachel told her, though she already knew the answer. "How about you?" Rachel said. "Is there someone special?"

Lucy looked slightly startled, laughed nervously, and glanced around the library. "His name is Jake," she almost whispered. "I go to school with him."

"Tell me about Jake," said Rachel, closing her chemistry book.

So Lucy filled Rachel in on Jake's astonishing good looks, athleticism, and popularity. "And," she said, "he's a musician. He plays at the coffee shop in town, and also at the church, at ECM."

Rachel remembered him from ECM. One of the Randall twins. She had pegged him as smooth and slightly arrogant. But she could be wrong. There were lots of good people at the church, perfectly sincere. Perhaps he was one. She remembered that poor Phoebe rather worshipped him from afar.

"You're dating him?"

"Yeah, for a few weeks." Lucy looked smitten.

Oh, Lucy, be careful, Rachel wanted to say. But maybe she was. Rachel was struck by how different Lucy seemed from her sister Phoebe, and from herself at that age. Rachel couldn't imagine being allowed at 15 to go to a public school, to dances, hang out in coffee shops, date boys. She had missed it all. And Phoebe was missing it too— even more, confined as she was to the house with her "condition." Something in Rachel was far more resentful for Phoebe than for herself.

"Earth to Rachel. Where are you, darlin'?" Ben's voice filled the cab of the truck.

"Sorry. I was thinking about the first time I met Lucy."

It was dark on the rural road, and she could barely see Ben's features. But his hand reached out for hers. "I'm excited that you two have been doing so well."

"She thinks I'll be ready for the GED in a couple of months. Sometime soon we'll start the practice tests."

The orange reflectors in the road approached, then traveled past them, only to be replaced by others. Forward.

"I'm proud of you, Rachel." It wasn't the first time he'd said it, but she couldn't get enough. She hoped she would not disappoint him.

Rachel was looking forward to this family dinner. Not her own family, but still, a comfort to her. She missed her siblings terribly, especially around the holidays. She looked at Ben. There was no way he could make up for that— those scars would be slow to heal, if they ever did—but perhaps they were moving toward something new that could, in a different way, be just as good.

"How far is it now?" she asked, peering into the night.

"Not far."

Ben's phone began to vibrate and chime. Rachel glanced down at the console where it rested; the name "Louisa" lighted the dark truck. Ben reached over and swiped at the red X, declining the call.

"Is that your sister?"

"It *was*." Rachel could hear the strain in Ben's voice and could just make out the tightening of his jaw.

"Are you talking again?"

"No, we're not. She tries about once a month, but I don't pick up."

"Ben, don't you think—"

Ben's response was calm, but firm. "Rachel, please just drop it. I can't talk to them. We're done."

Rachel didn't know who to be sadder for, him or herself. He had the chance at family—at least a few of them—which she didn't have, but he was far too stubborn. And too hurt.

"Here we are." Ben pulled into the driveway of a large Victorian house. The curtainless first floor windows were blazing, and Rachel could see the rooms were bare. Before they were even out of the car, the silhouette of a figure graced the threshold.

They climbed the steps and Alexa opened the storm door and ushered them in.

"Welcome. I'm so glad you could come." Alexa kissed and hugged them, throwing their coats over her arm.

Rachel had met Alexa when she'd picked Lucy up from the library. She was immediately drawn to the woman, as she imagined many were. Alexa was fine-boned like Lucy with the same large eyes, but Alexa's were gray, with tiny lines around them that showed when she smiled. Her smile was the thing. There was warmth, intelligence in that smile, and a sense of humor. She was quiet in her manner, yet moved in an almost liquid way that Rachel was sure made people stop and watch.

"I thought you'd like to see some of Ben's work before we go upstairs," Alexa said.

Lucy joined them for the tour. Rachel was impressed. Ben's woodworking was exquisite. As they strolled through the still-empty rooms, Alexa and Lucy were quick to point out the restored grand staircase, and the baseboard sections Ben had matched so well to the original that you couldn't see where the old work ended and the new began. Ben had repaired and refinished the original floors with inlaid borders whose patterns now stood out distinctly, intricate and beautiful.

They moved through to the kitchen, still in progress. The walls were up, the floors and woodwork finished. Ben was building off-white painted cabinets to Alexa's specifications. Some of the upper cabinets were already in place. Rachel could see they would fit the home perfectly.

They mounted the stairs and passed through a wide landing on the second floor. In a space meant for a bedroom, a small kitchen had been improvised.

"Have a seat," said Lucy, gesturing to one of the mismatched chairs around the antique table. She seemed pleased to have others joining them for the meal. The room held a tiny refrigerator and a low wooden dresser with a marble top, upon which sat a slow cooker, fragrant steam pouring from a vent in the lid. The woven tablecloth was set for five, and at one of the places sat a pleasant-looking older man with silver hair and mustache.

"Rachel, this is John Jeffers." The man stood to shake hands with them.

"John," said Ben, nodding. Obviously he and this man had met before.

Pleasantries were exchanged, and white wine was poured. Alexa raised her glass.

"Thank you all for gracing our table for this late, light Thanksgiving feast. We're grateful this evening for our family and friends, for the roof over our heads, for the food we eat, and the many hands which helped to bring it to our table." Then she laughed. "I'm afraid that no oven means no turkey, but we hope you'll enjoy this simple substitute."

John Jeffers bowed his head a moment when all was said; Rachel joined him and noticed that Lucy did as well.

Alexa's remarks were followed by a vinaigrette spinach salad with blue cheese, nuts, and cranberries. Next came the main course, a white chicken chili with shredded cheese and sour cream, served with crusty bread. And then there was something amazing called pumpkin flan for dessert, along with Ben's cherry pie.

Rachel asked how they liked Ecstasy, and they talked about their lives in Elm Ridge, their move to the house, their story of meeting Ben on the side of the road. The subject moved to Lucy's school; then Alexa began to ask Rachel about herself.

"There's not much to tell. I'm just a waitress."

"No such thing as 'just a waitress.'" John Jeffers said. "What are your interests, Rachel? What do you like to do?"

"Well, Lucy probably told you that I'm studying for my GED."

"And she's doing incredibly well," Lucy told them.

"Thanks to *you*." The young women looked at each other affectionately. "As for my free time, I used to do some cooking and gardening, though I don't have space for that now. Lately I'm fond of reading and dancing, both things I wasn't really allowed to do before."

"Allowed to do?" Alexa asked.

"Um, yes." How to explain? "I come from a religious family. That sort of thing was not encouraged at home."

"*Reading* was not encouraged?" Alexa asked, frowning.

"Certain things—the Bible, some other books—were okay to read."

There was a moment of silence as the others digested that.

"And you're from this area originally?" Alexa wanted to know.

"No ... well I've lived here for about eight years." She didn't mention how her family had made the decision to follow her Uncle Cyrus to Illinois from West Virginia. It still made her heart beat faster, made her feel guilty, disloyal, to think of them. *Old habits die hard*, her mother used to say. "I'm not in touch with my family anymore."

"And you live over on Center Street."

"Yes, at least … well, for this month."

"Oh, are you planning to move?"

Rachel must have looked embarrassed; Alexa regarded her with concern. "I'm sorry. I didn't mean to pry," she said.

"Oh no, of course not, you've been so kind." She swallowed hard, then admitted, "The truth is I need a second job pretty soon if I'm going to make my rent. I'm already behind."

"They charge her a fortune for that miserable place," Ben grumbled. "It makes me see red."

Rachel knew Ben was hoping that someday he and she might live together, but now was too soon, she felt, for both of them. Despite her new life, she wasn't sure she could do that before she was married, and in truth she had no interest in marriage. She'd been through the housework, the childcare, the drudgery.

"I have a great idea!" said Lucy, standing, tossing her napkin on the table. "Rachel should move in with *us*!" The entire party looked at her in blank surprise. "I'm not kidding," Lucy went on. "She needs a place; we have extra rooms. This room right here will be empty when the kitchen's done." She turned to Rachel. "It would be great! We could have our tutoring sessions here in the house. We need to start experiments now, and there's no way we can do that at the library." And then to her mother, "You wouldn't have to pick me up from the library, Mom. And," she reasoned, "it would help us out too. Financially, I mean."

Alexa colored slightly but recovered.

"I hadn't thought of renting rooms, but I suppose—"

"Oh, no, Ms. Moss, I didn't mean … " Rachel began. She could feel the heat rising in her face and neck.

They heard a door banging open downstairs, men's voices, and then footfalls on the steps.

"Mrs.? Mrs.!"

Rachel felt suddenly ill. She knew that voice.

"Mrs.!" More boots on the stairs, and then George Whitman's face appeared in the doorway. "There you are, Mrs., forgive me for interrupting. I came to pick up some things I need, and thought I'd drop off those paint samples you wanted. Here you go." He crossed the room to Alexa opposite and handed her an envelope. Removing his cap, he said, "Sorry, folks." He looked around the table, stopping short when he spotted Rachel. He stood unmoving for several seconds; his nostrils flared, and a muscle twitched in his cheek. He turned to Alexa.

"What is *she* doing here?"

"Papa?"

Rachel half-rose, trying in vain to catch her father's eye. He couldn't deny her, could he? Not when they were in the same room. But he did. He refused to look at her.

Ben was suddenly on his feet between them. His voice was icy.

"Don't you have something to say to your daughter, man?"

The two men stared each other down for a moment. Then Whitman closed his eyes and shook his head. He passed a hand over his forehead and Rachel could see the furrows there, the pain he was beating down—probably with scripture—in his mind. But he didn't relent.

"Your daughter?" asked Alexa.

Rachel felt her body begin to shake.

"Not anymore," Whitman said, woodenly. "She made her choice."

"No, Papa—" Rachel cried, as she rose and moved toward her father.

"Stay where you are!" he shouted. He held up his hand, still not looking at her. Rachel stopped and stood trembling. Whitman said again to Alexa, between his teeth, "*What is she doing here?*"

Alexa stood, squared her shoulders, and told him, "She's our guest." A moment later she informed them all, including—it was obvious—herself: "She lives here now."

Whitman looked surprised, then angry. He placed the cap back on his head. "Then you're a fool. You'll see what she is. You leave me no choice; I can't work for you anymore. We're off the job." And with that, he turned and headed back down the steps, calling gruffly to his men. "Boys, get the tools and the generator out to the truck!"

"Young lady, are you alright?" John Jeffers asked Rachel, who was dry-eyed but shaking badly now. He handed her his cloth handkerchief nevertheless, as Ben helped her back to her seat. "Alexa," John said, "you can sue for breach of contract."

"Good riddance," said Alexa. "We'll worry about that later."

"I'd better make sure he only takes what's his," John said, and went after Whitman and his men.

"She's pretty pale," Rachel heard Lucy say, just before the room slid sideways and everything went black.

* * *

She woke on the loveseat in Alexa's office, an afghan thrown over her, Ben kneeling next to her, holding her hand. As she sat up, her head spun, and it took a few minutes to clear her thoughts and realize what had happened.

Then she looked at Alexa and caught her breath. "Oh, Ms. Moss, I'm so sorry. Maybe he didn't mean it. If I'm not here, he'll come back. I'm sure he'll come back."

"Don't worry, hon; I wouldn't have him back," said Alexa, and brushed Rachel's hair from her forehead. Lucy, looking worried, hovered nearby.

Ben held and comforted Rachel until her shaking and dizziness had passed. When she was looking better, he stood and picked up his cell phone. "Give me a few minutes," he told them, and left Rachel briefly in Alexa and Lucy's care. He reappeared a short while later and went straight to Rachel's side. "Are you alright?" She nodded, though she couldn't say she felt very much at all. He took back her hand.

"I called some people I know, Alexa. You'll have a new team here on Monday. And I have to say—no offense, Rachel—they're a better group than the last."

"None taken." Rachel tried to smile.

On the ride back to her apartment, he drove one-handed, her head on his chest, his arm never leaving her still-trembling shoulders. He helped her up the stairs and into her room, fetched her nightgown, and helped her off with her things. He turned to let her change, but she barely noticed. She asked for a drink, and he made her a strong one. She drank it quickly, then lay down on her bed exhausted, numb.

He took off his shoes and lay next to her.

"You're staying?" she asked, and he nodded.

He kissed her, and she curled next to him, breathing his breath, and immediately fell asleep.

Rachel awoke several hours later, a high-riding moon slipping in between the broken blinds to stripe the room, her bed. Ben was asleep, breathing quietly. Her father's denying eyes arose before her. Despite being outcast for so long, she realized now that some part of her had been holding out hope of reunion. Tonight had put an end to that. The guilt, the fear, the absolute loss washed over her as if new. The moon moved on from her window, and the room grew dark.

She didn't know how long she lay there grieving. Images tumbled in her head. Phoebe in the ambulance. Cyrus, her parents, her brothers and sisters. Her cousin Caleb: "You made your bed." Her father: "You made your choice." She had never *chosen* to leave her family. Or her job.

But now there were others: Ben. Lucy, Alexa, the big old house. Could she really live with them? She yearned to be part of a normal family. But she herself was not normal. She was half a person, uneducated, alone. Besides the few dollars to rent the room, she had nothing to offer.

If there was ever a time to try prayer, it was now. "God?" she asked silently. "Are you there?"

She heard no answer. Only a distant rumble of thunder and the patter of rain beginning to fall on the roof. In her past life she might have taken that as a sign.

Ben stirred in his sleep. The scent of him was earthy, human. Watching him, Rachel was overwhelmed with affection. God may or may not be up there, but Ben was here in her bed. And there were some things she could offer him for his comfort and his kindness.

She pressed the length of her body to his and kissed him until he woke.

"Mmmm," he murmured, and pulled her into his arms. Outside, the night might be dark and starless, but here in their nest of blankets was her harvest moon. She touched his hair, his face, let her fingers roam his body, his flat belly. She felt his hand over hers. His eyes were open now.

"Rachel, are you sure?" he whispered.

"Yes," she answered, her body already building toward that radiant gold light.

14

Lucy: Sunday, December 1

Lucy marveled at the wall of pipes and the sound they made when the organist played—ancient, sacred, stirring something deep in her she could not quite identify. She'd been coming to church four Sundays now, and she was still amazed.

Sky Cathedral was awe-inspiring. The front of the space had angled white walls, a modern pipe organ on one side, a choir loft on the other, and a large silver cross with a violet light behind it—the ECM logo—in the center. Two huge screens magnified the pastor and other participants for the people in the rear. Lucy knew they broadcast at least one service a week on cable. The modern gray seats were like those in a movie theatre, and the carpeting was purple.

A glass ceiling gave the space weight and drama. Lucy's heart was lifted by the way the light came through it and seemed to bless what went on within. It was clear from the inside; you could see the sky, the sun, or clouds and rain, all without any glare. The outside was mirrored, reflecting that sky, so the top of the building disappeared, and the cross on the steeple appeared to float in the air. The pictures of it were all over the internet. In their first few months, she and Jake, holding hands, had wandered ECM's park-like grounds, admiring the architecture and the landscaped gardens and fountains.

Since Maddie and David's abortion attempt, things had changed. Jake had finally acknowledged her at church, but it was several weeks before he agreed to see her again. She knew it was punishment, and it sucked, but all she had now was Jake and her new friends. She couldn't afford to be cast aside in this foreign, rural place. She loved him and was miserable when she found him distant or cold.

Things had just warmed up between them when Jake learned that Rachel Whitman was living with them. Lucy explained their tutor/student arrangement and Rachel's relationship with Ben.

"But you know she's Cyrus Bell's niece, right?" he asked her.

"She is? I thought that contractor guy was her father."

"Yeah, that's right; he's married to Pastor Bell's sister."

Lucy was puzzled. "Okay. So is that bad?"

"Rachel Whitman was kicked out of her family. They won't have anything to do with her."

"Really? Rachel's so sweet."

"Don't let her fool you," he cautioned. "I heard she was living a sinful life: drinking, sleeping around, that kind of thing. She was supposed to be watching her handicapped sister, and something bad happened. No one will say what exactly, but everyone in that family holds Rachel responsible."

She had seen Rachel have a few glasses of wine, and she came in late when she was out with Ben. But nothing like Jake was describing. And Rachel always spoke of her little sister with love. Lucy liked having Rachel around but didn't want to argue.

"I didn't know about any of this. She's just renting a room from us."

"Well, maybe talk to your mother about getting her out. In the meantime, be careful you're not influenced by someone like that."

Lucy let it go, anxious to get back on Jake's good side.

Jake was off somewhere in the wings getting ready to play on stage. The late morning service was usually geared toward younger people, with upbeat sermons and readings, and Jake and his friends often provided the music. Before Lucy came to ECM, she'd envisioned church as something more formal, but this seemed genuine, organic. She found comfort in the traditional parts, but also liked the fresh ways the message was shared each week. The sanctuary held more than a thousand people, and she was lifted by the energy of so many coming together. She could feel that power and longed to be part of it.

She and her mother had always been essentially alone. They had friends in their neighborhood, in their condo building, but Lucy had never known anything like this purposeful gathering and celebration. She'd felt so disconnected when they moved to Ecstasy.

And now, because of Jake, Lucy had the chance to survive here. She knew he was disappointed with her, but he was patient. Spiritually, she was just a baby compared to him. She'd never met his equal, and she wanted to be worthy.

She cast a quick glance at his sister, who sat beside her. Jordan was in her element. She always looked ecstatic in church. She seemed so sure of her faith.

A few rows forward, Maddie and David sat together, flanked by both sets of their parents. Maddie had been taken out of school. Though David still picked Lucy up every morning, he hurried home each afternoon, leaving her to catch a ride with someone else or take the bus. He'd answer questions if she asked, and Lucy still texted Maddie, but they never mentioned the baby or their future plans. She could tell she was being kept at a distance.

Jake had admonished her. "Are you really surprised? They're expecting a child now—that you tried to help them destroy." Lucy winced at that. "You didn't know the harm you were doing, but you can't blame them for wanting to move on."

Despite all they'd been through, here with their families, in their church community, Maddie and David looked safe and supported. Lucy envied them that solid base.

A group of singers with a 3-piece combo came out to perform, the words of the tune projected on a large screen above them. The whole congregation lifted their hands and swayed as they sang.

It was the first Sunday of Advent, and one purple candle in a ring of four was lit among greens on the altar. "The pink one's for the 3rd Sunday," Jordan whispered to her. "The white one in the middle is for Christmas day."

Pastor Bell in his purple robes took the microphone. His voice was majestic, his audience rapt. His sermon was titled "Fire and Water." He talked about light, how Christ was coming into the world to light it with his love. Lucy was struck by the message: how God loved everyone—even her—so much that he sent a child into the world to comfort and save them. She felt she understood Christmas for the first time.

"You know," Pastor Bell continued, "that this season of waiting for the Christ child is symbolic. That Christ was born 2,000 years ago. He has already died on the cross for our sins and was resurrected. He is already with us, in us, part of us, even as we celebrate his birth. At least, he's a part of many of us here today. But," he said, gesturing toward the congregation, "what if that is not you? What if you have not accepted God's Christmas gift of his son into your heart? What if you are one of the ones still waiting?" Lucy leaned forward to hear what the pastor would say next.

"Well, it turns out this is your lucky day. Today you will have the chance to be forgiven your sins and cleansed in the name of the Lord. Sound good?" The crowd murmured and buzzed.

"Too simple, you might be thinking. Too easy. 'I've been a sinner all my life. How could God want me? How could I be worthy?' Well, the truth is that there's good news and bad. The bad news is we're *all* unworthy. We're *all* sinners." He paused for a moment to let that sink in. "But the good news"—he smiled a megawatt smile—"the good news, *literally*, is that Christ's sacrifice can save us. Was *meant* to save us, to save *you*."

Lucy felt singled out, as if Pastor Bell had pointed directly to her. A tingle ran from her chest down through her fingers.

"And so I'm giving you the chance today to accept the gift of Christ's love. I'd like those of you who are willing to let God into your hearts, to know the Lord, to receive the gift of Christ's sacrifice, to come forward, come to me. Don't be shy. We won't embarrass you. Just come on up to the stage here and stand to my right. You can have the gift of forgiveness and salvation. All you have to do is ask for it."

Lucy was overwhelmed, her eyes brimming.

"Oh my gosh, an altar call. He hasn't done one of those for a while." Jordan put a hand over hers. "Lucy, here's your chance! You should go."

Lucy shook her head. She couldn't. Could she?

Pastor Bell was looking out over the audience. A few timid souls had risen and were making their way self-consciously toward the front. The pastor was encouraging. "Good, good. There are some here who want to open their hearts to the Lord. Come right down sir, and miss, and you too, sir. I'm sure there are more—more of you who yearn for peace in your hearts. Don't hesitate if the Lord is calling. He's calling *you*."

A few more people stood and started toward the front. There were eight or ten in the aisles now, and more rising.

"Those of you already saved, please join us in singing and praying for these who are hearing the Lord's call at last."

Jake and his band took the stage and began to play. *Sin had left a crimson stain, He washed it white as snow.* The audience joined in the melody.

"You can be one of us," Jordan whispered. "You can be saved. Don't you want that?"

Lucy did want that. She wanted to believe. She yearned for some larger point to her life. And she wanted to belong to all of this, to *them*.

"You can be forgiven," Jordan insisted.

Forgiven by God. Even Jake couldn't argue with that. The music swelled majestically, tugging at something inside her. Lucy found herself on her feet, moving across the row to the center aisle. She felt lifted, propelled, her feet barely touching the ground.

There were more of them now. As they reached the stage and climbed the stairs, they were each hugged by one of the church elders and shepherded into a group to the pastor's right. Twenty-five, thirty, then even more, faced the audience, waiting expectantly. The congregation sang.

When the music stopped, Pastor Bell began.

He gestured toward those on the stage with a broad sweep of his arm. "Look at the way the Lord moves," he thundered. The audience broke out in applause, some raising their hands above their heads in tribute. Cyrus Bell's eyes glittered.

Turning to those on the stage, he said, "But this is serious business. The most important business of all. I'd like you now to bow your heads and close your eyes." All on the stage did so. "Picture this. You are standing on one side of a door, and someone is knocking. *God* is knocking. *Jesus* is knocking. Do you hear it?" he asked. "Do you feel it?" There were nods and murmurs of affirmation. Lucy's chest trembled as if someone were pounding on it.

"Do you hear it?" he asked again.

"Yes!" they said.

"Do you feel it?"

"Yes!" they agreed.

"Now," he said, "I want you to look inside your heart and decide if you want to answer. Take your time." He slowed his voice. "Listen. Listen. Do you want to answer?"

"Yes!" Lucy cried with the others.

"Those of you who feel ready to answer, please signal by looking up."

Those on the stage raised their heads, except for one young man, who was tactfully led off. Jake met Lucy's eyes and nodded approvingly. Her spirit sang.

"If you're ready to let Christ into your hearts, please signify by saying 'I do.'"

"I do," they all affirmed.

"Then I ask you to affirm that by repeating this prayer after me."

They repeated the prayer, admitting their sins, accepting Christ, and publicly professing their faith.

"Amen," Bell said.

"Amen."

Lucy felt light, clean, peaceful, as if a weight were lifted from her. A new group of nine or ten people filed onto the stage from the wings.

"These fine people," Bell told them, "have also found the Lord. They are scheduled to be baptized today." He turned to the crowd. "Let's show your love and excitement for them." The crowd applauded.

"And now," Pastor Bell continued, turning to the new converts. "*You* have the opportunity to be baptized, as a declaration of your faith. Not tomorrow, not next week, but today." Bell gestured to an area beside the stage, where a large platform with a basin was rising from the parted floor. The congregation murmured appreciatively. It was clearly full-submersion baptism. The new converts glanced at one another nervously. "Never fear," Bell told them. "We have everything you need." A group of people in purple polos emblazoned with the ECM logo appeared at the edge of the stage. "Our helpers will prepare you for the most significant moment of your lives."

As Jake and his band led another song, the group was ushered backstage. Lucy was carried forward with the others on a wave of raw emotion. Traversing the halls of the church complex, they looked around as if they had just awakened. They were split by gender, and Lucy's group was taken to a ladies' locker room, where there were stacks of baggy shorts, t-shirts, women's underwear, sports bras, and flip flops. The t-shirts were purple, with large white letters that announced, "I have decided." They were given lockers for their clothes and offered hair ties and make-up removal pads. Lucy and others swiped at their faces in front of a large mirror. Some of the women were pensive; others were talking or hugging. Piped-in Christian music helped sustain the mood. White towels were piled in towers by the locker room door, and purple-shirted helpers rotated in to carry them out in armloads. Lucy noticed Jenny Reynolds, her science teacher's wife, among them. They had briefly met one day after school in the lab. Mrs. Reynolds smiled and waved, as if to say, "I'm really glad to see you here today."

When dressed, the women were led back through the halls. On the way, they joined the men and were sorted, it appeared, by age, the youngest and fittest going first. Lucy was guided further up the line. The older or handicapped people who would take more time were helped to the back. Jake's band played as they filed into the sanctuary and through the aisles to form a line at one end of the basin. A woman vocalist sang now, while the words flashed across the screen. *I have decided to follow Jesus. No turning back. No turning back.* Jake caught her eye and smiled. She felt alive, electric. Higher than she'd ever been.

The line moved quickly. She mounted the platform and saw there were steps leading down into the rectangular basin, then up on the other side. Those to be baptized stood waist-deep in the water, and the assistant pastor dunked them backward as Pastor Bell stood behind and blessed them.

Soon it was Lucy's turn. A woman helped her into the water. The basin was like a large jacuzzi, without the jets. The water was surprisingly warm, as comforting as a bath. The assistant pastor put one hand on her back and placed the other, covered in a white washcloth, over her mouth and nose, gently pinching her nostrils.

"I baptize you in the name of the Father, the Son, and the Holy Spirit," he said, and bent her backwards into the water. She relaxed and trusted him.

Through her submerged ears, she could hear the others say "Amen."

In a minute it was over. She was helped up and out and offered a towel, and directed to stand behind Pastor

Bell with the rest of the dripping converted. Now she said amen as others were submerged to receive the Lord. When all were baptized, Pastor Bell said a final prayer of praise to God for bringing them all to Jesus.

"Is God not great?" he asked them, and the congregation heartily agreed. They were led shivering back to the locker room. Now hugs and tears abounded as the women greeted one another shyly or jubilantly in celebration. Lucy was given a bag for her wet clothes; they were hers now, she was told, including the "I have decided" shirt. She dressed, dried her hair quickly, and reapplied mascara and lip gloss, eager to return to Jake.

They were waiting for her: Jake and Jordan, Maddie and David and their parents. There were hugs and smiles all around. The twins invited her to get pizza afterwards. Maddie and David congratulated her but left with their folks; they were no longer allowed to see each other or their friends unsupervised.

Jake ordered their pizza "Chicago style" in honor of Lucy and treated her like a queen.

She was back. It felt great. She could feel the love in the pit of her stomach, in her chest, in her throat: love for Jake, for her friends, for the Lord, love for all mankind. She belonged now; she had a place and a purpose in this world. Jake held her hand.

After they ate, Jake said he had a surprise for her. Jordan would wait for them in the car. He guided her through the complex to the back of the Christian bookstore, to a display case where jewelry rested on a backdrop of deep blue. "Let's make it official," he told her. "I was thinking that one." He pointed to a beautiful silver cross on a braided chain, the loveliest in the store. Tears sprang to Lucy's eyes when the salesclerk handed it to Jake, and he clasped it around her neck.

"Now," Jake told her, "you're mine *and* the Lord's." He put his arms around her and kissed her right there in the store, before the clerk and the shoppers and God himself.

She had never been so happy.

15

Alexa: Monday, December 9

A lexa gathered her breakfast ingredients and set them on the island near the gleaming cooktop. It was a thrill to cook in her brand-new kitchen. The first floor had been finished for less than a week. The contractors were gone—no noise, no dust, no decisions to be made or defended—and every surface of the newly renovated kitchen shone. She especially loved her creamy white cabinets and honed slate countertops. Ben had worked her design and her vision into a warm and beautiful reality. Her curtains were hung; her furniture and selected antiques of Margaret's were moved in and arranged. She'd painted the walls an earthy neutral, then filled the rooms of the old Victorian farmhouse with creature comforts: a bright cushion here, a deco art print there, all in saturated colors, with a Bohemian touch that melded the modern and traditional.

Rachel strolled into the kitchen, smiled, and greeted her while filling the coffeemaker.

"Morning, Alexa."

"Hi, Rachel. How did you sleep?"

"Fine, thanks." Then seeing the ingredients laid out, she asked, "A big breakfast this morning?"

"Yes. Lucy's got the day off school. Teachers' meetings or something. Since you're off today, too, I thought we could have a brunch."

"Great. How can I help?"

Rachel was always eager to lend a hand. Since they'd moved here, Lucy rarely helped Alexa in the kitchen. Gone were the side-by-side mother-and-daughter meal preparations and talks about their day. Lucy cited homework, social events, or after-school activities, missing dinner entirely several days a week. Alexa, hoping it was temporary, didn't argue about it anymore. During the week, Lucy rarely made time for more than a granola bar for breakfast, but fortunately, she had not yet lost her appetite for brunch.

"You can cube those small potatoes for me," Alexa answered, gesturing toward a colander of scrubbed spuds in the sink. "There's a cutting board in the cabinet to your right."

While Alexa cracked and beat the eggs, she looked over at Rachel, standing at the counter with her head bent to her task. She wore a claret-colored tunic over faded jeans. Her loose, dark curls were pulled up and away from her face, her dimples in clear evidence even as she hummed along with the radio. Such natural loveliness: milky skin, blue eyes, graceful figure. She could understand why Rachel was approached, watched, remarked on constantly by men. No wonder she acted wary around them.

Rachel handed her the bowl of potatoes, then took plates and silverware from the cabinet and began to set the table, while Alexa melted butter and spices in the skillet and added the spuds.

Alexa had been skeptical about taking in a boarder. But Rachel was an upbeat addition to the house and a buffer between Alexa and Lucy. Rachel had arrived with no luggage, just a few plastic bags of clothes. She was usually gone for the afternoon and early evening, working both lunch and dinner shifts at Sandy's, taking the bus back and forth in her uniform. The rent Alexa charged her was minimal. Out of gratitude, perhaps, Rachel insisted on helping with the household chores in the mornings, freeing up more of Alexa's time to contact potential clients, work on projects, and start to build an architecture business here.

As she'd settled in, Alexa observed the curious mix of Rachel's traits and habits. While cheerful and kind to Alexa and Lucy, she often seemed pensive, even sad, when she thought herself alone. She was practical, yet sentimental; she seemed naïve about many things, yet was comfortable with the basics of life as few young people were. She blushed if someone swore, but drank vodka in her room every night. Alexa had noticed the carefully covered bottles in the recycling bin.

The potatoes almost done, Alexa poured the beaten eggs into a second skillet and stirred, turning the heat to medium and folding in bacon crumbles and fresh spinach. Rachel retrieved some paper napkins from the pantry and set out the salt and pepper. She poured several cups of coffee and started the kettle for Alexa's tea.

Yes, it was nice to have her around the house. And as a bonus they saw more of Ben, who was obviously Rachel's lover, though she never spoke about it.

Lucy was impressed as well, and a fast friendship had sprung up between the two young women. Lucy had always wanted a sister, and Alexa knew that Rachel missed hers. As for the tutoring, Rachel seemed to be doing well; something had clicked for her. Now she seemed to understand and even like biology and chemistry, and according to Lucy, was making steady progress toward her GED. Rachel was also respectful, and Lucy, she noticed, was a lot less sarcastic when Rachel was around. At this point, Alexa would take what peace she could get.

As if on cue, Lucy walked into the kitchen wearing her earbuds and flopped in a chair before her plate, lifting her hand in greeting to Rachel, barely glancing at Alexa as she thumbed through the tunes on her phone. Lately she'd been listening to Christian rock, suggestions from the boyfriend.

Alexa turned down the flame and added cream cheese to the skillet, then stirred her fried potatoes and readied some serving plates for the food.

Lucy had started going to church with Jake on Sundays, and often went to the youth-group meetings on weekend evenings. Alexa wasn't keen on the idea but stopped short of forbidding her to go. Lucy was a young adult now—highly impressionable, it was true—but she needed to experiment, to ponder things and find for herself where she fit. Alexa wanted to shape and guide that experience, while staying mostly out of the way. So far, those two intentions seemed at odds. She looked at her daughter sprawled at the kitchen table, her golden-brown hair falling longer over her shoulders now, her cheeks with a peachy glow. Alexa felt a sudden rush of love and protectiveness.

Maybe Jake wasn't the worst thing to happen to Lucy; she seemed to be settling into the community and appeared less homesick for Elm Ridge. He certainly had manners—in an Eddie Haskell kind of way—and this Christian group they hung out with had strong views on virginity. Most mothers would probably be relieved. But try as she might, Alexa could not get past her unease. She had noticed Lucy downplaying her interest in science, and suspected it was because Jake didn't approve. But she couldn't hide the light in her eyes when she and Rachel studied together and performed experiments. Alexa dearly wanted that to continue.

She filled the serving plates and brought them steaming to the table. Lucy sat up and removed her ear buds—a concession, Alexa knew, not to her but to Rachel. As they ate they talked of their plans for the day, and Alexa mentioned she wouldn't be home for dinner.

"That's okay," Rachel said. "I'll take care of the cooking tonight."

Lucy met Alexa's eye for the first time that day. "You're going out?"

"Yes. Remember I told you about the school-board candidate meeting?"

Lucy wrinkled her nose. "You're really going to that?"

"Mmm-hmm."

"Why?"

"Because it's important. I don't want to see the quality of education diminish for the very subject you're good at—or any subject, for that matter. It's hard to see how the colleges you've been dreaming of will accept you without a factual education in your field."

"It's factual, Mom. Don't do this for my sake. *Please* don't embarrass me."

"Excuse me?"

"It's hard enough to fit in here without you making a spectacle of yourself."

Rachel shot a surprised look at Lucy but didn't speak. Alexa was stunned. Suddenly her daughter was more concerned with what people thought than the principle at stake? Where was the Lucy she knew—the girl who wrote letters on the environment to local papers, who volunteered to clean up Chicago beaches and parks, who picketed in support of stem-cell research?

Alexa reconsidered. It would be a relief to stay silent, not get involved. But she wouldn't be doing her daughter—or herself—any favors by backing out.

"I'm sorry, Lucy," she finally said, "my mind is made up."

"What about my driving hours?"

Lucy had started Driver's Ed shortly before she turned sixteen in November. She'd passed her permit test, and Alexa had been taking her out to practice several times a week after school and on the weekends.

"You said you're busy this afternoon, and I don't know what time I'll be home this evening." Seeing Lucy's frown, she went on. "I don't think you're ready to drive in the dark just yet."

Lucy rose from the table and loaded her plate and fork into the dishwasher. "Why do you still treat me like a baby?" she asked.

Alexa chose not to rise to the bait. "You're not a baby, Lucy, but you *are* a new driver."

Lucy rolled her eyes, then brightened. "Maybe Ben can take us."

Rachel was learning to drive as well, so Ben had been practicing with both of them. To his credit, Ben was less nervous about it than Alexa, and willing to put in more time.

"I'll text him," Rachel volunteered, as she shuttled the skillets to the sink and immersed them in soapy water.

"Great," said Alexa. "I hope he's available."

It turned out he was. The school-board subject was dropped, at least for the moment. Alexa went to the den to put in a few hours of drafting work.

In midafternoon, she took a break and researched some topics in preparation for the candidate meeting that evening. She read countless pages where creationists vied for equal time with evolutionary theory in public schools—the "teach the controversy" approach that Cyrus Bell was employing. What was lacking in those arguments was any understanding of scientific method. If the method that produced the theory of evolution was faulty, then so was *all* of science— its discoveries, new technology and inventions—since it was based on those methods. And Alexa knew that biological science was essentially built on the principles of adaptation.

She found that Louisiana and Tennessee both had state laws allowing public schools to opt out of teaching evolution. Ditto for charter schools in Texas and Arkansas, and private schools in nine or ten other states, all of which received public funds. So taxpayers were footing the bill for "science" programs that didn't teach real science. Fortunately, Illinois was not one of those states. Yet. Alexa could see how that might be only one or two court decisions away.

She was thinking about those facts that evening when she walked into an echoing room in the county building in Ecstasy and sat in a metal folding chair in the second-to-last row. She was early, and her perch gave her a vantage point from which to see the other prospective candidates arrive. As they filed in and removed their coats, they greeted one another, shaking hands, clapping each other on the back, talking and joking in small groups. Alexa was reminded that this was a small town, and most of the residents had known one another for years.

Alexa found herself scrutinized by one such group. A 30ish blond man with pale blue eyes stared at her openly, then nudged his fellows. All four of them turned to look at her. The blond man seemed familiar. She could feel hostility rolling off him, and she seemed to be the target. She tried her best to ignore him, all of them.

A county representative took the podium, announced the start of the meeting, and introduced herself, then asked those running to stand and do the same. There were seventeen candidates, some for the school board, some for other county offices: thirteen white men, two white women, one Latina, and one black man. When it was Alexa's turn to speak, the blond man and his party stared at her, and continued to do so long after she took her seat.

Photocopied packets were distributed, and the facilitator spoke for 20 minutes, citing procedures for several different elected positions, and how to ensure that their names got on the ballot. School-board elections were held in April of every other year for four-year terms. The board would be filling four positions.

The topic turned to details and filing dates. Candidates needed to file a statement of economic interests with the county clerk. Alexa would need to clear a few hours to put that together; she made a note on her phone. A petition must also be signed by fifty registered voters, and notarized. The time window for this was ten days. She had no idea where she would get the signatures. Still, she thought of Lucy and resolved to meet the deadline or go down trying.

A low-key reception was held after the meeting. Groups chatted near the refreshment tables, and Alexa was again reminded that she was an outsider here. She chose a few cookies, then thankfully found hot water and a decent selection of tea bags. As she steeped her Darjeeling, she was joined by the black man, who chose Earl Grey and introduced himself.

"Malcolm Redd," he said, extending his hand. He looked to be in his early 50s, with salt-and-pepper hair and trendy round glasses.

"Alexa Moss."

"Running for the high-school board?" he asked. Alexa nodded.

"I am as well. Looks like an interesting election this year."

"That's for sure." They stood to the side as others came to the beverage table. Alexa was curious. "Tell me, Malcolm—if you don't mind my asking—what made you decide to run?"

Malcolm looked at her as if weighing whether she'd be receptive to what he had to say. He removed his glasses and rubbed the bridge of his nose with his thumb and forefinger. "I have a son and a daughter at the high school. What concerns me most is what they call the 'achievement gap' between black and white students. Black students at Pine Bluff have lower grade-point averages, don't score as well on standardized tests, and don't take honors or AP classes as often. And they're subject to more disciplinary actions." He paused then, appearing to wait for Alexa's reaction.

"Uh, yes … I'm familiar with this, actually. The Chicago suburb I've just moved from has been wrestling with this issue for some time."

Malcolm looked surprised. "Oh? Have they been successful?"

Alexa sifted her weight from foot to foot, chagrined. "I'm embarrassed to say that I really don't know. I haven't followed up on it." *Why hadn't she?* "I'm guilty, I guess, of focusing mostly on what affects my own child."

"As we all are," Malcolm admitted. "That's the thing in a nutshell. People don't see a problem unless it's a problem for them or theirs. There are no black members on the school board, so no policies in place which help black students. I hope to get elected and remedy that."

"I hope you do."

Malcolm spoke of methods used to address these problems at other schools, which ones were working, and which ones failed. Alexa learned quite a bit in those few minutes.

"Tell me, now," Malcolm asked at length. "What are your reasons for wanting to sit on the board?"

Alexa explained what she'd learned about the lawsuit against the high school, her daughter's interest in science, and her own fears that the facts of evolution, climate science, and more could be suppressed for a generation of students because of their parents' religious beliefs.

Malcolm tilted his head to the side, thoughtfully. "Well, Alexa, what do you have against students hearing both sides of the question? I'm an educated man. I support the teaching of evolution. But I grew up Baptist and find it hard to see the harm in saying some people think God had a hand in it."

"Ah, but whose god?" Alexa asked. "The Christian god, the Hindu or Norse gods? How about the Greek pantheon? If you teach the origin stories of one religion, aren't you obligated by fairness to teach them all and let the students decide what they believe? I don't see anyone suggesting that."

"True..." said Malcolm.

"The bottom line is that science class should be about *science*—how to arrive at facts and theories using *scientific method*. That should be the only criteria." Alexa silently thanked Lucy for her own science literacy. "Public-school science teachers aren't there to discuss whether there is or isn't a god, and their refusal to do so isn't taking away anyone's right to religion. Students can learn the creation stories of their faith at their churches or temples or mosques without imposing them on nonbelievers or other religious minorities in their publicly funded classroom."

"You make some interesting points," he conceded. "I'd never given it much thought from that perspective." He smiled. "Well, Alexa, it looks like we've educated one another some tonight."

Alexa agreed. Malcolm patted several pockets absentmindedly, then found what he was looking for.

"Here's my card."

It said Malcolm B. Redd, CPA; Managing Partner, Evans and Redd Accounting. Alexa gave Malcolm her card as well, and they walked together toward the entrance. They parted on the steps of the county building with a handshake.

"I hope we'll be working together on the board," Malcolm told her.

"I'd be delighted," Alexa answered. She returned his wave just before he rounded the corner of the building and disappeared out of sight.

It was a cold, clear night and the stars shone brightly, despite the lights of town. As she walked through the parking lot to her car, the wind picked up, and she shivered and turned up her collar. She heard footsteps behind her and turned to find the tall blond man from the seminar quickly approaching.

"Alexa Moss?" he asked. Under the streetlights his blue gaze was piercing, but cold.

"Yes. And you are?"

"You don't know?" The man smirked and shook his head. "I'm Aaron Whitman. I'm also running for the school board."

Rachel's brother. There was a vague family resemblance in feature, none at all in demeanor. He was wearing expensive two-toned wingtips. His large black overcoat was open, revealing a sleek, modern suit and a narrow tie, which he straightened now, lifting his pointed chin.

"Oh, I see. Pleased to meet you."

Alexa held out her hand. It was ignored.

"You're an outsider, aren't you? Where are you from?"

"We moved here from the Chicago suburbs."

Whitman's tone was condescending. "And just what would a Chicagoan know about the schools in our community?"

"I beg your pardon?" Alexa asked, and took a step back.

"Look," he said, grinning darkly, moving closer, bringing his face uncomfortably close to hers. "You don't belong here. Your candidacy will surely be challenged. Why don't you save yourself some trouble and go back to Chicago now?"

His voice was high-pitched and saccharine, but there was no mistaking the menacing undertone. Alexa looked around. Seminar attendees were still making their way to their cars. She hit the button to unlock her vehicle, guessing he wouldn't attempt to stop her—or strike her—in front of others.

"I don't think I'll do that," she said as she slid into the driver's seat. "Good night."

He caught the open car door and leaned against it, preventing it from closing. A chill went through her body.

"Well, that's a shame. But you'll see," he told her. "You'll learn."

She threaded her car keys through her fingers. Seeing that, he laughed, then suddenly stepped away and pushed the door closed. Alexa locked it immediately, but Whitman put his face and hands to the driver's side window.

"You'll learn," he sneered through the glass, his voice distorted.

And then he was gone.

Shaken, Alexa started her car, pulled out of the lot, and watched her rear-view mirror all the way home. She didn't know what Whitman was capable of, or how it would affect her candidacy. But the stars were still shining in the cold dark night, and oddly, perversely, the episode served to strengthen her resolve.

16

Alexa: Friday, December 13

C hestnuts roasting on an open fire …

So few radio stations here, and most were playing holiday tunes 24/7. Mel Torme was tolerable; "The Little Drummer Boy" or "Carol of the Bells" for the tenth time, not so much. She didn't know which was worse: the overplayed religious selections or the cheesy seasonal pop favorites. As if to press the question, she heard the opening chords of "Grandma Got Run Over by a Reindeer." Alexa sighed but couldn't stay annoyed for long. She enjoyed the holiday season.

She boiled water in her new copper kettle, steeped her Christmas-blend tea bag until the color was a rich, dark amber, and grabbed a couple of cookies from the jar Rachel had filled with her baking. Her sweet tooth would not be denied today. She carried the mug and the cookies to the den.

As she sipped she put her feet up, and her thoughts returned to her plans for the evening: Pine Bluff Humanists for Good. Chad was enthusiastic about the group. She'd accepted his invitation to their meeting tonight partly out of curiosity. She didn't know what to expect—a bunch of nonbelievers who did what, exactly? Alexa had never been much of a joiner. One of the perks of being nonreligious was escape from the dogma and dictates of large groups. Still, her experience had taught her the value of emotional and social connection, the power of like-minded people gathered together in one place. That was what kept most churchgoers returning to the fold. Maybe humanists had something similar.

She found Mark Robinson's card in her purse and googled the humanists' website. The home page was colorful and attractive. Under the group's name and logo was a motto, "good without a god." A photo slideshow showed the humanists in various settings: dining, speaking, volunteering, celebrating together. Pine Bluff Humanists for Good, the site said, was "dedicated to creating a community of and for ethical nonbelievers, advancing and teaching humanist principles and ideals, participating in service to others, and actively working for nontheist interests."

The site linked to the group's parent association, the National Humanist Organization, and their definition of humanism. The bottom line, as she understood it, was that humanists were people who followed the Golden Rule: "Do unto others as you would have them do unto you." And they didn't need to believe in a god to do it. Humanists did good things, not for reward or eternal life, but simply *because they were the right things to do.*

"Yes!" Alexa said aloud to the room. She jumped up and paced to the window, which overlooked Margaret's acreage. These had always been her values, and she was excited to find them phrased with such clarity. She'd been a humanist most of her life, without ever calling it that!

And she doubted that she was alone. She imagined that there were thousands, maybe millions more people who were humanists without even knowing it. She spent the afternoon reading everything she could find on the subject. The one-page Humanist Manifesto III on the national website summarized and crystalized her beliefs. Strange how so many things in life were clearer, easier, when you had the right language for them.

So at 6:15, with freshly minted interest, Alexa headed out to the meeting. She buttoned her winter coat against the chill as she walked to her car. The meeting was at The

Lodestone Pub, a restaurant/bar out past the north end of Ecstasy, several miles beyond ECM. Alexa hadn't been up that way since she'd moved to the area. She pulled out onto Collins Road, waiting for the engine to warm before she turned on the heat. Beside her on the passenger seat was a folder containing her petition to run for the school board.

As she entered the parking lot behind The Lodestone, it was swept by the headlights of the white van Chad and Jeremy used for their business. She grabbed her petition folder and met Chad on the gravel as he stepped from the van. He gave her a big hug.

"Glad you could make it! Come in and meet the crew. They're gonna love you."

The Lodestone Pub had an upscale rustic look, with plaster walls and exposed timbers, a deer head here, a dartboard there, a gleaming oak bar against one wall, and an equally impressive pool table in one corner. Strung across all were garlands of twinkling, colored lights, and wreaths of fresh pine adorned the walls. A decorated tree stood in one corner. The humanists were gathered at some high-top tables toward one end of the bar, one of which was spread with pamphlets and information cards. A private room was visible past some open French doors, with tables laid, she assumed, for the group.

Tonight, Chad informed her, was one of two yearly meet-and-greets for new and prospective members. The PBHG board and a few other members were already there, welcoming new people as they came in. Chad stuck close to Alexa, ordered them some drinks, and introduced her around. A clean-shaven, dark-haired man caught her eye and, smiling, came toward them: Mark Robinson, Heather's younger brother, he of the humanist business card. She remembered him as a child, playing with Legos and toy cars underneath the tables near his mother's desk at the library. He had grown into quite an attractive man.

"Alexa," he said, and kissed her on the cheek. "Long time, no see. You look fabulous."

"Thanks. You too."

Chad left them to greet another novice, and they spent a few minutes catching up. Mark was a widower of several years, a single dad with a daughter and a son. He pulled his phone from his pocket and showed her a photo of himself playing with two adorable children, five and seven years old.

"They're beautiful," Alexa said. She had a moment of wistful nostalgia for the days when Lucy was small. "And what are you doing now?"

Mark told her he worked at Pine Bluff Memorial as the head ER nurse, a position for which he "took some serious ribbing in this town."

"But I love the work," he told her. "I can't imagine doing anything else."

"It must be very fulfilling."

As Mark elaborated, Alexa's gaze was drawn to a man across the room with his back to her. He was dressed in jeans and a sweater, talking with one of the board members. The man was slim with broad shoulders, and the way he stood and moved held her attention and elevated her pulse. He must have felt someone watching him, because he turned mid-conversation and looked directly at Alexa. It was Eric Reynolds, Lucy's science teacher. A moment of recognition passed between them, and then something else, something that felt new and edgy and bright.

Just then, Chad approached with Mona Bauer, the group's president, and Alexa refocused her attention as Reynolds turned back to his conversation. But she remained intensely aware of his presence across the room.

Mona was a plump woman in her sixties, dressed in flowing clothes, her silver hair pulled into a stylish arrangement at the back of her head. She had a low, musical voice and beautiful translucent skin. Chad had told her that Mona was raised in the Quiverfull movement, which basically eschewed all birth control. She claimed to have over a hundred first cousins alone. She was a local artist who made humanist jewelry by hand, among other things. Alexa admired her "Happy Humanist" pendant.

After the pleasantries were exchanged, Mona asked, "Chad tells me you're running for the school board?"

"Yes, well, so far. If I get my petition signed … "

"Did you bring it with you?"

"Yes." Alexa retrieved the folder and handed it to her.

"I'm glad you're doing this," Mona said. Then she perused the paperwork and smiled. "Ten days, fifty signatures. A piece of cake. Leave it to me."

"Oh," said Alexa, "I didn't know whether you could …"

"Help a candidate? Well, not as a representative of the group. We're a nonprofit, so we can't, as an organization, endorse specific candidates. However, as a private citizen, I can support any candidate I choose." Mona looked her over and nodded. "And Chad suggests I choose you." And with that she tucked Alexa's petition into her large bag.

Alexa was happy that Mona, on such short acquaintance, seemed so eager to help her. After twenty minutes of watching this woman work the room, she already knew that Mona would deliver. Chad seconded her thoughts as Mona moved to the French doors and called everyone into the back room to meet and dine. Rectangular tables for six were set up, and Mona guided Alexa by the elbow to the seat next to hers. They were soon joined by three others: Everett Stark, a middle-aged man with a graying beard; Francesca Davis, a stylish black woman; and Oliver Maxwell, a skinny boy in his late teens or early twenties. Alexa looked up to find Eric Reynolds taking the last empty seat, perpendicular to her on her right.

Menus were passed and drinks refilled. Mona and Everett engaged Alexa in conversation. Everett Stark was a local science-fiction author whose latest book had just been released, and he discussed it at length. Reynolds, sitting next to her, was deep in a dialog with Francesca on his right. His shoulders were turned away from Alexa, but his knees were only inches from hers, close enough that she could feel the heat from his body. He was wearing a subtle, spicy aftershave. She thought about that day in his classroom: the confident way he ruled that space, the native intelligence in those green eyes, the reserve he tried to keep as he spoke with her. Something was there, and not just on her side. But her gaze fell on his wedding ring, and she pushed those thoughts away.

After the dinner orders were placed, Mona stood and brought the room to order, then welcomed and proposed a toast to the newcomers. The sound of cheers and clinking glasses filled the small space.

"I have a few announcements before the food arrives," Mona continued. "But first, I'd like to thank the owner of The Lodestone, Ed Hansky, as always, for being willing to host our group in his establishment." She gestured to a large balding man in a string tie, standing in the corner. "Ed calls himself a 'twice a year' Catholic—"

"Christmas and Easter, I'm there!" Ed joked.

"—but he's been hospitable to our group of nonbelievers in a way that many are not."

The group gave Ed an enthusiastic round of applause.

"Enjoy!" He smiled, gave them a little bow, and ducked back through the door that led to the kitchen.

Mona spoke as she went table to table passing out flyers. "Thank you for joining us. Pine Bluff Humanists for Good is a chapter of the National Humanist Organization. Our motto is 'good without a god.' Humanists are dedicated to living ethical and compassionate lives without religion. Contrary to what is rumored about us, no devil worship, no baby eating, no debauched or degenerate lifestyle." A number of "aw shucks" and "darn its" were heard around the room. "Okay, okay, at least most of the time," Mona said with a grin and a wink.

"Our local chapter," she continued, "strives first to build and maintain community among nontheists. We have social events, philosophical discussions, cultural outings, volunteer and activist opportunities. Do you all have a copy of the flyer?" she asked. People nodded. "Good. The first page is a list of our upcoming events. As you can see, our Humanist Holiday Gathering is slated for December 18th, right here at the Lodestone, in the bigger room at the front. In addition to conversation and general camaraderie, we'll have seasonal games and trivia, sing some humanist carols, and collect food and funds for the Pine Bluff Food Pantry. We'll also have a short candle-lighting ceremony, where we reaffirm our humanist beliefs. It's a great evening, and we always have a large turnout."

Mona continued, "In January, we'll have the next meeting of our Humanist Discussion Group at the Ecstasy Library. Our topic will be 'Where Do Humanists Get their Ethics and Values?' At our general meeting in February, we'll hear from climate lobbyists regarding manmade climate change and what we, as citizens, can do about it. Future topics for the spring include upcoming legislation that threatens the separation of church and state. Then we've got a group volunteer day scheduled at the local homeless shelter in early March."

Mona paused and sighed. "Unfortunately, our Adopt-a-Highway marker on Route 7 was vandalized again. The usual stuff." She held up a photograph of the sign, which had "Godless Burn in Hell!" scrawled across it in red. "You'd think they would get more inventive by now. Anyway, a new sign has been ordered, this time with a special coating that should repel attempts to mar it, including spray paint. This won't stop us from volunteering; we'll still do our bimonthly Sunday morning trash pickup along the same stretch."

Mona then introduced Everett Stark, the chapter's treasurer, who made a pitch for membership.

"Thirty-five dollars a year. Such a bargain! Not quite the 10% of your income a church would ask you to tithe. We have no building to maintain, no clergy to pay. All of our dues go directly toward support of our public programs."

He gave the web address for donations as well, then took his seat.

"And one more thing," Mona said, catching Alexa's eye. "Tonight we have with us a prospective new member, Alexa Moss, who is running for the school board. We as an organization don't endorse candidates, and we'll be happy to offer other candidates equal time. But since you happen to be among us, Alexa, would you like to say a few words?"

No, she really wouldn't, but she'd have to get used to this pretty quickly. Here, among like-minded people, was probably the best place to start. Reluctantly, Alexa rose. She kept it simple, explained about her daughter Lucy, her science classes, and their concerns about the lawsuit against the school. She made sure to point out the number of school-board seats available, and that each one would count in the decision about how to respond to the suit regarding intelligent design. Her heart was hammering when she sat down, but the people in the room seemed receptive—except for Reynolds, who was sitting lower in his seat and seemed to avoid her eye.

Mona returned to sit next to Alexa, and the group fell into conversation. Soon their attention was drawn to an adjacent table, where voices were raised. Over their drinks, Chad and Richard, a gray-haired man in a polo shirt, were arguing about atheism on the internet.

"We need those confrontations," Chad was saying.

"You guys are giving us a bad name, with all that snark and coarse language," Richard insisted. "Baiting Christians and making fun of religious people doesn't help our image. They see us as arrogant already." His eyes traveled to the atheist atom tattoo on Chad's forearm.

"Nonsense," Chad responded. "We have to call them out on their bullshit. I'm not worried about what they think of us. They'd burn us at the stake if it were still legal. And besides, debating them is fun. Most Christians know less about their 'buy-bull' than most atheists."

Richard shook his head. "I think we need a softer touch. Get allies first, impress people with our ethics and values. Let them see our humanity."

"That's one way. But some of these idiots only respond to a virtual kick in the pants." Chad smirked. "There are plenty of well-mannered atheist/humanist blogs and podcasts out there. I suggest you stick with those, if you're squeamish, and leave us reason warriors to do our thing."

They were interrupted by the servers bringing out the food. The room was abuzz during dinner with comments on Chad and Richard's quarrel. Most agreed there was plenty of cause for nontheists to be angry, but differed on the best approach to take with the religious. Alexa, although more like Richard, could see both sides of the issue.

After dinner, Mona and Everett encouraged the new people at their table to introduce themselves and tell their stories.

The young man spoke up first. "My name is Oliver Maxwell. I'm twenty years old, and as you can probably tell, I'm gay." He pushed his clear-framed glasses up on his nose and adjusted the burgundy scarf that was draped at his throat. "People have pretty much known all my life; I've been bullied since I was a kid." He sounded plucky but resigned. "But my parents are in complete denial. My grandparents are reform Jewish, hardly observant, and my parents weren't religious at all until Ecstasy Christian Ministries came to town. Now they've converted, and they're convinced they're part of a group of chosen Jews-turned-Christian who will be sealed with a mark on their foreheads in the end times."

A sympathetic murmur went around the table.

"My parents are now convinced that my being gay is a choice and a phase I'm going through. Fortunately, they've only been religious since I was sixteen, and by then I was old enough to resist conversion therapy. I was lucky. But they laid down the law—God's law, they like to say. No support, no money for school unless I'm straight. I don't have the finances yet to make it on my own, so I have a beard."

Oliver had no facial hair, and some quizzical looks passed among his listeners. He explained. "A beard is a woman who acts as a partner for a gay man, so people think he's straight. My sister's friend Laura plays that role for me. I'm in my second year of community college, and I've applied for a scholarship to Northwestern to study drama and screenwriting next fall. With that and grants, if I can find a job in Chicago, I can finally break from my parents." He lowered his voice and looked around. "I can't wait to get out of this town, but in the meantime, I have to be careful."

"Don't worry." Mona comforted him with a hand on his shoulder. "We don't out anyone here—for their sexuality, their nonbelief, or anything else. Plenty of people have to bide their time to get out of tricky situations."

"That's true," Francesca offered. "None of my friends or family know I'm an atheist." The diners turned toward her end of the table. She adjusted the lapels of her suit, then ran a hand over her chic, close-cropped hair as she continued. "I was raised in Ecstasy, and my family attends the Holy Word Baptist Church, which is 95% black. Everyone in the neighborhood goes there, not only for Sunday services, but weddings, funerals, gospel brunch, bingo night, you name it. That church does a lot of good for the community. They host an after-school program for kids, visit the sick, help care for the elderly.

"But I never bought into the religious part: all those 'amens,' folks holding their arms up and closing their eyes to be filled with the spirit, all that charismatic preaching. They're good people, but they only trust their own—with reason. Unfortunately, they don't understand or approve of people like Oliver here, and they're sure all nonbelievers are in league with Satan." There were nods of recognition at the table.

"I only know one other black atheist, and he's 90 years old. He didn't tell anybody until he was 80." They all chuckled at that. "Folks give him a pass. But it would be different for me. They love their religion. Nobody seems to recognize the irony of following the god of our slave masters. I make excuses most weeks not to go to church. But I don't want to lose that community. It's part of who I am, so I keep silent." Here she lifted her chin and smiled. "Still, it's good to know there's an alternative here."

"Yes," said Mona. "And believe it or not, there are several other black atheists who are members."

Francesca raised her eyebrows at that, then nodded thoughtfully. Mona turned to Alexa. "How about you? Do you have anything to add to your earlier comments?"

"I'm also glad to find this organization," said Alexa. "I've been a humanist all my life but didn't recognize it until I read your website. So many people seem to think you can't be a good person without believing in a god. It's great to focus on what I *do* believe in, rather than what I don't. And to learn that others feel the same.

"I admit that now I'm most motivated by this lawsuit at the high school, but also by the intrusion of religion in government. I'm amazed to find out how much of that is going on, all over the country. It will take a lot of effort to turn that around, but looking around this room tonight, I feel very encouraged."

Reynolds appeared to be listening politely, but still didn't meet her eye.

"Spoken like a politician already," Mona quipped. "I mean that in a good way, Alexa."

Oliver gave her a thumbs up and the others joined in support.

"That leaves you, Dr. Reynolds," said Mona. "What brings you here this evening?"

Eric Reynolds sat back in his seat and appeared to be weighing what he wanted to say.

"It's like this," he said. "I'm a scientist and a science teacher, married to a fundamentalist Christian." He seemed unaware that he was twisting his wedding ring around his finger. He paused and took a deep breath before he spoke again.

"Actually, we're separating. My family—" he paused, collecting himself, "my family is breaking up."

A sympathetic murmur broke from the listeners. Alexa's stomach fluttered.

"Please understand," he said, quickly, "I loved my wife. We met in college, and she was such a wonderful girl. Always sweet, kind, always wanting to do good." Reynolds rubbed his forehead with his fingertips, a gesture Alexa remembered from their classroom conversation. "She cared so much about everyone, and always obeyed the rules. So church was a natural fit for her. She took it very seriously. It gave her a foundation, lifted her up. I admired that, and went with her most of the time after we met. We married right after graduation.

"Things were fine at first—for years, in fact. We enjoyed each other, had two kids, a boy and a girl. They're young adults now; Katie is 21, James is 19. Jenny—that's my wife's name—got more religious as she settled down and became a mother, but still moderately so. Never an unkind thought. We went to the 1st Methodist, out on River Road. There were a lot of young families there, and like the Baptist church Francesca mentioned, it had a sense of community, so even though I wasn't into the theology, it seemed like a wholesome environment for the kids.

"Everything was going well until one new family joined. They were 'Bible-believing' Christians, and they formed new Bible study groups, insisting on a literal interpretation. Jenny spent all her time on that stuff and reading those crazy *Left Behind* books—you know, the ones that begin with everybody being raptured? She came to believe, as they did, that you have to take every word of the Bible literally. Being a scientist, knowing what I know of the earth, for example, I couldn't agree. She made new friends with very conservative opinions, and started speaking against abortion, gays, immigrants, even evolution. Eventually factions formed in the church, and the Bible believers started their own, which turned into ECM. Jenny went with them.

"The irony," Reynolds continued, "is that I saw a beautiful, loving person who wanted to be good, to do good, twisted into a creature who supports things that to me are clearly wrong. It's a damned shame." He looked at his listeners apologetically. "Sorry, it's a long story ..."

"Please go on," Mona said. "We're interested."

"Well, her new friends were always pointing out my heathen ways."

His listeners laughed knowingly.

"I'd given up my pretense of belief by then. The kids were split. James swallowed the whole thing. He's always been insecure with girls, and it didn't hurt that the new church gives men authority over women. Katie, on the other hand, wanted none of it. At first Jenny and James tried to convert Katie and me, then settled for taking pity on us as sinners. Their words were polite, but the underlying condescension was brutal. They spoke to us as if they were the only adults in the room."

Others at the table nodded, as if they'd experienced the same.

"Eventually Jenny decided we're 'unevenly yoked,' a biblical term which essentially lets you ditch your unbelieving spouse. She filed for separation. I'm still living there and fighting it. Jenny and I are already done; we both know that. But I'll lose my son James—in all the ways that matter—if we split right now. So far, she hasn't filed for divorce. But she's come down on the side of the church in this school lawsuit, and she's watching me, waiting to see if I will agree to teach intelligent design."

Here Reynolds stopped. "Sorry to run on," he said, coloring slightly.

"Nonsense," said Everett, waving his hand. "It's a tough spot you're in. And where would you talk about it if not here?"

"True," Mona added. "Our community was put together for just this type of support."

"We're on your side," offered Oliver.

Reynolds stole a look at Alexa, and she tried to keep her face sympathetic, yet neutral. They had a lot in common. They were both trying to do the right thing by their kids, but still—she could see that he might be in her way, in more ways than one.

The conversations in the room wound down, and the diners began to rise and collect their things. Mona declared the meeting officially over and wished everyone good night.

"Leave your petition with me this week," she told Alexa. "I'll call you when we have enough signatures." She put a hand on Alexa's arm. "You know, I knew Margaret pretty well. She was one of us in spirit." Alexa was warmed by Mona's remarks. They parted with plans for a follow-up conversation.

Mark Robinson walked Alexa to her car. The wind had stilled, and the sky had cleared. The threatened snow seemed to have blown past them. They lingered a bit in conversation, and he asked her if she'd like to have dinner with him the next Friday.

Why not? It had been such a long time since she'd dated anyone. He looked handsome standing there under the stars. She liked him. Best of all, he was single. And yet— "I've just moved to town in the last few months," she told him. "Do you mind if I take a rain check until I'm more settled?"

He reluctantly agreed and gave her a hug as they parted.

As she drove home, she turned up the radio and sang along with a trite old Christmas tune. She would never be religious, but there was plenty to be enjoyed about the season: home, family, food, music, tradition. Things were getting better for the first time since they'd moved. Okay, not so much with Lucy, and there was that nasty Aaron Whitman. But her freelance business was finding a footing, and she was making friends, becoming a part of the community. She dreaded her run for office, but saw her mission clearly, and after tonight's meeting really understood the stakes for the first time.

When she got home the back door was standing open, as well as most of the windows. An acrid odor lingered in the kitchen, and the counters were littered with Lucy's scientific equipment. Ben and the girls were huddled together in one corner of the room, and as she entered they looked sheepishly from Alexa to her new slate island, which now had a large scorch mark in the center.

Alexa moved to the spot and ran her fingers over the rough disfigurement.

"What on earth?"

"Lucy and Rachel were working on a chemistry experiment," Ben began. "Alexa, it will probably buff out ..."

"We're so sorry, Mom." said Lucy.

"We'll pay to replace it, Ms. Moss," offered Rachel, who looked like she would weep. Alexa held up her hand and stopped them there. Casting her eyes around the room, her gaze fell on the foil-covered pot of poinsettias she'd bought the day before. She grabbed it up and put it on a placemat in the center of the island, over the stain.

"There." She stepped back and admired the flowers, then smiled and turned to the young women. "Now it's home."

17

Lucy: Tuesday, December 24

The red bow slipped from the package again, rolled across the dining room table, and fell to the floor, where it lay mocking her. Damn. Lucy sighed and ripped off the paper. How did her mother manage it? Every present Lucy received as a child had been wrapped and ribboned perfectly. Maybe it just took practice, but Lucy knew she'd have to wrap a hundred more gifts to get this one just right.

Still, it gave her a chance to look at it again—Jake's dream, the Gretsch round-neck resonator guitar he wanted for playing gospel and blues. She ran her fingers over the sleek mahogany body, the rosewood fingerboard, the nickel-plated resonator with the cutout fan design. It was gorgeous, and she couldn't wait to give it to him. It had cost nearly all the money that Ben had insisted she take for tutoring Rachel. She just had a little left over for a new dress and a few other Christmas presents. She tried again, carefully folding and taping the paper along the guitar's curved sides and up the neck to the tuning pegs. The wrapping was lumpy but stayed put, and there was enough flat space between the pegs to anchor the bow securely. He would know what it was the minute he saw it, but now it looked all festive and Christmassy.

More than anything, she wanted Jake to be happy. December with him had been wonderful, with parties and concerts and Christmas shopping. She wore jingle bells and seasonal earrings to school, where excitement had run high for the whole month. Basketball season had started, and Jake led Pine Bluff's team in scoring. Lucy sat on the bleachers and cheered until she was hoarse. She loved watching him, walking down the halls with him, being part of his success and his world.

Their relationship had deepened and grown more intimate in these past few weeks since her baptism. Lucy pulled her new pendant from under her sweater and fingered the intricate cross. So far, she'd worn the necklace under her clothes—her secret. She had not told her mother about her conversion. Alexa knew she was attending church every Sunday, but nothing more.

She hadn't exactly been straight with her friends in Elm Ridge about that, either. Haley, Nicole, and Olivia had seen her online photos of Jake and were curious, asking about him every time they Skyped. They wanted details. Lucy was happy to brag about Jake's looks, his music, but so far she had left out the God parts. She wasn't sure they would understand.

Her thoughts were interrupted by the sound of Alexa answering her cell phone in the kitchen. She greeted Lucy's grandmother and wished her a happy holiday. Dealing with Sheila would keep her mother busy for a while. Alexa had been a merry pain for several weeks now, pressing Lucy to help her put up the tree and decorations, expecting to continue their Christmas traditions from the past. The woman who had dragged from her home, her school, her friends was disappointed that she didn't want to spend Christmas week making cookies or watching holiday rom-coms together. Too bad. And besides, those things were not important. Lucy understood the true meaning of Christmas now.

Alexa had invited John Jeffers, Heather and her family, and Rachel and Ben this evening for a Christmas Eve buffet in the now-finished house. But Lucy had something more important to do tonight. Jake was taking her to the six o'clock candlelight service at ECM. A big deal, she was told, with several choirs, lots of festivity. She would make it home when she could, and Alexa would just have to deal with that.

Lucy put Jake's gift under the tree. He texted her, saying he would be over at 3:00 to give her his Christmas gift. They would then leave early for the church, since he had some things to attend to there before the Christmas Eve service. He'd be on stage this evening, joining a larger group which played traditional carols for the sing-along. Lucy hurried upstairs to shower and put on the new green dress she'd bought for the occasion. While she put on her makeup, she glanced out the window to find the air dizzy with large white flakes spinning quickly down and covering the ground. Snow for Christmas!

By the time Jake arrived, a few inches had already accumulated. He bustled in and stomped his feet, then presented Alexa with a bouquet of red and white carnations and greens. Alexa brought in some eggnog and cookies as, despite his protests, Lucy took his coat and directed him into the living room. There Lucy sat Jake in an armchair before the tree and the fire and presented his guitar-shaped package to him.

"No way!" he cried. When he opened the wrapping, his eyes were shining. "Oh baby, you're the best!" He ran his hands over the intricate resonator reverently. "How did you know?"

"I asked Tyler what you'd really like."

"Man, I can't wait to use it." Jake started to tune it, then stopped and looked at his watch. "But it will have to wait." He stood and went to the door again and retrieved his coat. Lucy, confused and a bit disappointed, asked him, "Do we have to leave right now?"

"No, I just have to get something from the car." He threw on his coat and boots and dashed out again. Lucy stood at the door watching him, loving him, loving this moment. The smell of the new pine wreath on the door brought home every Christmas she'd ever known. Who would have guessed that this would be the best one?

Jake opened the hatch of his car and brought out a large, covered wicker basket topped with a big red bow. He crunched through the new snow back to the front door and entered, removing his coat and boots for a second time. He carried the basket to the living room and placed it near the fire. Suddenly it began to move. Lucy, startled at first, laughed out loud.

"What the ...?"

"Open it!" Jake urged her, and as she did, she squealed with delight. Inside was a fluffy, scruffy puppy, who jumped up at her, wagging his tail. She lifted him—or her?—from the basket and cradled him as he licked her face.

"Mom, Mom!" she called, and Alexa came into the room, then stopped short seeing the pet in Lucy's arms. A look of surprise, then hesitation crossed her face. She'd probably spoil everything. But Alexa looked from Jake to Lucy for a moment, then sighed and nodded.

"Well," Alexa said, "a new member of the family." She crossed the room to rub his head. "How are you doing, little guy?"

"It's a cairn terrier," Lucy told her. She'd memorized all the breeds of dogs—and cats and birds—when she was seven years old. Jake had remembered this was one of her favorites.

It was indeed a male. "I named him Samson," Jake said. "Hopeful thinking." They all looked at the tiny puppy and laughed.

He was perfect. The basket was filled with the things she would need to take care of him: food, pet dishes, a leash, a cushion for sleeping, doggie treats, even a small plaid puppy coat and booties for the snow.

"I figured you had your own newspaper," he joked. Then more seriously, "I made an appointment for him with the vet on Wednesday."

"That'll work," Alexa answered.

They all spent the next half hour passing the puppy between them, then put him on the floor to romp, trying to keep him away from the Christmas tree. "This'll be a challenge," Lucy said, but she was so up for it, so thrilled.

Rachel came home and joined them, taking her turn petting the little creature and feeding him treats. Eventually, completely worn out, the dog fell asleep on Lucy's lap, and they moved him carefully to the basket, which would contain him if he woke.

"Would you be able to watch him, Mrs. Moss, while we go to church?"

"Sure, Jake," Alexa answered. "You two go. Rachel and I can handle the preparations for dinner and take care of this little guy. Make sure you come back for food when the service is over."

"We will."

Once in the car, Lucy turned to look back at the house as they pulled out onto the road. She was charmed by the scene: the snow on the roof, smoke rising from the chimney, the shining tree in the window. It looked just like a Christmas card. Best holiday ever, for sure.

The ride to the church on Christmas Eve was one she would never forget. The night was still, and great flakes tumbled from the sky, sparkling and spinning as they fell. The world was muffled in glittering white, as if they were caught in a snow globe. And she was traveling through it alone in a car with the hottest guy in the universe, who was hers. There was so much to be thankful for.

The ECM campus was draped in glowing blue and white lights. A real-life nativity scene—with actual people—was staged near the entrance, the silver and blue of the set and costumes stunning against the backdrop of the white church. The doors opened to admit the waves of worshippers who shook the snow from their boots, coats, and hats. Lucy handed her wrap to a girl at the coat check. Inside the holiday spirit was high and infectious. Children dressed in their velvet best were running in circles while their socializing parents attempted to calm them. How futile that was, when Christmas Eve was finally here!

Jake left her to get ready for his part in the service. Lucy found Jordan and Brad and their youth-group friends in the sanctuary. Jordan was all smiles, thrilled that Brad was home. Together they admired the gorgeous decorations: pine boughs and wreaths with twinkling white lights, rich wine-colored ribbons, and white candles everywhere. A tree was set up at each end of the stage, trimmed in silver ornaments, garlands, and white lights. The ECM cross was temporarily replaced with a shining star of Bethlehem, backlit in the deepest blue. It looked beautiful on screen as the cameras panned the room. The organist played Christmas carols as all were seated, and the wall of pipes gleamed in the candlelight.

When the auditorium was filled, the lights were dimmed until it was dark. A hush fell, and then voices rose in harmony from the back of the room. *Oh, Come All Ye Faithful.* They sang without accompaniment, the altos, tenors, sopranos, and basses each individually ringing out and blending into one, their faces lit only by the candles they carried as they walked in procession down the aisles and up the stairs to the stage. Lucy felt chills travel the length of her body. They sang the last verse all together, Pastor Bell adding his rich baritone, to the wild appreciation of the listeners.

The night was filled with singing and celebration. Jake played an exquisite acoustic version of "What Child is This." Pastor Bell's sermon was elegant and joyful. He talked about how life without Christ was meaningless, but they needn't fear. "He has come," he intoned to the faithful, and Lucy's heart lifted in response. To end the evening, the contemplative "Silent Night" was followed by the jubilant "Joy to the World," and the congregation joined in merrily.

After the service, the teens filed out to the lobby. Brad met his family there and bid the rest of them good night. Maddie and David left their parents and crossed the room toward them. As they approached, Maddie held out her left hand. On her finger was a thin gold band with a tiny diamond; David had proposed before church. She was smiling, but her face, Lucy noticed, was swollen, and there were still some serious shadows under her eyes. Jordan asked about the wedding.

"New Year's Day," David answered. "We'll do it in the small chapel here, but—uh—it'll be just our families."

They all nodded their understanding and offered congratulations to them both.

Maddie's family had gathered their coats and came to fetch the couple. Hugs and "Merry Christmases" were shared all around.

"Wow, that was fast," Jordan said as they watched them leave.

"Do you think they're okay?" Lucy was concerned.

Jordan shrugged. "They will be. They're paying the price for what they've done. It'll take some time to get used to their new lives."

New lives were hard; Lucy knew about that. But she was adjusting, and she hoped that Maddie and David could as well.

"So many surprises today," she said, then brightened. "Did you know about Samson?"

"Samson—what? The biblical Samson?"

Lucy told Jordan about the puppy as they retrieved their coats and walked down the hallway to the backstage area, looking for Jake. They came to a door marked "Vestry. Restricted," with a bench outside it. "Wait here," Jordan told her. "I'll find him." She entered and closed the door behind her, leaving Lucy alone in the hall.

Lucy was part of this church now, but she was still a newbie who would have to earn the trust and privileges Jake and Jordan had grown up with. Across the hall from the bench, another door stood open a few inches. Lucy could hear the assistant pastor addressing a room full of people.

"Alright listen up, so we can get you home for your Christmas Eve. The last spontaneous baptism was so successful that we've scheduled the next for January 6th, Epiphany. After the sermon, Cyrus will give the altar call.

As soon as he does, you start. Sarah and Matthew, I want you to come down from the back. Position yourselves so you walk the longest, most visible route to the stage. Cheryl, Carlos, you do the same right afterwards from opposite sides. Then a few of you from the middle. The first seven or eight should go up, and if there are not enough volunteers from the audience at that point, the others should follow. Wear something attractive, but not too dressy. There are fifteen or so of you, all ages and ethnicities; that should be enough to get the unbaptized moving. When they take you backstage toward the locker rooms, you can slip out through the vestry area over here. We don't want you to be recognized being baptized a second time." His listeners laughed.

Lucy's stomach twisted and she covered her eyes with one hand.

"Remember, you're bringing people to Jesus. Okay!" He clapped his hands several times. "Thank you all and have a wonderful holiday."

Lucy heard chairs scrape the floor as people rose. Just then Jake and Jordan appeared from the private area, and Jake put his arm around her.

"Everything alright?"

Lucy smiled up at him. "Uh-huh. I'm just a little tired. Let's go home."

They walked down the hall just ahead of the people who came streaming from that room, laughing and talking. On the way home Lucy was silent, thinking. Jake was telling Jordan about the dog.

"I knew you couldn't keep a secret," he taunted his sister.

"I can so!" Jordan was indignant but laughing. "I'll come and see him tomorrow, Lucy, after our gift exchange."

"Mmm, what? Oh. Sure, okay." Lucy couldn't get her mind off the assistant pastor's words, or the way those people he talked to seemed to enjoy playing a role. Was she so naïve? Was she really a Christian now, or had she been played?

Jake dropped Jordan at their house, and they continued on to Lucy's for her mother's buffet. Lucy told him what she had overheard at the church.

"How could they do that? Was it all fake?"

Jake frowned. "It's not fake. You were baptized in the church, Lucy. Did you mean it?"

"Of course I meant it."

"Then don't overthink things. They have some people who get things started, help people make up their minds, set an example. Nobody forces anyone to the stage. You know that, right? *You* volunteered, didn't you?"

"Yes, but—"

Jake turned to her, softening his tone. "Lucy, we're having an awesome Christmas. Let's not ruin it."

She stopped then and kept quiet. Okay, he was right, as usual. What counted was what she felt in her heart, not how she got there.

When they got to her house, John Jeffers, Ben, and her mother's friends the McLearys had already arrived. Alexa had cooked and Rachel had baked; the guests had brought delicious-looking contributions as well. The kitchen island was loaded with colorful, fragrant foods and desserts. The fire was blazing and the tree was glowing. The party welcomed them.

The McLeary boys, fourteen and ten, were awkward at first, but they played with the puppy, delighted. Heather played some carols on the antique spinet, and soon Ben had them laughing and singing some goofy Christmas tune that got faster and faster. Dr. McLeary—Alan—entertained them with some of his ice-fishing and hunting tales. When they had all had enough to eat, Alexa suggested they play a board game.

Lucy declined, saying she wanted to take a walk with Jake before he left to spend the rest of the evening with his family. "We'll take the dog out," she told them. "It's a beautiful night."

They dressed the puppy in his new coat and booties and attached his leash, but Lucy chose one of the largest coats in the closet, placed the puppy close to her chest and buttoned it over him. "I don't want him to get too cold." Samson wriggled and licked her face, but allowed himself to be carried.

The moon had risen and sparkled on the snow in various shades of white and blue. The wind was still and the night was mild. They crossed the gravel driveway in the direction of the spring house, their secret rendezvous spot.

In the past several months, they had used the building for privacy. After Lucy's incident with the spider, Alexa had swept it out thoroughly and added a wooden bench along one wall. Lucy was fascinated by the thermodynamics of the place; it maintained a moderate range of temperature due to the moving water. In the summer it was cooler than the weather outside; in the winter, warmer, and the spring replenished itself fast enough in the basin that it didn't freeze.

They usually did most of their talking and kissing in Jake's car, when they could pry the keys away from Jordan. But when Jake came to Lucy's house, they knew Alexa was watching, so they often stole away to the spring house. The heat between them was incredible, and they'd progressed to fondling each other under their clothes. Lucy had pleasured Jake with her hands a few times as well. That was new to her, but she'd felt more than ready. She wasn't experienced like Sophia, but Jake said that was better. He would lead her, teach her.

Tonight the snow had drifted against the spring-house door, and Jake had to pull it forcefully to get it open. Inside it was warmer, and they sat on the bench and kissed for a while, the puppy snuggled between them. Soon their passion was more urgent, and Jake took the puppy from her coat and placed him on the floor.

"Do you think he'll be warm enough?" Lucy asked him.

"He'll be fine. It's not that cold tonight." He slipped his hand into her coat and ran his thumb over her breasts.

Lucy did feel warm. Her breasts swelled and tightened with pleasure, and she began to breathe heavily. Jake couldn't unhook her bra through her dress. Instead, he stood her up and held her from behind, with her backside pressed against him. He caressed her breasts and kissed the side of her neck below her earlobe until she thought she would burst.

"I love you," he told her. It was the first time he'd said it.

"Oh my God, Jake. I love you, too."

She wanted to turn and kiss his mouth, but he held her tighter, and she felt him stiffen against her. He ran his hands down her body and lifted her dress, moving his hands to her hips, then down inside her panties. There he rubbed her slowly until she was wet and frantic with desire. It both terrified her and made her weak with longing. Her legs were unsteady. She leaned on him and swallowed hard.

"Jake, maybe we should stop. I mean, David and Maddie ..."

Jake kept moving, but whispered, "David and Maddie were stupid. I would never let that happen to you."

"But ..."

"Shhh," he said. "I have a condom. Do you trust me?"

"Yes, but ..."

"Do you want me?" He kept fondling her. The puppy began to whine.

"Yes, more than anything, I do, but Samson ..."

"Lucy, relax. He'll be alright."

He bent her over the bench until her hands were resting on its back. Then he continued to touch her; the feeling built and built until she was gasping. The puppy whimpered and wrapped himself around their legs.

"Don't move," he told her. She obeyed, and he left her for a moment to tie the dog's leash to the door latch. Samson cried softly as Jake returned and guided Lucy's panties down to her ankles. She trembled as she stepped out of them, frightened and thrilled. She heard him unzip, then felt him move between her legs. She moaned, on the brink of exploding. Then there was something wet and cold between the cheeks of her backside. His finger was there for a moment and then he thrust himself inside her.

All pleasure left her, and she felt the pain stab up through her body just as she realized what he was doing. No, no, *not there!* This was all wrong. She cried out to stop him; she felt like she would rip inside.

"Shh," he told her. "I won't go in all the way this time."

But he pulled her tighter and pumped hard and fast, more urgently, until he finally grunted in satisfaction and relaxed. It was over in minutes, but the pain and humiliation went on. Lucy couldn't catch her breath and felt as if she would faint. The dog was crying loudly now.

Jake zipped up and spun her around to kiss her. She turned her head away. He took her face in his hands and turned it back, then wiped at her tears. "Don't worry. You won't get pregnant this way. I know it's not what you thought, but you'll get used to it. And you're still a virgin."

"Get used to it? How could anyone get used to that?"

Jake shrugged. "A lot of girls get to like it. You'll see."

Lucy picked up the puppy, who was shivering uncontrollably. Like herself. She had an urgent need to go the bathroom. Jake handed her panties to her; she put them on and ran for the house.

Jake followed her through the snow.

"Lucy ... "

"Don't come in," she called over her shoulder. Jake evidently thought better of it and headed for his car.

"Merry Christmas," she heard him say. "I'll call you tomorrow."

Inside she bumped into John Jeffers in the foyer. He looked her over, concerned. "What's wrong, young lady?"

"I don't know. Suddenly I'm not feeling too well."

Lucy put the shivering puppy in his basket and headed for the bathroom. As she sat there cramping, burning, trembling, her body voiding everything she'd eaten for days, she wondered what had happened and how. An hour ago, she was walking through the moonlit snow with Prince Charming.

"Lucy." It was Alexa, outside the door. "Lucy, are you okay? Mr. Jeffers said you're not well."

Lucy made her voice sound as normal as possible. "I'm okay, Mom. You don't have to worry. I think I just ate something that disagreed with me. I—I'll be better soon."

"Are you sure? How can I help?"

"You can just go back to the others. I told you, I'm fine."

"Alright, but come find me as soon as you're feeling better. I have a surprise for you."

She heard her mother walk away.

A surprise. The last thing she wanted was another surprise. What she could really use was a hug. But she was a big girl now and couldn't run to Alexa with every bump and bruise. An adult life had adult secrets, she was learning.

When she finally emerged from the bathroom, the group was playing a word game in the living room, shouting out clues and laughing uproariously. The puppy was still shivering and whimpering in his basket, but she didn't want to look at him now. Instead of holding him, she found a blanket and covered him, hoping he'd go to sleep.

Lucy wandered listlessly to the kitchen and looked over the food on the island. Her appetite had deserted her. She made herself some tea and picked at a Christmas cookie. Eventually the game wound down and Ben and Rachel wandered in.

"Hi Lucy, how are you? Your mom said you weren't feeling well." Rachel looked concerned.

"I'm okay. How has your evening been?" She felt like an automaton, exchanging polite pleasantries. All the real feelings of the day seemed walled off to her now, unavailable.

"We've had a lovely evening."

Lovely. Rachel did have an oddly old-fashioned way of speaking sometimes.

They were called to the foyer to see the McLeary family out. Wraps were sorted, thanks and season's greetings exchanged, and hugs and kisses doled out. The group watched as the family crunched out to their car. When the door was closed, Alexa turned to them.

"Now," she said, "Ben won't be with us tomorrow, so he and I have something to show you tonight."

"Tonight?" Lucy said. She really didn't know if she could stand it.

"Yes, actually it's your Christmas present. At least the big one. Ben helped me with it and wanted to see your face when I gave it to you."

Couldn't all this wait until morning? Lucy was so tired, but she didn't have the strength to argue. It was easier just to go along, until she could end this day. "Okay, okay."

"You'll need your coat and boots," Alexa told her.

"I'll bring the flashlight," Rachel said.

Ben led them through the backyard snow and up a small incline toward the orchard. The naked fruit trees wore a cover of sparkling white, beautiful, but cold and joyless to Lucy. Fast-moving clouds now covered the moon, and the wind had picked up. She turned up her collar.

There was an old canning shed at the edge of the orchard, which had been filled, when they moved in, with cobwebs and boxes. A small berm hid it from the house, and Lucy had found no reason to go there past the harvest season when the red and green apples fell. As they neared it, however, a new lamp over the door revealed that the shed had been freshly painted and the windows had been cleaned.

"Is that a new roof?" she asked, wondering when all this had gone on.

"Partly. We patched and sealed it," Ben answered.

Alexa opened the lock on the door latch, reached in and flipped on the lights, then stepped aside and motioned for Lucy to precede her.

It really *was* a surprise. Before her was a small but shining new laboratory. The entire inside of the shed had been repurposed and fitted with everything she would need to experiment and research. The canning shelves had been painted white and filled with cages and cases, beakers, pots, and bins, and all her science books (they must have moved them this afternoon!). On one wall, under a window overlooking the orchard, was a deep steel sink and long countertop, and an island with two stools stood opposite. On it were a new microscope and a high-end Bunsen burner with its own propane tank. There was a small electric heater in one corner and a vented fan in the ceiling. The walls held a whiteboard with markers, a colorful periodic chart, and some botanical prints. A small reading chair in bright turquoise with a yellow and orange paisley pillow finished the space.

"How did ...?" Lucy was speechless.

"Well, it wasn't easy," Ben told her. "But you were gone a lot, to school and such, and the electric and water were already here, although we had to patch a segment of pipe comin' in. The rest was pretty basic construction." Ben looked sheepishly proud of himself. "Your mom designed it, then figured out everything you'd need, and ordered it for you." He looked fondly at Alexa. "Talk about a kid at Christmas—she was so excited she nearly spilled the secret a dozen times."

So that's what was happening several weeks ago when the construction guys were digging up the yard. And why Alexa had what Rachel called "the cat that ate the canary" look all month.

"You and Rachel can do your experiments here now," Alexa told her.

"Oh, Lucy!" Rachel cried excitedly. "This will be wonderful!"

John Jeffers chuckled. "My goodness, Alexa. Guess you'd do anything to spare those new kitchen counters." They all laughed at that.

"I don't know what to say," Lucy said. "It's amazing. Thank you so much."

She turned to her mother and fell into her arms in tears.

"You're welcome, sweetie." Alexa held her and stroked her hair as Lucy cried and cried. She couldn't seem to stop herself. "Wow, you seem overwhelmed."

"It's been an unbelievable day."

They walked back to the house, and before John and Ben left they all sang a few more carols around the fire. Lucy excused herself for the evening, went upstairs and put on her red pajamas and robe. She opened her desk drawer and brought out her mother's gift: a gemstone necklace she'd chosen at a shop in town and wrapped in shining paper. She waited in her room until the others were all gone or in bed and the house was quiet, then slipped downstairs to the living room and put the present under the tree. She checked on Samson in his basket. The puppy was sleepy, but whimpering, and she picked him up, wrapped in the blanket. "Don't get used to this," she whispered as she carried him. On the way to her room she stopped in the den, and out of the pocket of her red robe took a flash drive, which she placed behind her mother's desk, with just enough showing to ensure that Alexa would find it.

"Merry Christmas," Lucy said to the empty room.

2020

18

Rachel: Saturday, January 25

R achel shrugged out of her winter jacket and looked around the room. She was 20 minutes early for the GED Science test. She'd been given a place to stow her phone, then directed to sit at one of the desks in the computer lab, but was cautioned not to turn on the unit until a proctor appeared. She was calmed by the dark old woodwork and the smell of papers, books, and chalk layered under the plastic and metal scent of technology.

Several others were already there, seeming as nervous as she was, shuffling their feet, tapping their pencils, or staring into space. A middle-aged woman smiled at her tentatively. So Rachel wasn't the oldest one, at least.

A large smart board in the front of the classroom contained the rules of the test: 90 minutes starting promptly at 10:00 a.m., no phones, books, or papers allowed, and no unauthorized calculators. One short break at the 45-minute mark.

Rachel was about to see if her months of tutoring with Lucy would pay off. She had pored over textbooks, taken notes, done experiments. She now knew that she was a visual and tactile learner. The mixing of actual chemicals seemed to anchor the facts in her brain much better than written formulas; she found it so much easier to understand what a "solute" was when something was dissolving before her eyes. Illustrations helped her more than paragraphs of explanation. In the past weeks, Lucy had made her take several practice tests online. Her grades started low, but eventually she got better and more confident.

The classroom filled with all types and ages of people who were quietly lost in their own thoughts or anxieties, "minding their own beeswax," as her mother used to say. Their faces reflected how important these test results were to their lives.

At 9:50, the proctor appeared, and they were allowed to turn on their monitors. There they found written instructions and a pop-up calculator they could use on questions requiring math. The proctor prepared to time them.

Rachel froze for a moment, panicking. So much was riding on this. But she could hear Lucy's voice in her head: "You're well prepared. You've got this. Just stay calm."

At ten o'clock exactly, the proctor said, "Go!"

Rachel began. This time the material looked familiar, even friendly. There were questions on chemical formulas, the laws of physics, the names for physical processes, all requiring rote memory. But in most questions there was a visual component. Graphs, charts, and diagrams triggered her memory and made the facts easier to recall. She worked quickly but carefully, finished early, and had time to recheck her work.

When time was called at the end of the test, she stood and stretched, relieved. She felt hopeful as she filed out with the others and retrieved her cell phone. Smoking a guilty cigarette, she waited outside for Ben to pick her up. Ben had been nagging her to stop, but she needed the nicotine to relax, especially this morning. Of course— assuming she passed the test—she never could have done it without Ben. He was good to her, always there to help her with any problem. And she loved that about him. She loved *him*. But lately, she longed to solve more of her problems herself. She had been dependent on others for so long.

If she passed the GED, she could find a better job, maybe even go to college. She'd grown fond of science the way Lucy taught it, and lately had daydreamed about becoming a nurse. Her stomach tightened with something like excitement. It was a daring goal for her. And yet, she hoped there was a way. If she went to nursing school, she could study seizure disorder and find a way to help her sister Phoebe.

Ben pulled up. She climbed into the truck and leaned over to kiss his cheek. He asked how it went. She gave him the details and accepted his enthusiastic congratulations. Nothing was official until the scores came back, but Ben was Ben; he never missed an opportunity to look on the bright side, and he wanted to take her for a celebratory lunch.

They drove out of town to one of the roadhouse restaurants Ben frequented, which offered simple food and an ample selection of beers. It was early for lunch, and there were few other patrons. She was glad. The plainness and calm of the place did her good after the stress of the morning. Rachel loved January; life was so sane and orderly after the holidays. No twinkling lights, no glitter, no big expectations, just the real world stripped bare and hunkered down for the winter. Somehow she felt most herself in this quiet month.

She and Ben sat by the window, warm and snug as it began to rain, then sleet outside, the silver clouds low to the earth. Ben talked about his new project. He was building himself a tiny house on Ray Ingersoll's property. Ray had given Ben the use of a plot on the edge of his woods, near the bluffs, in exchange for his help overseeing the property. Rachel had recently learned that Alexa had helped him with the plans.

He had started it in November. The shell was already built on the trailer. It would be quite large for a tiny home, over 300 square feet. Ben showed her the floor plans on his phone: a kitchen with full-sized appliances, a queen-sized bedroom on the main floor, a large shower, a sofa and TV area, a drop-down desk, a table with two chairs, even a washer/dryer. He would also have a sleeping loft and a deck. The view, he said, would be amazing.

Rachel listened with her chin on her hands. "Wow, I'm really impressed."

Ben grinned. "I've been saving for a long time, both money and materials. Ingersoll let me keep lumber and such in part of his sheep-shearing shed. I salvaged every piece of wood, pipe, wire, or tile I could find. Alexa gave me all the scrap from her project." He took great pride in the fact that the home would be energy self-sufficient—off the grid. "Very eco-friendly: rainwater collection, graywater system, solar panels, composting toilet." Rachel asked how a few of the systems worked, and Ben was delighted to fill her in.

"But the best part will be the privacy," he said at last. Rachel blushed a little at that. "We'll be able to be alone when we want to, darlin'." He reached across the table for her hand, his blue eyes gleaming.

Since Rachel had moved to Alexa's, it had been a challenge to find time alone. Ben had been hinting that Rachel could move in when his project was finished. But Rachel still wasn't sure she was ready for that.

Ben's phone rang and he silenced it; it was probably business, but she wondered about his sister Louisa, and if they would reconcile. She couldn't believe that Ben could stay angry forever.

Ben needed a few supplies, so they finished their lunch, bundled up, and headed to Dawson's on Main Street, an old-fashioned general hardware store that carried nearly everything. Dawson had spent 60 years in the business, and not only knew every nut and bolt in his store, but also almost everyone in town. At nearly 90, white-haired and stooped, he still greeted each and every customer. When Ben and Rachel entered the store, he came out from behind the register and clapped Ben on the back.

"Great to see you, boy. Great to see you." He looked genuinely delighted. "And who's this? Rachel Whitman? My goodness, you're all grown up!"

Rachel had made frequent trips to Dawson's with her father, before she took responsibility for her younger brothers and sisters.

Ben asked Dawson some questions about converting from solar panels and was directed to the electrical products aisle. Rachel followed, and rounding a corner, ran into her cousin Caleb. Occasionally Rachel saw him in town, but she hadn't expected this sudden face-to-face meeting. Ben was already extending his hand. It seemed he and Caleb had met before, on construction sites. A licensed electrician by trade, Caleb oversaw the buildings at ECM, but also worked some freelance jobs around town.

Rachel noticed he looked tired. Tall and fair, he still looked more like a country singing idol than a church keeper. But he seemed to have aged five years since she saw him in August.

It appeared that he and Ben liked one another. When Caleb realized she was with Ben, his eyebrows shot up in surprise, but not disapproval. Caleb was polite to Rachel but didn't meet her eye. She explained their kinship to Ben and asked about Caleb's wife and family. He said they had another child on the way, a girl. They would have three girls. Caleb made some sort of joke, but Rachel barely heard it. She was focused on the one thing she needed to know.

"And Phoebe?" she asked, as she had so many times before.

Caleb looked uncomfortable, but—probably due to Ben standing there—finally answered, "She's okay."

"Really? Are you saying she's better?"

"Well, it depends on what you mean by that," he said.

"I mean, is she having fewer seizures? Have they gotten that under control?" Maybe Phoebe was finally on medication, seeing a doctor.

Caleb winced. "No. Not that." He hesitated. "But she's quite the celebrity now, in some circles," he told them. His voice was neutral, but his eyes said something else.

Rachel was confused. "What do you mean?"

"Well, they're saying she has the gift of prophesy. Aunt Eunice says that happens sometimes with fits. Phoebe has visions and interprets people's dreams and fortunes. She speaks in tongues." Caleb lowered his voice. "They're going back to the old ways more lately," he said.

Rachel knew that "the old ways" meant the things they had done in the church in West Virginia. The Bells were actually Pentecostals, with a history of faith healing, speaking in tongues, and more that wasn't shared with ECM when Cyrus Bell was hired. The family had thought that might not play as well in Illinois.

"A lot of people believe it," Caleb was saying. "I can't judge. Only the Lord knows her heart. She goes into kind of a trance after a seizure and says strange things. They film it and put it up on YouTube. They call her 'Angelica.' Cyrus says she's an oracle. There's no connection to ECM. But people on the internet ask for her guidance and contribute."

"My God, Caleb. How is she taking it?"

Caleb flinched at her language but continued. "At first, she didn't like it, but she seems to have adjusted to the idea, to be proud of it even. She does everything they ask." Caleb looked up and saw Rachel's distress. He said more softly, "Maybe it makes her feel special, like there's a place for her, like all she's had to endure is worth something, good for something. I don't know. We all want her to be happy, and there's no sign that it actually harms her."

"That's bull. I need to see her, Caleb."

"Rachel, you know that's not possible. Cyrus will never allow it." But he looked at her sympathetically for the first time in years. Something seemed changed in him.

"How have you been, Rachel? I heard you're working at Sandy's."

"Yes." She told him she was living with friends, that she'd been well, but she didn't mention the GED test she'd just finished taking that morning. Caleb seemed concerned about her welfare, but she couldn't be sure she could trust him. Cyrus was still capable of hurting her greatly. Caleb seemed to read her thoughts.

"Don't worry, Rachel. I won't repeat any of this to them." To her surprise, he added, "You can text me once in a while if you want; they aren't paying attention now." Then he turned and left the store quickly without buying anything.

Ben was troubled by the conversation, and they discussed it as he drove Rachel back to Alexa's. "Your family's on a dangerous path. This could be both physically and psychologically damaging to Phoebe."

Rachel was outraged, but not particularly surprised, that they were allowing Phoebe to keep having seizures and using them—among other things—to make money. She was more determined than ever to help her sister.

Ben said he understood. "Whatever I can do to support you, darlin', I'm there."

They were almost to the Moss house when they passed a red Honda SUV on the shoulder. It was parked in a spot with a clear view of the property. Rachel recognized the car as one of those from Cyrus's compound. She turned as they passed to see the driver; it was one of her brother Aaron's underlings. Were they tailing her now? Had Caleb broken his trust with her already?

Ben was not so sure. "I would never have thought that of him, Rachel. Maybe he's not behind this."

"Turn around," she told Ben. "I want to talk to the driver."

Ben executed a U-turn, but the red SUV had already taken a perpendicular side road north of the property. When they got to that road, the SUV was nowhere in sight. Well, Rachel would be watching from now on. Shunning her was one thing, stalking was another. They headed back to Alexa's. Ben told her to call if she needed him. When he dropped her at the door, he kissed her and whispered, "Be careful."

Samson came to meet her as she entered the house, lifting her mood for the moment, and she picked him up and cuddled him. He was certainly adorable, but somehow Lucy, though taking excellent care of him, hadn't taken to him the way they thought she would. So Rachel had been filling the void, and the dog was attached to her.

She heard Lucy call, "Rachel, we're in the kitchen."

Alexa and Lucy were at the island, and they both jumped up when Rachel entered and asked how the test had gone. Lucy squealed with delight when Rachel told her she thought it had gone well. Rachel thanked Lucy profusely.

"I couldn't have done it without you. You're the best teacher I've ever had."

"Rachel," Lucy remonstrated, "exactly how many teachers have you had?"

Rachel laughed. "Well counting kindergarten, about three."

"Yeah, I thought so." Lucy smiled. "I'm sure you passed."

"Well, let's not count our chickens, as my mother used to say. It'll be a few weeks until I get the results."

Alexa just beamed at her proudly, her reaction so different from the one her own mother would have. It was touching, but at the same time made Rachel a little sad.

She needed time alone to think and research, and asked Alexa for permission to use the desktop computer in her office. Scrolling through websites was difficult on the tiny screen of her phone. Alexa agreed.

Rachel closed the office door and logged on with the guest ID. She had never watched YouTube, but she'd heard of it, and the search engine took her right there. She searched for oracles, prophets, epileptics and came up with thousands of entries. Then she remembered Caleb had called her "Angelica," and she paired her search terms with that.

A video came up quickly and Rachel gasped. She almost didn't recognize her sister. Phoebe had grown considerably, and was even thinner, but beautiful, in an ethereal kind of way. She was dressed in a flowing peach-colored robe and wore dark eye makeup—a shock to Rachel—though the rest of her face was pale. Her blond hair was long and wispy, floating around her head as if electrified. She was propped up in bed, against a pile of cushions. Her glassy expression and the sheen of sweat on her forehead made it clear to Rachel, who knew her ailment, that she had just had a seizure. Phoebe was physically lethargic, but intensely focused, babbling incoherently.

She was, the video's narrator claimed, filled with the holy spirit and speaking in tongues. Rachel remembered the nonsense syllables, the rolling eyes, from her days in the Apostolic church in West Virginia. But Phoebe's look was different, riveting: knowing yet innocent, ancient, but also oddly contemporary.

The off-screen narrator translated. "The tribulation is coming. A great nation will be torn asunder. Foolish people will turn from the Lord. Only the righteous will be saved. They will follow the consecrated, the anointed ones, and be taken to sit at the right hand of God. All others will perish."

As Phoebe's eyes steadied, her words began to form themselves into English sentences. She talked about events to come, fantastical objects, faraway places, a lyrical drumbeat of words. Rachel recognized passages from the Old Testament and Revelations.

The narrator asked her some leading questions, and she answered by rolling up her eyes, and trembling as she stated "yea" or "nay."

Then Phoebe was helped to a high-backed, throne-like chair. She sat erect, ready, the narrator said, to make more personal predictions and pronouncements. Again, she would answer only "yea" or "nay" to the questions her followers had posed. The narrator rephrased some questions, guiding her responses.

Near the end of the video, the narrator stated that epilepsy isn't always caused by possession by demons; in fact, it can herald the holy spirit, a gift from God—the gift of tongues and of prophesy, as it was in "Angelica." How did one tell the difference? If the viewers knew someone so afflicted, he asked them to contact him, "Reverend John," for a private consultation. The video concluded with a web address where followers could send in questions and donate money. The voice of the narrator was Cyrus Bell's.

There were four YouTube videos of "Angelica" so far. Rachel's stomach churned as her mind raced. How could she stop this? It was surely a form of abuse, but she knew the local police—Cyrus's cronies—would ignore her.

Phoebe had been hidden away from the world all her life, as if seizures were something shameful. Closing her eyes, Rachel relived that Sunday in West Virginia when Cyrus preached a sermon about evil spirits and then had Phoebe brought in. At his direction the congregation surrounded her, chanting and shouting at the "demons" inside her until the child was sobbing, terrified, and began to convulse. Cyrus and the others laid hands on her and commanded the demons be gone. When the throes of her seizure faded, he declared the ritual a success. But within a week, her condition continued—an embarrassment to Cyrus.

He tried every few years to free her from the spirits. When Phoebe entered puberty, Cyrus claimed she'd become even more a vessel for evil, and he was determined to cure her. He and Aunt Eunice strode into the bedroom the two girls shared, and Rachel was pushed out. She sat in the hallway, hugging her knees, and wept to the sounds of flesh being struck, and Phoebe's cries of fear and pain. Cyrus again claimed victory over the demons, but Phoebe, covered in bruises, went back to seizing within days.

That's when Cyrus, searching for answers, first cast his eyes on Rachel. Wasn't she sinful, and therefore the likely cause of Phoebe's affliction? Worse yet, Phoebe had almost begun to believe it. She, like Cyrus, wanted a reason, an explanation that might make sense of her world.

And these "prophesies," for Phoebe, might be just that. Wouldn't suffering be more tolerable if it served a purpose? And if that purpose was to please God, spread his word, convert followers—do what Phoebe thought might be some good in the world—wouldn't that be comforting? Rachel couldn't blame Phoebe. But she could blame the family, the church. Rachel scrubbed her face with her hands.

How could she get Phoebe away from Cyrus? She was only 16, and legally under her parents' jurisdiction. Were there exceptions to the law in cases like hers? Rachel spent several more hours researching, but just ended up confused. She found no definitive legal statutes and didn't know where else to look. She was holding her head in her hands, frustrated, when Alexa knocked and peeked in the door of the office.

"Oh, I'm sorry, I didn't know you were still on the internet. I'll come back."

"It's okay, Alexa. I'm finished. I'm afraid I'm not good at this."

"Can I help you? What are you trying to find?" Alexa's eyes searched hers.

Rachel hesitated, then decided she could trust Alexa. She motioned for her to take a seat, swore her to secrecy, then spent the next half hour pouring out her story, ending up by playing the video.

Alexa, watching it, was visibly shaken. "Oh, Rachel, this is terrible. No wonder you're upset."

"I have to help her, Alexa, but I don't know what to do."

Alexa hugged her, then they sat together and Alexa tried as Rachel had to find more information. The result was much the same.

Alexa finally sat back in her chair. "What you need is some legal advice." She thought a moment. "John Jeffers is going to stop by one evening this week for dinner; he has some things to go over with me. Why don't we call him and ask him if he'll take a look at this?"

Rachel brightened at first, then her shoulders slumped. "I don't have any money to pay him."

Alexa shook her head. "John's retired, and aside from managing Margaret's estate, he only does pro-bono work. He won't charge you for a consultation. He has access to legal information that we would never find. At least he could help you understand your options."

Rachel sighed at this, but agreed, and Alexa pressed a few buttons on her cell phone.

"John? It's Alexa. How are you? ... Good. Listen, do you have a few minutes? Rachel and I have some questions for you; I'm putting you on speaker phone."

"Sure Alexa. Hi, Rachel. I'm in the car on my way home. I have some time. What's up?"

They filled John in as he drove, gave him some background, and summarized as succinctly as they could. "Can we send you the links to the videos?"

"Sure, I have the afternoon free, except for one client call. I can research a few things for you. Rachel, can you send me your specific questions by email?"

"Yes, I'll do that right away."

"Alexa, are you willing to feed an old man supper tonight? I can be there at 7:00."

Alexa looked to Rachel, who nodded. They both knew Lucy would be out that evening, and that was for the best.

"What old man? I can feed *you* this evening, if you'd like. Chicken parmesan?"

"My favorite! Okay, I'll see you then. You and I will talk for a bit, get our business done, and then I'll speak with Rachel."

"Thanks so much," Rachel told him.

"Yes, thank you, John. I'd better start cooking." Alexa laughed.

"Get to it," teased John, and hung up.

At a few minutes to 7:00, John showed up and hung his wet coat and umbrella in the foyer. The sleet had started up again and pelted the window as they seated him before the fire and gave him a glass of wine. Samson curled atop John's feet as if to warm them. The cutlery and glasses clinked as Rachel finished setting the table.

"Smells great," John called to Alexa in the kitchen.

"Ten minutes," she answered.

When his glass was refilled and they were seated at the table, they began by trading bits of news and pleasantries over dinner. They discussed and toasted Rachel's assumed success on the GED. Rachel smiled, appreciative, but couldn't relax. The test, which she had so anxiously anticipated, seemed like a week ago. She could think of nothing now but Phoebe's face on that video. Rachel could barely wait to hear what John would tell her. Patience had never been one of her virtues, though she had been trained to act as if it were.

So she was relieved when the meal was finished and she could clear the table for Alexa's paperwork. Loading the dishwasher, she could hear them documenting expenses for the will. The house part of the renovations was complete. The lab was a bonus, even with the extra insurance required, John was saying. Now they just needed to focus on the land itself and the carriage barn.

Drying her hands, Rachel came into the dining room as John was packing Alexa's documents into his briefcase. He pulled out a smaller sheaf of handwritten notes.

"Let's pour a glass of wine and go sit by the fire."

"Alexa can join us," Rachel offered.

"I think I'll head upstairs, if that's okay with you," Alexa countered. "I'm happy to support you in this, but I think there are some sensitive issues you need to discuss first with John."

"A good idea," John said, "at least for now."

Rachel conceded, and they pulled two armchairs into the glow from the hearth. She gripped the arms of the chair and leaned toward him.

"So, Mr. Jeffers, how can I help Phoebe? What can I do?"

"This is a rather knotty issue," he began, running his hand across his silver mustache. "I researched some Illinois statutes, and they pretty much confirmed what I had thought. And by the way, the state laws are the most important here."

Rachel's eyes never left his face as he continued.

"Illinois has an exemption to the child abuse and neglect laws for parents who refuse medical treatment on religious grounds. Also for those whose children are treated only by means of faith. You mentioned that you know about that. Children can't be taken from their parents solely on those grounds. And Illinois courts, unlike in some other states, are not allowed to step in and order treatment for the minor. The law is clear on this point."

Rachel closed her eyes and nodded.

"In this case, with the videos, there may be ways to make the family uncomfortable, make things public enough to shame them into getting her care. The ECM congregation might take exception to all this. But if Phoebe's a willing participant, you would probably not have a case in court against your parents. What they are doing to Phoebe is deplorable, but likely not illegal. Also—though I hate to say it—Cyrus Bell is particularly well-connected, and you might not get a fair shake from certain judges in this county."

And whether she succeeded or failed, Cyrus would make sure the rest of her life was hell.

"What about what Phoebe wants? She's sixteen. Doesn't that count?"

"In some states or cases, it might. So the next thing I researched is medical emancipation, where a child under the age of 18 petitions to make her own health-care decisions."

Rachel perked up immediately.

John shook his head. "I'm afraid I have some bad news here as well. That petition is only possible when the child is living *independently*, away from the parents, or the parents grant permission, *and* when the child herself wants medical treatment the parents won't allow. Since Phoebe still lives with her parents, they have authority in these matters, and though you are a relative, you likely wouldn't have standing to bring a case. It's very unlikely you could sue for custody of Phoebe under those circumstances, and even if you did, well ..." He shook his head.

Rachel paled. "What? Mr. Jeffers, be honest with me. I need to know."

John exhaled slowly. "Rachel, you're only 23 years old." He held up his hand. "I know, I know, you love her. You've cared for Phoebe most of her life. But think of this from the court's perspective. You're barely an adult yourself, without a spouse, a home or apartment of your own, or sufficient income. You would not be able to show you could support her and would most certainly be ruled against. I wouldn't advise you to proceed under those circumstances."

Rachel's eyes began to brim with tears. "So what do you suggest?"

"I know you'll hate to hear this, but I advise you to wait until Phoebe turns 18. That's what—a year and half? She can leave her parents then, if she wants to, and make her own medical decisions. It gives you time to get ready for her, if you want to take her in. Lawyers for her parents would likely use every tactic to delay proceedings anyway, waiting for her to reach legal age, when the case would be consequently dropped."

"I understand what you're telling me, but a year and a half is too long for her to suffer. What if something worse happens?" She raised both hands to her forehead. "I can't just do nothing!"

John Jeffers put his hand on Rachel's shoulder.

"I understand how you feel, dear. But the best thing you can do for her is get stronger yourself—emotionally, educationally, financially. You've taken the right first steps, like the GED today; I commend your spirit, as well as your concern and care for your sister. You've come a long way since you were abandoned by these people, and I know you'll be there to help Phoebe when the time comes. The time is just not right now, Rachel. I'm sorry."

Rachel swallowed hard. She shook John Jeffers' outstretched hand and thanked him for his help. He donned his raingear and bid her good night. As he drove away, she watched his taillights, reflected like a hundred stoplights in the drops on the living room window. She poured herself a drink, returned to the fire, and sat before it, thinking, until the last glowing embers fell.

She was disappointed but not deterred. She kept coming back to the same conclusion. In order to seek medical emancipation, Phoebe must live away from the family. That meant Rachel would have to go and get her.

19

Alexa: Wednesday, February 19

Alexa set the stack of brochures on the vintage oak table in the library's foyer and fanned them out carefully. The early morning sun poured through the beveled windows and lit her own face staring back at her from the glossy white trifolds bordered in red and blue. Did all political handouts use these colors? She suspected so; one couldn't allow one's opponents to appear more patriotic. She'd spent a chunk of money on these materials, which listed her qualifications—such as they were—for the school board, along with her positions on district issues.

Mona had referred her to the photographer who took her head shot. It wasn't a bad picture. She wore a charcoal-colored sweater which contrasted well with her fair complexion and gray eyes. The lighting brought out the red highlights in her hair. She'd chosen a pose with a hint of a smile that made her look friendly, yet capable and serious. At least that was what she hoped it conveyed. Chad had suggested the slogan positioned above her head: "Make the Most of our school with Moss."

She appreciated that the candidates were allowed to display their literature here. It was not in her nature to seek the spotlight, and she'd kicked herself nearly every day for making the commitment to run. But she *had* made that commitment, and self-promotion was a necessary evil.

Heather had left the wide double doors to the main room open for her, and as she entered the heart of the library, she relished the hush and the scent of books she remembered from her childhood. The high windows, massive columns, and dark wood paneling lent a classic air to the architecture, which—fortunately, to Alexa's mind—had not been updated to something sleek and modern.

She spotted Heather near the front desk, her blond waves masking her face as she sorted through a cart of returns. Her mother, Barbara Robinson, Ecstasy's head librarian, was working on a computer at the front desk.

Heather straightened and noticed her.

"Oh hi, Alexa. I'll be right with you," she said as she rearranged a final few books.

There'd been recent cuts to the library budget as well as the staff, and when Mrs. Robinson, who was near retirement, found herself short-handed, Heather helped out.

Mrs. R. came around the desk and gave her a hug. "Alexa! So good to see you."

"Ditto. It's always a pleasure."

"I'm right in the middle of something," she said, patting Alexa's arm, "but I'll join you for coffee as soon as I can. I want to hear all the latest." She returned to her computer and began to type again.

Heather led Alexa into a small staff area in the back, where she made herself a cup of coffee and offered Alexa some tea.

"How have you been?" Alexa asked her.

"Crazy busy." Heather blew at a strand of blond hair that had fallen across her face. "Work at school is always hectic at the start of a new semester. And my kids are in sports, so late afternoons and evenings it's all uniforms, gear, and carpools. Forget about family dinners." She took a carton of cream from the mini fridge and sighed as she added it to her coffee. "Probably just as well. Alan is at the clinic most nights and weekends anyway. It's flu season. And measles. Measles in 2020, for heaven's sake!

Even in bright red Central Illinois, we have anti-vaxxers. I had to marry a pediatrician." She shook her head and laughed. "Other than that, I'm pretty good. How about you and Lucy?"

"We're okay." Alexa spooned sugar into her mug and stirred. "The reno of the house is done, and I've picked up a few clients. Also, Lucy seems to be finding her niche here." She looked at Heather. "I wish I was sure it's the right one."

Heather's brows met. "You have concerns?"

"As a counselor, you probably know these kids she hangs out with better than I do. They're certainly attractive and polite—it isn't that. It's just that she's focused so much on this group, especially this boy she's dating, Jake Randall. It's way too intense. I actually heard him claim to be the 'spiritual head' of their relationship."

Heather laughed, then said, "I'm sorry. I've known a lot of teenaged boys, and the idea that they're equipped to be the spiritual head of *anything* at that age is pretty funny."

"That's so true," agreed Alexa. "The whole group seems a little bit too wholesome." She laughed. "I know how weird that sounds. Lucy's been going to ECM activities with them. I wouldn't worry about that so much, but her attitude at home has not been great. She's been so distant." Alexa paused a moment, caught by a now-familiar ache in her chest. "I *miss* her." She shook her head.

"And her grades, particularly her science grades, have been slipping. The national science talent search is coming up, and she hasn't spoken about it at all. This is something she's been looking forward to for her whole life. It's not at all like Lucy, and it worries me. At the same time, she tutored Rachel for the science portion of the GED, which it appears she passed." She shrugged. "Go figure."

Heather nodded. "It's really tough to parent teens, but most of what you describe is pretty normal. They get obsessed with stuff, experiment, push away from the family. Do you want me to ask her what's happening?"

"Oh." Alexa hesitated. "I don't know ..."

"If the grades continue to slide, I'd have a legitimate reason to discuss it."

"Well let's see how the first few weeks of this new semester go."

"What about you? How's the campaign going?" Heather asked, switching subjects.

"It's hard to tell. Better than I had anticipated. Mona helped me with the signatures for my petition, and people have been more receptive than I thought. I've had quite a few emails and phone calls about the direction this school board is taking, which surprised me."

"Yeah, there are more liberals and moderates in this town than you'd think, but we pretty much keep our heads down. Are you nervous about the candidates' forum tonight?"

"More like terrified," Alexa said with a rueful smile. "My worst experience in college was speech class. I always did well, but I never got over the fear of it. And tonight, reporters from Wednesday Gazette and WXT will be there. The moderator is Principal Franklin."

"Lynette Franklin is moderating? I didn't know that. Well, if it makes you feel any better, your nerves aren't showing."

"Yet."

Mrs. Robinson joined them and poured herself a cup of black coffee. She looked much the same now as she had when Alexa was a child: an elegant nose, wide-set blue eyes with straight no-nonsense brows.

As they sipped their drinks, Alexa asked, "Can you tell me what happened here with the humanists?"

Mrs. R. shook her head.

"First, you have to understand the library board is subject to the same pressures as the school board. It also has its share of right-wingers and fundamentalists. Some of them mean well, some of them don't, but they have strong opinions on what books the library should carry and how the facilities are used.

"As you're probably aware, the Pine Bluff Humanists don't have a building, so my son Mark, as the VP, books a lot of their programs here. They hold discussion groups in the small meeting room, and when they have prominent speakers, they use the large one. Or at least they did. We don't charge for nonprofit groups, so the price is right," she added. "Alexa, you were here for the January event. The one about ethics and values?"

"Yes, it was interesting. People were really animated and made some wonderful points."

"They did. But I noticed that one of the regulars from ECM was also there—Jenny Reynolds."

"Eric Reynolds' wife?"

"Yes, the blond with the bright pink lipstick. She looked uncomfortable with what was said and left early without speaking to anyone." Mrs. Robinson opened a package of cookies and offered them to the others, who declined.

"Coincidentally—or not—the next day ECM's people tried to book all the meeting rooms for the next six months. For Bible study groups, they said. They know the reservation system is first come/first served. When they were asked to leave some open dates for other organizations, they contacted the library board and claimed discrimination. The board didn't want to deal with that and held an emergency meeting. They voted to solve the problem 'in the interests of fairness,' by ending access to these spaces for *all* religious, political, and philosophical groups. Of course, ECM didn't need the rooms in the first place. They just didn't want the humanists to have them." She sniffed. "I had no say in any of this, though I report to the board."

"Wow," said Alexa.

Heather took their cups and began to wash them in the small sink. "That's why it's so great you volunteered your carriage barn, Alexa," she said. "Mark is pretty excited about it. A steady place to meet will help the group a lot." She arranged the wet dishes on a small drying rack on the counter. "How is that project going, by the way?"

"Well, once I found the plans again," Alexa said, exchanging a look with Heather, "I hired Ben Miller to head up the project. The framing is mostly done, and the electric and HVAC are in. The plumbing won't be completed until the spring, when the ground is soft enough to trench. I'm hoping that the building will be ready by mid-May. There will be an office for me on the second floor with a separate entrance, as well as a small one for the humanists, and a big gathering space on the first floor. One bathroom, a kitchenette, and a gravel lot next to the building for parking. The carriage barn reno was required for the inheritance, so I had to do it anyway. There was no stipulation on how to use the property. The humanists will pay me a small rental fee, so it's a good trade."

"I'll say. A happy day for the group. They've been looking for space to rent for a while now, but everything has been too expensive." Heather looked at her watch. "Oops, 8:05, time to go." She turned to her mother. "I had Alan drop me off this morning so I could ride to the high school with Alexa. She wants to check out the auditorium for tonight. You have a good day."

Heather kissed her mother's cheek and they donned their coats. After saying their goodbyes, they climbed into Alexa's car and headed for Pine Bluff High School. On the way, Alexa asked Heather about the Methodists. "Speaking of churches, I read something online about the United Methodists meeting in St. Louis this month. Specifically, the article said they're going to discuss LGBT issues."

Heather groaned. "This is the bane of my existence. And may be the death of our church—again."

Alexa adjusted her visor to block the morning sun. "Really? I thought the Methodists had gay ministers."

"Some do, and some forbid it. There's no gay clergy in Ecstasy. We've pretty much avoided the issue here."

"So what will the Methodists be doing at this conference?"

"Among other things, the delegates will decide on whether LGBTQ+ individuals can be ordained, and whether same-sex couples can be married in the church. The Methodist Book of Discipline says that homosexuality is 'incompatible with Christian teaching.'" Heather used air quotes to emphasize her point. "There are three different plans proposed to deal with the controversy. They'll need to pick one of them." She paused, pulled down the visor, and quickly refreshed her lipstick in the mirror. "Sorry. I'm sure you're not really interested in the details."

"I *am* interested, actually," Alexa reassured her.

"Well, okay. The first one is the 'Simple Plan,' which recommends we just remove the language from the Book of Discipline. That would mean all Methodist churches would need to accept gay clergy and weddings. That would cause a firestorm in some parts of the world. The second is the 'One Church Plan,' which would keep the denomination together, but allow each church to make its own decisions. That way people could choose the church that aligned with their beliefs. The third one, the 'Traditional Plan,' would leave things the way they are, but all Methodist churches would need to comply to remain in the denomination."

"Wow. That *is* a big deal. How do you think they'll vote?"

"I don't know. I'm hoping for the One Church Plan, where each church gets to choose. I don't think the Simple Plan can pass; the delegates come from around the world, including Africa, Asia, and South America, and they're almost all more conservative there. Not to mention the U.S. southerners. I don't think they'll vote to change the wording. And the Traditional Plan, where the Book of Discipline wording remains, could rip a lot of North American Methodist churches apart. I'm keeping my fingers crossed, but it doesn't look good."

"I'm really sorry, Heather."

They drove the last few blocks to the school in silence. As they pulled into the parking lot, Heather pointed out the employee spots. "You can park there for now. I'll give your license plate number to the office, so you don't get towed."

Alexa pulled her shopping bag full of candidate materials from the trunk, and they entered the building by the teacher's entrance to avoid the morning crush of teen humanity. Heather pointed Alexa in the direction of the auditorium and gave her a hug.

"Good luck tonight. Don't worry, you'll be wonderful. And I'll be right there in the audience, although I won't be commenting. Being on staff here, I have to appear to be neutral."

"Understood. Thanks so much, Heather. See you then."

Alexa waved and headed for the north wing of the school. In the auditorium foyer, there were tables dressed and ready for the candidates' literature. She put out brochures and some peppy *Alexa!* buttons Chad had talked her into ordering from a little shop in town. They did look good, she had to admit—fun, yet professional.

She pulled open one of the double doors to the empty auditorium and walked down the carpeted center aisle. Pine Bluff was not the largest high school, but they took their theater seriously. The fixtures were silver gilt, and the deep-red stage curtains and seating looked like velvet. She walked up the steps to the stage and turned to the rows of seats, imagining herself before the crowd. In ten hours, those seats would be filled with parents wanting to know who she was, what she stood for, what she could do for them and their children.

A wave of panic washed over her. What was she doing? How could she hope to influence hundreds of people she didn't know? She shuddered, bolted down the stairs, and fled to the door.

* * *

That evening, Alexa sat at the table on the stage, wishing she were anywhere else in the world. She'd spent a long afternoon pacing and prepping, reviewing her material, hoping she'd covered the bases. With some guidance from Mona, she'd already researched every argument for and against religious intervention in public schools. She'd read the Illinois school-board website one last time to familiarize herself with the district issues. As the afternoon sun began to set, she showered and dressed in her favorite sage-green dress and did her makeup carefully. Eating was out of the question for her nervous stomach, but she mixed herself one good stiff drink and knocked it back standing at the kitchen island before she left the house. It helped to steady her nerves.

Now there was no turning back. The auditorium was filling with parents, administrators, faculty, and students. Alexa could see Heather and her husband in the audience; also Mona and Chad, who had promised to be there for moral support. They smiled and waved to her. She caught sight of a flash of white teeth toward the center aisle and recognized Rodrigo, the man from the service station who had fixed her car, smiling and chatting with an older woman seated next to him.

Eric Reynolds sat in the third row with his wife Jenny, a pretty blond with large blue eyes, wearing vivid lipstick. This time it was a coral shade that matched her sweater. She leaned toward her husband, talking, their heads together. They must have reconciled since the humanist meeting in December. Alexa tried to ignore the sinking feeling in her chest as she watched them. What, after all, was she to him? As if in answer, Reynolds looked up and met her eye, gave her a polite nod, then looked away. So that was that.

When she arrived, she'd been glad to find Malcolm Redd's tent card next to hers at the candidates' table. Now he slipped into the seat to her left and greeted her cordially. She was happy to turn her attention to a friendly face. He spoke and joked with her, dispelling much of her tension, his eyes crinkling at the corners behind his glasses.

The seven candidates, vying for four spaces on the board, sat in a row at the table, shuffling cards, smiling, and waving to supporters, waiting for the forum to begin. Two of those four spaces were open due to retirements, and two were held by Aaron Whitman and Brittany Spencer, a PTA mom, who were running as incumbents.

The other five candidates were first-timers: Alexa; Malcolm; Scott Planek, a young man who had been a student at Pine Bluff; an older man named Gary Gustavson; and Jessica Lopez, a woman around Alexa's age. Each of them seemed unlike the others, and Alexa was surprised by the variety.

She was thankful that Aaron Whitman was seated at the other end of the table. That didn't stop him from glaring at her, though he had to bend forward and crane his neck to do so.

"Looks like you have an admirer," Malcolm joked.

Alexa shuddered, remembering their encounter. She steeled herself and met Whitman's eyes briefly, steadily; then she ignored him. She had as much right as he did to be there.

Lynette Franklin, Pine Bluff's principal, sat center stage in a cobalt-blue suit and a chunky gold statement necklace. Her carefully drawn eyebrows were slightly raised as she looked out over the crowd. She held a stack of colored cards: questions for the candidates.

At the opposite end of the stage sat the three incumbent board members not up for reelection: Glenn, a military type with ramrod posture; Celia, past leader of the PTA, now president of the school board; and Stacy, a young woman with a background in social work. Alexa had introduced herself to all of them on the candidate information night, but only Stacy had welcomed a conversation. Now they sat watching and taking the new candidates' measure.

Ashley Hale, the reporter from WXT, took notes and photos of the school board and candidates, then parked herself near the stage exit. If things got too boring, Alexa assumed, Ms. Hale could make a quick getaway.

At a few minutes after seven o'clock, an expectant hush went through the crowd. The principal looked at her watch but didn't move to the microphone. Alexa's drink was wearing off, and she suppressed an anxious tremor.

Just then, the door from the lobby swung open and in walked Cyrus Bell, surrounded by what could only be described as an entourage. He shook hands and clapped shoulders as he walked down the aisle, smiling all the way to his reserved seat in the front row. Removing and folding his great coat with a flourish, he turned and waved to those assembled before he took his seat. He wore a dark-gray pinstriped suit and a lilac shirt with a clerical collar that accented his silver-white mane.

Principal Franklin rose to her feet and tapped the mic. Alexa realized Franklin had been waiting for Bell to arrive. The principal greeted the public, made some announcements, then laid out the forum rules: two minutes to respond to questions with a one-minute follow-up. Franklin asked those in the audience to hold their questions for the Q&A session at the end.

For the next two hours, the questions ran the gamut of school-board issues. Gary spoke on the topic of school security and garnered both applause and groans when he talked about arming teachers. Scott prioritized new technology, updated facilities, and equipment. He was humorously self-deprecating, and his quips kept the audience laughing. With kids on athletic teams, Jessica Lopez was focused on the budget for extracurriculars. She liked to use personal anecdotes and tended to run out the clock with her responses.

Malcolm was a dynamic speaker, his manner impressive and to the point. He discussed the problems of standardized testing, academic tracking, the achievement gap, and the inequity in disciplinary action between students of color and whites. The audience looked uncomfortable but, to his credit, they seemed to pay close attention.

Aaron Whitman spoke forcefully of the need for traditional values: school spirit, the flag, student prayer groups, and "wholesome" extracurricular activities. His rant was well-received by a certain portion of those in attendance. Brittany Spencer seconded many of his concerns, though she focused more on the social functions at the school and the prospects for "students with promise" to get into good colleges.

Alexa found some topics came more naturally to her than others; she knew little of quarterly budgets, but as an architect was able to speak to the importance of the arts and sciences. She didn't argue directly with Whitman or Spencer, but stuck to her strengths and directed her answers to academic standards when she could. She maintained that a strong, fact-based curriculum was crucial, for college-bound students as well as those going to jobs straight after high school. Much of the audience seemed to approve, and Alexa relaxed a bit.

Just before 9:00, the principal's questions to the candidates concluded, and she announced that there would be a short break before the audience Q&A. People rose to stretch their legs and visit the refreshment tables in the lobby. Alexa and Malcolm walked out together, and he introduced her to Rev. Clemmons, pastor of Holy Word Baptist Church, and other prospective constituents, who greeted her warmly. They congratulated Malcolm on a job well done.

Alexa found Heather, then Mona and Chad, and thanked them for attending. The consensus was that she'd held her own. Now there were only the audience questions to get through. Aaron Whitman stood across the lobby and shot glances at her as he spoke to Cyrus Bell. Bell looked up, met Alexa's eyes, and sent one of his dazzling smiles her way.

Ushers shepherded the audience back to their seats for the Q&A. The vice principal, a tall, thin man with curly hair, traveled the auditorium with a cordless mic. Questions were directed to the candidates, who were able to clarify their positions and qualifications for the room. About ten minutes into the Q&A, Cyrus Bell raised his hand.

"My question is for Mrs. Moss."

Bell cut a charismatic figure, with his stylish clothes and deeply-timbred voice. Ashley Hale, the reporter, stood and moved up the side aisle, filming on her cell phone. The audience went quiet to hear what the preacher would say. Alexa's pulse telegraphed her dread to every part of her body.

"I've heard, Mrs. Moss, that you are an atheist. Is that correct?"

Some mumblings and even a gasp or two could be heard from the audience. Alexa kneaded her knuckles under the table and drew a deep breath.

"I prefer the term humanist."

"I see. But you admit that you do not believe in God."

She kept her voice steady and answered simply. "Yes."

The audience murmurs grew louder, and all eyes now were fastened on her.

"And tell me, would you agree that the rest of us"—he turned and swept his arm across the audience—"have the right to worship the Lord?"

Alexa sensed a trap.

"Certainly. As long as those beliefs aren't used to harm others."

"Ah," the pastor held up a finger. "So why would you oppose those beliefs being taught with yours in the classroom?"

Alexa was taken aback. "I beg your pardon—when have *my* beliefs been taught in the classroom?"

Cyrus smiled and shook his head, as if she were daft. "Every day. Secular institutions teach secular values. Our Christian children are led to believe—or at least behave—as if God does not exist. They are fed false 'theories' and 'facts' which contradict the Lord's holy word."

Reverend Clemmons lifted his chin, and Alexa knew that Bell's words had been chosen to elicit that response.

Alexa, though fearful, was not going to give Cyrus Bell an easy win if she could help it. "Would you mind giving us some examples?"

Bell looked at her shrewdly. "Let's start with the *theory* that man evolved from monkeys. Or that the earth is billions of years old and an *accident*." His voice started low, then built to a crescendo as he spoke. "That man, rather than God, has determined the climate, and that man should decide which babies are born, *and which are not*."

A few yelled out, "You tell them, Pastor!", "That's right!", or "Praise the Lord." But there were some who rolled their eyes.

It was the anti-science greatest hits. Where the hell should she start? She looked to Eric Reynolds in the audience, but he was clearly struggling to keep his face as neutral as possible.

Neutral. That was the answer.

"I assume you're talking about science classes, about the teaching of biology, evolution, cosmology, climate science," said Alexa, then paused in thought. "So okay, this is America. People of all beliefs have the right to hold and express an opinion, and there are plenty of places for that." She turned to address the audience, rather than Bell. "But public-school science class isn't one of them. The job of science educators in public schools is to teach science, not religion; and what defines science is scientific method. Anything taught in a science class should be supported by scientific method, which includes experimentation and evidence. By these standards, so-called Creation Science or Intelligent Design is not science at all, it's theology." She heard a rumble from the crowd, and one "yeah!" from the back of the room. Encouraged, she continued.

"And by federal law, the schools must maintain a neutral stance on theology. The school can't tell the students that there is or is not a god. No one at Pine Bluff is telling your kids which to choose. Take evolution—we're talking about a scientific process. Students can decide for themselves whether a deity had a hand in it. If your children want to believe that a supreme being created that process—or the physical laws of the universe—they can. All science is saying is that the process—and those laws—exist, that they can be proven using scientific method, and that we can teach students how that works."

To Alexa's surprise, there was some applause from the audience, as well as the anticipated boos.

Principal Franklin had paled during this discussion, shuffling her cards and shifting in her seat throughout. Now she quickly intervened, declaring that it was time to move to the final question. Cyrus Bell opened his mouth to protest, then evidently thought better of it. He smiled and waved the mic away, as a few people raised their hands.

The final question was for Scott Planek, whose jokes about technology did a lot to relieve the tension in the room. The event concluded with some final information from Principal Franklin about the election. As the audience headed toward the exits, Alexa noticed Ashley Hale looking in her direction, then Cyrus Bell's, as if weighing who to interview. She decided on Cyrus and scurried up the aisle after him. Alexa, relieved, donned her coat, and a few handshakes and short conversations later made her escape.

In the parking lot, she looked over her shoulder several times, watching for Aaron Whitman, but he didn't appear. She assumed he was still inside with the reporter and Bell. She started her car uneventfully and drove home, still tightly wound from the forum. The first half had gone better than she expected. The second half had been trickier, though she felt she had done alright. Some had liked her; some had not. She had known the minute she opened her mouth she'd be seen as controversial—with or without Cyrus Bell. But who knew? She might even get elected. She had no delusions, however, about Whitman and Bell. They'd take every opportunity to cast her as a heathen and a city liberal, and tear her down, even more so if she won.

As she neared Kranston's Market, she remembered some things she needed, including a birthday card for one of her friends in Elm Ridge. The store was open late tonight, though the place was nearly deserted. She took her time choosing the greeting card, then picked up a packet of stamps and some of Lucy's favorite snacks. When she got to the checkout counter, the cashier gave her an odd look.

As she pulled out of Kranston's lot, she turned on the radio. Her exchange with Bell had already hit the airwaves. But not the whole thing, not the part where she defended science. Only Cyrus outing her as an atheist and his subsequent "secular" rant. She supposed it would be all over the TV news by morning. She punched another button, but the local news was over. The national news was running a story on a virus that was spreading in China and now the Philippines; a cruise ship with thousands of passengers was quarantined off Japan. These things never came to much in the States; she hoped this would be the same. Still, it certainly put her own problems into perspective.

As she pulled onto her property, she exhaled slowly, calming herself. There'd be other events and appearances, but thankfully not another forum.

She left the garage and started up the path toward the back door. It was a crisp, clear night and the moon was almost full. She stopped a moment to look at it and the surrounding stars, so much brighter here than they had been in the suburbs. A heavy feeling returned as she thought briefly of Eric Reynolds, but she shook it off. She'd survived this evening, in more ways than one.

As she pivoted, taking in the sky, she glanced in the direction of the carriage barn, and stopped. What were those shadows across its face? A cold sweat beaded her forehead. Those weren't shadows; they were letters— huge black letters scrawled on the side of the barn. Heart thumping, Alexa stepped closer to make them out, then raised a hand to her throat. The words read "Humanist SCUM" and beneath that, "Atheists go home!"

20

Lucy: Saturday, February 29

Lucy rang the doorbell a second time, waiting for someone at Jake's house to answer. The tall colonial portico gave no shelter from the wind, and she was laden with her purse, a small suitcase, and a dress bag thrown over her arm. She hoped that the dress wasn't wrinkling.

Finally, she saw movement through the sidelights, and Mrs. Randall opened the door. Lucy had hoped it would be one of the kids; Jake's parents had been polite but distant since the whole abortion thing. And then the humiliation of her mother on the news.

"Good afternoon, Lucy. Jake's not here. Jordan's upstairs in her room."

"Thanks, Mrs. Randall."

She felt the woman's frosty gaze follow her up the steps.

Jake and Jordan's house featured a two-story foyer. The stairs led to an open catwalk on the second floor, from which you could see the family room and kitchen beyond. It separated the master suite from the other bedrooms. Jordan called it "the drawbridge."

Lucy hung a left and followed the sound of Christian rock to Jordan's lavender bedroom. Jordan sat at her vanity in fluffy slippers and an open robe, which showed her pink lace bra and panties beneath. She was playing with her blond hair, lifting it high before the mirror.

"Up or down?" she asked Lucy.

"I thought we agreed on down."

They'd spent the last few weekends preparing for the Sadie Hawkins dance, choosing their dresses and trying out new hair styles and makeup techniques.

Maddie had been allowed to join them in some of the planning, but only at her parents' house. David was attending school and living with his parents until the end of the semester. Maddie, though, was pretty much on lockdown. She was homeschooled now and would not be returning to Pine Bluff. She had begged her parents to let her go to the dance with David. This would be her last chance to be a teenager, she said, before the whole world knew she was pregnant. So far only her chest was bigger, but that couldn't last for long. She would miss her entire senior year, her prom, her graduation. College was out of the question, at least for now. She and David had not had a wedding reception. She wanted one night, she told her family, before she became a mother. Her parents finally agreed, as long as they could chaperone.

Jake, Jordan, and Lucy would meet them and the rest of their group at Maddie's house and drive to the dance from there. David and Maddie would be riding in her parents' car and not attending any post-dance activities.

It was a wonder Jake had agreed to go at all. When Lucy mentioned the idea, he was not a fan. They were standing in her living room after school, taking off their coats and unwinding their scarves.

"Girls ask boys?" he asked her. "Isn't that backwards?"

"C'mon, Jake, that's kind of the point. Sadie Hawkins is one day every four years—February 29th—when the girls can ask the guys. All the other girls are asking their boyfriends. Jordan is going to ask Brad." Jake rolled his eyes. "Plus," Lucy reasoned, taking his hand, "I'm dying to dress up and dance with you."

Samson came in and jumped on Jake's leg, excited to see him. Jake rubbed the dog behind his ears, but then when Samson persisted, he pushed him away.

"There's always prom."

She was thrilled he was thinking that far ahead. It was a good sign. But she really wanted to do this.

Samson continued to jump on Jake, his tail wagging furiously. When Jake ignored him, the dog sat at his feet and whined. Jake frowned. "Can't you school that dog?"

Lucy carried Samson to the kitchen, gave him a treat, and closed the new dog gate. Samson eyed her reproachfully but gave up and worked on the treat. Jake was seated on the sofa when she returned.

"Please, Jake? I'd really like to go to the dance. Will you go with me?"

He looked up. "Come and sit with me."

As she sat, he pulled a sheet of notebook paper and pencil from his backpack. On the paper he drew four umbrellas, a large one on top and then three others, progressively smaller, descending underneath. He labeled the top umbrella "Christ"; the next one, a bit smaller, said "Pastor"; the third one, underneath that, was labeled "Husband"; and the fourth, the smallest, was "Wife." Under the wife's umbrella he wrote "children." Across the top he printed "Umbrella of Protection."

Lucy had noticed that same chart on the wall at ECM. At Jake's suggestion, she was taking a private Bible study with Cyrus Bell, and she was amazed at the time and attention the pastor was giving her religious education. She hadn't mentioned the class to her mother. Alexa would not have understood—especially after her clash with Pastor Bell at the candidate forum.

Jake pulled her close and pointed to the chart. "So this is actually for a family, but it works for relationships, too." He tapped his finger on the top umbrella. "You see that we're under Christ's protection. He heads and instructs the church." He waited for Lucy to nod, then continued. "Underneath his protection is the pastor, the spiritual authority who runs the church and oversees the husband. The pastor is under Christ's protection, and the husband is under the pastor's. It's the husband's job to protect and provide for his family, following the pastor's example and God's word. *He makes the decisions*, heads the family, and instructs them in God's plan. The wife, the bottom umbrella here, manages the home and children, comforting, teaching, and nurturing them. She is their protection. Do you understand?"

Lucy searched Jake's face. She knew the church said stuff like this. But him? Was he serious? This was the 21st century.

"Don't you believe that women are equal?" she asked.

Jake sighed, as if he'd been through this discussion a hundred times before. "Men and women are equal in God's eyes, but they have different roles. It's in the Bible. Women need men's protection, just as men need Christ's."

Lucy noticed that, according to his own diagram, the only reason a woman would need a man's (or a pastor's) protection was if Christ's big umbrella failed. Otherwise, she was covered. But seeing the look on Jake's face, she decided not to mention it.

"Lucy, in any relationship, there has to be a leader." He pushed back a lock of her hair. "I want to protect you."

She did like the sound of that, especially since her dad had never been around. She'd seen plenty of situations, however, where there didn't need to be one leader. What about friendships? Business partnerships? Sibling relationships? Why should romantic love be any different?

But they weren't married—yet, anyway. Once he went to college, she knew, he'd see the world outside Ecstasy, and forget a lot of this stuff. So for the moment she said nothing, and he looked satisfied. She tilted her face up and looked into his eyes.

"So you'll go to the dance with me?"

Jake laughed and kissed the top of her head. "Okay, this once, because I can see what it means to you. Also," he said, nuzzling her, "I can't wait to see you in your dress."

Now, she placed that dress on Jordan's bed, unzipping the bag and smoothing out the wrinkles.

Jordan turned from the mirror and shrugged. "I guess you're right; I'll leave my hair down. Brad always likes it that way."

"How is Brad? Is he in town yet?"

"Yeah, he's at his parents' house. He'll meet us later at Maddie's. We only got to spend a few minutes together last night." She sighed. "I barely get to see him now. He can't come home from college every weekend, and my dad refuses to let me visit Blackrock alone." Jordan sat on her bed and pouted. "It's so unfair. The few times I got to go, I had to take Jake along, and he didn't give Brad and me any time alone. He said my dad would have his hide if he did."

"Yeah, Jake told me it was rough—that he wanted you guys to have a good time, but he'd made a promise to your father."

Lucy was lucky. When Jake was at college next year, she doubted anyone would chaperone when she went to visit him.

Jordan got up and closed her bedroom door. "We can't even have any intimate time together; it's been since Christmas. When he was at Pine Bluff, we did it all the time. Now we never have the chance. His parents give him a ton of stuff to do when he's home, and my parents watch us like a hawk, especially since Maddie." She frowned. "It's going to be so hard to wait 'til the summer. But we'll be together next year. At least there's that."

"So, um ... you guys really did it all the time?"

"Sure, don't you and Jake?" She turned toward Lucy and laughed. "Don't tell me you don't; I won't believe you! I know my brother."

Did she really know her brother, though? After Christmas Eve in the spring house, Lucy had avoided Jake. For a week, she didn't pick up when he called. When he texted, she told him she'd caught a cold and couldn't go out with him on New Year's Eve.

Jake came to see her on New Year's Day, and her mother, clueless, had let him in. He found Lucy in front of the television, perfectly healthy, watching old black and white films, and he asked her to go for a drive. When she hesitated, he whispered in her ear, "I won't touch you.

I promise. I just want to talk." The look in his eyes was so sincere that she agreed. It was a cold, clear day and they drove to the bluffs and stayed in the car, running the heater and drinking a thermos of spiked hot chocolate Jake had prepared at home. Lucy stayed as close as she could to the door on her side of the car.

"Look," Jake told her, trying to take her hand. "I made a mistake. I'm sorry." He did look sorry; she had to give him that. "I really miss you. I realize now that it wasn't the right thing, the right time—"

"You didn't ask me."

"Uh ... I know. I just thought that, well, we were so excited. I mean, I *did* ask you if you wanted me."

"Not *that*, though. You didn't ask about *that*." She leaned away from him and crossed her arms.

"You're right, I should have." His voice softened. "I know now that you're a nice, clean girl. I respect that, and I won't ask that of you again, if you don't want it. Can you forgive me?"

She wanted so much to forgive him. "Do you promise?"

"Yes, I promise. Could we, um, just go back to the way we were? We were enjoying each other so much."

She was not sure she could trust him when he was excited. She had needs too, and sometimes she could barely trust herself.

When she got home that day, she made a list of the pros and cons. Cons: there was the gross sex thing; Jake was also anti-science, and she had to hide those activities from him. She'd never even shown him her lab. And he often told her what to do. Pros: there was so much she loved about him: that tousled blond hair, his sexy smile. Being seen with him was amazing; being alone with him even better. He made her feel special, understood. And his music! She wanted to climb into his arms every time he played.

The best part was that he wanted *her.* There were plenty of girls who'd change places with her in an instant. Sophia's new boyfriend was rarely in town, and lately she'd shot some pretty steamy glances in Jake's direction. It wouldn't take much to lose him.

So they did, eventually, go back to the way they were. Lucy kept him satisfied with her hands and mouth, and Jake, though they fumbled and rubbed together, did not try to pressure her into doing *that* again. So far.

"Lucy?" Jordan was looking at her.

"Oh, I'm sorry. What did you say?"

"You and Jake. You do it, right? You have sex?"

Lucy swallowed. "Well, not *exactly* that."

"Obviously not *exactly* that. You need to remain intact." Jordan raised her eyebrows and nodded knowingly.

Lucy was floored. "And you don't mind," Lucy whispered, examining her fingernails, "Um—the *other*? I mean ..." Her voice trailed off, embarrassed.

"I know what you mean." Jordan shrugged. "It hurts at first, but it keeps them happy. It's the best way. Look at David and Maddie. They were stupid to risk so much." She paused. "Though at least she's *married*," she said rather wistfully.

Lucy remembered her last conversation with Maddie. "They don't seem all that happy at the moment."

"Yeah, well. I'm sure they will be when the scandal dies down and they have their new baby in their arms. I'm going to help Maddie pick out things for the nursery." Jordan outlined her large green eyes and brushed mascara onto her lashes.

An old-fashioned word, *scandal*—one that Lucy had heard used for politicians. It was only a "scandal" if you got caught.

They heard a tapping at the door, and Jordan opened it to her younger sister, Claire.

"Can I come in?"

"For a little while," Jordan answered, stepping aside. "Why are you wearing that?"

"I wanted to show Lucy my dress."

Lucy remembered that Claire, 13, was going to the ECM purity ball the next night with her father. Claire idolized her big sister, and most of Jordan's friends. The chubby blond girl stepped into the room and twirled before them. Her dress was midcalf white lace with a satin bodice, covered by a white lace jacket with scalloped sleeves and edge. She wore white satin pumps and a decorated headband of the same material.

"Beautiful!" Lucy told her. "Do all the girls wear white?"

"Duh," Jordan said. "It's a *purity* ball?"

"Oh right, makes sense, I guess. What do they do there?"

"First, there's a procession," Claire explained excitedly. "We all walk in wearing our dresses and sing a song for our fathers, thanking them for their guidance and protection. Then there's prayer, and dinner, and a speaker, and then we sign our vows."

"Vows?"

"The chastity pledge. Some call it a virginity pledge," Jordan told her. "They both sign."

"Yeah. And then there's cake, and my dad gives me a gift." Claire's eyes gleamed.

A gift from her father. Lucy envied her.

"What kind of gift?" Lucy asked. "A ring like Maddie's?" Maddie wasn't wearing her purity ring anymore.

"I don't know yet. I hope it's a necklace like Jordan's."

Lucy turned to Jordan, who waved her hand. "I'll show you later."

"And then," Claire told her, "there's ballroom dancing. I learned how to waltz." She held her arms up for an imaginary partner and began to dance in the center of Jordan's bedroom. "This is the box step. Mrs. Schultz said I was the most improved—"

"That's enough," Jordan told her. She opened the door and called, "Mom!"

Mrs. Randall called from downstairs, "Claire, it's time to come out of there now."

Claire stomped her foot, making the faux pearls on her satin headband bounce. But she obeyed her mother.

"Have fun at the ball," Lucy told her on her way out.

Jordan closed the door and locked it. "She's such a pest."

Lucy took Jordan's place on the bed, drawing up her knees. "I think it would be fun to have a little sister."

Jordan shook her head. "Not usually."

"What necklace was she talking about?"

"Oh, you know, you've seen it a million times." She walked to her jewelry box and pulled out a silver pendant in the shape of a heart with a keyhole in it. Lucy had seen it often around Jordan's neck, when she wasn't wearing her cross. She'd always assumed it was from Brad.

"The father keeps the key," Jordan told her.

"What?" Lucy wasn't sure she understood.

"See the keyhole? The father keeps the key, until his daughter gets married. Then he gives it to the husband."

"Seriously?"

"Yeah." Jordan moved back to the mirror and began to pencil her eyebrows. "My dad has mine."

Sometimes this group took the Christian thing way too far. Still, they were raised with something to believe in, unlike her.

Lucy applied her makeup under Jordan's direction, then they helped one another into their dresses: Lucy's a tea-length in muted teal with beads and sequins around the neckline, Jordan's a pale rose with pleated bodice and spaghetti straps. Jordan's had a little jacket, which she'd sworn to her parents she would not remove. The doorbell rang as they finished their preparations.

Jake and Brad stood in the foyer, awkwardly holding corsage boxes as the girls descended the stairs. They looked good in their suits: Jake in dark gray, and Brad in royal blue. They slipped the corsages onto their wrists, and Mrs. Randall took pictures before they left.

When they got to Maddie's, her father, Mr. Gibson, ushered them in. He and his wife were dressed up to chaperone. Logan and Tyler were already there with Emma and Beth, the girls who'd invited them to the dance. David and Maddie sat on the sofa, a few feet between them, David pulling hard at his collar. Maddie stood to greet them. For her "last dance," as she called it, she'd chosen a dark blue lace dress with an empire waist to hide her fuller figure. Her mother took enough photos to break Instagram, then they drove to the dance in several cars, Maddie and David with her parents.

The gymnasium was decorated in turquoise, white, and silver, with streamers, balloons, and strings of lights, transforming the space into something magical. A deejay was in throwback mode, playing hits from the 70s, 80s, and 90s, and people were actually dancing to them—a different vibe from her old school. Their group staked out territory near the stacked-up bleachers. Long tables with bottled beverages and refreshments were set up along an adjacent wall. Opposite them was a platform with chairs for the chaperones, who took turns patrolling the dance floor.

Brad and Jordan were the first couple in their group to dance, Jordan's prim little jacket left on a chair. Several songs later, Jake and Lucy joined them.

The fast numbers turned to slow ones. When the deejay played "I Hope You Dance", Lucy saw Maddie lead a reluctant David to the floor. They started out stiffly— arm's length at first—then moved close together, despite disapproving looks from Maddie's folks. It must have been surreal for them: married soon-to-be parents dancing in a high-school gym. But Maddie looked happier than she had in months. Lucy was glad of that.

Then Mr. and Mrs. Gibson's gaze turned to her. Lucy was conscious of Jake's arms around her, the press of their bodies, their mingled breath. Lucy didn't care who was watching. It was so romantic to be here with him, dressed in their finest, dancing together under the twinkling lights. This month had been heavenly. Jake had surprised her on Valentine's Day with a special song—"For Lucy"—which he sang to her at the coffee shop: *Ten years from now, I vow, we will be together.* Jake slid his hand down her back as they danced, sending a thrill through her body.

Brad and Jordan hurried by them, headed for the door that led to the hall. Jake turned to watch them. "Jordan isn't happy. I wonder what's up." That twin thing—it was like radar. Jake turned to go after them.

Lucy caught his hand. "Maybe—whatever it is—we should let *them* work it out."

Jake's brow furrowed, then relaxed. "Yeah, you're right." He pulled her close again, touched her hair, her neck with his lips as they moved to the music. Lucy closed her eyes to savor the feeling.

When she opened them, she noticed Dr. Reynolds on the chaperone platform, looking at her. Lucy couldn't meet his eye. He'd kindly offered to mentor her for the national science talent search, the competition she'd been prepping for since grade school. The one that would launch her bright scientific future. She and Reynolds were supposed to discuss her research project six weeks ago. She'd blown off two appointments with him, and never made a third. Her mother would kill her if she knew. The national competition would take all her time and attention. Jake wanted her to work with him as a counselor at the ECM summer camp. There was no way she'd be able to do both.

Lucy nuzzled Jake and tried to stay in the moment.

That moment, however, was over too quickly. Jake made a face, and she followed his gaze. Near the bleachers, her lab partner Sam, in black pants and tuxedo jacket, was dancing with Eva Lopez, her teammate from the cross-country squad. They had come as a couple, a rare occurrence, Lucy imagined, at hetero-norm Pine Bluff. Jake's football-player friends, the Bison, were scowling at them from different parts of the room.

At that moment Jordan flew back into the gym, heading straight for her brother. She'd obviously been crying.

"Is it true?" she asked him angrily. Lucy and Jake let go of each other and stared at Jordan.

"Is *what* true?" Jake asked her. "What happened?"

"Is it true what Brad says—that Dad said I can't go to college?"

"Brad told you that?"

"Yeah." Jordan saw Jake's expression and started to cry again.

"It's too loud to talk in here." Jake grasped Jordan's arm and steered her out into the hall. Lucy followed. David was leaning against the lockers, staring into space. He looked surprised to see them, then concerned.

Weeping, Jordan turned to Jake and said, "Tell me."

Jake looked at his shoes. "I know Dad's thinking in that direction. Your trips to the college worried him. He doesn't want to risk your virtue, for a degree you won't use once you're married." Jake raised his head and put a hand on his sister's shoulder. "He just wants what's best for you, Jordan."

Lucy stared at Jake, open-mouthed.

"Best for me? *College* is best for me! I've wanted to be a kindergarten teacher since I was five years old." Jordan's voice grew desperate, and she grabbed Jake's arm. "You've got to help me. You've got to change his mind! I already have my sorority picked out. It's not fair! Why should you get to go to college and not me?"

Jordan choked on her tears, then blew her nose on the tissue Lucy handed her. "Dad told Brad he can see me here if his intentions are serious. But I can't go to Blackrock anymore."

Jake frowned. "And what did Brad say to that?"

"He said he loves me, but that we should see other people."

"What?" Jake balled his fists at his side. "I'll kill him, I swear. Where is he?"

"No, Jake, don't. I don't know where he is. It's not his fault."

"Stay here." Despite protests from Lucy and Jordan, Jake took off down the hall in search of Brad.

David put his arm around Jordan, supporting her. She leaned into his chest, tears flowing.

"I'll take care of her," he said to Lucy. "Why don't you tell the others what's going on? We'll probably need to go."

Lucy ran back to the gym and scanned the crowd. She noticed with relief that Dr. Reynolds was standing between

Sam and Eva and the Bison. She couldn't locate Maddie at first, then spotted her dancing to a fast number with Logan. Lucy decided to wait until they returned to their seats. Maddie deserved every minute of this evening she could get. Tyler, Emma, and Beth were at the refreshment table. When she explained the situation, they were sympathetic, but decided they wanted to stay. When Maddie and Logan returned, she filled them in. Maddie looked disappointed, but worried for Jordan. The girls grabbed their purses and the three of them headed out into the hall. The others were nowhere to be seen.

Logan noticed the door to one passageway was propped open. "Let's try this way."

As they hurried down that corridor, they heard the faint buzz of voices. Just before the hallway led into the auditorium foyer there was an open staircase, where Jordan and David sat together, their backs to those approaching.

Jordan's voice was still tearful. "But what will I do without him?"

"You'll be okay, I promise." David put his arm around her. "I know this isn't the time or place, but there's always me." He paused a moment. "I love you."

"I love you too, David. Thanks for being here."

"No, I mean I love you, Jordan. I'm *in love* with you. I have been for years."

Jordan twisted her body in surprise. "Wait—what?"

The others, unobserved, stood perfectly still.

"I love you, Jordan. Maybe we've been with the wrong people all along."

At that moment Jake caught up with them, and asked, "What's happening?" Jordan and David turned and saw the four of them standing there.

Jordan gasped, "Oh, Maddie ..." and started down the stairs toward her.

Maddie, wild-eyed, yelled, "No! Leave me alone, all of you."

She fled through the auditorium foyer, out the exit doors, into the night. Jordan stood there, stunned. Jake,

Logan, and Lucy followed Maddie out, in time to see her speed off in her parents' car.

Jake started back to the building. "We'd better find her mom and dad."

Jake and Lucy helped Mr. and Mrs. Gibson find a ride home with another chaperone. Logan decided not to abandon his date and stayed at the dance. Jake and Lucy took Jordan home. Both of the girls kept texting Maddie, but she wasn't answering.

Jake had phoned ahead. Mr. Randall was waiting to talk to Jordan and steered her into his home office. Her muffled pleas and her father's resolute responses could be heard from the family room. Jake turned on the TV, and he and Lucy sat together, listlessly flipping through channels. The news was grim: people dying in Italy from the new coronavirus, the U.S. issuing travel restrictions for affected countries. Someone near Seattle had died. The president was downplaying the outbreak. "It's going to disappear. One day, it's like a miracle, it will disappear." Their local TV anchors agreed—news of the virus was exaggerated and politically motivated. Lucy, knowing what she did of genetics, doubted that. Jake changed the channel.

It seemed the whole world was in turmoil. Lucy kicked off her high heels and curled her feet under her. She didn't feel like cuddling with Jake. She wasn't sure what role he had played in this whole no-college thing. Or in Sam and Eva's troubles, for that matter. She texted Maddie again, but there was no answer.

It seemed hours later that Jordan emerged red-eyed from her father's office and went straight to her room. Lucy rose to follow, but Jake put a hand on her arm.

"It's time I drove you home. Your mother will worry."

As Lucy put her shoes back on, Mrs. Randall, in tailored pajamas, came down the steps toward them, talking on her phone. Her voice was stressed.

"And what do the doctors say? ... Oh, that's something, after all. I'm so sorry you've been through all this, Gretchen. For months already. You must be exhausted ..."

She held a finger up to Jake and Lucy. "Yes, tell them you need a Christian counselor. Can't it be that one they've been seeing? ... Oh ... Well, yes, we've got our own drama here. Nothing like what you're going through ... No, it was a shock to her. She doesn't feel the same way about David, and she feels so bad for Maddie ... Yes, okay, I'll tell them. Keep us updated. We send our love to you all."

Mrs. Randall sat heavily on an armchair near them and ran her fingers through her long blond bob. "Lord!"

"Was that Maddie's mom?" Jake asked her.

"Yes." She shook her head. "And I have some bad news. Maddie's in the hospital. She cut her wrists this evening."

"What?" both Lucy and Jake cried at once.

"Her parents got home quickly and found her, so fortunately she didn't lose too much blood."

"Will she be okay?" Lucy asked.

"Yes, they think so. They're holding her in the psych ward for observation."

Jake frowned. "The psych ward? Is that really necessary?"

"Can we visit her?" Lucy asked.

"No, I'm sorry, they won't allow it. Gretchen said she'll be there for several days." Mrs. Randall sighed. "Hopefully they'll give her some help. She's certainly put her family through enough."

Lucy winced at that but held her tongue. Mrs. Randall looked at her. "You two should call it a night."

Jake agreed.

Mrs. Randall rose and walked to the stairs, then stopped and turned with her hand on the railing. "Oh. There's some good news, though," she announced. "The baby is doing fine."

21

Alexa: Sunday, March 1

The window slid open effortlessly on its new sash cords, and Alexa leaned out into the unseasonably mild spring air.

"Thanks, Ben, for all your repairs on the windows. They're working great."

Ben turned from his work on the carriage barn, grinned, and touched the brim of his painter's cap. He and Rachel had almost finished priming, and those horrid letters were finally covered over. In the last week, Ben had worked tirelessly to get the siding repaired, caulked, and ready for paint. Fortunately, the weather was accommodating, with higher temperatures and cool, dry evenings. At this rate, the humanists should be able to move in by midsummer.

Alexa shuddered at the thought of someone creeping onto her property to deface the barn. Two uniformed policemen had come to the house to take her statement. One of them, seeing the word "atheist," had narrowed his eyes and acted as if she somehow had this coming. She assumed he had seen her exchange with Cyrus Bell on the evening news. Though stiffly polite, neither officer was sympathetic, and she doubted they would investigate any further.

Fortunately, Chad and Jeremy were free the next day to install a security system—something she never thought she'd need in the country. There were cameras now on the barn and the house, and alarms on all the windows, doors, and the porch. She was still getting used to the codes and settings, but she slept better knowing that the house was actively monitored, and the three women wouldn't be caught off guard by an intruder.

At ten o'clock, she heard Heather's car on the gravel drive and went out to meet her on the porch. Heather, an avid gardener, had agreed to help her identify what was growing on her property and offer suggestions for new things to plant. Except for a few herbs and flowers she'd grown on her Elm Ridge balcony, Alexa was unfamiliar with the flora of the world. Her classes in landscape architecture had been few and long ago. John Jeffers pulled up in his SUV, unloaded huge bags of soil and mulch, and then, after greetings, joined in Alexa's tutorial.

Heather pointed out perennials in the north yard as Alexa worked up a plan on blue grid paper. They looked over the beds by the spring house and carriage barn, then stopped to greet Ben and Rachel and compliment them on their work. Although Rachel had a good idea who'd done the damage, John Jeffers explained that there wasn't sufficient evidence to file suit against ECM. "But if there's a next time—and I hope there won't be—we'll have them on video."

The trio moved on to the back yard. The grass, encouraged by the early spring, had already started to green. "Margaret had her vegetable garden there." John pointed to the slope behind the kitchen. "It's long gone to seed. She couldn't keep it up, with the Parkinson's and all. I tried to help for a while, but eventually she just let it go and bought her produce at the market. You may find some of the sturdier plants have survived." He pulled up some shoots and placed them in the women's hands, drawing their attention to the roots, then indicated several places on the ground to watch, as Alexa took detailed notes. He turned and paced to the berry bushes above the garden. "It was a sad season when she gave up canning. I sure do miss those raspberry preserves." He looked momentarily bereft, his straight shoulders sagging as if pulled closer by the earth. Alexa wondered again about his relationship with Margaret. Were they lovers? She would probably never know.

They climbed to the orchard to inspect the cherry and apple trees. To Alexa's surprise, there was a pear tree, too. The cherry trees were already beginning to bud. Behind the orchard was wooded acreage—"a project for another day," Heather told her.

Alexa unlocked Lucy's laboratory shed to show Heather the improvements they'd made.

"Wow, Alexa," she said. "I had no idea."

"Oddly enough," Alexa told her, "she doesn't use it as often as I'd thought. Maybe she will when her national competition project gets started."

Circling the house to the south, they stopped at Lucy's planting beds, where some green was beginning to show. "This side of the yard is all hers," Alexa told them, "for her research." John and Heather looked impressed.

They ended at the front porch again to check out the rose bushes, lilies, and azaleas. Heather guaranteed there would be color all summer, as long as the plants were properly cared for. She gave Alexa instructions and promised to help her shop soon for some annuals for the garden beds near the road.

John had errands in town and said his goodbyes, and Alexa invited Heather in for a late-morning cup of tea. They washed the earth from their hands and settled in at the kitchen table with mugs of Irish Breakfast and some muffins that Rachel had baked. Heather's blond waves caught the sun from the bay window.

"I can't thank you enough for your help this morning," Alexa told her. "So, what's been happening with you and yours this week?"

Heather caught Alexa up on her job and her family. They chuckled at stories of her teenaged sons learning to do their own laundry, and anecdotes from her husband Alan's pediatric practice. Then Heather grew more solemn.

"Both my husband and brother are concerned about this new virus," she told Alexa. "There's a case in New York now, as well as those in Seattle. The medical community is taking this way more seriously than the government. Mark said they've had several meetings at the hospital and are preparing for a good-sized outbreak in the States."

"I know they expect it in the larger cities. Do they think it will come here? Does Alan think it's a danger for children?"

"It's mostly affecting older people, from what they can tell, but it's highly contagious, and you don't want kids exposed if they don't have to be. I understand it attacks the lungs and causes pneumonia."

"Wow. Well, I hope they'll be able to contain it."

Heather knocked on the table. "So do I."

Alexa took a sip of her tea and finished off one of the muffins. "So, you attended the early service this morning?" Heather nodded. "What's been happening with the Methodists?"

"Oh, it's heartbreaking," Heather answered. "The 'One Church Plan,' where each church gets to choose for itself, was not adopted. They voted for the 'Traditional Plan,' the one banning same-sex marriages and gay clergy. And they added rather ominous 'accountability measures' for those churches that violate the rules."

"Wow. So what will happen now?"

"A lot of churches will leave the denomination. There's too much of a schism, I'm afraid. It now looks like the traditionals will form their own new branch." Heather squeezed some lemon into her tea and stirred distractedly. "The church will be voting on a plan to split at the general conference in May. If it goes through, individual congregations can decide to stay or leave with a two-thirds vote."

"Which do you think your church will choose?"

Heather sighed and looked out the window. Alexa followed her gaze. A robin was busy in the garden where John had disturbed the earth. "I'm really not sure. Most of us have been following this closely, but very few have openly taken sides. I'd say we're probably pretty evenly divided." She turned again to Alexa, her blue eyes troubled. "We all know we're going to have this debate, and I'm not sure our church will survive it. Either way, there won't be many left to carry on."

Alexa reached out to touch Heather's hand. "I'm really sorry it's come to this."

"Yeah. You'd think well-intentioned Christians could allow each other to follow their own consciences."

Alexa gathered the teapot and mugs and took them to the sink, emptying the tea leaves that had accumulated in the bottom. If only she could actually read the future in them. She understood how the hope for answers could drive some to believe in omens.

Heather brushed some muffin crumbs from her shirt. "By the way, Alexa, Eric Reynolds stopped by my office on Thursday. During the course of the conversation, he mentioned that Lucy seems to have lost enthusiasm for his class. She canceled two appointments they'd made to discuss the big science competition. I'm concerned."

Alexa leaned against the counter, astounded. "I don't know why she'd do that, Heather."

Lucy had come in late from the dance last night and gone straight to her room. Alexa had seen her briefly this morning as she grabbed a pop tart and a cup of coffee and headed back upstairs.

"I don't know what's gotten into her lately, but I'm afraid it's her friends. This boy. She's so involved with this church. I barely know her anymore." Alexa put one hand to her face and rubbed. "And she's been super upset, embarrassed, by me being on the news. It's bad enough I 'don't believe in anything,' but now I'm ruining her life by running for the school board."

Heather had helped Alexa through her anxiety since the forum segment with Cyrus Bell had first aired. The TV pundits had torn her apart. Twitter and Facebook were filled with religious vitriol against her.

Mona Bauer, the humanist leader, had implored her not to give up. "Unfortunately, that's part of the risk of running now. The election is a full month away. A lot can change by then." And she was probably right.

"My biggest concern is Lucy's future, Heather. She's worked toward this competition for most of her life. Why am I doing this if not for her?"

"Maybe it's time for a discussion. The three of us."

Just then, Alexa's phone rang—an unfamiliar number. The caller left a voicemail and she excused herself to the living room to listen. Someone named "Traci with an i," assistant producer for WXT's weeknight show, *Southerland Tonight*, was inviting her to appear on the program. Tomorrow. She'd sit on a panel with Cyrus Bell and another guest to discuss the addition of intelligent design to the Pine Bluff curriculum.

Alexa winced. It would be a total ambush, she knew. And yet it was better to make her own case than to let them do it for her.

She glanced at the kitchen, where Heather sat at the breakfast nook, lost in thought. Alexa hastened to the powder room, where her pale face taunted her from the mirror. Maybe Lucy was right; she could still quit the race. No one would really care.

She sighed. Wrong. *She* would care. She pulled herself together and went back to the kitchen to talk it over with Heather.

"I don't know if I should do this or not." Alexa sat down, then got up again and paced. "I suspect I'll spend the entire program defending my religious choices, and that won't save our science curriculum."

"That's possible," Heather agreed. "I've seen those shows. You'd have to be very disciplined to stick to your message under fire."

"They should have asked a scientist instead of me. Or a science teacher. Oh—they should have Reynolds on the show! That would balance things out. It might force him to fight for his science program for a change."

Heather shook her head vigorously. "He can't, Alexa. Remember? Despite how much he cares about this—and he does—all of us who work at the high school have been forbidden to talk about the lawsuit. And, as you've pointed out several times, he has personal reasons not to do it." Heather held up a finger. "But you could make the argument for him. For us all." She looked up to the ceiling, thinking. "Talking to him might be useful. You could ask him to help you prepare."

"Oh—" Alexa replied, alarmed. She wasn't sure she'd be comfortable spending time with Eric Reynolds. Or that *he* would be comfortable with her.

"Let me call him." Heather pulled out her phone and tapped some numbers before Alexa could protest. Alexa's stomach knotted at the thought of disturbing Reynolds, at home with his family on a Sunday afternoon.

After what seemed like a dozen rings, Reynolds answered, and Heather put him on speaker.

"Hey, Eric, how's it going?"

"Good, Heather, what's up?"

"Alexa Moss is here with me." Heather proceeded to fill him in on WXT's invitation.

"Hold on a minute," Eric said. They could hear him walking up or down stairs and closing a door. Alexa assumed he didn't want his wife or kids to overhear the exchange. When he came back on the line, he was businesslike. "How can I help?"

"We were hoping you could give her some fodder for her argument."

He was quiet for a moment. Alexa held her breath, embarrassed.

"Yeah, sure. I have to go in to the school today. Alexa, can you meet me in the lab this afternoon?"

"That would be great," she told him. They set the time for three o'clock.

Heather hung up and rose to leave. Alexa hugged her, thanked her for all her help, and watched her drive off with a feeling of trepidation. Then she called Mona Bauer, who agreed to see her the following day.

Alexa's cell phone rang. It was her mother. She ignored the call, unwilling to stress herself out any more today.

At three o'clock, Alexa drove to the high school and pulled into the lot, careful not to park too close to the only other car there, a dark blue hybrid she assumed was Reynolds'. She refreshed her muted lipstick in the visor mirror, tamed a few stray strands of hair, and adjusted the neckline of her sweater. That took care of the outside.

The only thing more unsettling than her first TV appearance was the idea of facing Eric Reynolds alone. She'd thought of him often, especially when the girls were asleep and she had only the late-night sounds of the country for company. It was a different life here; there were fewer events, fewer friends and neighbors. She'd been lonely, so an attraction to a man like this was probably inevitable. But there was no indication, beyond a few looks and gestures, that the feeling was, or would ever be, returned.

The wide oak doors of the school were locked, but Reynolds was waiting for her; he ushered her in and led her silently through the hallways to the lab. Today he wore slim black jeans and sneakers, and a fitted blue Henley which emphasized his lean frame and broad shoulders. She noticed he was not wearing his wedding ring.

The lab smelled like the mix of chemicals, plants, and animals she remembered from her previous visit. A radio on a corner shelf was tuned to a classical music station, Gershwin playing softly in the background. The afternoon sun streamed through the high windows, spotlighting a case of labeled seashells in fancy shapes and a collection of geodes, their green, purple, and silver depths sparkling like diamond dust. Alexa had to drag her eyes away from them to browse the opposite wall.

"I see the *Brassica* plants have grown since I've been here last."

He smiled. "Actually, those are different plants. They're the F2 generation for the second semester. The kids took the plants from last semester home."

The ones Lucy had in her lab had come from the school then. "Oh, I didn't know."

"No reason you would. They're also called Wisconsin Fast Plants. They have a 28-day life cycle—a new generation virtually every month. We use them in experiments because they reproduce so quickly. It lets us see the results of our genetic crosses in a manageable period of time."

Reynolds offered her a seat but remained standing. He apologized for having no coffee or snacks. "I'd be happy to run to the teacher's lounge."

"No need," Alexa reassured him. "And I'm the one who should apologize, for disrupting your afternoon with your wife and family."

Reynolds looked startled, then shook his head, looked down, and shuffled randomly through the papers on his desk. "My daughter and I are living with my sister at the moment. You didn't disturb anyone."

Alexa felt the color rise in her face. "Well, it's good of you to see me. I appreciate your time."

"Of course," he said. "I've been meaning to talk to you anyway about Lucy."

"I just learned this morning that she hasn't met with you about the competition. I have no idea why, but I'll talk to her."

Reynolds nodded. "She seems distracted lately." He paused, but Alexa didn't know what to add. "We still have time to get started on a project if she's interested. But we'll need her results and analysis by October to apply."

"I understand," she told him.

Then he asked about the TV program. Alexa had little information beyond the format and guests. The show's host, Dusty Southerland, was an aging conservative, famous in these parts for his gray goatee, his "gotcha" questions and opinionated responses to the issues of the day. He loved an argument and must have thought that a preacher and an atheist would provide some juicy TV.

"I'm afraid I'm the proverbial sitting duck," she told him. "But allowing WXT to 'control the narrative,' as they say, has not turned out well for me."

"I've seen the video clip from the candidate forum. I noticed it was heavily edited."

Alexa laughed. "Yes, indeed. The one condition I made for appearing was that they show the video, uncut, in its entirety."

Reynolds looked impressed. "A smart move, Alexa." She warmed all over, both at his praise and his use of her first name. She reminded herself to be careful.

"Maybe. Now I need to make my point and survive the night, without losing too many feathers."

Reynolds chuckled, then regarded her thoughtfully. "Proponents of intelligent design usually attack evolution as a theory. I can help you with that."

"That'd be great." She took a small notepad and pen from her purse, ready to record every word.

"What they don't recognize," he began, "is that virtually all modern biology is based on evolutionary theory. It's our fundamental understanding of so many processes in life, our planet, the universe. We are already using it, and have for years, to grow food, fight disease, improve life in general."

He motioned her over to the *Brassica* plants, which were separated into two groups. She left her notes on the table and stood next to him. A brown wave fell forward on his forehead as he bent over the specimens. His voice was deep and measured.

"Take this experiment we're doing. Most of the farmers in the area already use a form of *artificial* selection. They understand the concept: that certain varieties of corn or wheat or soybeans are genetically specialized for maximum yield, climate, soil type, etc. And yet they refuse to see past the GMOs to centuries, millennia when *nature itself* produced conditions that favored some organisms over others, and the ones best suited to those conditions lived on to reproduce. That's *natural* selection. That's evolution."

He picked a leaf from the bottom of one plant and then from another and, taking her hand, placed them in her palm. One had spiky projections on its leaves; the other did not. But she barely noticed; she was riveted by the touch of Reynolds' hand. A thrilling electricity coursed through her. He felt it too; she read it on his face as his eyes met hers. He dropped her hand and took half a step back, as she did.

He recovered first and pointed to the plants in her palm. "Do you see those hair-like projections on the leaves?" Alexa nodded, trying to concentrate. "Those are trichomes. Currently we're selecting out for trichomes—that means we're counting the trichomes on each plant, then crossing the plants, and counting the trichomes on the leaves of the resulting generation. Students can see genetics in action through several generations."

"What are the trichomes for?" Alexa asked.

"Science is exploring their purpose, but it appears they discourage insect infestation, help keep mites off grapevines, for example. That alone ... could make a big difference in a crop yield. And they have other properties ..." His voice trailed off as his eyes again met hers. He seemed to have found something fascinating there. The silence became almost palpable, and heat rose as some signal passed between them. Reynolds smiled slightly, then returned his gaze to the plants, shaking his head as if to clear it.

Alexa found her voice. "Wow. So some of this has pretty immediate practical applications."

"It doesn't always work that way, but in this case, yes."

Alexa forced her mind to return to her subject. "So what would you do if you had to teach intelligent design?"

"I'd have to find some way to bring a supreme being into all this. That's pretty impossible, even if I believed it. I challenge these ID people to tell me what experiment we'd do to show that a god created the *Brassica* plant. What data could we use, what characteristics could we measure? God is a hypothesis that can't be scientifically studied. And eventually, every accepted theory must be able to make testable predictions about nature. Intelligent design is incapable of that."

Alexa's phone chimed. Lucy needed a ride home from a friend's house.

"I'm sorry, I have to go." She turned reluctantly and gathered her things, folding the leaves he'd given her into her notes. He preceded her to the door of the lab and walked her down the hallway.

She turned to him at the outside door. "I can't thank you enough for your help and your time, Dr. Reynolds."

He grinned and said, "I think it's time you called me Eric."

They both reached for the door handle at the same time, fell awkwardly against one another, and laughed. Smiling, he grasped the handle again, one hand on the small of her back as if to guide her out, but then he seemed to think better of it, and turned toward her instead. He removed his glasses. His eyes were the color of sea glass. She turned her face up to his and lost herself in his gaze. The moment seemed to last a lifetime; the scent of him made her head spin. He drew her closer. Their lips were inches apart.

"These days, I need to ask your permission," he whispered.

"Um, let's see," she teased him. Then seriously, "You have it."

He kissed her softly at first, and then more deeply, their bodies moving closer together, their breaths coming faster, the heat returning, rising—

Her phone buzzed again. Lucy. "Where are you?"

"Eric, I'm sorry," she told him. "I have to go."

He groaned, but finally relinquished her with a grin, and Alexa walked squinting into the bright afternoon.

"I'll watch tomorrow. Good luck," he told her. "Feel free to call me anytime."

"Thanks. I'll do that."

She smiled and waved, and then he was gone. She was warmed by more than the sunlight as she drove to pick up Lucy. Her cell phone rang—her mother again—but she ignored it.

Lucy was angry when she got there. "What took you so long?"

Alexa told her about the Southerland show, though she didn't mention her meeting with Eric Reynolds in the lab.

"Oh, great!" Lucy said sarcastically. With a heavy sigh, she slumped down in her seat and spent the rest of the short trip texting. Once home, she grabbed a snack and headed, as usual, to her room. Rachel was working, so the house grew quiet, while Alexa's thoughts grew loud. What was she doing? Agreeing to be on Dusty's show might be her worst mistake yet.

The landline in the kitchen rang, and Alexa picked it up unthinkingly. It was Sheila.

"It's about time you answered. Why haven't you returned my calls?"

"Hi, Mom." Alexa tried to keep the annoyance out of her voice. "How are you?"

"Well, I'm alright. Some aches and pains, as usual, but you don't want to hear about those."

Alexa sighed. "Anything serious?"

"Nothing for you to worry about. I just called to see how things are going. Did you finish the house? Do you have a job yet? When do you think you'll be giving this up and coming back to civilization?"

"Yes, several, and not anytime soon."

"You're not still thinking of running for the school board?"

"I'm still a candidate."

"Well, it's your life, but I can't understand why you'd want to do that. And who would vote for you?"

"Maybe no one, but I've got to try. Lucy and I are doing just fine, by the way."

"I know Lucy's good. That girl finally has her head on straight. I saw on the television that she's baptized."

"What are you talking about?" Her mother was losing it for sure.

"We get Pastor Bell every Sunday morning on the TV in the community room. He changed his intro this week, and I saw Lucy on there, getting baptized. I told everybody that was my granddaughter! They all wish her well, by the way."

"Are you sure it was her? I don't think—"

"Are you saying I wouldn't recognize my own family?" When Alexa didn't answer, she probed, "Don't you know about this? Weren't you there?"

"No, Mom. I don't think it's Lucy." The top of Alexa's head began to pulse.

"See for yourself. They rerun the program at seven." That'd be six o'clock here. It was 5:51.

"Okay, Mom. I've got to run. I'll call you later in the week."

Before her mother could protest, she hung up, her whole body tense. Why would Sheila say this? What was she up to?

Alexa fumbled for the TV remote and scrolled through the channels until she found it: *Morning at Sky Cathedral.* She'd only watched the broadcast once, when she first learned about ECM. She remembered her dismay at the size of the whole operation, the campus, the hype, the vast number of people in the seats.

The theme music started: a modern hymn she didn't recognize. Scenes of church activities flashed across the screen, and she held her breath at each new picture, willing it to be over. But then there it was: a group of individuals being baptized. There was no mistake. The one in the water was Lucy. Alexa gasped. And that wasn't all. In several shots a youth group was gathered around Cyrus Bell. Lucy was with them, listening, rapt, her eyes shining like the silver cross pendant on her breast.

She paced the living room for several minutes, throat aching with stifled rage. Composing herself at last she went to the stairs.

"Lucy!" she called up. No answer. Then louder, "Lucy!"

"What?" Lucy came to the top of the steps, frowning.

"I need to speak with you, please."

"But Mom ..."

"Now," Alexa said quietly.

Lucy came down the stairs. "What's going on?"

Alexa pointed at the television, then ran the video back to the start of the program. Lucy stood in front of the set watching curiously, then started when she saw herself. Alexa paused the recording.

"Would you care to explain this to me?"

Lucy winced. "I didn't know anything about this. Honest."

Alexa raised her eyebrows. "Really? You didn't know you were baptized?"

Lucy looked at the floor. "I didn't know they were recording it, that they'd—I can't believe ..." She sat down heavily on the sofa, twisting her hair.

"We'll get to that part." Alexa resumed her pacing but tried to keep her voice level. "Start at the beginning, Lucy. Tell me what you've been doing at that church."

Lucy swallowed hard. "Don't freak out, Mom. I've just been going to youth group with my friends and to church on Sundays. Jake says—"

"Jake says?"

Lucy raised her chin. "Yes, *Jake*, Mom. He's shown me a deeper, more spiritual way to live." She stood and walked to the bay window and looked out for a moment, then turned to face Alexa. "You wouldn't understand."

"I think I do."

"No, you don't! You raised me with *nothing*—no church, no religion, no family!"

Alexa was struck. "The family part is what it is. I can't change that, Lucy. And you know why I didn't raise you with religion. It was forced on me. I didn't want that for you."

"You didn't believe, so I had no choice! Don't you think I should have?"

"The idea was that you'd choose when you were older."

"Well, I'm older now, and making my own decisions."

"I see. And what have you decided, exactly?"

"That my spiritual life is more important than this life you'd have me live, this house, my so-called career—"

"Wait, is this why you've cancelled your appointments with Dr. Reynolds?"

Lucy stepped back. "You know about that?"

"It's a small community." Alexa felt nauseated. "Tell me the truth. *Are you giving up your science?*"

Lucy was defiant. "What if I am? I've been on this track since I was little, but maybe it's not the right one. Maybe I want to have friends, have a life. I'm not going to apologize for anything. These are good people. Pastor Bell—"

"That man! Where exactly does he fit in all of this?"

"He's been giving me private Bible study. He says that I have spiritual potential."

Alexa's hands became fists at her side. "Well, that's going to stop immediately. He has no right! You're underage, Lucy. You need my permission. And legally, he can't use you in that video without my consent." She softened her tone. "Can't you see that he's using you to get to me? Convincing you to keep secrets from me? He's trying to tear us apart."

"It's always about you!"

"It's actually about you, Lucy. I love you. I don't want to see you hurt."

"You're the one who's hurting me! You're determined to ruin my life!"

Alexa snorted, despite herself. "Oh, I think Pastor Bell has got the jump on me there!"

Lucy shot her a scathing look. "You can't stop me from going to church! Or seeing Jake, or my friends!"

And with that she turned and stomped up the stairs. Alexa sat in the armchair, stunned, exhausted. Lucy's bedroom door slammed.

22

Alexa: Monday, March 2

W XT was housed in the Jefferson building, the
tallest structure in Ecstasy, a 1930s Art Deco affair
with an aging limestone façade. Alexa admired the classic
setbacks and decorative spandrels, the bronze relief of Atlas
that appeared to hold up the building.

The lobby held more exquisite bronze: a bank of vintage
elevators between chevron sconces that would set her
architect's heart aflutter if it wasn't already pounding. She
entered the first car on her right and pressed the ivory-
colored button for the seventh floor, as instructed. The ornate
elevator ascended slowly, and Alexa eyed her reflection in
its mirror-bright brass panels. She'd dressed carefully in
a black suit jacket with a gray sheath dress underneath.
Her auburn hair was partly clipped back; the silver and
moonstone earrings she'd chosen echoed the color of her
eyes and softened an otherwise no-nonsense look.

Her calm appearance belied her inner warrior. Lucy had
slipped out early today without facing her, but the fallout of
their argument sat heavy in Alexa's bones. She held Cyrus
Bell responsible. She was fueled by her hurt and armored
by her anger. The stakes were personal now.

In her mind, she ran over her conversation with Eric
Reynolds, grateful for his input. She had studied the notes
from their meeting all morning, then gone to town and
lunched with Mona, who'd brought some research of her

own. It turned out that Mona kept a file on separation of church and state violations going decades back. Now, since the dawn of the current administration, it was bursting with items on local, state, and federal legislation and court cases. Alexa was shocked.

"Yeah," Mona said. "They've been busy."

The information was invaluable, and Alexa internalized as much as she could. But despite Reynolds's help, despite her discussions with Heather and Mona, she felt as if she was riding into a crucial battle alone. People she knew would be watching; they were counting on her, and if she failed, she could do more harm than good.

The entire seventh floor was occupied by the TV station. The receptionist directed her down the hall to a makeup room, where stylists sat her in a barber-type chair and fastened a paper cape around her neck. Assistant producer Traci-with-an-i arrived and went over the format. Alexa would appear on the show's second segment, which would begin with the video. The panel would consist of herself, Cyrus Bell, and Garrett Baker, a lawyer from the American Center for Freedom and Liberty—the Christian right's answer to the ACLU—remote from Washington. The show's host, Dusty Southerland, would ask the questions.

Alexa allowed the stylists to neaten her hair but explained between the producer's remarks that she had done her own makeup, since she wasn't sure the station pros would know what to do with her birthmark. Shaking their heads, they insisted she'd look washed out on camera without more color—at least more emphasis on the eyes and lips. Traci agreed, and Alexa bowed to their expertise, though she found the finished look a little clownish. They clipped a microphone to her lapel that was wired to a box under her jacket.

At 5:45, she was taken to a small green room where water, coffee, fruit, and snacks were spread out on a modern glass buffet table along one wall. Above it, in black and white, were row upon row of photos of Dusty Southerland, posed with two former governors (including the one who had just been released from prison), various state and local politicians, and a bevy of lesser-known celebrities, including a shot with Cyrus Bell, arm in arm. "Bastards," she said, but then self-consciously fell silent, wondering if the room was monitored. Traci had mentioned that Bell was waiting in another space. They would not see each other until they were on camera. Alexa sat on the stylish but uncomfortable sofa, which faced a massive TV screen. A clock on the screen was counting down: seven minutes until the show started. She crossed her legs, uncrossed them, stood up and paced, sat down again.

The show opened with the now-familiar theme song and shot of Dusty, alone at the acrylic news desk. The first segment always covered a single topic from the national news, discussed in depth with an "expert" or political pundit. The topic tonight was the novel coronavirus. "Real Threat or Hysterical Hoax?" read the screen to Dusty's left, followed by a video montage of the president insisting "it will work out fine," and comparing the new virus to a seasonal flu. The surgeon general was quoted: "For the general public, the immediate health risk is considered low." The administration had ordered a "do not travel" warning for Italy and South Korea and banned all travel to and from Iran. Dusty and a Republican representative, beamed in from a remote location, discussed whether the virus was a real concern for Americans or just the latest overblown alarm by the Democrats.

"It's a real virus, but probably not very dangerous to the average person. After all," the bow-tied congressman asserted, "the regular flu kills 32,000 people in the U.S. every year. And we make it through just fine." He and Dusty chuckled.

A young man poked his head into the room and called "five minutes." When he was gone, Alexa opened the door to the corridor and looked down the carpeted hallway. If she ran now, she could get away before anyone saw her. She sighed and closed the door again. She would face Bell and do her damnedest.

Traci arrived to lead Alexa to the set, and guided her to her chair at the desk, between Dusty and Cyrus Bell. Cyrus wore a dark, expensive suit with a clerical collar. Dusty was similarly dressed, with a power tie that complemented the red-white-and-blue backdrop of his set. Both men smiled and shook her hand before she sat, as if they were all old friends. Then they eyed each other over her head: two foxes sizing up the hen, as Rachel's mother would have said.

The producer told them which camera to look at and counted them back in from commercial break. Alexa felt the tension ripple through her. First up was the video of Alexa's exchange with Cyrus at the candidate debate. Alexa cringed inwardly at the footage, knowing how a humanist would be viewed by Dusty's conservative audience. She hoped it wouldn't spur more vandalism. But true to their word, the show's producers had run the entire exchange, which mitigated the first part and got much of her point across.

Dusty introduced the panel, including Garrett Baker of the ACFL, remote from the capitol. Alexa's credentials were paltry compared to those of the two men, and hung orphaned in the air for a few seconds. Reading from the teleprompter, Dusty went on to recap the high-school lawsuit, then directed his first question to Cyrus Bell.

"What prompted ECM to be involved in this lawsuit at this time? In short: why here, why now?"

"First, Dusty, let's make it clear that ECM is not a party in this lawsuit. We are simply involved in an advisory capacity." Cyrus retold the story of the young unnamed woman, and reiterated his role as her concerned pastor. "The plaintiff was having to sit in class and be spoon-fed 'science' she doesn't believe. She knows, as most thinking people do, that something can't come from nothing, that life on earth can't be some meaningless, random, statistically improbable combination of molecules. But she must turn in homework, participate, answer test questions as if that's true. That is discrimination."

Dusty nodded thoughtfully. "A valid point."

"She's not asking for intelligent design to be the only theory taught in her classroom. All she wants is a balanced curriculum, one that allows for exploration of many scientific theories. *Critical thinking* rather than blind adherence to one theory, evolution. *Academic freedom,* Dusty."

In the first two minutes, Bell had hit all the buzzwords, all the creationist talking points of the Christian right. Alexa could guess what chord they would strike with Dusty's audience.

Bell continued. "Evolution as a theory is full of gaps and inconsistencies that proponents of the current science curriculum won't admit. Why not let students examine *all* theories about the origins of life? Intelligent design is evidence-based and a better scientific theory than evolution. *Teach the controversy,* and let the students decide for themselves. It's time to end the unchallenged reign of secularism in our schools."

Dusty turned to Garrett Baker. "Let me ask you, then, Garrett. So far, Pine Bluff's Principal Franklin, though sympathetic, has not honored the request to teach intelligent design in the classroom, claiming it's not in keeping with previous court decisions on the subject. And indeed, there have been some major court decisions—*Kitzmiller v. Dover* for example—which have gone against the teaching of intelligent design in public schools. What is different in your case, and why do you think you have a chance to win?"

Garrett Baker adjusted his glasses. "That's a great question, Dusty. For many years the courts have been packed with liberal activist judges, some opposed to any and all religious freedoms. Laws have been passed which force Christians to act in ways that don't line up with their beliefs, which deny them the right to do business as they see fit or challenge their right to public expression of their values and concerns."

Alexa recognized this rhetoric from the many court cases revolving around gay rights. And if those decisions didn't hold, women's rights, civil rights, atheist and minority religious rights were sure to be targeted next.

"But it hasn't always been that way," Baker continued. "It's important to note the Supreme Court has never actually ruled on intelligent design. *Kitzmiller v. Dover* was a mid-level federal court case in Pennsylvania, and their ruling didn't extend to the rest of the country. What the U.S. Supreme Court *did* conclude in the 1987 *Edwards v. Aguillard* case is that teaching a variety of scientific theories about the origins of life was constitutional, as long as there was 'clear secular intent' to provide the best science education, and as long as schools did not exclude evolution.

"Fortunately, in the past few years, our current administration has appointed many federal and supreme court justices who will uphold the *religious freedoms* guaranteed in the Constitution. And with these new court appointments, we think there will be a return to the core values of our founding fathers."

Dusty asked, "Alexa Moss, how would you challenge that?"

Alexa gathered her wits. Here's where her preparation with Mona could pay off.

"Some judges do pose a real danger," she said, "but not those Mr. Baker references. The founding fathers deliberately created a wall of separation between church and state. Several other court precedents have upheld it. In 2005, a U.S. district judge ruled against the use of warning labels questioning evolution which were placed on science textbooks in Cobb County, Georgia. More relevantly, in 2000, a Minnesota district court dismissed the case of a high-school biology teacher who wanted to teach what he called 'evidence both for and against' the theory of evolution. The judge ruled that the teacher's right to free speech did *not* override his obligation to teach the state science curriculum—which is based on evolution—and that the school district was not guilty of religious discrimination in requiring him to do so. Illinois' origins of life curriculum is also based on evolutionary biology."

Bell looked nettled. He obviously hadn't expected her to know her stuff. Alexa felt a wave of new confidence.

"And how would you answer those who say evolution is just a theory?" Dusty asked.

"A scientific theory is not speculation or a guess. It's a way of explaining natural phenomena that has earned acceptance through *scientific method*. That includes, yes, a hypothesis, but also repeated and careful research, observation, experimentation, analysis, and peer review. Also the ability to make testable predictions about nature. Gravity, for example, is a scientific theory, but few people would argue with it. Intelligent design has yet to be tested and verified by scientific method."

Alexa went on to talk about the *Brassica* experiment the students were doing and to give Reynolds' example of the artificial selection the farmers in the area already used. "Most of them rely on that science—evolutionary biology—to maximize their crop yield."

Garrett Baker spoke up: "That may be so, but intelligent design, rather than evolution, could easily explain that. ID doesn't make religious claims; it's simply *alternative science*, based on evidence like irreducible complexity." He smiled. "Not to get too technical for you, Mrs. Moss ..."

"It's Ms., actually," said Alexa.

Garrett Baker smirked.

"Alternative science?" Alexa countered. "Irreducible complexity has been refuted by the scientific community. And intelligent design by definition presupposes a designer. Since that designer is not part of the natural world, it's *super*natural, and therefore ID is theological, not scientific." She posed Reynolds' question: "What kind of experiment could you do to prove the existence of a designer? What exactly would you observe and measure?"

"That's hardly the point," Bell interjected. "You as much as admitted on the video that you can't prove there's *not* a designer—that students could make up their own minds on that point. So why not just allow the teacher to say so?"

"Which designer should we talk about?" Alexa queried. "And how do we explain the process? Every religion or culture has its own creation story. Do we teach them all?

To do less would be unconstitutional. There are theories that aliens brought life to earth, built the pyramids. Would we also be required to teach those?"

"Certainly not!" Cyrus answered. "That's nonsense and everyone knows it. There is biblical support for intelligent design, writings that predate science books by thousands of years. The idea that life is an accident, without conscious intent or moral obligation, is the problem in this country. And I think your daughter, who's a student at Pine Bluff High School, would agree." Bell's eyes glittered with self-satisfaction. He knew that most of Ecstasy had seen Lucy's baptism photo on his show.

A white-hot anger burned through Alexa, and she alternately clenched and stretched her fingers under the desk. Deep breaths. She couldn't let him win this one, take her out using her own child as the bait.

Alexa turned and spoke to the camera. "No. My daughter and I disagree about a lot of things. Those who have teens at home will understand. However, she's a scientist who follows scientific evidence, and the evidence for evolution and the big bang are overwhelming. They're the very *fundamentals* of life on our planet."

Cyrus opened his mouth to answer, but Dusty noted, "Wow. It's been a great discussion, but we're almost out of time. If you would each please take one minute to sum up. Garrett, we'll start with you."

"Yes, thank you, Dusty. We agree that educators must keep up with science. And the *new* science points to an intelligent designer as the architect of our magnificent universe. We fully expect that ethical judges will support our reasonable and just requests, so our students can have all the information they need to make decisions, from all quarters."

"Thanks so much, Garrett, for the legal perspective," Dusty said. "We can always count on you to illuminate us. Cyrus, your remarks?"

Bell turned to the camera, employing the dulcet depths of his voice. "The problem," he said, "is the secular agenda foisted on us by big-city liberals controlling our state governments. Where in our schools are the values we cherish: God, country, family? Where is the place for the tender young girl who believes that we are created in the image of God? Is she to be denied a voice? All we ask is our religious freedom, as guaranteed by the constitution. All we ask is equal treatment. I hope you'll support us. I hope you won't allow godless outsiders to take that away from you."

"Thank you, Cyrus, for that heartfelt appeal. Alexa, as the dissenting voice, you have the final word this evening."

"Thank you, Dusty. I agree with Garrett that we must keep up with science, but not just the new science, the *true* science—science that's been subject to the methods that define the discipline. We're all entitled to our religious beliefs—or none at all—on our own time, with our own money. But public institutions supported by our tax dollars must remain neutral on these issues. True science is necessary in all the facets of life: technology, manufacturing, farming, health care, to name a few. It is imperative that our children are scientifically literate, not just when they're in school, but throughout their lives, to meet the challenges of this planet. It's the only way to move forward into the future."

"Thank you, Alexa. And thanks to all our panel tonight. You've given us much to think about. We'll be here tomorrow: same time, same place."

Dusty lifted his hand to his forehead and gave his signature sign-off salute and catchphrase.

"And to all our viewers this evening, an American good night."

The theme music played for a moment or two before someone said, "We're out." Dusty shook their hands again and thanked them for appearing on the show. Staffers stepped in to unwire them, and quickly escorted the show's guests in opposite directions, Alexa back to the small green room to pick up her things and then to the elevator. She was out of the building in ten minutes, without seeing either Dusty Southerland or Cyrus Bell again.

Before she even got to her car, her phone began to ping: "Atta girl!" Chad texted her. "Nice job tonight," from John Jeffers. "Thank you, Alexa," Mona wrote. "We'll talk tomorrow." Heather texted, "Kudos," followed by star emojis. "Call me later." There was nothing yet, however, from Reynolds or Lucy, the two whose opinions meant the most to her.

When she got home, Lucy was up in her room and didn't come down. "Did she even watch?" she asked Rachel.

"Oh, yes, we both did." Rachel said. "She took it so seriously. She was actually pretty embarrassed at first, but I think you surprised her. She didn't like Cyrus's treatment of you, especially when he mentioned *her*. Don't tell her I said so—but in the end, I think she was rather proud." Rachel stepped toward her and hugged her. "I'm proud of you, too. It's not easy to go up against Uncle Cyrus. You were wonderful! We recorded the show."

"Thanks, Rachel, I'll watch it later. Right now I'm still really wired. I need a glass of wine and a bath."

"There's a casserole in the oven waiting for you."

"That special one of yours that I like?"

"Yes, just for you."

So Alexa sat at the kitchen island with Rachel, decompressing, eating her casserole, drinking her wine, and answering Rachel's questions about the show. Alexa couldn't help but wish that Lucy were with them. Rachel mentioned that she'd met Dusty at the ECM complex a couple of times. He and Cyrus were given to conversations behind closed doors. "I'm surprised they were as polite to you as they were."

"It did go better than I thought," Alexa admitted. Her preparation had paid off. Maybe she was learning something. Maybe she could be an effective contributor on the school board. Ha. That was probably still a long shot. She was suddenly very tired; the adrenaline of the evening had worn off.

She thanked Rachel and climbed the stairs to Lucy's attic bedroom and knocked on the door. "Can I talk to you?"

The music paused as Lucy called, "I'm doing my homework. Can't stop now." Then the music resumed.

Alexa muttered under her breath as she descended to her bedroom and gathered her pajamas and robe. She'd forgotten the heavy on-camera makeup and startled herself in the bathroom mirror. She took a selfie before scrubbing it off, a memento for a later time, when she might see the humor in it. Wrapping a towel around her hair, she settled into a bubble bath in the clawfoot tub, her back and shoulders, then her neck, relaxing at last. As she soaped herself, she thought of Reynolds— Eric, rather—and a different kind of tension mounted in her body, one heightened rather than relieved by the steaming water. She closed her eyes. It had been a long time, but she felt something reawakening, opening in her like a flower ...

Her reverie was disturbed by an insistent knocking on the bathroom door.

"Mom? Mom?"

Alexa sighed and opened her eyes again to the white-tiled bathroom. *Now* Lucy wanted to talk?

"Mom? I think you'd better come and see this."

"What?" It was hard to keep the irritation out of her voice.

"Just come. Now."

Lucy's tone had her out of the bath and dried off in thirty seconds. She donned her pajamas, terry-cloth robe, and slippers, and met her daughter in the hallway. Her cell phone began to vibrate and ping in her pocket.

Lucy simply beckoned to follow her down the stairs. In the living room, the nine o'clock news was airing and an image of herself flashed across the screen. Rachel stood before it, biting one knuckle. Lucy ran it back from the beginning.

All the stress returned as Alexa sat on the sofa and unwound the towel from her hair. What could this be now? How could there be more? Her phone was vibrating constantly in her pocket. She had texts from Heather and Mona with links to the news. She silenced it and concentrated on the TV.

"Earlier this evening, on *Southerland Tonight* ..." One of the interchangeable blond reporters on WXT ran video from Dusty's show. Of course they showed Bell's final plea, out of context, but other than Alexa's overdone makeup, which made her—let's face it—look tawdry, there was nothing to be that upset about. She glanced quizzically at Lucy, who gestured back to the screen. The program cut to an interview with Cyrus Bell in the parking lot of ECM. He was just getting out of his car. Aaron Whitman was with him.

"Pastor, what do you think of the Zaleski tweet?" the reporter asked.

Cyrus smirked into the camera, drawing himself up to his full height.

"Horrified, but not surprised. This is what happens when we allow outsiders and atheists into our community. We get a school-board nominee who not only doesn't believe in God, *but takes the life of her own children.* Now she moves here and wants to keep the facts of God's glory out of our schools. We have evil in our midst, make no mistake."

"What?" Alexa was on her feet, yelling at the TV. "What the hell is he talking about?" She looked at Lucy, then at Rachel. Neither one would meet her eye. "What's happening?"

The program moved back to the reporter and the screen beside her. "In case you're just joining us, Pastor Bell is reacting to this tweet tonight from an old acquaintance of Moss's."

The screen held a giant shot of someone's Twitter account.

> Caught Alexa Moss on the Southerland show. Dont buy her bull****, dont let her tell you what to do with your kids. Knew her in Chicago in the aughts. Stuck up selfish single mom ...

I used to watch her kid. She got pregnant with another one she didn't want so she got rid of it, fired me because I knew. Not a good person please beware. #alexamoss #ecstasyschoolboard #pinebluffbadapple #southerlandtonight

Alexa gasped. She looked at the twitter handle, @chitownmZaleski, and then at the picture. Older, but recognizable: Michelle Zaleski. Alexa sat down again on the sofa. It was too much, this. She squeezed her eyes closed.

She could barely hear Rachel's voice over the pounding in her ears. "Alexa, are you okay?"

Then Lucy's. "Mom? Mom, is that true? What is this all about?"

Rachel put a cushion behind her head. "Alexa? Alexa?"

Reluctantly, she opened her eyes and looked at the girls. "I'm fine," she said.

"Mom, who is this woman?"

Alexa was exhausted. She understood that her candidacy was over. Every limb ached, yet it was time to climb this mountain of rubble and see what could be salvaged. She sat up straight and tried to compose herself.

"I guess I owe you an explanation," she told them. The girls sat down on the sofa, attentive.

"Lucy, there are some things I never told you."

"Obviously." Lucy shot her a look, arms crossed.

"As you know, your father and I divorced when you were a toddler. I told you he went to Eastern Europe to do charity work, but that wasn't exactly the case. The truth is, after I worked to put him through medical school, he fell in love with somebody else and left me. They were caught performing procedures that were unethical, maybe illegal, and decided to leave the country to avoid the consequences. They probably went to Belarus, where she'd been raised.

"You were about four years old at the time. He stopped contacting us—I assume, so he couldn't be found. Also, he said he loved you, and it's possible he felt some remorse for bringing shame on you."

Lucy looked stunned. "Why didn't you tell me before? Don't I deserve that?"

"I knew you had no real memories of him, and I didn't want to fill in the blanks with bad ones."

"But what about the baby? What happened to it?" Lucy's tone was frightened but accusatory.

"There wasn't a baby; that was the point."

"But this woman, this Zaleski person—"

"Between the time your father left me and when he moved out of the country, he used to see you. He would show up unexpectedly, bring you big presents, and throw some cash at me. I was still in love with him, after everything. I know that was stupid. One night, they'd had an argument, he and this woman. He came to our place and told me he'd made a big mistake to leave us, that he wanted to give things a second chance. To make a long story short, we slept together."

Lucy groaned. "You mean the baby was his? I could've had a brother or sister?"

"Please let me finish," Alexa said quietly. "He stayed the night. The next morning, we had an early breakfast and talked about plans for the future. He said he would go to get his things and move back into our apartment. He was supposed to call me at 1:00 to let me know when to expect him. I was thrilled at the thought of getting back together. One o'clock rolled around, and I hadn't heard from him, then two o'clock. I ended up calling him about three. To his credit, he picked up the phone. I knew right away from his voice that something was wrong.

"He told me that they'd reconciled. He cared about me, about you, he said, but he was in love with her. The night before had been a mistake on his part. He suggested I think of it as our last goodbye. He promised to send us money and then hung up. I can't tell you what that did to me. You seemed to sense it, and you crawled into my lap, took my face in your hands, and kissed my cheeks. I still remember that moment."

Rachel was crying openly now.

"So that Zaleski person was his girlfriend?"

"No, that was your babysitter."

Lucy looked confused.

"After we originally split up, I worked part time and went back to school for my degree. Michelle Zaleski lived across the hall from us. She was also a single mother. I thought of her as a friend at the time. She had a daughter a year older than you, and she took in kids to babysit. You seemed to love her."

"Okay, but what does she have to do with this?"

"Despite my despair that afternoon, I was thinking clearly enough about one thing. We hadn't used protection when we were together the night before. It was unlikely I would get pregnant, given the time in my cycle, but I couldn't risk having another child. I was already short on time with you, and money. Fortunately, in Illinois, the morning-after pill was available. I was lucky—in another state I wouldn't have had that option. I desperately needed to find a pharmacy where I could get it, before they all closed at 6:00.

"Michelle was home; I told her what had happened and begged her to look after you for a couple of hours. She agreed.

"I got the prescription. No one but Michelle ever knew about it. The odds are that I would not have conceived; the pill was just extra insurance. I didn't end a pregnancy; I prevented one. And I'm glad I did. That was the last time I ever saw your dad."

Lucy was digesting this. So many emotions crossed her face that Alexa could not keep up. She finally asked, "If Michelle was your friend, why would she do this to you?"

"When I picked you up after work one day," Alexa answered, "you had a bruise on your cheek. Michelle claimed you'd fallen, but when we got home, you told me that she hit you and started to cry. You didn't want to go back to her. Although I couldn't prove anything, I pulled you from her care. Another parent came to see me; her son had had marks and bruises too. And then, it turned out, there was a third child. One of those parents called Child Protective Services, and Michelle ended up losing her childcare license and her business. She blamed us all. I heard she went back to her hometown, which isn't far from here, actually. That might explain—"

They were interrupted by lights in the driveway, then footsteps on the porch. The doorbell rang insistently and there was pounding on the door. The new alarm system started beeping, then went off. Rachel moved to the control box, trying to silence it. Before Alexa could stop her, Lucy had opened the front door. They were blinded by bright lights and could barely see past the microphones shoved in their faces. Alexa moved in front of the girls to shield them.

"Alexa, Alexa!" Her name came at her from every direction. Flashes went off like fireworks. Questions flew.

"Did you really do it?" "What does your family think of this?" "How will this affect your chances for election?"

Alexa tried to stay calm. She shouldn't talk to the press under these circumstances. What would the ever-composed Mona Bauer do?

Rachel finally silenced the alarm. Alexa stepped out on the porch and pulled the door closed behind her. Tightening her belt, she stood before the media in her bathrobe, her damp, tangled hair spilling over her shoulders. She could see the WXT reporter Ashley Hale front and center, with a snarky smile on her face.

Alexa straightened her posture and lifted her chin. When she cleared her throat, they fell silent.

"This development has come as a surprise to me." She worked to keep her voice level and firm. "I will not address Ms. Zaleski's allegations this evening, except to say they're completely untrue. It's late," she said, and gave them a small appreciative smile. "I will make a full statement to the press in the next few days. Until then, I have nothing more to say."

She reentered the house and shut the door on their protests, hoping they'd go away. After shouting questions to the closed door, some of them dispersed, but not before they did live shots for their networks in front of the house. The rest moved their vans out to the road to camp there with their crews. Alexa knew they would be there until morning.

Lucy was peeking out through the blinds, fascinated but trembling. Too much excitement for one day. For all of them. Alexa coaxed her away from the window, suggesting she join Rachel in the kitchen for a piece of her pie.

"I have some calls to make," she told her daughter

Lucy followed Rachel toward the back of the house.

Alexa turned on the TV and saw promos of herself for the ten o'clock news. They sure hadn't wasted any time. She picked up her cell phone and dialed John Jeffers, who answered on the first ring.

"Alexa, hi. I was just watching."

"John, I really need your help."

"Yes, I think you do."

Alexa explained what had happened and the history behind it. "Do I have any legal options?"

"Media's not my area, but I have some connections. Let me see what I can do." He told her he'd call her later.

She texted Mona, letting her know the developments, including what had just transpired at her front door. Mona was disgusted, but not surprised.

"You were set up," she told Alexa. "They've obviously had Zaleski in their pocket for some time. Your strong performance tonight is why they sprang this now. Let's watch the ten o'clock news, and then we'll talk."

The story led the local news on all the channels but got the royal treatment on WXT. Alexa was brought to a boil by Ashley Hale's smug footage in her front yard. The coverage was exactly what Alexa had recently come to expect. Except for one thing. As she stood on her front porch facing the press, she'd forgotten she wasn't wearing any makeup. On the video, under that uber lighting, her flame-shaped birthmark stood out in sharp relief on her pale face.

Damn. Another bit of herself to explain, to be picked apart by people who didn't know her. Her candidacy was finished.

She expressed as much to Mona when she called.

"Maybe," Mona told her. "Only the wackos will care about the birthmark. And anything about abortion, true or not, will outrage some of them. Those people never fail to obsess over what others do with their bodies. But they're the ones who wouldn't have voted for you anyway."

"I'll withdraw, Mona. Someone else can take my place."

"Too late for that. I know a PR person in another humanist group. I'll give him a call. He can advise you on which parts of your story to tell, and how."

"Oh. Well—"

"Also, a heads up," Mona continued. "WXT just announced that they'll be taking a poll of the voters, something they've never done for a school-board election. It's strategic on their part. We'll have to see where that leaves us. You've really stirred them up; they're afraid of you."

"I have to say that feeling's mutual."

"I don't blame you. I'm sorry it's come to this, Alexa. Try to get some sleep. Big day tomorrow. I'll be in touch in the morning."

Alex sighed as Mona disconnected. When she'd decided to run, she had never imagined all this. She'd filed her paperwork, spoken at the forum, appeared on TV, championed her cause, and dealt with the press; now she'd have a lawyer and a public-relations person. She meant well. She was in this for good reasons. Yet now, she must maneuver to protect herself, stand before the public, and pick and choose which truths to tell. Somewhere along the way—despite all efforts to the contrary—she'd become a politician.

She checked her messages and there were two from Eric Reynolds. He had texted earlier, probably when she was in the bath. "Impressive performance!" the first one read. In the second one his words were simpler. "Hey Alexa, I'm with you." She checked the time he sent it. 10:25. After

Zaleski, the porch appearance, and the birthmark. That was something.

She walked into the kitchen, where Lucy and Rachel were huddled over their phones, looking angry and shocked.

"You'd better sit down, Mom."

"What is it?" Things could hardly get any worse.

Rachel turned her phone to Alexa. "It started on Christian social media. Now it's on Facebook, Twitter, and Instagram."

Pictures of Alexa's face, birthmark blazing, were juxtaposed with the horrified faces of characters from *The Omen*. "Mark of the Beast?" the copy read. Others were simply labeled "The Fires of Hell."

Well, why not? For the first time in this horrible day, Alexa was tempted to laugh at the absurdity of it all. But the look on her daughter's face stopped her.

"Those assholes!" Lucy cried, and flung her phone to the kitchen table. "They made you a meme."

23

Rachel: Sunday, March 22

R achel woke to the smell of bacon and the clattering of pots in the tiny kitchen. She rolled over and stretched in the clean sheets, reveling in the luxury of the queen-sized bed and marveling again that it fit in the space.

Ben and his team had worked double time through the late winter months to finish the tiny house. They'd mostly built it in Ingersoll's barn, then moved it to the site last week, hooking up the plumbing and attaching the solar panels. The place still needed window coverings and a few homey touches, but it was attractive, snug, and functional. They had christened it several days ago with Rachel's first overnight visit, and Ben had hardly stopped smiling since. He began to whistle now as he cooked breakfast.

Rachel felt both excited and apprehensive about her day. She pulled on clean clothing from her overnight bag, used the composting toilet, and brushed her teeth in the miniscule sink, balancing her tube of toothpaste on the rim. If they were going to stay here, she'd need a medicine cabinet, or at least some shelves. She tied her hair up, made the bed, and shuffled the few short feet from the bedroom to the tiny living area.

Ben had laid the small table with a fringed blue cloth and some colorful Fiesta dishes they'd picked up at a flea market. An earthenware vase held three yellow tulips, enhancing the cheerful still-life quality. Ben seated her, kissed the top of her head, then served her scrambled eggs, bacon, and his specialty, biscuits and gravy.

She was too nervous to be hungry, but she couldn't deny him the satisfaction of seeing her eat what he'd cooked. She eyed him across the table as she dug in. "I can feel the pounds piling on as I lift my fork."

"That won't hurt you any," he told her. "Sandy's been runnin' you off your feet at that diner."

"I'm glad I'm one of the few she kept for the pick-up window." She knew how fortunate she was, since the governor had been forced to close bars and restaurants to eat-in patrons, as well as schools and non-essential businesses. So many had lost their jobs already, and this was only the first full day of lockdown, or "shelter in place," in Illinois.

"And besides," Ben added, "we'll need the extra energy today. No tellin' what time it'll be when we eat again."

After the meal, Rachel stepped out on the deck to smoke. Even the nicotine failed to calm her completely. It was too early for vodka, and besides, she needed to give that up, starting now. The early morning sun began to warm the air as it streamed over the bluffs to the greening fields and forests below. Birds twittered in the trees; spring had arrived. Strange how beautiful—and now deadly—the natural world could be. The universe looked exactly the same, but so much had changed in the space of a couple of weeks.

She enjoyed the view for about a minute before her worries kicked in. They had nothing but their wits to pull this off, and she couldn't even think about failing.

Back inside, she hung her jacket on a peg next to Ben's and hugged him from behind as he scrubbed the skillet in the sink. She felt the hard leanness of this body, his heat warming her through. She kissed his neck and breathed in his subtle woodsy scent, which had come to be the elixir of her world.

"This is a beautiful place. I'm so grateful."

"Anything for *you*, darlin'."

It was true. She knew that now.

They turned on the radio and washed and dried the dishes. Today's topic was the effectiveness of the drug hydroxychloroquine, which the president had recommended, part of the "tremendous control" he claimed to have over the virus.

There were cases all over the country now. The locals claimed that the virus was an urban thing—as if those New Yorkers, those Chicagoans, deserved it—and they doubted they would ever see it here in their hometown. But Rachel had noticed Lucy glued to the national news, spending hours on the internet listening to the scientists. Like birds that sense bad weather, Lucy seemed to know what was coming.

Since January, when Rachel saw Phoebe's videos, she'd been determined to free her. Then Phoebe could file for medical emancipation, and Rachel could become her guardian. Rachel thought about it constantly, playing out various scenarios in her mind.

Ben was not so sure about the idea. "Darlin'," he said, "I know you're concerned about Phoebe, but I'm guessin' that John Jeffers is right. Legally, you probably have no options."

It didn't matter. She couldn't allow her sister to suffer, to be exploited. "I don't have a choice, Ben. She needs me."

They'd argued for weeks about it—their only disagreement. At one point, the two of them didn't speak for several days after Ben called Rachel's focus on the topic "obsessive."

"How could you say that?" she asked him, when they finally reconnected one late evening on the phone. She'd had more than a few vodkas and struggled to keep her voice low so she wouldn't disturb Lucy and Alexa. "Since when is loving someone, caring about them, too much?"

Ben sighed. "When it sucks the pleasure, the purpose, from the rest of your life, even though you can't do anything about it. I know you love your sister, but—"

"Do you, though?" Her tone was sarcastic, her words slightly slurred.

"What do you mean?"

"I thought you knew how it felt to lose your family. But *your* sister and brother are reaching out, and you're refusing to talk with them. I don't think you understand at all. I don't think we're really anything alike."

"Darlin', I'll excuse that, this time, because you've been drinking. We *are* alike. I can't tell you what to do about Phoebe, but I suggest you think about it carefully, soberly. The alcohol isn't helping this situation."

He was right about that, yet her pain required some relief. She stopped talking to Ben about Phoebe, but she thought about her, worried about her, more than ever.

Rachel was concerned when the World Health Organization declared a pandemic. But it was the announcement, a week ago, that the virus had reached several neighboring counties, that finally made up her mind. Busloads of worshippers traveled to ECM from those counties.

Coronavirus, or Covid-19 more specifically, was marked by fever, coughing, and shortness of breath. Fevers were Phoebe's nemesis. High fevers made her hallucinate, seize more severely and more often. During a seizure she often stopped breathing, even without a temperature.

Rachel knew her family. They would not wear masks or take other precautions. They wouldn't move Phoebe if family members caught the virus, or take her to a doctor if she contracted it, no matter how sick she became. None of them would get the vaccine when there was one.

Rachel had to get her sister. Now.

"Please help me, Ben," she'd begged him one night, crying. "Phoebe's life may be at stake." And then, when he hesitated, she added, "I'm going to figure out a way, whether you're with me or not."

Despite his reservations, Ben had finally agreed. "Whatever you're going to do, Rachel, I don't want you to do it alone."

But where would they go? How would she support her sister? She had passed her GED, as expected, but how far would a high school diploma get her? They were on the sofa at Alexa's one evening, Rachel's legs draped over Ben's, when he'd offered her the use of the tiny house.

"I can continue livin' with the guys for a while. Later, when Phoebe's used to things, maybe I can move in. At least it'll get you started—give you a chance to see a doctor, get her on some meds. You can figure things out from there."

"Ben, I couldn't. How would I pay you? I'm sure what I make won't be enough. And I'd hate to move out suddenly on Alexa," she said. "She and Lucy have been so good to me."

"I've been saving up for a long time, Rachel. The house is mine. There's no mortgage." He sat up straight, faced her, and took her hands. "You know how I feel about you. It was only a matter of time until I asked you to move in." His blue eyes were earnest. She trusted him. "Alexa will understand."

Rachel was overcome with emotion at Ben's generosity. With his help, this could happen. She kissed him and agreed. Now they needed a plan.

In the weeks that followed, they'd considered rescuing Phoebe from her parents' house. She was always at home—but so were the others, in the compound Cyrus had built on the outskirts of town. The place was monitored by cameras and closely guarded; the houses were on a cul-de-sac and there was one road in and out. Rachel knew Aaron and the boys had guns and were prepared, probably eager, to use them. It would have to be at the church then, the one other place that Phoebe was allowed to go.

Oddly enough, it was Cyrus himself, two nights before, who had given them an opening. In a response to the governor's shelter-in-place order, Cyrus took to the airwaves to announce that he had no plans to shutter the church. Draped in his most elegant vestments, he faced the cameras and delivered the news like a sermon.

"We will gather to praise the Lord," he intoned. "This is not a time to abandon God. He will be with us and protect us. This plague will pass over the righteous among us.

The faithful need not fear." Lenten and Holy Week events would not be cancelled. Services would be held on Sunday as usual. "We will exercise our religious freedom, despite the Illinois governor's intent."

Rachel knew Cyrus. That meant there would be media coverage in addition to the broadcast of the service. The congregation would be packed in the pews as usual, buses from other counties bringing in the faithful. Cyrus would make sure of it; he had a point to make.

That also meant that Phoebe might be overlooked. She was taken to the church each Sunday, but left to watch the service remotely from a room with a monitor. Cyrus didn't want Phoebe seizing in public, where he had no control. Especially not with the cameras around. That could work in their favor.

After talking to Caleb at Dawson's hardware, Rachel was sure her cousin was sympathetic to Phoebe's plight. Fortunately for them, he oversaw security for ECM. Rachel had called him on Saturday and begged him to let her see Phoebe at the church the next day, if only for an hour.

Caleb refused outright. "You know what you're asking."

"Please, Caleb. It's been two years. I just want to visit with her and see that she's okay." She appealed to his conscience. "You know that what they're doing to her isn't right."

Caleb hesitated. "Actually, she's been asking about you," he admitted.

"I miss her too. She needs to know I love her. All I'm asking for is an hour."

"You know how dangerous this is, what Cyrus will do if he finds out."

"I'm certainly not going to tell him, and I don't think Phoebe will."

"No. You're right." He paused, and she could sense him wrestling with his thoughts. Finally he relented. "We'll have to be careful."

Rachel gave a thumbs up to Ben, exhilarated.

"Anything you say."

"Come at ten minutes after eleven. Cyrus will be preaching by then. Use the north door, the one with the handicap ramp." He proceeded to give her the door code. "I'll put the security footage for that area on a loop. They use room 17 for her now. It's just to the right of the door, across the hall." Rachel remembered the layout of the church. "Find a way not to look like you. I'll create some distraction so she's alone. But 35 minutes is all I can give you. You have to be out again by quarter 'til."

Rachel agreed.

"I'll text you right before that all is clear. You text me when you're out."

"Okay."

He sighed. "And Rachel?"

"Yes?"

"Don't let me down." She knew what he meant, and what it could cost him in the end.

"I won't," she told him, and hung up.

She had lied. She had to. Phoebe's life might be in the balance.

Now, today, it was really happening, and Rachel was uneasy. To visit the church, even Phoebe, would impact her in ways she dreaded. And if they were caught, Phoebe was destined for more years of misery and abuse.

Ben understood her apprehension. "We'll have to get it right, then," was all he said, but he held her close.

When it was time, Rachel donned a large old coat of Ben's and tucked her hair under a wide "church hat" she'd picked up at thrift store the evening before. When she walked, slightly stooped with the cane Ben gave her, she could pass for one of ECM's senior congregants. Ben would be the son helping his mother. He had a hat of his own, and they both put medical masks in their pockets, which would further prevent recognition.

When they got to Longview Road at 10:30, cars, trucks, and buses were lined up for several blocks to get into the church parking lot. Cyrus would get his big day. Fortunately, Ben's pickup was one among many and wouldn't call attention to them. At the gate they turned right and skirted the huge complex to park near the north door. Worshippers were shepherded to the main entrance on the east side of the building, where reporters were conveniently camped to film and interview them. No one was wearing a face mask but the TV crews, so theirs would only call attention to them. They needed to stay in the truck, unobserved, until the service began. The north door was briefly opened to admit disabled attendees, then closed again.

As they waited Rachel relived her last day at ECM, and her stomach tightened with the memory: the grip on her arm, the sneering tone of the church guard as he escorted her from the property, those first moments on the street, panicked, not knowing where she would go. A familiar sorrow washed over her.

At 11:07, Caleb texted the all-clear. They made their way to the north door unchallenged, the picture of a young man escorting his mother. Ben entered the code, but the door didn't open. Rachel cast nervous glances around them as he tried again. They were exposed here, the only living beings on this side of the building. She thought they were still unobserved, but she couldn't be sure. After several heart-stopping attempts, Ben's efforts were successful, and the door swung wide. They entered a long, white hallway in ECM's north wing, their footfalls muffled by the signature purple carpet. They found room 17. The door was closed.

Rachel drew a deep breath and entered the room as quietly as possible. Inside, Phoebe sat in a wheelchair, her back to the door, watching the church service on the screen. She was alone. She was singing with the Christian rock band onstage. The Randall kid. Ben closed and locked the door behind them.

Rachel waited until the music stopped.

"Phoebe," she said softly.

Phoebe started and turned. Rachel pulled off the hat, and Phoebe's eyes went wide with recognition. "Oh! Oh!

Rachel!" With barely a glance at Ben, she rose from her chair and threw herself into Rachel's arms. She could walk. Thank goodness. She looked better than she had in the videos. Rachel immediately started to cry with relief. Phoebe cried too, and Ben was in a similar state as the young women clung to each other.

On the screen Cyrus raved about church closures. *"Under the constitution, we are guaranteed freedom of assembly."*

"Is it really you?" Phoebe said. "I've missed you so much!"

"Yes, it's me. I couldn't stay away forever."

Rachel held Phoebe at arm's length and looked at her. She'd grown three or four inches since Rachel had seen her last and was nicely dressed, with a tasteful amount of makeup, which neither of them had ever been allowed to wear before. Her long blond hair had been cut more stylishly. She was still very thin, and the dark circles under her eyes remained.

Cyrus went on: *"Food for the soul is more important than food for the body. There can be no physical health without spiritual health."*

"By the way, this is Ben."

Phoebe smiled shyly and extended her hand. "How did you get in? Do they know?" she asked Rachel. "Are you allowed to see me now?"

"No, and we don't have much time," Rachel told her, noticing Phoebe's purse on a chair. "Grab your things, I've come to take you out of here."

"Where? For how long? Can we go to a restaurant or a movie?" She looked excited, then suddenly deflated. "I have to ask them. They'll never let me go."

"Liquor stores and abortion clinics are essential businesses and we are not? I guarantee that Jesus Christ is essential!"

"Not to a store. With me. Forever. I've seen the videos. I know what they're doing to you. You can come with me; you can go to a doctor, get medicine, quit having seizures. You can live with me."

"Live with you?" Phoebe looked confused.

"Yes. We have the truck here. You can come with us now."
Phoebe sat down in one of the room's gray padded chairs and looked at her sister. Some understanding seemed to dawn in her eyes. Then she frowned. "Rachel, I can't live with you. I can't leave here."

Rachel and Ben sat too. Ben glanced at the clock on the wall. Twenty minutes left.

"What do you mean? Phoebe, there's a whole world out there," Rachel reasoned. "You can go to school, to dances, to restaurants, stores—well, after this virus is gone." Rachel had pictured it a thousand times in her head. Her little sister, healthy, having friends, graduating from high school, living a normal life. Surely Phoebe wanted that as much as she did!

"They need me here." Phoebe lifted her chin, straightened her shoulders. She suddenly looked more adult. "I'm an oracle."

"What?" Rachel brought a hand to her forehead. "Phoebe, I know what they're doing—those videos. You don't have to go along with that. In fact, it's abusive."

Phoebe pushed her blond bangs out of her eyes. She appeared to be looking at something far away. Or something inside her. "I have a gift. A 'calling,' Uncle Cyrus says. I'm helping people. It's important."

"Honey, I understand the attraction—"

"I'm famous. I get hundreds, sometimes thousands, of views a day." Phoebe watched for Rachel's reaction. When it was not what she'd hoped, she asked her, "Why aren't you happy for me? Are you jealous?" Her voice was petulant, and she was a teen again.

And a teen didn't always know what was good for her.

"Look, things are pretty scary now with this pandemic," Rachel told her, taking another tack. "I'd like to make sure that you're safe."

"I'm fine. The Lord will protect me."

"God has seen fit to visit this plague on the cities, not on us. Render unto Caesar the things that are Caesar's. We cannot live by the dictates of the secular world."

Rachel stood. "Come on," she urged Phoebe, desperate, her eyes on the clock. She caught Phoebe's wrist and pulled her up. "I love you. This is your chance. Please take it," she pleaded.

Phoebe squirmed away and took several steps back. "I loved you too, but you're disfellowshipped."

Phoebe turned her eyes to the screen. Cyrus, in his purple robes, was stabbing the air with his finger. *"The first commandment is to love the Lord. He will not abandon the faithful; we must not abandon him."*

"Phoebe, please."

Phoebe refocused on Rachel and narrowed her eyes. "They told me you were a heathen now, but I didn't think it was true." Then she reached for a cord around her neck, pulled out a medical alert device, and pressed the button.

The Christian band began to play again.

Ben put his hands on Rachel's shoulders. "We have to leave now." He urgently tried to ease her away from her sister. But Rachel continued to plead as Ben tried to guide her toward the door.

"Rachel, she's not coming with us; we have to go."

The doorknob rattled, and someone was knocking. "Phoebe, are you all right in there?"

Ben and Rachel exchanged looks. They were trapped.

"Caleb, where's the key?" It was Aaron's voice.

A moment later they unlocked the door. Aaron's face lit up with a cold smile when he saw them.

"Well, well."

Caleb entered the room behind him, and moved to Phoebe's side, his face composed. Ben and Rachel glanced at him, then ignored him, careful not to let on he'd been involved.

"They tried to take me," Phoebe reported. "But I wouldn't go with them."

"Good girl." Aaron turned to Rachel and gestured toward Ben. "And who the hell is this?"

Caleb identified Ben as a local carpenter. Rachel kept silent and refused to meet Aaron's eyes. The church guards arrived, guns drawn, talking on their radios. To Rachel's sorrow, Phoebe was taken away down the hall in her wheelchair, and Rachel and Ben were marched in the opposite direction to Cyrus's outer office.

"Keep them here until Pastor Bell gets back," Aaron told the guards, and disappeared.

They sat in pearl-gray chairs, across from the mahogany desk of Cyrus's secretary. The room brought back memories: all the times Rachel had waited here anxiously, summoned by her uncle for minor offenses.

The door opened and two guards came in with Cyrus and his lawyer, Topher Kent. One of the guards was unfamiliar to Phoebe, middle-aged with reddish hair and mustache and a bulbous nose. The younger, taller, leaner one was clean-shaven, with a head of tight blond curls—Mick Gandy. Rachel recognized him as the son of Griff Gandy, the Ecstasy police chief, who fished and played golf with Cyrus Bell. They barely glanced at Ben and Rachel as they went through to Cyrus's inner office and shut the door. A low rumble of voices came from the room, but the words were indistinct. Ben and Rachel were offered water and allowed to use the restroom with a guard outside the door, but that was all.

Forty-five minutes later, the two security guards emerged from Cyrus's office. "We're going to ask you two some questions," one told them, and they ushered Ben and Rachel into a windowless conference room across the hall. Bell's lawyer Kent entered a few minutes later with Aaron. Aaron, as usual, wore a custom-tailored suit and his expensive two-tone wingtips. Cyrus himself was absent; he was probably still talking with the press. Caleb brought them coffee and pastries and left again. They accepted the coffee but passed on the treats.

"You can't hold us," Ben said to them. "It's not legal. You're not the police."

Gandy scowled. "It's just a friendly conversation. No need for the police just yet." Rachel guessed the chief was already informed, but Cyrus didn't want cruisers in the parking lot while the TV cameras were rolling.

The red-headed guard introduced himself as Patrick Ferrell. "Now then," he began, as he finished a cruller. He licked his fingers and took a large swig of coffee. Tiny bits of icing remained in his mustache. "What brings you here today? And let's have the truth—we know you weren't worshipping."

Rachel had a lot to say about Phoebe's illness, about her restricted life, the video, the virus. But now she thought better of it. She would find the appropriate outlet later: DCFS, the courts, the press—whatever worked.

"Cat got your tongue?" Ferrell asked her. "Well, at least one sister is talking. Phoebe says you tried to take her from the building. Since she's underage, technically that's attempted kidnapping."

Rachel's stomach dropped at the thought of Phoebe's accusation. "Kidnapping?" she said sadly. "We didn't force her to do anything. We only talked to her. You're the ones holding her prisoner."

"And yet," the guard continued, "she claims you grabbed her by the wrist and wouldn't let her go. And this guy," he pointed to Ben, "locked the door and stood in front of it so she couldn't exit the room." Cyrus's lawyer sat quietly taking notes.

Rachel reflexively jumped to Ben's defense. "No. That wasn't what happened. I mean, technically he was between my sister and the door, but—"

Aaron gave the lawyer a smile and glanced up at the security camera in the corner. Rachel followed his gaze. They were being recorded.

"Rachel," Ben interrupted, "we need to talk to our lawyer."

"Yes, you're right." She had already, stupidly, said too much.

"You can do that at the station if you choose," the curly-headed Gandy announced. "Right now, we need some answers."

They remained silent as the guards continued to question them. How did they get past security? What had they planned to do with Phoebe? Charges would be pressed if they didn't speak. Rachel looked at Ben, who appeared relaxed, but under the table his knee was pumping. After fifteen minutes more of this, security guards entered the room and drew Ferrell out into the hall. When he came back, John Jeffers was with him. Rachel almost wept with relief.

"They texted him," Ferrell told Gandy.

It must have been Ben, when they went to the bathroom.

"Figures. Their guards should have taken their phones. We'll deal with them later."

John Jeffers was acquainted with Bell's attorney. "Topher, I'll need a few minutes with my clients." He motioned to the security camera. "Privately."

They were moved yet again, this time to a small, unmonitored file room nearby. John asked them what had happened, and how, and wrote it down without comment. Rachel could read disapproval, exasperation in his lined face, but he treated them both with compassion and respect. Rachel told him everything, including her conversation with Phoebe, her fears for her sister's health during the pandemic, and her outrage at the videos, which John had already seen.

"Rachel, I cautioned you," he told her, shaking his head. "But let's see what we can do now."

Topher Kent was called in, and Ben and Rachel were asked to return to the conference room. There were sandwiches now; they still had no appetites, but refreshed their coffees while the two lawyers hashed things out. Rachel was trembling and Ben held her hand to calm her. She wondered if they were going to jail. Maybe she deserved it, but Ben surely didn't; she was truly sorry she'd gotten him involved. After what seemed like hours, a guard came to summon them back to the small room. John Jeffers was there alone.

"We've reached an agreement, if all the parties accept." Ben and Rachel stood and listened. "It doesn't look good for you. You were already banned from the property,

Rachel. They don't have video of you entering the church or talking to Phoebe, until she summoned them with the medic device. Then the camera started working again."

Caleb. He must have taken it off the loop at that point. John looked at them quizzically. "They can't figure out how you did that." They didn't answer.

John shrugged and continued. "They do have footage from that point, of Ben between Phoebe and the door. The door was clearly locked when they arrived. In addition," his gaze softened as he looked at Rachel, "your parents are willing to press charges, and Phoebe herself is willing to testify that you restrained her."

Rachel's ears began to ring. Ben leaned against a filing cabinet and rubbed his neck.

"Now, it may not get very far in the courts. You were distraught and feared for her safety, and you didn't force her out of the building. But even if a judge throws it out, there will be an arrest, a booking, and an arraignment. And," he sighed, "Bell knows quite a few judges in this district; I can't tell you which one you'll get, or what the outcome could be. An attempted kidnapping is a class 3 or 4 felony, with a sentence of 18 to 36 months. And the man has media connections. He's stirred up a lot of people today. Public opinion will go against you."

"I don't care what happens to me," Rachel countered. "I'm worried about Phoebe's *life*."

"I know," John told her.

"So where does that leave us?" Ben asked.

"They've agreed not to press charges if you sign a nondisclosure agreement, forbidding either one of you to speak publicly about Phoebe, the church, or the videos. The latter would be a PR problem for Bell—his congregation doesn't know about those videos—but they wouldn't be ruled illegal if Phoebe has given consent.

"Also, I'm sorry," he said, looking at Rachel. "There will be an order of protection—a restraining order on Phoebe's behalf, barring both of you from approaching her, her home, and the ECM properties. That would be in place until Phoebe turns 18, at which time she herself could file again."

"What do you recommend we do?" Ben asked

The reality of losing Phoebe was hitting Rachel hard. "Do we have any choice?"

"I think you should take the offer," John told them. "I don't think you want to go up against Cyrus Bell at this moment in time. I can get the documents ready for you to sign in my office tomorrow." He looked at Rachel with sympathy. "I'm not asking you to give up, just to wait it out. Phoebe will be 18 in a year and a half, and a lot can change by then."

Rachel searched Ben's face, and he nodded. "I couldn't stand to see you go through all that, darlin'. Especially since Phoebe turned us down. It would be different if she wanted to go."

Rachel looked at the floor. She knew he was right; she couldn't save someone who didn't want to be saved. She swallowed hard and agreed.

John disappeared for a few more minutes, then came back with the guards, who escorted them to their vehicles, and followed them in the ECM cars, all the way out to the road. As they traveled back to the bluffs, Rachel was silent, tears sliding down her cheeks and chin as she stared out the windows at the waning light. They'd been held all afternoon and into the evening. Sunrise, sunset. Hope and heartache. A half a turn of the world in between. Ben tried to comfort her, and then in the awkward silence, turned on the radio. As he changed the channel, Cyrus Bell's voice rang out from the evening news.

" ... a great day here at Sky Cathedral, and many more to come. This is the house the Lord has built, and his children must always be welcome."

24

Lucy: Wednesday, March 25

Lucy peeled the stiff, yellowed tape from a carton marked "photographs." An interesting old-paper smell wafted into the room.

"I hope they're in good shape," Alexa said as she pulled a handful from the box.

The photos were bundled and tied with ribbons of various colors, with stacks of old-time postcards and letters as well. Sheltering in place on a Wednesday morning had motivated Alexa to explore the attic. There were boxes of Margaret's they hadn't found time to open. She'd dragged them down to the dining room table and invited Lucy to join her.

Lucy supposed it was better than nothing. They'd been stuck inside for ten days already. Her classes had moved online, but most of her teachers had limited technical expertise, so connections were still random and chaotic. This was the time she'd normally have gym, but the school hadn't worked out a plan for that as yet. She wasn't due to log on again until after lunch.

Two weeks ago, they were all in class, looking forward to the end of the school year: parties, plays, concerts, sports, and graduation for the seniors. Now there was nothing. She couldn't see her friends. They were texting and video chatting, but even that, like the empty streets, was kind of spooky and weird. Her friends back in Elm Ridge felt the same. They'd called Lucy more this last week than all the other months combined. All the schools in Illinois were closed until the end of March.

But that, in all probability, was only the beginning. She knew enough about microbiology to doubt they'd be back in school by the end of the month. She was watching the experts—the virologists, the epidemiologists—and the experts were saying things did not look good. She believed them, and the numbers, whether anyone else in this county did or not.

"Wow." Alexa handed a photo across the table: a handsome young man with a tall young woman, dressed in 70s-style jeans, leaning against a boxy Dodge in the drive. The picture's color had faded some, but the faces looked fresh, alive. "That's my dad—your grandfather—and Margaret. I think that was his first new car."

Lucy had only seen pictures of them when they were older, and never together. Margaret had a long, graceful neck and a beautiful smile that looked a lot like Alexa's. Her grandfather wore a patterned shirt with an enormous collar. He looked kind, though, and slightly amused.

She passed the photo back to her mother, who handed her more from that era. There were picnics, holidays, and family gatherings, and Lucy was surprised to see a younger version of her grandmother Sheila in a halter top—evidently before her holy roller days.

She noticed her mother looked better today, the lines on her forehead less prominent, her shoulders more relaxed. Alexa was used to working at home, at least for her drafting, but some of her clients had already put their projects on hold. So she, too, had more free time, especially since the school-board election had been postponed. Lucy knew Alexa was rethinking her candidacy.

She couldn't blame her. She hated the way her mother had been treated. After "the night of the living reporters," as Lucy had dubbed it, Alexa had held a press conference to address that woman Zaleski's allegations. She'd had to defend her personal life, which was so unfair. It hadn't stopped the media from calling her a godless baby-killer, and it hadn't stopped the memes. Those clueless morons were still insisting the morning-after pill induced abortions. It was bad enough for Lucy, who had to face the world at school—"spawn of Satan," they'd teased her—but was so much worse for her mom. She'd like to slap that reporter from WXT.

This lockdown, in a strange way, had been a respite from all that. Rachel had been staying at Ben's tiny house. So Lucy was quarantined with Alexa, just the two of them. So far it wasn't so bad.

She helped her mother sort the photos and memorabilia into piles; there were old report cards, diplomas, birth and wedding certificates. Old black and white portraits had notes on the back in Margaret's elegant cursive: names, dates, and places Lucy had never heard of. One photo was of a much-younger John Jeffers. "For my dear Margaret," it was inscribed, "with love, from John." She held the photo out to her mother, who smiled and shrugged. If she wanted to know about John and Margaret, she'd have to ask John herself.

A chime sounded: Jake's special ringtone. She walked to where she'd left her phone on the sideboard but declined the call. She still cared for him, but lately she'd seen sides of Jake that concerned her. He wasn't supporting Jordan in this whole no-college thing, and his sister had dubbed him "the traitor." He made fun of Lucy's science projects, calling her "my little nerd," and she was beginning to doubt that he could ever be enlightened.

And he was insisting, despite the lockdown, on playing with his band at the church. He bought what Pastor Bell was saying about the virus being some urban plague that God would not allow to reach them. She wasn't about to set foot in that place until all this was over. And now he was furious Lucy wouldn't go out with him. She'd made it clear she intended to follow the shelter-in-place order until it was lifted.

And then there was Maddie. Lucy couldn't forgive Jake for the things he'd said at school and church about

Maddie, how she'd once again "endangered the life of her child." He got that language, she was sure, from Pastor Bell. Jake didn't know she was video chatting with Maddie daily, giving her whatever support she could. Maddie felt abandoned, alone, and fearful of having a baby in a pandemic, but she knew now she was better off without David. She had filed for a separation more than a week ago. Strange how things turned out. Maddie wasn't the only one sequestered at home with her parents; now they all were.

Her mother handed her one more picture, this one a color school portrait from the 80s. The little girl was eight or nine, with large gray eyes and a ponytail pulled to one side. In the middle of her left cheek was a deep red, flame-shaped birthmark. Lucy had seen very few pictures of Alexa as a child. She was overwhelmed with sympathy for this little girl, who looked as bright and curious as she herself was at that age. She smiled at her mother across the table. Alexa, surprised and pleased, beamed back at her.

At half past noon, they went to the kitchen to make a chef's salad for lunch. Lucy carried a bowl upstairs to her computer and logged on to her Zoom AP English class. Mrs. Kirchner, sitting in her plant-filled living room, adjusted her camera a dozen times and muttered mild expletives before she realized her mic was on. Embarrassed, she cleared her throat and addressed the class. Today's story for discussion, Joyce Carol Oates' 'Where Are You Going, Where Have You Been?' was an interesting one, and despite the disjointed format, Lucy lost herself in the topic for an hour. When Mrs. Kirchner signed off, Lucy had a fifteen-minute break before Bio with Dr. Reynolds.

Lucy had finally met with Dr. Reynolds in early March. He was still willing to mentor her for the national science talent search. The 2020 talent search had been postponed. They were waiting to hear how the 2021 search would fare. Lucy needed to work on a project now for that competition, for the spring of her senior year.

At 2:10, she signed in for Bio. Dr. Reynolds Zoomed from the lab, panning the camera to show them the progress of their plants and animals. Since they couldn't physically participate, he did the experiments on camera, asking them to name the steps and predict the results. They reviewed cell chemistry for their finals, also genetics, filling out Punnett squares—her favorites—to work out various crosses.

When her science class was over, Lucy often went out to her canning-shed lab and recreated the work. She was also learning to film some simple experiments for YouTube. Her idea was to reach grade-school and middle-school science students who didn't have access to labs or equipment right now. She focused on procedures that could be done with common household objects and products. The experiments were the easy part; the video production, she'd found, was harder to get right.

But today, as soon as Reynolds logged off, Jordan Skyped her. She was wailing again; this seemed to be Jordan's default mode in the last few weeks.

"Oh my God, they've canceled prom," she sputtered.

"What?" The dance was scheduled for late April, and Jake had already asked her. "Are you sure?"

"Yeah, you can check for yourself on the Pine Bluff homepage. They just announced it."

"Maybe they just postponed it," Lucy offered.

"It says cancelled. But it says they can revisit the issue later in the school year if things change."

Lucy threw her pen across the room, then retrieved it. She was vexed but not particularly surprised.

"Why are they doing this to us?" Jordan cried. "We don't have the virus here."

"Actually, we probably do. They have cases in neighboring counties."

"But that's not *us*. I have my dress already. Why should our senior year be ruined? What's next, graduation?"

"I'm sure they'll let you graduate."

"Well, I'm starting to wonder. No prom, no graduation, no college ... Arhhhh!" Jordan growled. She pouted, then suddenly brightened. "Wait. If the school won't hold prom, maybe we can do it at the church. They haven't closed."

"I'm not sure that would be a good idea."

Jordan frowned again. "Well, I'm going to ask them. This isn't fair."

"Yeah." Lucy thought about her science competitions. "There's a lot that isn't fair lately."

She spent fifteen more minutes calming Jordan, then went out to the yard and planned her garden for the rest of the afternoon. She was learning that sometimes solitude was a good thing.

Alexa and Lucy had just settled in after dinner with a Netflix movie when Jake called her again. When she didn't pick up, he texted "Emergency." She excused herself and went to her room.

"need ur help js in meltdown"

Jordan. Lucy sighed.

"k will call her," she texted back.

"we need u here"

"cant come there"

"tell ur mom ur going to walmart meet u in the parking lot"

"when"

Lucy looked at her watch: it was 7:15.

"7:30 see u then"

They could socially distance in the parking lot, have conversations from their cars, but still ... "not without masks," she texted him.

There was a long pause. "thats nuts but ok b there"

Lucy gave a thumbs up and went down to Alexa. Thank goodness she'd gotten her license in February.

"Someone just called and reminded me: I need some things for school. Can I take the car and go to Walmart?"

"I can go with you if you like. I could stand getting out of the house."

"No, Mom, it's okay; you watch the movie. I'll be back in a little while."

"Okay, but you haven't driven alone much at night. Be careful."

"I will."

On her way out, Lucy stopped in her lab to get face masks. She'd sent her N95s to a local ER, but she still had a stack of disposables for her experiments. She put one on. Her small cross-body shoulder bag was big enough for several others and some Clorox wipes in a baggie. She knew this would probably be the drill until there was a vaccine.

She'd traveled a quarter mile from her house when she stopped at a stop sign and was startled by a man's figure in her high-beams. Her heart skipped hard, and she quickly reached for her cell phone.

But it was Jake. He motioned for her to roll down her window.

"Hey," he said. "I'm right over there," pointing forward and to the right.

Now she saw his car, which was parked on the shoulder on the other side of the crossroad. She pulled Olive in behind him and cut her engine.

Jake opened both his front car doors and slid into the driver's seat. "C'mon, get in," he told her. She handed him a mask through the window and refused to enter the car until he put it on. As they traveled, he turned east, then north, away from Walmart and his house.

"Where are we going?"

"You'll see."

They drove out of town, encountering almost no one on the road. It was an eerie feeling. This time of year the evenings were still pitch black in the countryside. After several miles, she saw lines of cars on both sides of the road, and Jake pulled over.

"Where are we?" Longview Road was dark except for the early moon reflected on the windshields. She could hear loud music nearby.

"Don't worry, Jordan's here," Jake told her.

They got out of the car and walked on the shoulder to a gravel drive. A sign there, unlit now, said "Jensen's."

This was Sam's house. Her mom had a nursery on the property and a stand on the road where she sold plants and produce. The music was louder as they approached the house.

A party. Lucy stopped twenty feet from the building. "What's happening?"

"They cancelled our prom, so we're having our own. C'mon." He grabbed her arm, but she didn't move. She actually dug her feet into the gravel.

"This is crazy," she said. "We're on lockdown. Why would Sam's parents let her have a party?"

"They're out of town this week. Lucky us!"

"I thought this was about Jordan. You lied to me?"

"No, it is. She's here. I told you."

"Jake, you need to take me back."

"I'm not gonna do that, Lucy." She glared at him. "Okay, stay for a little while," he said. "Just fifteen minutes."

Lucy still refused to move, so Jake called Jordan, who came to the front door and walked unsteadily toward them down the drive. She threw her arms around Lucy and whispered in her ear, her breath reeking of alcohol.

"I'm so glad you're here. Brad's here, but he won't pay attention to me, the bastard. Please come party with me. You're the only real friend I have left."

"No, Jordan, that's not true." She turned to Jake. "Let's take her home."

But Jordan shook her head vehemently, and Jake crossed his arms. Lucy was miles from anything, without a way home, unless she convinced someone else to give her a ride. Or called her mother—but if she did that, everyone here would be busted.

"Fifteen minutes," she said to Jake, and allowed Jordan to walk her up the gravel drive to the house. Before she entered, she texted Alexa.

"Ran into Jordan. Talking with her. Wearing a mask. Will be a while, don't worry."

Then she stepped across the threshold. Jake ditched his mask at the door and motioned for Lucy to do the same.

"No way," she told him.

"Hey, everybody, Lucy's here," Jordan shouted, and the crowd turned to her. On seeing the mask, they were silent for a moment. Jake shrugged and rolled his eyes, and taking their cue from him, they raised their drinks to her, then carried on.

There must have been seventy or eighty people; every room was packed with bodies talking, laughing, dancing, making out. The music was too loud to talk over, and already the place smelled heavily of beer and sweat, with an undertone of vomit. Jordan took her arm and they shouldered through to the kitchen, where the booze was laid out on the island, the beer and wine in coolers near the door.

"Where's Sam?" Lucy shouted in Jordan's ear, as Jordan poured her a red plastic cup of Everclear and fruit punch. She hadn't imagined Sam would go for this.

"Don't know, actually. Haven't seen her."

Fortified, they worked their way back through the partying crowd, holding their drinks aloft. Several students ribbed her about her mask.

"Hey, gonna rob a bank?"

"Hiding your mark of the beast?"

Lucy ignored the comments as she and Jordan moved through the first floor. She'd been here before, with Sam and Logan, working on a bio project. She'd admired the old-fashioned farmhouse: the gray-green walls with wide white woodwork, the tall white fireplace mantel, the graceful stairway, the colorful artwork and décor in every room. But tonight all that was hidden by cups and bottles and bodies. The carpets were a sticky mess, like every other surface in the place. Where the hell was Sam?

Jake was in a corner of the living room, surrounded by the popular girls, who were laughing and flirting, pawing at him, Sophia first among them. Someone had brought him a drink already. Brad, in a corner, played the big man returned from college. A cheerleader danced for him as he watched, her drink sloshing out of her red cup as she moved. Jordan headed toward him, stumbling several times. David appeared at her elbow, and Jordan shook him off. David looked mortified.

Lucy turned away, sickened. Everything she'd come to be sure of in this place was falling apart. Glancing back, she saw David on the window seat in the dining room, his mouth twisted, one hand raking through his short, red hair. He drained his drink, and his eyes glazed over with tears. Lucy made her way back to him and sat down. He seemed glad to see her.

"Hey Lucy, have a drink with me."

Lucy took a few big swallows as David told her all his troubles, and asked about Maddie, who wasn't speaking to him. He claimed he still loved her and the baby, but he was "so messed up,"—manspeak, Lucy realized, for really scared and confused. This had to be hell for him, too. But it was probably best that he and Maddie weren't quarantined together.

When he was calmer, she excused herself to find the facilities. The powder room downstairs was full, and several people were waiting. She knew there were bathrooms upstairs, in the master bedroom and the hall. She climbed around the drunk juniors and seniors perched on the steps. The second-floor hallway was jammed with people, and the bedrooms were filled with kids in various states of intoxication and undress. She didn't see Sam or Eva in any of them. She walked into the master bedroom; the master bath door was locked. One of the seniors was knocking. "C'mon in there! Some of us have to go!"

"Yeah, yeah, in a minute," a boy called out. A girl giggled.

The bed was rumpled; more than one couple had probably hooked up here already. Lucy felt a cool breeze and stepped through the open French doors to a balcony overlooking the backyard. In the moonlight, she could make out the greenhouse in the distance, and closer, a white wood gazebo, unused this time of year. Beside it was a koi pond, rimmed in natural stone, the water rippling silver in the evening's breeze. Sam had shown it to Lucy, who'd found the fish and the setup fascinating. The fish were gone; Sam had helped her parents move them to a heated tank in the greenhouse for the winter. It was a beautiful night, warm for the season and moonlit. With the perfect person, it would have been romantic. But she didn't know any perfect people anymore.

Someone had taken her place in line for the master bath, so she headed to the guest bath down the hall. Opposite was a stairway to an attic or bedroom topped by a closed door. Three of the Bison sat on the steps. Their loud talk and raucous laughter rang out, peppered with expletives. They stopped their revelry when they saw her, looking her up and down as she entered the bathroom. Their laughter exploded again as she locked the door. When she emerged, they went silent until she moved past them.

Why would they be here when Sam was not? Something was very wrong.

She made her way back to the living room, where Jake was slow-dancing with Sophia. He dropped his arms when he saw her, looking guilty. Sophia left the room.

"Lucy, I'm sorry. It was nothing," he said in her ear.

Lucy really didn't care at the moment. "Jake, where are Sam and Eva?"

His face closed. "Dunno. I'm not their keeper." He smiled and put his arm around her. "I'm glad to see *you*, though." She wriggled free. He looked annoyed, then shrugged and turned back to his friends. "Suit yourself."

Lucy headed for the kitchen, where she saw that Logan had arrived. He was wearing a mask, but she could see the frown lines on his forehead.

"Hey, Lucy," he greeted her. "What a nightmare. Where's Sam?"

"I don't know. I'm worried," she shouted over the music. She gestured toward the back door, and he followed her out into the night, where they could talk. The moon had disappeared in the clouds and the backyard looked far less enchanting.

"I knew something was wrong," Logan said, "when I saw all the cars. Sam told me her parents were gone for a few days to pick up her sister at college. Their dorms have closed."

"Did she plan this party?"

"Not a chance. Eva was going to come over; that was all." Lucy thought about that closed door at the top of the steps. "I have a bad feeling about this." She started around the side of the house, beckoning for Logan to follow. She spotted a lighted third-floor dormer window. There were small stones in the flower bed against the house, and she bent and picked up a handful. In the dark they were different shades of gray, smooth and cold in her fingers, smelling of earth. "Logan, could you hit that window with these stones?"

"I think so."

The first few fell short, but he was able to tap a couple of panes with the next ones. Shortly afterward Sam's head popped out of the window.

"Oh, wow. I'm so glad you're here," she called down when she saw them. "We're trapped. They took away our cell phones and locked us in."

"Who?" asked Logan, visibly angry.

"The Bison," she answered. "The door opens from the outside. One of those guys has the key. You need to get the key."

"Okay," Lucy said. They'd figure something out. Distraction, confrontation ...

"Lucy," Sam called, "can you ask Jake? The two of you might be able to convince them."

"Fat chance," Logan muttered, but Lucy said, "I'll try." She didn't want to believe that Jake was a part of this.

They quickly passed back through the house to the living room, but Jake had disappeared. The party was starting to wind down, with some kids sitting along the walls, clearly wasted. Logan motioned up the stairs with his thumb and Lucy nodded. When they got to the second-floor hallway, the crowd had thinned. They passed the master bedroom, where Jordan sat on the bed talking with David. Down the hall they could see Jake's back and hear him talking to the Bison, all five of them.

"Let them go now, guys."

"Who asked you, Randall?" one of them slurred. "We're doing them a favor, aren't we? Locking them up together?" The others snickered. "Too bad we couldn't see anything through the keyhole."

"This isn't cool. I understand where you're coming from. But this won't solve the problem," Jake told them. "You can't just hold them prisoner."

"We should all go in there and show them what they're missing. Straighten them out," said another one. Lucy hoped he was joking.

"C'mon. Don't risk your scholarships. You want to play football next year, don't you?" Jake reasoned, swaying a little. "Why risk it all for a party?"

"Too late. We can't have them calling the cops. We'll let them out when we're done here."

"Hey!"

The Bison noticed Lucy and Logan and moved together to surround them. She could smell their sweat and their breaths as they closed in. One of them ripped off their masks. Jake said nothing.

"Let them out," Logan said quietly.

The biggest one punched Logan hard in the jaw. He fell to the floor and several Bison jumped on top of him. Lucy turned and ran down the stairs. As she fled through the kitchen, she realized Jake was after her. She clutched her purse tightly, pulling out her phone. He caught up with her in the back yard as she was dialing.

"No!" he yelled at her.

"I'm calling the police."

"No, you're not!" he told her. "They're my friends. They're harmless. I've known them since kindergarten."

Jake grabbed her arm and twisted it, making her release her phone. In one swift motion, he threw it into the koi pond.

Lucy faced him. "It doesn't matter. Someone else will lend me theirs." He stood between Lucy and the house, blocking her path. "Let me pass!" she shouted, as she tried to go around him.

He grabbed her arm, hard, and pulled her close to him. "Don't make me do something both of us will regret." Lucy struggled to pull away, but Jake held her tightly.

One of the Bison stumbled out into the yard. "There you are," he said. Then, taking in the situation, "Can't you control that woman?"

Jake laughed. "I've got this. She needs to learn a few things, like her mother."

Lucy scratched at Jake's face with her fingernails, drawing blood. He tightened his grip. They stared at each other, panting.

"Let her go, Jake." Jordan was on the balcony of the master bedroom, watching them.

He looked up at her. "Stay out of this, Jordan," he yelled.

Suddenly there was another voice. "911. What's your emergency?"

Jake glanced at the koi pond, confused.

Jordan held up her cell phone. The call was on speaker. "Hello," she said into it, staring straight at Jake, "I'm at the Jensen farm on Longview Road. There's an underage party here and a possible assault in progress."

"What's happening now?"

Jordan gave the details to the dispatcher.

Jake exchanged a look with his buddy, who took off. "Shit!" He dropped Lucy's arm and ran into the house, warning the crowd to get out. Lucy hurried back in, fighting the tide of people trying to leave. The Bison came barreling down the steps, elbowing people aside to get to the door. Drinks were abandoned as everyone made for the exits. Lucy climbed the stairs and found Jordan, Logan, and David, the latter two roughed up but still standing, unlocking the attic door. Sam came out, followed by Eva, who went straight for the guest bathroom.

"God," said Sam, running a shaky hand through her short hair. "What a night." She looked around her. "What did they do to the house?"

"Don't worry about that now," Lucy told her. "You're okay; that's what matters. I'm sure your parents will see it that way, too."

Sam shook her head. "I don't know ..."

"What happened?" Logan asked her. They heard sirens approaching.

"Those guys showed up at the farm stand today," Sam told them. "They must have heard me tell someone my parents were out of town. The five of them came back about 6:30, when Eva was here. They locked us in the attic, then called all their friends. They took our phones. No one could hear us yelling over the music."

Eva came out of the bathroom; Sam excused herself and went in.

Eva was visibly shaken and leaned against the wall. She turned to Lucy and Logan. "We're lucky you found us. I didn't know what they'd do to us ..." She wobbled slightly. The boys moved to her side to steady her. Sam came out of the bathroom and put her arm around Eva, who leaned against her.

They heard the cops on their megaphones, instructing the partiers. They went downstairs, where the front door was standing open, and police, in face masks and gloves, were herding students into the yard. Longview Road had been blocked by squad cars; no one was getting away. Logan went out to meet the police.

A short time later, he brought two officers, male and female, back with him. Their group was handed face masks and asked to remain in the living room. Their personal information was taken, and they explained what had happened. David gave the officers the key to the attic; the Bison had wiped it and dropped it the moment police had been called.

The female officer took the girls aside and questioned them. She suggested counseling for Sam and Eva, to process the evening's events, then called their parents. It would be up to them and the girls to decide if they wanted to press charges. Eva's mother, Jessica Lopez, arrived in fifteen minutes. Lucy recognized her from the school-board race. Mrs. Lopez invited Sam to spend the night and arranged to come back with a cleaning crew in the morning.

The Bison were loaded into squad cars. As people were released to go, Jordan and Lucy realized that Jake had left without them. Fine with her; she was done with him. She'd learned a lot in these past few months. Sometimes evil wasn't what you did; sometimes it was what you allowed.

Logan offered to take them home. The policeman shook his head.

"No, young man, that bump on your chin is swelling, and the cut above your eye might need some stiches." He looked David over as well. "I'll drive you both to the clinic where my wife works. They're open late, and they can patch you up." The boys agreed.

"I'll take the young ladies home," the policewoman told him.

Lucy looked at the vandalized house, at the battered faces of her friends, at the bruises forming on her arm, at her fingernails crusted with Jake's blood. She was suddenly more weary than she'd ever been in her life.

"If it's alright with you," she told them, "I'd like to call my mom."

25

Alexa: Saturday, April 4

The little red-haired boy pulled at his face mask and pointed to a box of animal-shaped pasta and cheese. "We need that," he told his mother. She nodded and readjusted his mask so it covered his nose. "And that, and that," he said, pointing to his favorite packaged foods on the shelves. She shook her head and made other choices. Alexa handed the mac and cheese to her, along with a small bag of rice and a box of spaghetti, then checked the starches off the woman's list.

The little boy whined and clung to his mother. "I want to go to the *real* store."

She hushed him, clearly embarrassed. "We have to do things differently today." She and her son moved on to the canned goods, and Heather, to Alexa's left, helped them to applesauce, red beans, and a jar of marinara before they crossed the aisle to the fresh produce.

"Was that the boy who wanted to be Batman?" Alexa asked Heather, remembering him from their October day in the park.

"Oh yeah, I think it was. Same little plaid shirt."

Volunteering at the food pantry wasn't new to either of the women, but shopping there was to some of their customers. So many had lost their livelihoods in the past month that the lines for the pantry went for blocks, filled with people who'd never imagined finding themselves there.

The humanists had stepped up their donated hours during the crisis. Mona Bauer was a beacon of light on the registration desk, where she and Francesca Davis helped patrons navigate the process and generated shopping lists based on each family's size and needs. Chad and Jeremy worked the other end, helping people to their cars with their groceries. Alexa helped Heather stock the shelves and serve the customers. Everett, the older sci-fi writer, and Oliver, the young acting student, now fast friends, worked to "rescue" unsold food that the grocery stores saved for the pantry.

The humanists and Methodists volunteered at the pantry together, since some of the other churches objected to working with nonbelievers. ECM people worked their own day at the pantry, Thursdays, unsullied by any heathens. The Methodists, despite their disagreements, had promised to host the pantry in their basement for the duration of the pandemic. But Heather was worried about the pantry's future.

"What will happen when the church splits?" Alexa had asked her when they were preparing to open.

"It's unclear which faction will get the building," Heather answered, as she rearranged cans and jars on the shelves, "so, unfortunately, it may not continue here."

Alexa unpacked a carton, restocked the shelves behind her with staples, and set up samples on the folding table before her.

"Holy Word Baptist has volunteered to house the pantry if we can't," Heather continued. "I hope they will. The main thing is to keep it out of ECM. You know what it'll become if they have their way."

Alexa nodded. The ECM volunteers reordered things to their liking, flouted established procedures, and patronized the shoppers. They'd been trying for years to get the pantry moved to their own church campus. The pantry director, no fan of Bell, had been fighting to keep it out of the megachurch.

Cyrus Bell had been on the news every day. With the school-board election postponed to May 5th, he took full advantage of the extra weeks to vilify Alexa. Her lower poll numbers, published and maybe fudged a bit by WXT, reflected that. But now Bell, it seemed, had bigger things on his mind. While the administration raved about the "invisible enemy" and did nothing, while stores were shuttered and the stock market tanked, while the U.S. topped the world in Covid cases, Bell thundered about the "tyranny" of the lockdown and "the end of religious freedom."

Despite spread of the virus into every county in Illinois, Bell was defying stay-at-home orders, keeping the church open and the televised services packed with worshippers. He encouraged protests against the governor's orders. The county sheriff was threatening the pastor with charges, to no avail. Palm Sunday services were scheduled for the next day. Bell still claimed that the virus would not affect the faithful. "Those right with the Lord, those pure in heart, do not need to fear this plague."

"Oh yes they do." Heather said, as they tidied their stations. "Mark said our ER is already seeing Covid cases directly linked to the church, and they're getting more every day. Ditto the hospitals in the counties near us. Amos Windows is still open and also a concern. Mark's really worried; they only have two ventilators and very few ICU beds. Like everywhere else, they're short of masks and test kits. People think it can't happen here, but it's already started. And it's not just older people. My husband Alan has seen a few cases in kids."

ECM. Thank goodness her daughter seemed to be done with that place. Lucy was angry at Bell's refusal to close the church in a pandemic. Also at his defense of those Bison boys at the party. Jake had been questioned, but hadn't been charged like the others, mostly due to Bell, who denounced Lucy's friends Sam and Eva as unwholesome elements. There had been no sense in grounding Lucy after the party; they were all grounded now.

But the thing that seemed to bug Lucy most was Bell's treatment of her mother. Alexa was touched by her outrage. Lucy had set up a table outside the food pantry and was now handing out Alexa's campaign buttons and brochures, and information on mail-in balloting. She'd taped a poster on the wall behind her—the meme of Alexa's face that had gone viral—but she'd deleted the Omen actors and changed the wording to read: "Alexa Moss: *on fire* to save your children's education." She'd had some success with it online.

For Lucy's sake, Alexa wished she cared more. At this point she just wanted the election to be over. She had little chance of winning, and what if she did? She'd be subject to scrutiny and abuse for the duration of her term. She'd had enough of preachers, reporters, and—let's face it—people in general. It was time to end this and get back to her quiet life.

Nevertheless, a number of people smiled at Alexa, promising to vote for her, as they filed through and filled their baskets. There were so many patrons today; they went through cartons and cartons of food and household products, and still, the line kept coming. The director asked the volunteers to work for a few more hours. Most agreed, not wanting to turn away anyone in need. Toward the end of their shift, an older couple came through and stopped at their station. Alexa admired the woman's bright yellow blouse and paisley mask.

"Which vegetables do you want?" the husband asked.

She stared at the selection, trying to focus. "Peas, and ... I think ... lima beans ..." Her voice trailed off and she looked unsteady. She began to sway on her feet and clutched at his arm.

"Are you okay? Are you having those pains again?"

His wife passed a hand over her forehead. "I'm not feeling so good, Harold." Then she leaned against him, and her knees seemed to buckle as she slid to the concrete floor.

Alexa was around the table in an instant. Heather was already dialing 911.

"Janice, Janice!" the man called out, distraught.

The woman was still conscious but moaning. Alexa took off her cardigan and handed it to the man, who gently lifted his wife's head and placed it beneath.

"Help is coming," Heather told them. Volunteers diverted the crowds, taking those in line back the way they'd come.

The paramedics arrived quickly, took the woman's blood pressure and pulse, and listened to her heart. "Ma'am," one of them said when he was sure she could understand, "you're having a cardiac incident. We're going to take you to the hospital."

The woman looked terrified and pawed at her husband's arm. "The virus," she managed to say.

"She won't go to the hospital," he told the paramedics. "She's had pains on and off for days, but she's scared to death to go to the ER."

"I understand," the paramedic told him, "but there's no choice if you want her to live." He put a gloved hand on the man's shoulder. "There are separate areas for the Covid patients."

Harold, resigned, agreed and they put the woman on a gurney and wheeled her out to the waiting ambulance, her husband holding her hand. "Janice, honey, they're going to take care of you."

Harold, who had no other transportation, was helped into the ambulance cab. They left the parking lot and started the siren as they reached the main road. Once they were gone, the volunteers had little time to react or to process. The people in line were brought back in; families needed to be fed. Lucy came in to help Heather and Alexa, and they worked side by side, serving as many customers as they could. At three o'clock, the last patrons went through and the doors were closed, and the three of them began to sweep up and put things away. They looked up to find Mona Bauer in the doorway, holding her phone and shaking her head.

"Bad news?" Alexa asked her, gripped by dread. "Is it about that couple?"

"No, not that," Mona told her.

They gathered around to watch the latest: reporters, in covering the long lines and the emergency call at the pantry, had caught Lucy's modified meme on camera. They loved it, or at least thought it clever enough to air on several TV stations. Cyrus Bell had wasted no time in responding.

"The atheists are the reason God has sent these plagues to get our attention: grasshoppers in Africa, murder hornets, coronavirus, sickness, floods, unrest. This is the beginning of the end times. God's children need to wake up, repent, and vanquish the godless. To do that, they must support their churches." His parishioners had recently received their government stimulus checks.

Alexa sighed and shrugged. More of the same. "I'm done responding to him, Mona. There's so much more to worry about now. I'll stay in the race, but whatever happens, happens."

"No, Mom, don't say that. You can win," Lucy told her. Alexa appreciated her enthusiasm, which was matched only by her youthful naivete.

"Alexa, you have an unusual opportunity," said Mona. "It's all about earned media and public perception now. Lucy's meme is just the type of thing that can make a difference."

"What about issues, Mona? No, I'm done with this. I have nothing more to say." She held up her hand to indicate the conversation was over. The others stayed quiet.

They finished their cleanup and headed back out to the parking lot. The last of the patrons were lined up to be helped to their cars or to buses with their groceries. The reporters were waiting and chased Alexa and Lucy to their car, firing off questions about Cyrus Bell's remarks. They ignored them, but the camera crews blocked their vehicle, making it impossible to leave. Alexa took a deep breath. She was not going to let them bait her, rattle her. Eventually they would go away. She could sit here all night if she had to.

But one reporter banged on the window, making Lucy jump and cry out.

That was it!

Like most Americans, Alexa was doing her best, but was stressed beyond measure by her country. All they asked of their leaders was decency, accountability, the truth. What they got was a 24-hour news cycle dominated by despots, both national and local, their greedy enablers blocking what the American people wanted and knew was right. It was more than exhausting, and every person she knew was "on fire" or tinder waiting to light.

Somebody had to do something. A *lot* of somebodies had to do something. But this time it was her.

Alexa got out of the car.

"Why don't you take off your mask," Ashley Hale from WXT taunted her, "and show us the ugly truth."

"Step back," Alexa told them, and when they did, she complied. She had not applied her foundation today, as she'd found it just smeared the mask. Her left cheek burned bright red in the afternoon sun.

"You want the ugly truth?" Alexa asked them. "Here's my truth: I have a birthmark; I'm a woman; I use birth control; I don't believe in a god, but don't care if you do as long as you don't force your beliefs or restrictions on anyone else. I care about science, education, health care, the environment, our community, and about other people's hardship and suffering. I care if you lose your job or get sick from a virus.

"Here's the ugly truth about Cyrus Bell: he frightens people with talk of Armageddon, encourages them to risk their health by gathering together, threatens factual education, condones bad behavior in our youth, and conspires with corporate interests to keep people working dangerous jobs in a pandemic. He opposes women's bodily rights and *anyone's* rights if they don't believe as he does. He and his church fleece people out of their hard-earned money, while demanding special privileges and not paying a cent in taxes." She restrained herself from mentioning

Phoebe, or her family's lack of schooling or medical care. "He's in league with those in power who would threaten our civil liberties and divide our people. He's symptomatic of what's wrong with this country, and those who tolerate his behavior are every bit as guilty as he is.

"Vote for me or don't," she told them, "but please quit defacing my property and harassing my family and supporters. Thank you, Pine Bluff. That's all I have to say."

The people in the parking lot cheered as she got back into her car and drove away.

26

Rachel: Sunday, April 5

Rachel packed her summer clothes in her newly purchased suitcase, along with several pairs of shoes. She stashed her toiletries and personal items in a small tote Lucy had lent her. She would miss this house, this room. The view of the orchard was beautiful now, with the fruit trees starting to bloom.

She carried her suitcase down the stairs and began to collect the dog's things in his basket. Sampson watched her, his shaggy head tilted to one side. Alexa's invitation to stay was tempting, but Rachel and Ben were essential workers, and more likely to be exposed. Why risk infecting Alexa or Lucy, who were based at home? Phoebe would not be coming, and Ben would be gone, at least for a few weeks—part of the crew refurbishing a shuttered hospital in the suburbs of Chicago. She would need a companion, and lately Sampson had more of a bond with Rachel than with Lucy. Lucy was kind to the dog but detached; Rachel thought it had something to do with his being a gift from Jake Randall. So when Lucy had insisted that Rachel take him, she didn't refuse.

Ben texted her he'd be there in an hour with the truck. They had planned a romantic evening together before he left for Cook County in the morning. Over the past weeks, Ben had nursed her through her disappointment about Phoebe. John Jeffers had kindly advised them, and they'd signed the papers. She would never get over her worry about her sister, but she was beginning to adjust to the weight of that grief. She could make a plan for the future. When Phoebe was ready, she would be ready too.

Now, while she waited, Rachel unloaded the dishwasher and cleaned the kitchen island with disinfectant. Alexa and Lucy would be home from the grocery store soon and would need a clean place to wipe down their purchases. Saying goodbye to those two was going to be hard; she had grown to love them both. They had extended their home and their hearts to her when she needed it most, and they were her family now.

Rachel turned on the TV in the breakfast nook while she worked and found Uncle Cyrus in the middle of breaking news. Palm Sunday services had let out over an hour before, but the ECM parking lot was still filled with people, yelling and protesting, barefaced, shoulder to shoulder. As the camera zoomed in, Rachel realized that the main door to the church had been padlocked, with uniformed men in brown standing guard, the noon-hour sun glinting off their epaulets. The news crawl on the screen said that the church's bank had taken over the building, which was now being guarded by the county sheriff's police. In the live shot, the reporter explained.

"The bank president has declined to comment, but a well-placed source informs us that the bank has required the church to comply with Illinois orders and guidelines, or they intend to call in the loan. The bank president's wife, it should be noted, is a pulmonologist at Pine Bluff General, where they've seen a consistent rise in corona cases in the past two weeks, many of which they claim have been linked to ECM. Three people have died, and many are gravely ill."

ECM's security guards in gray stood to the side, watching Cyrus for further instructions. The local police, in blue, stood next to them. So many uniforms, so many badges and guns. It looked like every emergency vehicle in the county was parked in front of the megachurch.

"ECM will seek an immediate injunction," the reporter continued. "The lawyers will be fighting this out in court."

Cyrus, with his lawyer, Topher Kent, and Aaron, was standing before the crowd, talking and gesturing furiously, but he was drowned out by his own protesters, who were chanting now: "Churches are essential," and "We have the right to worship." There were posters and signs with similar messages: "Open Illinois," "Freedom over Fear," "End the Tyranny," "Give me liberty or give me COVID," "Thou shalt not close the churches." These people were well prepared; this looked a lot like the protests in Springfield, or the ones that blocked ambulance access to ERs in New York City.

Two officers stepped up to flank Cyrus. The reporter pressed her earpiece. "I'm just learning that Pastor Bell may be charged by the county sheriff." The officers took Cyrus's arms and led him down the church steps to a squad car. Rachel noticed they didn't cuff him.

"There is evil afoot in Ecstasy," Bell thundered. "Beware!"

They put a hand on his head and guided him into the cruiser, which flashed its lights and blipped its siren as it moved slowly through the crowds out to the road. The protesters stayed, but without their leader, quickly lost energy.

Rachel wished that Cyrus was really, finally, going to jail, but she knew his buddy, Griff Gandy, the local police chief, would not let him be held long. She was sick of everything to do with ECM. She turned off the news.

At one o'clock, she took her luggage out to the front porch to wait for Ben. Samson trotted after her, then disappeared around a corner of the house, barking, probably after a squirrel. It was a beautiful spring day; the tulips and crocuses were blooming, the azaleas near the porch showing their first color. Ben was nowhere to be seen, but up the road a red Honda was idling—the same car from Cyrus's compound Rachel had seen there before. How dare they watch the place! When Ben got there, he could help her run them off.

Samson was barking and barking, but not at the car. The wind shifted, and Rachel smelled something burning. She jogged down the porch steps and rounded the corner of the house, where she had a view of the north side of the property. Gray smoke billowed from the carriage barn! The dog was still barking; she grabbed him by his collar and put him in the house for safety. Then she ran to the building. She could hear a roaring and crackling and feel the heat from several feet away. Backing up, she called 911 and gave the address. "Fifteen minutes," the dispatcher told her. Rachel realized she'd just seen Ecstasy's fire trucks at the ECM protests on the opposite side of town. The barn might burn down by the time they got to it.

Flames appeared at the windows and along the roofline. She ran to the spigot on the side of the house and attached the garden hose lying coiled beneath. It was a powerful hose, long enough to water the garden, but Rachel knew as she ran that it probably wouldn't reach the barn. She was right; she adjusted the nozzle, but the arc of the water fell short. The flames began to lick at the old clapboard siding they had just painted. She heard something like a muffled howl and looked around for Samson. He was there in the window of the house where she'd put him, still barking frantically.

What now? She couldn't think. The spring house! Rachel ran to the spring house and filled a bucket from its basin. As she neared the flames, she realized what little good her bucket would do. Still, she had to try. She threw it at the barn wall, and then ran back for another. She was on the fourth or fifth one when Ben pulled into the drive. He ran to her.

"What happened?"

"I don't know. It went up so fast."

They coughed as the wind blew smoke toward the house. Before she could run back for another bucket, Ben, assessing the situation, asked her for a rake. "In the garden shed."

When she returned with more water, he had stuck a rake handle into the ground and fixed the garden hose to the tines with duct tape. It was wetting down one corner of the house and roof. "There might be sparks on the wind," he shouted. "We can't do much by ourselves to save the barn, but we can save the house."

As they both ran back to the spring house, they heard the sirens. Two fire trucks and an ambulance pulled in. The firemen alit from the trucks and motioned them back. At that moment, Alexa and Lucy returned from the grocery store. They got out of the car and stood in the driveway, Alexa's hand to her mouth as Lucy clung to her. They'd arrived just in time to witness the carriage barn roof falling in.

With hoses, ladders, and protective gear, the firemen battled the blaze for another hour. Rachel and Ben stood back, then huddled with Lucy and Alexa as they watched. Three of the walls were left standing, but the building was a total loss. As the firefighters waded through the debris putting out small fires, one called out.

"There's someone in here!"

The firemen ran into the barn. When they came out, the paramedics went in.

"Did you know anyone was in the building?" one of the men asked them. "Is someone missing?" They shook their heads. "Looks like a white male. He was trapped underneath a beam. Any idea who it could be?"

Alexa looked at the others. "No, none at all," she answered. "Is he still alive?"

"We'll wait for the EMTs," the fireman told her. "But it doesn't look good."

Lucy looked pale and fragile. "Oh my God."

One of the paramedics came out and went back in with a gurney. It was another 20 minutes before they brought out a body, the head covered with a sheet.

Rachel recognized her brother's expensive wingtips. Aaron was dead.

27

Alexa: Friday, April 10

Lucy mixed the ingredients for the blueberry filling on the stove, while Alexa rolled out the pie crust. Rachel directed them via video chat on Lucy's laptop. It turned out Rachel's secret to pie crust was lard. Alexa hoped she'd gotten it right; if the pie was half as good as Rachel's, she'd be pleased.

"I wish I could help," Rachel told them. "This tiny house kitchen is well-equipped, but there's no space to roll the dough. I'll have to bake him a cake or two instead."

John Jeffers' cook and housekeeper, the headstrong, capable Florence, was down with coronavirus, and they were stepping in to keep him fed. Alexa had assumed John was in his sixties, but it turned out he was 73, an age group even more vulnerable to the virus. Having been exposed, he had wisely decided to quarantine himself. They were chatting with him daily, insisting he report his temperature, as well as any symptoms he might develop. He was still doing pro-bono work from home, mostly with unions now, as they fought for safe conditions for their workers, but he wasn't seeing clients or going shopping. He didn't cook—anything more than boiling water, he claimed, was "damned tricky"—so Rachel, Alexa, and Lucy were bringing groceries, hot meals, and other treats to his door.

"I told her not to go to church," John had said. Fourteen members of the ECM choir had contracted

Covid. Six were currently hospitalized, three of them critically ill. Several others had died. Test kits were scarce in their area, so who knew how many other local cases there were. At least the authorities had put a stop to the ECM gatherings for now. Amos Windows had closed for a week, then reopened without any protocols in place. It was likely they were also a source of the outbreak. The local hospital's beds were full, and cases were being transferred to facilities in other counties.

The national lockdown had been extended to April 30th, and the president's back-to-normal-by-Easter dream was history. The death toll was near 25,000 and climbing.

Alexa preheated the oven and pressed the rolled dough into the pie pan. Lucy spooned the pie filling into the crust. Then came the latticing of the carefully cut pieces for the top, and the trimming and pinching of the perimeter, under Rachel's supervision. At last, they slid the pie into the oven, and Alexa sighed with relief.

At least, if they were housebound, they had video; Ben had bought Rachel a laptop so she could chat with him while he was away, and Lucy had helped her, remotely, with the setup.

Alexa thanked Rachel for her guidance.

"Don't mention it," she said, picking up Samson and allowing him to sniff at the screen. Alexa and Lucy both talked to him, and he wriggled with excitement to hear their voices. "How's the election going?" Rachel asked them.

"I'll let my campaign manager answer." Alexa gestured to Lucy.

Lucy grinned. "Well, you know WXT has been running that online poll." Rachel nodded. "The more liberal candidates are doing better than we thought, including Mom, especially after her comments in the food pantry parking lot. We're getting a strong response online with the younger voters and the parents, and we're slowly but steadily creeping back up from that Zaleski fiasco. We released the info on why that woman had it in for Mom; it never appeared on WXT, but the other stations carried it."

"I saw that. I hope it helps. Hold on," Rachel said, and disappeared for a moment. She came back to the screen holding a gray and blue card aloft. "I finally got my registration, so I can vote," she told them, clearly pleased. "The state wouldn't issue the card until I got my driver's license, and I couldn't get that until I had my birth certificate." They knew John Jeffers had worked for months with West Virginia to get Rachel's home birth documented.

"That's great!" Lucy congratulated her. "With the election postponed to May 5th, there's a chance for us. That's enough time for people to get a mail-in ballot." Lucy was proud of the work she'd done to spread information about the mail-in process, both by pamphlet and on social media.

"How are you doing, Rachel?" Alexa asked.

"Oh, I'm fine. It's a little lonely with Ben gone on the weekdays. He got a ride to his job this week and left me the truck, but right now there are not many places to go. At least I get to see people at work. It's just Sandy, the two cooks, and me and another girl filling take-out orders. We've been busy. I'm decorating this place when I'm not working, and Samson keeps me company in the evenings." Alexa noticed that Rachel hadn't mentioned her brother. It had to be hard, especially today, when her family was gathered for Aaron's funeral, and she was not allowed to be there.

"I actually meant about Aaron," Alexa said gently.

Rachel shook her head briefly, then cleared her throat. "Well, I know it sounds awful, but I stopped feeling much for him a long time ago. Being older and male, he thought he had authority over me. He made my life hell when I wouldn't obey him. My cousin Caleb stuck up for me, or I would have had a much harder life." Her tone became wistful. "I do wish I could be there today, mostly to comfort my mother. Uncle Cyrus and Aunt Eunice couldn't have children, so they just took Aaron and treated him as their own. My parents didn't have much say." She looked off into the distance for a few moments, then back at the screen. "Maybe it was my aunt and uncle, maybe he was born that way, but the truth is, Aaron wasn't a good man."

That much was true. The police were still investigating the security footage from the carriage barn, but there was no doubt that Aaron had set the fire.

"I'm sorry for all you've been through," Alexa offered, nonetheless.

"Me too," Lucy added.

"Thank you. You two are the best." Rachel paused. "About Aaron …" she said, "I was wondering if you'd watch the funeral with me. I need to see it, but I don't want to do it alone."

"Sure," Alexa answered. "It's starting soon, isn't it?"

"About 15 minutes."

The timer went off. Alexa donned her mitts and carefully took the pie from the oven, setting it on a rack on the counter to cool. It smelled heavenly. She was glad they'd found Margaret's stash of canned blueberries in the root cellar under the pantry.

"It looks great," Rachel told them.

They both tuned their TVs to WXT. To get around lockdown orders, the service was being held at the drive-in theatre out on Longview Road. Alexa assumed Good Friday had been chosen so more people would be free to attend or watch. The decision was sound: folks were lined up for miles to get in and listen to the proceedings from their cars. There was a stage where the movie screen should be, with immediate family set up on one side, extended family on the other, supposedly socially distanced. It was a sunny but breezy day, and the participants looked cold. Rachel identified members of her family for Lucy and Alexa. She pointed out her mother, Ruth Ann, whose face was buried in her husband's shoulder. Also her siblings, and her former best friend Sarah, who was helping with the service. Phoebe sat in a wheelchair, closest to Cyrus. On the other side of the altar, she identified her cousin Caleb and his family.

"Oh my gosh, there are his two little girls, Melissa and Melanie." Rachel sounded sad. "They've changed so much. And the baby …" Caleb's wife was holding a newborn. "I don't even know her name."

The casket, covered in roses and lilies, stood in the center, before a makeshift altar. Cyrus Bell stood behind it, resplendent in his purple vestments. He'd been charged with a misdemeanor—a slap on the wrist—and was awaiting a court date, which she guessed would leave him unscathed. He spread his arms over the crowd as if he were a god himself.

When all were assembled, he opened a Bible with a large gold cross on the cover and began. His eulogy was eloquent and impassioned. He praised Aaron as his right-hand man, a servant of the church and of God, one who always did what the Lord commanded. After listing Aaron's virtues, he recounted personal anecdotes, bringing tears to his own eyes and those of his listeners. Then Cyrus talked about Aaron's death in the fire. Alexa and Lucy both sat up and listened more carefully.

Cyrus claimed there was something suspicious in the way Aaron died on "that atheist property." He implied that Aaron might have been restrained there and set on fire. "God has condemned that wicked place," he thundered. "That's why he brought the virus to this town." He called for an investigation by local authorities. The people in their cars honked their horns in agreement.

"We've allowed this evil to germinate and grow, to sprout from the dirty cracks of this town like a greedy weed. We must stop it before it takes over. We must pluck it out." A chill ran through Alexa's body, and Lucy gave a small moan.

"This virus is penance for the wicked," he shouted. "Those with true faith need not fear, need not close their doors, need not be vaccinated."

Lucy gasped.

"Our God is a healing God, with a plan for this world. Give this town back to him, and he will deliver you." The honking horns were deafening.

He went on to the closing prayers and gave a last benediction. The pallbearers carried the casket through the crush of cars to the waiting hearse. Bell followed after, his Bible held aloft. He got into a car behind the hearse with his wife, his lawyer, and Phoebe, and the procession left for the cemetery. The news cameras zoomed in on various drivers, who all appeared irate. Those interviewed at the site were riled up, ready to take on those who did not share their viewpoints and beliefs.

Lucy looked to Alexa with fear in her eyes. The pastor's words were meant to raise an army. Or a mob. They were alone. Alexa told Rachel they'd call her back for the interment.

"Lock all the doors and windows, Lucy, and look for anything that we can use to defend ourselves." Alexa had never had a gun and wouldn't know how to use one. She hoped that wasn't a mistake. "We shouldn't assume the worst of our neighbors, but we need to be prepared."

Alexa dialed the police department and spoke to one of the officers who had taken their statement after the fire. The policeman seemed unconcerned. "Relax, that's just some fire and brimstone from the old boy. People around here aren't the violent kind. Is anything happening now?" he asked her.

She peered out the window, as far as she could see up the road, and admitted that so far there was no problem. But then, there probably wouldn't be until after the funeral. She reminded him that, in fact, setting a fire on one's property was violent.

"Look, if you're nervous, we'll send a squad car to patrol the area. Keep a lookout. You let us know if you see anything. But I don't think you have much to worry about."

"Thank you. I hope you're right." Lucy's softball bat and some kitchen knives were not going to help very much.

Lucy had gone out to secure the lab. It had survived the carriage barn fire, despite being next to the site, because it was slightly upwind. Alexa had been sick at the thought that it might be damaged. Lucy returned with a few small vials of acid. "I don't think they'll be much help," she said, "but you never know." They armed the security system, then retreated to the kitchen. They had done all they could.

Alexa put her arm around Lucy's shoulders. "We'll be alright," she told her, though she wasn't sure of that at all. She tried to stay calm for Lucy's sake, but she could feel fresh sweat trickling down her back. They both turned back to the television, where the funeral procession had reached the cemetery. The casket was taken from the hearse and moved to the graveside, while some of the mourners exited their cars. Evidently only immediate family was allowed to gather on the grounds. They reconnected with Rachel, who had noticed that the Bells and Phoebe were absent. For some reason, the assistant pastor had taken Cyrus's place by the casket.

"That's strange," Rachel remarked.

Just as the prayers began, the station cut in with their logo.

"We have breaking news," the announcer told them. "A controversial video has been made public this afternoon." There was a photograph behind her, a still from the home security video Alexa had given the police.

"Rachel, we're changing to channel 3." Alexa flipped to another local channel, one more reliable than WXT when it came to truthful reporting. Rachel did the same.

A news anchor was covering the story. "A leaked video appears to show the late Aaron Whitman setting the Moss family carriage barn fire. Whitman died in the Palm Sunday blaze." They ran the clip, which was taken by the security camera on the back of their house, overlooking the yard and barn. It clearly showed Aaron—grainy but recognizable—with a pump spray can, dousing the outside of the barn with some kind of accelerant. Then he stepped inside.

Fortunately, it was not the first time Rachel had seen the video. "I can't imagine why he did that," she said, "why he did the outside first. 'Common sense isn't so common,' my mother used to say about him."

The video, fast forwarded, showed the smoke, the flames, the vain attempts by Rachel and Ben to put out the fire. Then the fire department arriving, battling the blaze, the roof falling in, and the final scene of the paramedics wheeling the covered body out in a gurney. Edited to a couple of minutes, it was powerful stuff.

There were several closeups of Aaron's unique two-tone wingtips, one while he doused the barn, one on the body on the gurney, juxtaposed with a closeup of those same shoes, worn by Aaron in public as he stood alongside Cyrus in several recent news clips.

Then the station ran ECM footage from Palm Sunday, the day of the fire. As Cyrus stood before the padlocked church, he whispered something to Aaron, who nodded and left through the crowd. One camera had followed Aaron to a red Honda, his wingtips clearly visible as he entered the passenger side. The car left the ECM lot about 45 minutes before the fire.

"The driver of the red Honda, seen near the Moss property at the time of the fire, is now being questioned. We go now to Ecstasy's police chief, Griffin Gandy."

The police chief acknowledged the video was authentic. "We are still investigating," he said, though not with the conviction of his early statements on the subject. He was sweating profusely and mopped his head with his handkerchief. He admitted that the Honda driver was, indeed, being questioned. The town's mayor stood uncomfortably next to him.

A masked reporter asked him, "What about Cyrus Bell? Will you be bringing him in for questioning?"

The chief's face reddened from his fleshy cheeks to the roots of his iron-gray hair. "Pastor Bell is a pillar of our community and is not at this time under suspicion of any crime." He coughed several times into his handkerchief, wiped his forehead again, and recovered. "However, we'll be speaking to him shortly, for clarity." The reporters clamored for further information, but the chief declined to answer their questions. "It's an ongoing investigation; I can't say more."

The scene returned to the news desk, where the anchor announced, "We now have the county coroner."

The coroner, a tall woman with a long face and a short dark bob, stood at a microphone in front of the county offices. "Despite his burns, and injuries from the falling beam, it was determined that Aaron Whitman died of smoke inhalation, complicated by coronavirus." There was a loud buzz from the reporters. "Whitman was in the early stages of the virus, but his lungs were already too compromised to handle the combination of smoke and accelerant. It's likely he passed out due to these reasons before he was able to leave the property." She handled a few more questions, then the program cut back to the news desk.

"Our anonymous source decided to leak this video when they heard Pastor Bell's incendiary words at Whitman's funeral this morning."

The station went into a news loop, alternately running Cyrus's eulogy, the security video of Aaron, clips of Cyrus's whisper to him, and Alexa's "ugly truth" food-pantry rant while the humanists helped families to their cars with their groceries. Alexa was grateful for the coverage, but afraid it might be too late. Rachel had signed off some time ago; they assumed she'd had enough.

Lucy paced the living room, looking through the blinds out to the road. "Mom!" she called out. Alexa moved to the window and saw dozens of cars parked along Collins Road in front of the house. She ran upstairs. From a second-floor window, she could also see cars lined up along the side road on the north of property. They must have come straight from the funeral. Alexa thought of the many countries where atheists were put to death. Dread rolled through her body.

She ran back down the stairs, thinking furiously. Lucy was posting video on social media. "We're not going down undocumented," she said.

Alexa dialed the police again and alerted them, then wracked her brain for solutions. She remembered the trap door to the root cellar in the pantry, under a rug.

"If they start for the house," she told Lucy, "I'll go out to them. You take your cell phone and hide in the root cellar under the pantry. I'll put the rug back over the door when I leave."

"No, Mom—"

"This is no time to argue. Just do as I say. I'll text Rachel you're under there in case you can't get a signal."

Lucy hugged Alexa, and their hearts thumped together as one. There were voices outside, shouting, and people getting out of their cars.

"Look! They're all wearing masks!" Lucy said.

Not a good sign. These people would only wear face masks to hide their identity.

Alexa had fought many battles in life—mostly against herself—but she never suspected she'd have to face literal physical violence. Now, a clarity came over her, replacing her fear with a resolve born of pure adrenaline.

"Get ready," she said to Lucy.

Her phone rang, but she ignored it. It rang again. She turned it off and dropped it in her pocket. There was a woman in a mask, coming up the walk. It couldn't be …

It was Mona Bauer. She walked up to the front porch and rang the bell. Was this some kind of decoy? Alexa looked at her from the front window. Mona motioned to her to open the door. Alexa shook her head, and Mona pointed to her phone. Alexa turned her own phone on and looked at the messages.

"It's us," Mona had texted. "All these cars are us. Really. Open your door."

Alexa fumbled with the buttons on the security panel, disarming the system, and opened the front door.

Mona removed her mask for a moment and grinned. "The cavalry has arrived," she said. "The ECM people can't get near you. Come with me."

Alexa and Lucy grabbed their masks and jackets and followed Mona to the road, where hundreds of people sat in or stood next to their cars. They cheered and honked their horns in the happiest cacophony Alexa had ever heard.

The three of them moved through the line of vehicles, greeting everyone. Eric Reynolds was parked right in front of their house; he must have been among the first to arrive. He raised both arms in celebration and gazed at them fondly as they passed. Despite the face masks, Alexa recognized most of the humanists; also, Chad and Jeremy; Jessica Lopez, her daughter Eva, and brother Rodrigo; Heather and Alan and a lot of the Methodists from the food pantry; plus Malcolm Redd and his constituents. Lucy saw some of her teachers and most of her high-school friends, including Logan, Sam, and Jordan. Even Ivan, the electrician, was in the crowd. Alexa was truly amazed and choked up by their support. They stood apart from one another, but sang and clapped and hollered, the gathering more like a fair than like the mob she had expected.

"How did they all know?" Alexa asked.

"It was Rachel," Mona answered, pointing to the end of the line. Rachel sat in the bed of Ben's truck in his camouflage hat, holding his hunting rifle. "She alerted me, Chad, Heather, and Malcolm. John Jeffers too. And even Jordan Randall. And we told the others."

When they came abreast of the truck bed, Alexa called up to her.

"Thanks, so much Rachel. We owe you!"

"Hey, my family got you into this. It was up to me to get you out," she answered. "A few of the ECM people did show up," she said, laughing, "but they saw us and turned tail. We outnumber them twenty to one."

"They saw *you,* looking fierce," Lucy told her.

"Well, I have a few scores to settle."

A squad car pulled up and the officers alighted, guns drawn. "No need, fellas. We got this," Mona called out. They took a few moments to understand what was happening, but eventually stood down.

Alexa noticed Rachel was on her cell phone. "Damn," she said, hanging up. She got down from the truck and stood several feet from Alexa and Lucy. "That was Caleb. Cyrus took off. They're on the run," she said. "And they have Phoebe."

28

Rachel: Sunday, April 26

Rachel let Samson back into the house, put some food in his bowl, then climbed back into bed with Ben, who was snoring softly. A buttery early morning light slipped through the blinds, and she watched a tiny moth flit against the window. It was so peaceful here. The bluffs were isolated from town, this part of them lush with foliage and birds. Sundays were her favorite now, their mutual day off.

She missed Phoebe, ached for her, and worried every day she was gone. All she could do now was wait. And plan. She'd registered for community college in the fall, in the nursing program. She was nervous about the math and science placement tests, but Lucy had agreed to help her study. John had told her about state grants—she'd never heard of such things before—which would pay for her courses and books. Both he and Alexa had written glowing letters of recommendation for her. She didn't know what she'd done to deserve this good fortune, but she knew how to pay it back: by finding Phoebe, by helping her and others lead healthy lives.

Rachel inhaled, exhaled slowly, quieting her mind, and watched Ben as he slept, her heart beating with the rise and fall of his chest. He was beautiful. His kindness and humor had lifted her, guided her through her despair and given her hope. They'd just gotten better and better, stronger together. As if he heard her thoughts, Ben stirred and woke, stretched his lean, muscled frame and took her into his arms. "Mornin', babe." He kissed her softly and they made long, languid love in the morning light.

Afterwards they talked and played in the sheets together until Samson nosed the door open and climbed onto the bed. They dressed and ate a lazy brunch, then Ben took Samson out for a walk and Rachel sat down with her laptop.

She checked Sandy's schedule first; she was on most of the week. Thankfully the diner was still busy during the lockdown, with Sandy's grilled entrees translating well to take-out. Rachel was grateful every day for her job. Since she'd been staying with Ben, she was able to save a little money in a special account earmarked for her education.

She checked her email. There was one from Lucy, with links to several sites for practice tests, and one from the financial aid office at the college confirming her grant. A woman she used to work with at Amos had copied her on a memo about the spread of the virus at the plant. Both Tom and Orrin were in the hospital. Yolanda was home sick. Scores of other workers had tested positive.

Rachel sighed. She opened a kitchen drawer and took out the box of nicotine patches she'd bought several days before. The virus had finally convinced her. Smokers were more susceptible to Covid, and she needed to stay strong. Until a vaccine was developed, she'd have to take what measures she could. She peeled the backing from one of the patches and placed it high on her arm under her sleeve. Then she ran her cigarettes under the faucet and dumped them in the trash. Another parting.

Returning to her email, she read a notice from an online group she followed—people "recovering" from religion. Rachel had found such comfort in that group. It turned out there were hundreds, thousands like her, who had grown up or found themselves in restrictive faiths: ex-Muslims, Christian fundamentalists, orthodox Jews,

Jehovah's witnesses, LDS, and even some Amish, like Ben. Most were surprised to find how full and meaningful life could be without religion—if you could, in fact, adjust. It was a process. These people understood what no one else could, and found solace and support in one another. She really needed that, especially now.

She steeled herself, clicked on Google, and began her daily search. She typed in Cyrus Bell and every other possible version of his name; evangelical pastors and churches; "Angelica"; seers, oracles, and epileptics. Then she did the same on YouTube. Cyrus was still running, but they'd find him eventually. He, Eunice, and Phoebe had been traced by police to a private flight to Cincinnati, where they'd fled in a black van. The van was later abandoned in a Denny's parking lot in southern Ohio.

They were probably holed up in Appalachia—West Virginia or Tennessee most likely—where Cyrus was born and raised. He knew trails in the mountains beyond any civilization, beyond paved roads, electricity, running water. Beyond Wi-Fi, if he was smart. But knowing Cyrus, he'd want current information. And eventually, attention. That's how he'd be found. Chad and Jeremy were scouring the internet for him, including something creepy called the "dark web." If he or any videos of Phoebe appeared, they'd know. Rachel just needed patience.

In the meantime, she had her life to live, even in a pandemic. The virus was horrible, the economy a mess, but even quarantined, she was freer than she had ever been with Cyrus or her parents.

Her cell phone rang; it was Caleb. She was glad they were talking again. Her cousin was trying to run the church—oversee the physical facilities, pay the bills, keep track of the congregation—despite the fact that his wife was down with the virus, and he was caring for their three girls by himself. The baby's name was Megan.

"Rachel, I'm calling to let you know your dad's in the hospital."

"What? When did this happen?"

"It was late last night. Your parents were so sick they actually went to the ER. Both of them tested positive for Covid-19. Your mom's got a terrible cough, but they sent her home. Your dad though, he's in bad shape. They didn't have enough ICU beds, so they flew him to Mercy General. He may need a ventilator."

Rachel knew they must have been desperate if they'd gone to a hospital; they never would have done that—for themselves or their children—when Cyrus Bell was around.

"Can I see him?"

"No, it's not allowed." He gave her a number. "You can try to call. It's hard to get through; the staff is overwhelmed."

"Thanks for letting me know, Caleb. How are you?"

"I'm okay for a man who hasn't slept in a month. Newborns are not for the faint of heart."

"Let me know if there's anything I can do."

"The community is pulling together. They drop off groceries and diapers for me, and whatever your brothers and sisters need. But a lot of them have family members sick with this thing themselves."

"I feel for them. I'll keep trying Mercy. Let me know if you hear anything."

"Will do."

Ben returned with Samson and wiped the dog's paws. Rachel filled Ben in on what had happened.

"Caleb's a good man," she told him, scratching Samson behind the ears. "I'm so sorry all this has landed on him, though he's better for the congregation than Cyrus ever was. He told me this week that he found three sets of books when he did the accounts."

"I'm not surprised. Your uncle is a pretty shady guy."

"There's probably more than one reason he took off."

Unfortunately, the problem wasn't just Cyrus or ECM. Perhaps the congregation would choose a better pastor. But one with a similar doctrine wouldn't substantially change things. Cyrus believed everything he preached. That was what made him dangerous. So much of the harm that had been done was the logical, inevitable consequence of that fundamentalism.

Rachel put Samson on the floor. "I'm going to call the hospital." She dialed them several times but couldn't get through.

She was frustrated she could do nothing else for her family. She no longer believed in prayer, in a higher power who chose who lived and who died. Now she must put her faith in scientists, doctors, nurses. Humans were the answer.

Rachel tried the hospital intermittently as they spent the afternoon tackling various projects—painting a wall in the tiny bedroom, hanging a few new pictures and shelves—and again before they donned masks and gloves and headed for the grocery store. There, they bought ingredients for a special dinner Ben wanted to make for Rachel.

Just as they got to the house, Ben's cell phone rang: Louisa. When he denied the call, as usual, Rachel couldn't keep silent.

"Ben," she began, as they brought in the groceries, "don't you think it's time to talk to your family?"

Ben grimaced as he washed his hands in the sink.

"So many people now can't see their loved ones if they want to," she continued, soaping and rinsing her hands as well. "Families are split, and some, like me, can't even make contact with sick parents. What if someone has Covid there? Wouldn't you want to know?"

They unpacked the porterhouse steak, potatoes, and green beans, and wiped down their purchases.

"They didn't tell me the last time. Why would they do it now?"

"I don't know. The whole world is different now. We need to appreciate the things we've got. This is no time to be holding a grudge. Look at *me*, Ben. Look what that's done to me."

He turned and wordlessly took her into his arms. They held one another as if they were the last people in the world.

"She texted me to find out if I'm okay," he admitted. Rachel raised her eyebrows at him. "Alright," he finally said, "I'll think about it."

Rachel reined in her impulse to say more.

She had bought the ingredients for Ben's favorite cake, which she mixed and put into the oven. She finally got through to the hospital, but there wasn't much to learn. George was indeed on a ventilator and sedated. Rachel left her number, and the nursing staff agreed to call her if there was any change.

When Ben went out to grill the steak, she frosted the cake, set the table with flowers and candles. She could see him on the deck through the kitchen window. He put on the steak, then picked up his phone and tapped it a few times. She heard him say, "Louisa?" then watched as he paced the deck and talked, stopping every few minutes to flip the meat.

When the steak was done, he came back inside and put on some music for mood. When they sat, she looked up at him expectantly.

"I'll tell you about it later," he said. "Tonight is just for us."

They dined and talked like normal people; the tiny house, this moment, a small island of peace in a sea of uncertainty. After dinner, Ben produced a bottle of champagne, which he had hidden on the deck, and poured them each a glass. "Maybe just one for now," he told her, and Rachel nodded.

Then he excused himself momentarily and came back to the table with a package. Rachel drew in her breath. It was small and square, wrapped exquisitely in gold. She opened it with trembling hands. The diamond was round-cut and modest, set in a simple platinum band. Rachel loved it, and Ben, with all her heart.

He had tears in his eyes as he knelt before her. "Rachel, I love you. Will you do me the honor? Will you marry me?"

Rachel put her hand over his. "I love you so much. And I want to marry you." How could she tell him? What could she say that was kind? The simplest way was probably the best. "But Ben, I'm not ready yet."

He rose from his knees and reseated himself, never dropping her hand, never taking his eyes from her face. He looked sad and puzzled, waiting for her to continue.

"You're the best thing that ever happened to me," she told him. "I don't want to lose you. I want to go on as we are. You've been wonderful, almost *too* wonderful. You've picked me up and held me up, supported me through tough times. But the thing is, I've never stood on my own, or at least not successfully." Some understanding began to brighten Ben's eyes.

"There's still so much I have to do. Not just Phoebe, although she's part of it. I need to find out who I can be, and what I'm capable of." There was so much she'd missed, so much to learn and experience. Marriage, even to Ben, would close some doors forever. She had even thought, once the virus was over, of moving back to Alexa's. But she had plenty of time to make that decision.

Ben looked at her for a long time, quietly, absorbing all she'd said. "I can't say I'm not disappointed," he finally told her. "But I think you're right. You got a late start on life, darlin,' and you need a chance to live it. You need some room to grow. I know I've got some growin' to do myself." He smiled, rather poignantly. "The good news is, if we grow in the same direction, we'll still have each other." He pulled her to her feet and kissed her, then whispered in her ear, "I can't wait to find out."

29

Lucy: Friday, May 8

"**D**ouble sixes." The best way to start the game. Lucy moved her white backgammon pips to the bar points. "Do you want to concede now?"

John Jeffers, who was playing black, laughed. "Don't be smug. The game's not over yet."

"Not even if I double you?"

"Try it and see." Lucy knew better than to double John so early in the game. He was pretty good. She enjoyed playing online backgammon every day with him on her lunch break between Zoom classes. The game site was colorful, easy to use, and made pleasant clicking sounds like actual pieces when you moved. They Skyped while they played.

She'd grown fond of John and worried about him quarantined alone, though so far, he seemed Covid-free. She was amused to see that his silver hair was longer, and he'd more or less stopped shaving; his beard was growing out, though being John's, it was neatly trimmed. He looked like a movie wizard, or a prophet. They'd come a long way since they met on that rainy moving day in August. She admired him immensely, and he seemed to feel the same. He had signed off on the inheritance, providing they rebuilt the carriage barn within the year, and told her she could start looking at colleges. His role as estate executor was almost over, but he was family now.

John rolled a five/six and ran, escaping her block with one man.

"Who's lucky now?" she teased him.

He wiggled his eyebrows at her. Then he asked how her classes were going.

"Fine. It's weird online. Some classes work better than others. We're spending most of our time reviewing for finals." She took a bite of her sandwich and rolled again, hoping to build a prime to trap his hindmost man in her home board.

"What about the national science competition?"

"We're waiting to hear about the 2021 applications. Most of the students won't have lab access, so things will be different this year. I've been talking with Dr. Reynolds about a couple of possibilities."

"Oh? And what are those?" It was John's turn to roll doubles and he secured several strategic points.

Lucy chewed the last bite of her sandwich, took a swig of her soda, and pushed her plate to the side. "Well, I could continue with more generations of the *Brassica*—our Wisconsin Fast Plant project. There are other traits I could cross for, or conditions I could impose that would qualify as original research. I've already done some of that work.

"*Or*—there is public data on scientific sites that has not yet been analyzed. The CDC is one of those sites. Contact tracing is underway in some areas. I'm thinking about how those data sets might be combined; for example, if there's a particular genetic predisposition to contracting Covid, or suffering certain symptoms or severe outcomes."

"Now that sounds interesting. And right up your alley."

"Yeah, I think it would be."

"Sounds like you have a lot of work to do. I'm proud of you, Lucy."

"Thanks, John." She had managed to cover most of her home board and put two of his men on the bar. She doubled him.

"Ouch. Well, I think that's it for me," he said. "I concede. That's 4 to 3, you. Do you have time to finish the set?"

Lucy checked the clock on her computer. "No, I only have ten minutes 'til class. We'll have to finish tomorrow."

"Okay, dear, give my regards to your mother, and tell her I'll call her this evening. I need to thank her for all that amazing food. Oh, and it looks like the election results may be in tonight. Fingers crossed."

"Fingers crossed," Lucy said, and signed off. She enjoyed having someone like a grandfather in her life.

The afternoon went quickly, with AP English—review of the romantic poets—and Bio. She noticed Dr. Reynolds' wedding ring had not reappeared on his finger. That was good, since he'd been calling her mother a lot late in the evening. Alexa, who took those calls in her room, didn't think Lucy knew about that.

As usual, Jordan called her right after class. She sat at her computer in her lavender bedroom, her blond hair in a messy bun, painting her nails as she complained about school, prom, graduation, and her family. Lucy was sympathetic, knowing Jordan's disappointments, and willing to listen. Jake was sick with coronavirus—*karma*—and was past the worst of it, but their dad had gotten it too, a pretty bad case. The two of them were sharing the family room downstairs, keeping their distance from everyone else in the house. Jordan, Claire, and Mrs. Randall were still okay and hoping to escape infection.

"Not that I could go anywhere anyway, even without the lockdown. Everyone is mad at me for calling the cops on the party." She painted several nails, then held them out straight-armed for inspection.

"They'll forget about that by the time we're out," Lucy offered, hoping it was true.

Since Jake wasn't charged, he hadn't lost his scholarship. He was going to Blackrock Christian College with Brad next year, so Jordan might be allowed to visit. She said she was weighing her options. Her eyes clouded over. "My dad's not budging on the college thing. I told him, 'I'm eighteen; I could get on a bus and leave.' He laughed and said, 'Who'd support you?' He's right about that part—but anything would be better than hanging around Ecstasy with high-school kids until he marries me off." She let out a long sigh, then cringed. "Oh sorry, Lucy, no offense. I didn't mean you."

"None taken." She'd probably feel the same way herself. "I might be able to talk him into community college." Jordan finished one hand and blew on the nails.

"I hope so." Lucy tried a more positive subject. "How's the video coming?"

"Great! I got about sixty students to model the prom clothes they never got to wear and send their videos to David. He's going to edit the clips together with dance music as part of the graduation video." Leave it to Jordan to curate fashion in the middle of a pandemic.

Pine Bluff High School had lawn signs made for all the seniors—"Class of 2020 PBHS graduate." A virtual graduation was scheduled, with speeches from the principal, teachers, and valedictorian, and the video created by the class. Every name would be read, just as if they were actually there. There would also be a decorated car parade in the parking lot the day before graduation.

School would be different next year without Jake, Jordan, and David, but she'd still have Logan, Sam, and Eva. Maybe Maddie would be around. When the topics of prom and graduation were exhausted, Jordan moved on to Maddie's baby shower.

She dipped her brush in the pale blue varnish and started on the other hand. "We're doing a Zoom shower for her on the 17th. Small, but you're invited, of course. There will be games and stuff. We'll drop off her gifts several days before and she can open them on video. She doesn't need anything big; this is just for fun. Her parents and David's already bought her all the furniture and equipment."

Lucy knew from her chats with Maddie that she still refused to see David. She would have to let him spend time with the baby once he was born, but she wouldn't talk about that yet. They knew it was a boy. Maddie hadn't chosen a name; it seemed she was still in denial in some ways.

Jordan held out her wet nails for Lucy's approval. "What do you think of this color for the shower?"

Lucy smiled. "I'm sure Maddie will appreciate your attention to detail."

Jordan had one final subject. "So you gave away the dog Jake got you? Why?"

Lucy hesitated. "The short version is that Samson really bonded with Rachel. It made sense for her to take him." She would never tell Jordan the real story. "Anyway, Eva's cat just had kittens, and she's got a cute gray one picked out for me. That might be a better fit."

"I think Jake still loves you, Lucy. Couldn't you forgive him?" Jordan used her famous pout, though it wasn't really working for her these days.

Lucy shook her head. "No. And you know that Jake is back with Sophia, at least on Skype."

"Okay, okay. You guys were such a great couple. Guess I'll just have to get used to this."

"Yes, you will."

"I'll call you tomorrow."

"Okay, see you then."

Lucy took her lunch plate downstairs to the kitchen and grabbed a granola bar. Alexa was in her den, working, with the door closed. Lucy missed Rachel, and even Samson begging for a bite of her snack. Her life had once been busy with school and church and friends. And Jake. All of that was gone now, or changed beyond recognition.

The TV in the breakfast nook was on, the sound muted. Alexa must have been checking for election results. Lucy wondered why it took three extra days to count the mail-in ballots; their town wasn't very big.

In the national news, the virus was still the biggest story. Over 75,000 people had died, and the administration was pushing the states to reopen. Two days ago, the president had issued an executive order making churches essential businesses.

In the local news, the screen flashed a picture of Cyrus Bell. The police were still looking for him. Lucy's chest felt heavy as she watched. Only a few months ago, she and so many others had depended on him for guidance. She had almost given up her science, misled by the stirrings of her heart.

She'd had some time to think about that and had come to some conclusions. Yes, her experience was authentic; at the time, she'd believed the things she'd said and felt. Yet now, with some perspective, she'd examined the church's claims and found them wanting. A lot of her willingness to believe had been tied to her love for Jake.

But, surprisingly, not all of it. She rejected the Bible stories. Yet her spirit had been awakened to something beyond herself. Her head knew the facts, the science; her heart longed for something larger to give them meaning. Could she have both? Could a person be spiritual without being religious?

"This is a big debate among humanists," Alexa told her, "and I think it's mostly semantic. We all understand that 'spirit' can mean the essence of something, even if you don't believe in souls. I don't believe in a god, but I find meaning in music, art, architecture, in my relationships with people. Others find it in poetry, nature, the cosmos. Some people use the word 'spiritual' for that feeling of awe and connection."

She thought her mother might be right; nature, the genome, the night sky all aroused in Lucy that feeling of something more.

Alexa had stroked Lucy's hair, her gray eyes shining. "You're young; you have years to work this out. Talk to Mona," she said. "Talk to Heather, too, and other believers who aren't bound up in dogma. There are so many ways to celebrate life, to feel wonder, to be part of something larger. In the end, though, your beliefs are less important than how you treat others."

Lucy wouldn't be returning to ECM; that much was for sure.

Her phone pinged. It was Logan. She joined him, and Sam and Eva popped up on the screen as well.

"Hey," Logan said. "We're getting together an online movie watch party tonight. Eva wants to see *The Blues Brothers*; Sam says *The Breakfast Club*; I vote for *Casablanca*. What do you think?"

"Ooh, let's do *Casablanca*. I've never seen that one."

Logan raised his arms in victory, then coughed into his sleeve. His dark hair was longer now and stood out on his head. The cut over his eye had healed, leaving a faint red line.

"Do you still have Covid symptoms?" Lucy asked.

"Not really," he answered. "Just a little hack sometimes." He scowled. "That freaking party. My only comfort is that all the Bison got it, and from what I hear, way worse than me."

"The mayor too, my mother says," Eva added. "He got it from Chief Gandy."

"Oh really? The mayor almost deserves it," said Lucy. "He's done squat to protect the community from the pandemic."

Sam said her great aunt was in the hospital with Covid, in the ICU. "I think she got it at the church. She's not in good shape."

They were all silent for a moment.

Another window popped up. Two more kids, a brother and sister.

"Hey, everyone," Eva said. "These are my friends, Cybil and Henry Redd. They'll be joining us for the movie."

They recognized them from school and greeted them warmly. Henry was in their class; Cybil, a year behind, was on the cross-country team with Sam and Eva. The group talked about their online classes and what they'd been doing since the lockdown.

"It's going to take some next-level planning to get us through the summer without going nuts," offered Logan. "I've been making a list, googling stuff we can do online or outside with social distancing." Seeing their smiles, he grinned and shrugged. "What? I've got nothing else to do. I'll send you the list when I'm done."

"Cool. Speaking of which," Eva said, "how about 10:00 for the movie? We can log on at 9:30 to hang out." The others agreed.

"I'll make the popcorn," Logan told them. They all laughed and logged off.

Lucy went out to her lab to check on her plants and animals. Her recent additions were two guinea pigs and a couple of brown field mice she'd trapped in the orchard. She spent a few minutes filming their activities and a voiceover on their progress. One generation of *Brassica* was ready to be pollinated; she'd start on that tomorrow. As she recorded some measurements, she thought again about Logan, who crept into her mind more than usual these days. They video chatted often, and he looked better to her every time. He was relaxed and funny, and they had a lot in common. Lately, he'd been flirting with her. Maybe he had been all along. Maybe she'd have something to tell her friends when they Zoomed from Elm Ridge.

None of them knew how this year would play out: whether the virus would stay or fade, whether there would be a second wave. They might be back in the classroom this fall or still in front of their computers. She was lucky, actually. Yeah, she and Jake were over, and she was on lockdown. But if she hadn't moved to Ecstasy, she wouldn't have a big house, a lab, and 20 acres to roam. She missed her old friends, but loved her new ones, and lately she didn't even mind her mother. Funny how things went. Only sixteen months until college. She might just make it here 'til then.

Alexa called her for dinner: tacos, Lucy's favorite. As they sat down at the table, Alexa's phone vibrated. She checked it out, then said, "Turn on the TV, Lucy, the votes have come in."

30

Alexa: Wednesday, May 20

A lexa said goodbye and disconnected from her five-p.m. video meeting, the board members' voices still thrumming in her ears. It would take her a while to get used to the various personalities and agendas. As disparate as those were, however, the members were bound together by the pandemic crisis, and each in this moment felt the charge to make thoughtful, responsible decisions for the district. The eerie absence of Aaron Whitman went unacknowledged.

Alexa was both delighted and apprehensive when she was elected. She and Lucy had watched over dinner two weeks before as the final returns came in. When the mail-in ballots were fully counted, Malcolm Redd, Scott Planek— the funny young tech guy—and Alexa had been elected. Brittany Spencer, the PTA mom, had narrowly edged out Jessica Lopez, Eva's mother, for the fourth spot. With the new members, there were three solid conservatives and three liberals on the seven-member board. It appeared that Scott would be the swing vote. He sided with Alexa about science education, though, so despite the fact that Grace Hubbly had not dropped her lawsuit, Alexa knew that the new school board would fight it.

Lucy had rejoiced in her mother's victory, dancing around the kitchen in jubilation. Alexa had a lot to thank her for. In the end it was Lucy who saved her campaign and taught her some things about rising from the ashes. That night Lucy had tasted her first champagne as they celebrated on video with their friends. Rachel and Ben, John, Heather and Alan, Mona Bauer, and Chad and Jeremy had all raised a glass to Alexa's success. John in particular was "proud as a peacock."

All that was great, but after this evening's school-board meeting, she needed to unwind. It was already seven o'clock; too late to cook. As she scanned a take-out menu from Sandy's, Heather rang her on video chat.

"What's new with you? How's your brother?" Alexa asked her.

Mark had been hospitalized with Covid after months of nursing others who had refused to mask or stay home.

"The fever's still there, and the breathing is getting much worse. They're talking about a ventilator. I'm afraid for him."

"Oh, Heather, I'm so sorry to hear that. Are his children still with you?"

"Yeah, and they miss their dad. He wanted to protect them by leaving them with me, but it's been months now, and really hard on them, especially since they lost their mother a couple of years ago." She passed a hand over her face. "How about your mom? Have you heard from her?"

"Just a few days ago, actually. Her retirement home in Michigan was safe for a while, but now a couple of the staff have tested positive. She refuses to leave. She's sure it'll 'pass over' her."

Others evidently thought so too. The virus was surging in states that had reopened or never closed. Over 100,000 were dead; Sam's great aunt and George Whitman, Rachel's father, were among them. Those who attended ECM or worked at Amos Windows accounted for dozens more. The most heartbreaking case was Mark, whose kids could be orphaned, though Alexa knew Heather would take them as her own.

"How did the board meeting go?" Heather asked Alexa.

"It was fascinating," Alexa admitted. "Issues that seemed critical three months ago were put aside as we talked about getting the kids back to class in the fall. Our main job is to support the administration as they develop plans for both on-site and distance learning. We don't have any idea which it will be. The board may have to meet once a week, or more, during the summer."

Alexa circled her choice on the Sandy's menu, then called up to Lucy to come downstairs and do the same.

"Sounds like a lot of work."

"Yes, but thankfully we have the chance to do it. I'm not fooling myself. We were lucky enough to hit a very small window. This pandemic showed Cyrus—and a lot of local officials—for what they are, and we more progressive candidates rode that backlash into office. I don't think it would have happened otherwise. It's still a pretty conservative community, and as a nonbeliever, I'll always be seen as suspect."

And the battle too for the country was far from over. With the death toll climbing every day, and the political landscape littered with false information and party divisions, it was going to take work far beyond a local or national election to make things right. But this was a start.

"How's your business going?" Heather asked her. "Did that new client work out?"

"Yes, and two more this week. The Schaefers are putting on an addition, rather than put their mother in care. And I'm taking over a kitchen remodel another architect abandoned." She shrugged. "Seems all that notoriety was good for business. But the biggest news is that on Ben's urging, I submitted some drawings to Ray Ingersoll for the new clinic he's financing north of town. He really likes them. Looks like I'm in the running."

"Oh Alexa, that's fabulous!"

Alexa's phone signaled that she had a call. "Hang on."

Her insurance company. She'd call them back. They were going after ECM for the carriage-barn fire, although with Bell still on the loose, it was anyone's guess how they'd end up working that out. They had assured her she was covered.

"By the way," she asked Heather, "has your congregation decided about the barn?"

The moderates in Heather's church were slightly outnumbered and would be out of a building by the fall. They could stay Methodists—most of them favored that—but they were also looking at Unitarian affiliation. Alexa had offered them use of the carriage barn on Sunday mornings, when it was rebuilt and this virus past.

"Not yet," Heather said. "It would give us a chance to get back on our feet, while we decide what to do. We'll take a vote on it this Sunday. I've pretty much got them convinced. Some objected to sharing space with humanists, but I pointed out that while our beliefs are different, our values are aligned. We're much more like you than we're like the fundamentalists, and we've got to stop giving them a pass." Heather paused and gave a small laugh. "It's pathetic, isn't it?"

"What?" Alexa asked her.

"I was willing to overlook so much—challenges to the school, to the community, all that bigotry and dogma—just to keep the peace. I couldn't see the extent of the damage. Until it was me. Until it was my church, twice. My friends. My brother."

"We all have our blind spots," Alexa told her, thinking about her conversations with Malcolm Redd.

Lucy came bounding down the stairs and into the kitchen, breaking the mood. She waved to Heather and picked up the Sandy's menu.

Heather smiled. "Someone still has some energy. Well, I'll let you go, Alexa. I'll keep you posted."

"Okay, Heather. Our love to the family. And Heather," she said, "call me if you need me."

"Thanks, Alexa. Bye."

Lucy called their order in to Sandy's and offered to pick it up. "Rachel's working. It'll be good to see her."

It was fifteen or twenty minutes until she had to leave. Lucy wandered to the jigsaw puzzle laid out on the dining room table. They'd rediscovered some simple pleasures during the lockdown, as many families had. Alexa joined her and fitted a few pieces into a corner spot, then watched Lucy sift through pinks and oranges to complete a garden in the center of the picture.

Lucy was a picture herself. She'd cut her own hair—after watching a video on how to do it—producing a wavy shoulder-length style which, though casual, made her look more sophisticated. It swung out neatly as she bent her head over the puzzle. Her eyebrows drew together in concentration the way they did when she was a child, but she'd shaped them now, and her hazel gaze, when she looked up at her mother, was direct and adult. She'd changed almost exponentially in the past few months, yet there was some essential Lucy—the scientist, the daughter, the friend—who hadn't been lost, but had come back into herself, full circle. Alexa was grateful to have another year with her.

When Lucy left to get the food, Alexa poured herself a glass of wine and headed out to the porch. The sky was still light; summer was almost upon them. A warm breeze ruffled the oaks and maples, and made the budding lilies sway on their stems. She sat in one of the old rockers, thought about Margaret, and lifted her glass. She remembered that day in the Elm Ridge condo when she'd gotten the notice about the will, how she'd doubted Margaret's sanity, then her own when she'd accepted. There were times along the way when she thought she'd lost Lucy. But Margaret had believed in her, she realized now, as no one else ever had. Alexa could not have imagined the journey before her. Not that it was done—not by a long shot. They were building and rebuilding: the house and the carriage barn, yes, but also connections, relationships, community. Friends and family.

Her phone chimed: Eric, on Skype.

Eric called her every night, and they often talked until the small hours of the morning. He had filed for divorce.

He'd realized, he told her, that the girl he had loved so long ago didn't exist anymore. Hadn't for years. And though he was worried that Jenny would turn his son against him, he had to face the fact that James was 20 now and accountable for his own decisions. As a parent, she sympathized.

Their attraction to one another was undeniable and their frustration with keeping a physical distance was growing. But it gave them time to get to know one another, to form a different sort of intimacy, and their bond grew every day. He was funny, kind, and intelligent, and he seemed fascinated by her. When she talked about architecture, his eyes lit up.

"Hi. How was your day?"

"It was good," she told him, and filled him in briefly about the school-board meeting. "How was yours?"

"Interesting. My daughter Katie and I found an apartment. It's temporary," he said quickly, "a place to get out of my sister's hair. A month-to-month rental until we find out if Katie will be back on campus in the fall."

"I think that's wise."

"And until then, I have an idea: we can form a pod."

"A pod?"

"A small circle of people who are only exposed to one another. You and Lucy, Katie and me, maybe a couple of others."

"We could see one another then?" Alexa beamed.

"We could if we're careful," he said with an impish smile. Then he grew serious. "I don't think you and Lucy should be alone too much, after what almost happened there. People are misinformed; the mood can be ugly. School boards are the eye of the storm in so much of the country. And not just science is being attacked. History and literature are at risk, too. Your position and beliefs make you a galvanizing figure."

"Yes, you're right. I think a pod is a good idea. At least for the short term. It's hard to figure out where this is going."

He pushed his glasses up his nose and nodded. She admired the shape of his jaw, his shoulders, the slight curl in his brown hair. He made her feel like melted butter inside. She caught a view of herself in Skype's small window: flushed, alive, eyes shining.

"I know. But we can plan, and hope, and stay flexible—and in the meantime, spend some time together." His green eyes crinkled just a bit at the edges when he smiled.

Alexa saw her car up the road.

"Lucy's back with dinner. Talk later?"

"Definitely." He waved to her and hung up.

Lucy climbed the porch steps with several bags in her arms.

"How is Rachel?" Alexa asked.

"Good. She told me Chad and Jeremy found a video of a dark-haired girl resembling Phoebe. They're hoping to trace it to Cyrus."

"Wow."

"I'll tell you all about it in a couple of minutes." She hefted the bags a bit higher. "Rachel threw in some appetizers and desserts," she said. "Wait here."

She disappeared into the house, and the screen door slammed. A clinking of china and glassware came from the kitchen. Alexa looked around her in the deepening dusk. The world, at the moment, was frightening and unpredictable. But this was solid: the house, the land, the carriage barn, the lab. Margaret had a vision. Alexa was living it; Lucy would live it too. And then, eventually, they would find their own. Alexa felt her place in the world, between these two women, linking the past and the future. She had work to do. For now, at least, this was where she needed to be. It was home.

Lucy came back to the front porch with a white cloth, silverware, plates, and candles. Alexa watched as her lovely daughter drew up a table, lighted the tapers, and laid the feast out before them.

Author's Note

I have played with time a bit for this novel. Candidates for school board elections in Illinois are required to have lived in the district for at least one year. Alexa does not meet that requirement in Ecstasy. Also, although the split in the Methodist Church is real (the more conservative new Global Methodist Church announced a split from United Methodist Church in March, 2022), I have compressed the timeline of events to fall within the scope of the story.

The references to Covid-19, and state and national leaders' response to it, are dated as they were reported in the news.

Acknowledgements

It's been a long journey from the seeds of this idea to the finished novel, and I've had much help along the way. Huge thanks to my writing group and beta readers, novelists Julia Buckley, E.C. Diskin, and the late Emma Gates, for their continued enthusiasm and expert feedback along the way. I could not have finished this novel without them. I am particularly grateful to Elizabeth Diskin for her publishing guidance, to Ari Fernandez for her marketing skills, and to Linda McCauley Freeman for years of writing camaraderie and encouragement.

Special thanks go to author and zoologist Abby Hafer for help with questions of science and evolution. Any mistake contained in these pages on that subject (or any other) is my own. A big thank you to Wells Street Press for taking me on. I am indebted to my editor, Kerry Cullen, without whose expertise and insight this novel would be a far worse offering. CreativeIndie deserves a special shout-out for their terrific cover and interior design, and their endless patience in working with a debut author.

Thanks to Luis Granados, former editor at Humanist Press, and Hemant Mehta of The Friendly Atheist, whose calls for humanist/atheist voices in fiction inspired me to write the book. I am grateful, as always, to American Humanist Association, for providing a philosophical home for myself and tens of thousands of other humanists and freethinkers.

Lastly—and most importantly—my writing life itself would not be possible without decades of love, patience, support, and encouragement from my husband. For him I am grateful every day.

Discussion Questions

1. Alexa is willing to uproot her life, and her daughter's, to go to Ecstasy. How is the town of Ecstasy like other small towns you've known? How is it different? How have those towns changed in recent years?

2. Alexa feels that Lucy's—and all students'—public school education would be compromised by the teaching of intelligent design. Do you agree? Why or why not?

3. Alexa finds that the current ECM website doesn't wholly reveal what its leaders believe and enforce as policies. Do most churchgoers know the tenets of their faith? The policies of their churches? Why or why not?

4. Why, in a few short months, is Lucy so willing to give up her science? What factors drive her to get baptized? Are these factors personal to her or universal?

5. Lucy is shocked and upset by her liaison with Jake in the springhouse on Christmas Eve. Why doesn't she confront him more forcefully after the incident? Why does she continue to date him?

6. The story of Alexa and Lucy could have been told without Rachel. Why do you think the author included this character? What does she add to the narrative?

7. Rachel's family raises her in a repressive religious home and then disfellowships her. Why doesn't she turn on them? Why do you think she's so focused on her sister Phoebe?

8. Jake and Jordan were raised as fundamentalists. Are they perpetrators of the church's edicts or its victims? Why?

9. Cyrus was raised in a strict religious environment. Do his background and beliefs excuse his actions? Do you think he will be held accountable? Should he be?

10. The town has accepted Alexa enough to vote her onto the school board. Will this acceptance last? Why or why not? What has Alexa learned since moving to Ecstasy?

11. Alexa is an architect, and buildings are a motif in the novel. How do they contribute to the story?

12. ECM overshadows the town of Ecstasy in many ways. How does fundamentalist religion impact those beyond its congregations? How and why is that accepted? Do you think that will change?

About the Author

Lydia Gordon is an award-winning poet and writer living in the Midwest. She holds an MFA in writing and literature and her work has appeared in a number of literary publications. *The Fundamentals* is her debut novel. Ms. Gordon is the founder and current president of her local humanist organization.

Made in the USA
Monee, IL
06 February 2023

27131619R00217